DATE DUE		

NOCTURNAL BUTTERFLIES
OF THE
RUSSIAN EMPIRE

NOCTURNAL BUTTERFLIES
OF THE
RUSSIAN EMPIRE
A Novel

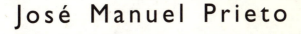

José Manuel Prieto

Translated from the Spanish by

Carol and Thomas Christensen

Grove Press / New York

Originally published in Spanish as *Livadia* by Literatura Mondadori, Barcelona, in 1999.

Published simultanesouly in Canada
Printed in the United States of America

FIRST EDITION

Library of Congress Cataloging-in-Publication Data

Prieto González, José Manuel, 1962–
      [Livadia. English]
      Nocturnal butterflies of the Russian Empire : a novel / José Manuel Prieto ;
translated from the Spanish by Carol and Thomas Christensen.
         p. cm.
      ISBN 0-8021-1665-5
      I. Christensen, Carol, 1947–   II. Christensen, Thomas, 1948–   III. Title.
PQ7390.P76 L5813 2000
863'.64—dc21   00-042957

Design by Laura Hammond Hough

Grove Press
841 Broadway
New York, NY 10003

01 02 03 04   10 9 8 7 6 5 4 3 2 1

It is good for a man not to touch a woman ...
> —St. Paul, First Letter to the Corinthians

In the hands of my superior I must be malleable wax, to be shaped to any form, whether to write letters or to receive them.
> —Ignatius de Loyola

NOCTURNAL BUTTERFLIES
OF THE
RUSSIAN EMPIRE

FIRST LETTER

I

LIVADIA

Seven sheets of rice paper illuminated by afternoon light. The page in my outstretched hand was full of fine writing, the blue lines recalling the azure field that represents the sky in heraldry. The ink had flowed irregularly, swelling at commas, spilling over at points, giving the text a sort of rhyme, so that I could slide from top to bottom with ease.

She had folded the letter twice and sealed it in a white envelope (no airmail mark), which I had opened with a clumsy tear at one corner. I was pleased when I found that she had not used one of those awful writing pads sold in dime stores, with a bouquet of violets or lilacs on every sheet. This was a fine-grained paper, with faint veins and blemishes, obviously handcrafted, a lovely feel to it. This letter of hers, the soft rice paper, the round feminine forms, put me in a good humor. With this letter, I said to myself, I would feel less alone.

Going to my pension, I kept sticking my hand in my pocket to confirm that the envelope was still there, the letter V. had written on paper she had specially chosen, probably copying over a first draft with its mistakes and revisions, so she could send me . . . a perfumed letter? I stopped short. What if I hadn't been able to smell it in the stiff breeze off the beach? I bent forward—not a thing. All right, this was no love letter she sent, but now I wanted more than a scent: to see her, to talk to her. She showed much subtlety in sending this letter. I had never gotten one like it.

In the beginning was the date, which she didn't forget, as I often do. Over this head was a white space, creating a perfect visual balance, a clear sign of educated taste. My name had been written with an ornate capital and extra flourishes, tight swirls that showed long training in calligraphy, something I hadn't suspected in her. On the rare occasions that I write letters, I usually number the pages by drawing a circle around the figures, in the top right-hand corner of the page. She put hers at the bottom of each page, with the numbers centered between long rules. A seven-page letter, and with such cramped writing it was really twice as long, but I read it all in a wink, the wind pulling it out of my hands, not getting the deepest sense of every passage, saving the speeches for a second reading, my chest filling with a gas lighter than air, floating toward the end along her violet lines, touching down on the signature, to check the identity of the sender again— Yes! Absolutely!—and flying home.

She had skipped the good-byes, spared me the usually empty promises, "I'll write" or "You'll hear from me." And instead sent a letter with no word about her abrupt departure. It came as a shock, this reappearance, like when a person you thought you'd never see again, someone you thought was hundreds of miles away, suddenly comes back, says the flight was canceled, there's a snowstorm in Strasbourg, the airport's closed.

Should I tell her that I was on the the balcony at the Maritime Terminal in Odessa, that I saw her run away? "I did not know at the time," I could write, "that you were the girl making a dash for the streetcar."

It was getting darker every minute. I bounded up the stairs in the pension, kicked open the door to my room, and cleared the table (tossing a book and two shirts on the floor). "I'll write a reply," I told myself, "right now." I felt truly inspired, like I could fill sheets till dawn.

. . .

From the balcony of the Maritime Terminal in Odessa, the two ships on the horizon had looked like they were about to collide, slowly sliding toward this meeting as if on a sea of oil, gray, *black*. As they started to dissolve into each other, someone came out on the balcony. It must be V., I thought, and did not turn around, but she walked away. It wasn't V.

I saw a woman below, by the laurels along the esplanade that ran past the terminal. Hadn't I seen that dress before? I pictured V. getting out of the boat after our escape from Istanbul, testing the boards of the gangplank with the toes of her high-heeled shoes, her white blouse reflecting the first rays of a sun that was still bright now, at five in the afternoon. I shifted my eyes back to the unknown woman walking in the shade of the laurels, the path striped by their shadows. I saw her run a little way to catch a streetcar, leaping onto its platform. The streetcar started to move away, raising a cloud of dust, turning the corner of the esplanade, so that it was perpendicular to me, disappearing into the distance, cables quivering.

My mind cleared, brightening like a southern sky, imagining V. standing at the mirror in the lady's room, splashing water on her face, smoothing her hair with damp palms, touching up her lipstick, maybe thinking about buying a new swimsuit. I rolled my eyes heavenward. It looked like a wonderful day ahead, great weather in store. I was wrong: it rained three days straight. We were planning to take the ferry to Yalta and then drive to Livadia. How could I have guessed that V. was counting out rubles at that very moment, buying a plane ticket home (to a small town, ten thousand people)? Completely oblivious of that, I went back into the waiting room, wandering over to a bookseller (another retiree, same casual outfit, short-sleeved shirt and straw hat) to inspect his merchandise. I was bored from the long wait. If I had known I was losing V. when I picked up the book from his stand, I would have tossed it aside instantly, my rejection as fierce as my former drive to read, back when I could read the directions on emergency exits, the signs on city buses, the labels on jelly jars over and over again.

Lately I had been amazed at people who could get lost in a book, for example, during a St. Petersburg–Helsinki trip when I could think of nothing but the blue uniforms of the customs officers, my eyes gliding past the birches out the window, lakes and more lakes: Finland, the land of lakes (had it been a good idea to hide the musk sac in the pot of jam I left out on the lap-table?). I had watched the woman in the seat ahead of me open a book as dull (I managed to make out the title) as the correspondence between Sibelius and Aalto. The woman read until the words *Passportny kontrol* shouted in Russian at the far end of the car made her shut her book and me shut off my nerve endings, shrinking down like a mollusk into an armored shell, safe from the tricky questions of the customs agents, the iron hooks of their sneaky inspections.

These days, showing any interest, simply picking up a book, reading the title, opening it, meant cracking this stony cover of mine, already loosened up a bit, it's true, by the last few days in Istanbul.

I went downstairs and sat on the bottom step outside the Maritime Terminal, reading in the late afternoon sun, warm breeze through the laurels, completely engrossed in *No Return Address,* a novel by W. S. Chase. A hair-raising scene of betrayal in Malibu; I looked up from my book and saw the light; at last it struck me (Chase's fictional deception was the tip-off): V. had been gone more than an hour; I too had been betrayed. Now I saw myself (in a crane shot this time), a white point—brushed-linen shirt and pants, soft leather sandals—bounding up the steps of the Odessa Terminal, taking them two at a time, running into the waiting room, the door slamming behind me.

For an instant I imagined that V. was waiting, asleep on the bench where we'd been sitting, her head resting on her arm. Must I add that when I saw the empty space, my hand automatically went to my pocket, checking for my wallet, the wad of bills?

Women always run off with your money, I knew that from the Chase story, and I also knew that earlier, when I had bent over (like an idiot) to try to kiss V. (who'd sat perfectly straight, her back glued to the bench, so that my mouth pursuing hers left slithery traces in the air), she could have lifted my billfold, undoing the cord with pointy fingernails. Had she taken advantage of that moment, my weak knees, to rob me of nights on the steppes, butterflies fluttering foolishly against the illuminated sheet? While I mimicked their blind flight, drawn toward the pale rose of her mouth, a tight bud admitting nothing, not the warmth of a smile nor an affectionate word, not the faintest hint about heading home, sinking into her favorite chair, moving her feet closer to the heater, watching the snowfall out the window. No. I still had my cash, so that all of my plans, which had seemed to fall apart, were soon reconstructed, each with its own little compartment: the trip to Livadia, the hunt for the *yaẓikus*. . . . Only one cell was still empty, the one belonging to V., and a warning light flashed. I had two visions: in the first, I was leaning over V. in an endless kiss, feeling her start to warm up, lose the chill that had locked her arms (which were now around my neck, holding me fast), sensing her servomotors kick in and start to pump furiously, correcting the angle of her neck, filling her mouth with juice, and making her body glow (speeding up oxygen combustion); and in the second, I was alone, walking along a path by the sea, waves breaking below the cliff, a hawk crying high above me, a desolate figure in white scanning the horizon (like Ovidius Naso in Tomi).

The discovery swept me away, flooding over me in waves, carrying me off, doubled over, clasping my feet, nearly drowning me, and during the whole trip to Yalta, the whole time, words kept spewing out of me: I kept talking to myself, shouting so loud that people looked at me, pumping the emptiness from the pit of my stomach, tears starting up in my eyes, staring unblinking at the coastline.

While the ferry was preparing to cast off, I was still thinking of returning to shore, running back to the terminal: I had imagined finding her on the steps—maybe we had just missed each other when I raced upstairs, jolted by Chase's tale of treachery. (I even waited on the dock at Yalta for three days, hoping she would get off the ferry.) Now, leaning over the rail, reading the ship's wake, I saw that I had been tricked by a . . . I automatically switched to Russian, fearing the Spanish word would permanently tarnish the time we'd had in Istanbul, the risk we'd shared. Like a cook throwing slop in the ship's wake, I hurled a torrent of curses, the stream of bile souring my stomach, without a scrap of conscience. I enjoyed spitting out furiously, swearing violently in the Russian I had learned years before in the meat-packing plants of St. Petersburg, sticking slippery pig quarters with a four-letter purge.

I had been way too easy on V., I thought, when what she needed was a couple of *súkas* (bitches) from me—yelled out harshly, through clenched teeth, or flung lightly, carelessly—to grab hold of her wrists and shake her memory of the past, make her see I had her, she was mine. Then she wouldn't have slipped off in Odessa: slick as a professional robbing a client in a hotel room (the Divan, in Istanbul). At the height of my misery I saw myself clearly, as if in a spotlight, playing the fool, helping her off the streetcar after our walk through the Grand Bazaar, the grateful look she threw me (practiced night after night on customers who stuffed bills in her garter, mesmerized by her winking navel), the friendly squeeze she gave my hands when she saw me off. My face burning with shame, I redirected the stream of *súkas* that I'd been pouring into the sea and felt it fall on my head like a rain of ashes.

2

LIVADIA

I kept taking dream journeys, plowing through the sea, covering thousands of miles in trains so long that on curves you could look across at the engine at the front of the arc, pulling an endless line of coaches. Me riding in the ninth, having tea. For a few brief seconds, while the train went around the corner, I tilted my head, pressing my cheek to the windowpane and watching the engine throb laboriously. Afterward I had the feeling that my car was continuing on by itself, with the cries on the platform, the very look of the city I'd left, all carried along as if in a single block. Aboard I was like a time traveler in a capsule cutting through various ages like a stack of pancakes. Hours in the car, hours talking to my fellow travelers, shrank to nothing when I arrived at my destination, evaporating the moment I stepped onto the station platform. One trip from the Black Sea to the Baltic, three days of biting cold, disappeared as if by magic the moment I saw the first golden cupolas of St. Petersburg. The worst was waking up after a dream trip full of strange beauties—all swindlers trying to steal my bags—worn out from wrestling with them, a terrible anxiety pressing down on me. I opened my eyes not knowing where I was and lay staring around a room without a single painting or personal touch. In the corner I saw copper heating pipes: two tubes thick as a finger that fed the radiator in my room. Had those parallel lines provoked my prolonged glide along the rails in the dream? The little window I'd left open when I came to bed was rattling, the shadow of a beech tree fell across the glass, a woman in the garden was shouting in Tartar. I had finally reached the end of my journey: Livadia.

Without enough energy to rise, I looked out the window at a beach dotted with early-morning bathers, many with dogs. I was keenly aware of everything; I hadn't been here long enough to have registered the changes, this pension room, Livadia. It hurt to see those swimmers with their dogs, I confess. I didn't have a house, my books were gone, I didn't even have a dog. These strangers coming out of the woods bothered me, walking their dogs on the beach. I don't think anyone in the pension had one. All rovers, like me, without a dog.

...

Before moving to this pension I had checked out the Oreandra, a hotel in Yalta. I left in disgust: I would never stay in such a high-priced place, a hotel for foreigners (a *jungestill* built in 1905 where the rooms cost more than a hundred a night). I was not exactly a foreigner. I had lived in Russia too long. I knew, for example, that if you want a room, you have to look at the ads on lampposts, the concentric layers of signs tacked up there. I needed a pension that had rooms for single men (Russian, many specified, but that was a small snag, no problem). I pulled up layer after layer, as carefully as if they were the Dead Sea scrolls. They worked loose easily, soft from the rain. I found a sign about a pension in Livadia—perfect—with the name and number repeated on a fringe at the bottom, so you could tear off a strip. Only one strip left, that wasn't so good: the room could be gone.

I went back to the Oreandra. From a phone booth in the lobby, I looked out the window and saw that the day was turning nice again: big beams of light shot out like fans from the bottom side of gray clouds, that sort of thing. If you had been looking out this same window an hour earlier, you would have seen a downpour splashing on the flagstones, but when I dialed the number and someone picked it up on the second ring, the sun burst out from behind a cloud, the rays so bright they hurt, and I had to half-shut my eyes. The booth had a list of prefixes—typewritten with penciled corrections—for the major Russian cities. I could say I was calling from Simferopol, I realized, for a better bargaining position, so I'd be under less pressure, the rain less of a threat.

"I'm calling about the ad." (Why else would I be calling? I ought to introduce myself first, but that meant a name. I could invent a name: say, Andrei Gavrilov. Maybe I should start with a greeting: "Good afternoon, but it's probably already evening . . ." No, straight to the point, no preliminaries.)

"Yes," she responded dryly. (Fifty or fifty-five years old, fleshy, full breasts, in a dark housedress and slippers at the moment. Flinty blue eyes. I could just picture her.)

"Can you tell me about it?"

"I don't give out information on the phone." (Seventy, no, more than seventy years of Soviet rule).

"But do you have any rooms?" (Several years in Russia myself. I can elbow my way on to a city bus, if need be, and haggle over a kilo of figs in the market, with the best of them.). "I have a letter of recommendation," I added. The lie occurred to me as I watched a multi-colored helium balloon go up across the bay.

"Oh, good!" Meaning, that changes things, and in more than one sense: she knew it was false, totally false, but wasn't that a testimonial to my ingenuity? Anyway, they didn't use letters of recommendation in Russia anymore. Since 1917, maybe a little later. Only the state wrote letters for or against you, promoting you to a ministerial post or dumping you in a distant outpost, ruining your reputation and your career.

She suspected I was a foreigner, which gave her a bit of confidence, enough to open the door a crack, so she could throw me out, face first onto her lawn, telling me:

"I don't think it will be possible. We don't have any vacancies. But you can come by anyway."

Before I left the phone booth, I ran my finger down the list for the Astrakhan prefix. A second balloon was now rising, rocking back and forth, as slowly as a coin falling to the bottom of a glass (not quickly, the way a bubble rises from the bottom of a glass—how odd!). The revolving door of the Oreandra pushed me toward the street with feigned friendliness, but instead of hurrying out before it slapped me on the back I continued the circle and returned to the lobby. I had decided to write myself a letter of recommendation on the spot, at one of the tiny marble tables in the lobby.

I used my best Russian penmanship, imitating the shaky handwriting of a seventy-five-year-old man, Vladimir Vladimirovich, a friend in St. Petersburg. A single paragraph was all I needed, and I turned it out in the stiff superficial style of official letters, applications for jobs (and dismissals from them). And addressed it to Maria Kuzmovna (just like that, Maria, Kuzmá's daughter, with no last name), the name on the ad.

The coast road ran past blue mountains with pine trees growing up them (and the sea below). Sometimes there was a clearing and I would have a perfect view of the tourists' sailboats and a large-hulled ship coming into the harbor. The wind carrying the balloons across the bay hit me in the face, a few raindrops still floating in it, but warm again. The asphalt ribbon of the highway slipped off onto the shoulder without a curb, irregularly, like it was pinned down by pine needles. A good road. I was glad it was asphalt not concrete, very much alike, but the asphalt was softer, making my walk easier. The lady at the front desk in the Oreandra had told me that a trolleybus went to all the little towns and beaches on the coast, Livadia and beyond, as far as Alupka. A strange route for a trolley. I let her tell me where to catch it—go five blocks down, wait at the movie house—and decided to walk.

It would take a half hour, I figured, by the road through the pines. I walked against the traffic. That way I could see the cars coming toward me (as a safety precaution), and the shuddering of the cable long before the trolley appeared around a long curve, an ancient model, its wires held on by rope.

Following its line I couldn't get lost. I walked past several pensions, practically on the road. The trolley didn't make regular stops, just pulled over when the driver saw anyone who wanted to go into Yalta, or the other way, to the mineral baths in Alupka. I had been to Yalta before, but it didn't count. I had made a quick circuit of the peninsula, driving along the coast in a prewar convertible, hardly stopping at all. Without visiting Livadia, for instance. There is a Grand Palace in Livadia, built in 1911. Surrounding it is an English garden with the road down the middle. I stepped onto its grass and ran downhill, full tilt, so I wouldn't fall. I slowed down at a gravel path. "It's not far from the Palace, in fact, just 800 meters from the left wing." Nice location, near a palace. I went a little farther, down to the sea. And found the two-story house I wanted: "Livadia" (the pension's name, too).

The Black Sea was a good place to live, lots of family-style pensions, very cheap since the crisis. The only problem was that these pensions, these solid houses built on stone foundations, with ten to fifteen rooms plus a kitchen, were not really family-run. Not any more. Not since the turn of the century. Now they were administered by the state, with the rooms listed on the vacation plans of unions from all over. Schoolteachers and retirees could stay practically free, paying with vouchers for meals, plus every service from laundry to midnight snacks: a cold glass of milk and some cookies.

Vladimir Vladimirovich had spent a month there, I told Maria Kuzmovna. She didn't remember him, naturally, but my dollars, which she could change into the new local money, widened the opening my fake reference had given me. I just let her know I didn't approve of the old voucher system. I would pay in cash and in advance for board and bedding.

She didn't have to read the letter twice, I noticed, not this Kuzmovna. Her fear was gone, most of it anyway. She was just cautious, probably had to be, without the false trust so many people invested in the newly opened market. The swarms of old soviet economic police were being replaced by fiscal inspectors, and I had seen many people slip up on deals that seemed safe. She gave me a sharp look. She was about fifty, with a broad chest like a landing strip for airplanes with soft tires, nearly flat. She yelled: "Mikhail Petrovich!"—another retiree in loose shirt and sandals—"Come here please." She wanted a witness to our deal. So at least she wasn't overcharging me. She wanted to know the purpose of my visit. No answer. She had to ask, she explained, since I was staying so long. I said, "I need a room with a view." It could mean anything: a poetic nature, an interest in astronomy, a respiratory disease. "I have a room facing the sea," she admitted at last. She folded the letter and put it away, slipping it into the pocket of her dress. Mikhail Petrovich, the retiree in the round glasses, couldn't be her lover: he was too old and feeble to move Kuzmovna's massive hips. I was in. A pair of unsuspecting vacationers showed up for the room, pockets full of vouchers, and she sent them packing: someone's always messing up, Moscow or somewhere, sending two guests for the same spot (lie!); try the big sanatoria, maybe, or the Palace.

I soon discovered that the boarders exchanged notes, which they attached to the doors of their rooms on little self-adhesive papers with a strip of glue that stayed sticky. I went sneaking from door to door, reading these little notes, forming impressions of the other guests. Kuzmovna's always had a peremptory tone: "Mikhail Petrovich, don't ever leave the oven on again!" Kuzmovna was bright enough ordinarily, but could not seem to learn my name. I let on that it was Joska, which ended the stammers provoked by a strange name, and soon notes started to appear, topped by that simple name, and decked with three exclamation marks (indicating amazement, urgency, incredible importance): "Don't forget to empty the wastebasket!" or "How many times must I tell you, your breakfast gets cold by eight-thirty in the morning?"

3

The woods led down to the beach. I was cold walking through them, among the pines. When I came out on the beach, I was shocked by the heat, unimaginable under the trees. Just the sort of contrast you would remember years later, and made a (mental) note: "This sure beats the tropics, those dry lonely beaches." At least I liked it better now, the nice combination of sunny beach and woods, the chance to withdraw to the shadows, light a fire in a clearing. The mere hint (mental) of the August sun made me queasy. By September, maybe before, the market would be full of fruits. That, too.

I had traveled too much the past two years, I thought, when I was back under the trees. I had hurried away from great cities, with their museums and galleries, without seeing them, in and out in three days, not a moment to spare. Always rushing to catch a plane, the ferry leaving at 18:37, the train at 13:45. Always in some cab, the backseat heaped with bags, flying toward the dock, the station, the airport. Or else, I had floated through too many cities: Helsinki, Prague, Vienna, Stockholm, Berlin, buying and selling, immersed in liquidation sales when the Wall gave way, chasing after cut-rate antiquities in Kraków, barely alighting in its cobbled streets, soaring to Vienna on sandals winged with 500 percent profits. My sole activity: crossing the membranes of states (borders), taking advantage of the different values between one cell (nation) and another. And after a few days' inactivity, taking off charged with oxygen, a terrific payoff with a minor toll on my nerves. I did not, for example, take the opium bars an Uzbeki tried to push on me in Samarkand. I had read how every hour in prison seems endless, and also, of course, about men in solitary confinement with nothing to do, a lifetime of letter-writing ahead.

The problem of borders fascinates me, the practical angle, of course. In one night hundreds of people, hundreds of smugglers, crossed the Estonian border. A dream. The newspapers didn't say a word about the incident or its political significance. Russia had set its colonies free, shrinking away from its customs posts, its barbed wire, its dogs. Crossing into Estonia or any of the other Baltic republics, you were suddenly in a foreign country. Across the border a dark mass of smugglers had gathered, suitcases stuffed with illegal merchandise, trucks with tarps covering their loads. Like the army of the night preparing an attack, with every precaution. In Ivangorod, the ancient fortress that now marked the end of Russian territory and the start of the Hanseatic League, you could walk down the main street in broad daylight and not see the preparations: the forces camped along the border, the jeeps with their lights out and their map boxes open, the index fingers tracing a sinuous route by which a few soldiers were taking out three helicopters with muffled blades. People had been filtering across this "transparent border" (as *Izvetia* called it) for a long time, gradually "draining the lifeblood from Mother Russia" (*sic*), but one moonless night the first divisions of smugglers began pouring out of the heart of Russia, overrunning the country like an an army of lemurs, and months later in Warsaw or Berlin, people were still talking about it. A single night. Some of them took more than one trip. A cargo of osmium oxide, for example, a rare earth, at seventy thousand dollars a kilogram, making a killing overnight. Estonia and the other Baltic republics took the weapon fate had given them and paid Russia back with smuggled goods. I traveled through Ivangorod when memories of that night were still fresh, inspiring long hours of stories in the train-station café. That day was over, but some people had seized it, as well as a fortune. I heard about it the afternoon I arrived, a few months too late, from a drunk selling fried meatballs, twirling his aluminum fork, and talking about crossing that border on foot, no problem. "A walk in the park!" (he winked), but with just two bottles of vodka in the pockets of the checked jacket he was wearing. By now, he told me, he could have been a millionaire in Tallin . . . "Kolya! My friend Kolya . . . We drank together here many times . . . Zubrovka . . . I visited him three days ago in his office in Narva, five minutes from here: two secretaries, *nogui, vo!* (legs up to here, this long), cellular phone. The transparent border!" he spit out furiously.

It was no less transparent now, but you needed quick wits to go through: you might have to toss the goods and run. Russia had brought in soldiers from all over, garrisons in the Urals or Bashkirya, raw recruits with no real sense of customs, ready to take your watchband to stop the looting of their country.

. . .

A curious incident, something that happened to me on one of my trips: a woman in Brussels tried to return some goods I supposedly sold her in Liège, some bad caviar. I had never gone to Liège, nor would I want to. Nor had I ever sold any caviar. Well, all right, one time someone gave me a bargain on a few tins of the finest caviar—beluga, anyone who eats caviar knows what that means. But this woman, on that trip to Brussels, saw me in the plaza by myself, cool and assured, singing the praises of my goods. (I'm embarrassed to admit, but at first, when I was starting out, I stood in plazas selling my merchandise, before I found clients who would buy whole shipments from me, items like

Hasselblad cameras, two hundred dollars apiece. I should add that I'm interested in optics, that's why I went to Russia, to study optics, but I didn't graduate.) The lady could have been seeing double, suffering from some kind of optical aberration, maybe a temporary disphasia. Like déjà vu, the same physical principle. The theory is that one eye (we'll say the right, but it can be the left) sees the image first, a split second ahead—a young man in a khaki jacket, a black watchcap over his ears, excellent teeth flashing a disdainful smile, thinking he won't make very much here, he should go big time—and his image travels along the optic nerve to the brain, where it is received, processed, and stored; and then a bit later, the left optic nerve gets a second image (which looks the same, but is actually different, secretly altered—the young man thinking he ought to get better stuff, a bigger profit, at least a hundred grand a year), and that one reaches the brain, and hey! seen that one before!; and next thing you know the person, the fifty-year-old fury walking toward me, is sure she's met me, and what's worse, I'm the man from Liège, the one who sold her the lumpy caviar that tasted like asphalt.

It took me completely by surprise, like déjà vu, providing an aftertaste, a faint hint or a big hit, of nostalgia or euphoria. The woman didn't have the nerve to throw her caviar in my face—she had the cans in her bag, maybe planning to present them in the lower house of the Belgian parliament, material evidence in a complaint about smuggling, tainted goods coming into the country from the east, Russland. Seeing me there—and inexplicably taking me for whoever had sold her the caviar in Liège—she spoke to a pair of teenagers, explaining the dirty trick I'd played, shaking an angry finger as she came toward me (twisting the top of my thermos in irritation, gripping it with the fleshy fingertips protruding from my cut-off gloves), and spat out a big speech in Walloon, brandishing the cans I had never seen (much less sold).

Then she switched to plain English: pay her back or she'd call the cops. I started to explain that I never sold caviar, it wasn't my line. And showed them the sort of things I sold, handing infrared telescope sights to the boys, who might want to follow their debut as bodyguards with a little turn at surveillance. Since the stuff had sidestepped customs, the woman wanted to have it out with me—the accused swindler— herself. Let's just see, I thought, if she'll call the police. I gave her a cutting answer, in English (I must say, English has an edge, I like that, at least in the tough novels I've read, Micky Spillane, plenty sharp): *"What's the problem? The money? You want your money back? Okay. Give me those damned cans and get your money back."* I knew I could unload them on some other Sunday stroller short the francs for caviar from Belgian shops. I'd never been to Liège, I hadn't sold her those cans, but the old lady tapped them with a crooked finger and pointed at my chest, establishing a mysterious link between me, the caviar, and an unknown city (Liège).

She took me for someone else, I figured. A month later, in Stockholm, a man came up to me, quite friendly, claiming we had met on the ferry, saying I had promised him some folk music tapes from southern Russia. He seemed to be suffering from some delusion, too, like the Chinese who can't tell Western faces apart, or maybe it was a blindspot, like the Westerners who can't tell Chinese faces apart— although I don't look Chinese; that's just an example.

Later it was my turn: I was sitting in the bay window in a Greek restaurant, right here in Livadia, and simultaneously seemed to be in some faraway place. Like when you're sitting in an armchair at home and suddenly feel like you're in a pasture in Inner Mongolia, all the same physical sensations, wind bending the tall grass, small ponies grazing. I would really like to find an explanation for this phenomenon.

4

LIVADIA

What I didn't grasp were the empty points, the amazing stretch between the time when I had left V. on the Odessa steps, or actually, between the moment she left me in the Ferry Terminal, and the point at which she reappeared, yesterday afternoon when the window opened and the thin arm of the Post Office clerk reached out to hand me her letter.

I had gone into the Post Office to make a long-distance call (since Post and Phones are in the same Russian ministry, in the same gray Moscow edifice). While the operator was making the connection, I was inspecting the model telegrams displayed under glass on her desk— announcements of train arrivals and departures, notes of congratulation—and it occurred to me I might have a letter at general delivery (*poste restante*). I looked up from a sample of a 500-ruble money order, located the general delivery window, and suddenly heard a voice: "Sir, there's a letter for you." This *gospodín* (sir) was unusual in Russia, so I figured it was directed at someone else, certainly not me. Some person behind me, somebody who had come in for his mail. And they addressed him with an expression starting to spread in Russia, the old-fashioned: "Sir." (I was just plain "mister" to the streetcar drivers and porters of Petersburg). And "a letter for you," that was odd, too. From whom? I wasn't expecting one. No one knew where I was (except Stockis, who never wrote to me in Russia, for security reasons. We only spoke on the phone, our words—he was sure—going off into thin air), so I could hardly be getting mail here. It had been ridiculous to come to this window. Not only that, my call must be going through. Going back to stand by the desk, I heard some pounding—metal rapped against the window behind me (the handle of the postmark stamp, I found out later)—and then the voice piped up again, much louder: "*Muzhina*, I believe we have a letter for you. Isn't this yours? Here, take a look. Aren't you J.P.?" and a hand was extended, sliding a pale yellow envelope through the slot in the glass. I approached it slowly, shock flooding me with a vague conviction . . . "My God, It's incredible!"

"Yes, I believe it's for me. You're right, it's for me." She must have noticed me yesterday, when I had come in to place a call to Stockholm, which had never gone through. Then she got a letter with a foreign name and concluded it was mine.

I stood there speechless, as if I had been descended upon by an angel (her rustling wings with their white tips and tailfeathers quite a sight in the gloom of the Post Office), who had handed me an envelope that had the sender's name (which I saw at once), but no return address (in the bottom right, where they put it in Russia). I had not been expecting a letter from her. She had disappeared without a trace in Odessa, leaving me with an uneasy feeling, like when you drop a letter that contains vital information into the indifferent mouth of a mailbox, afraid it's gone for good. But no, it reaches its destination and weeks later, out of the blue, you get a response. (The response to its disappearance and, more than anything, the real and true response to itself.)

I have never read letters very carefully. Nor had I had any interest in other people's letters, in collections of letters. I didn't know a thing about letters. I'd read novels, books of short stories, but never letters (nor plays; I never go to the theater). Whenever I get back from one of my trips, with a huge stash of cash in my clothes, I'd just glance through the few letters I'd received, from all over the world, Japan, New Zealand (and even Cuba!), maybe looking twice at a word or phrase if I couldn't make it out. I'd never gotten a letter that affected me like V.'s. I read it over and over, like the chess player who defeated twenty opponents at once, blind, and can't stop repeating the moves in his head, returning from ending to opening gambit again and again, in an endless loop, to the point of madness. In a lucid moment I held the thin rice paper up to the light, hoping to discover its secret, some mesmerizing device between its layers. I classified it (erroneously) as a love letter, but then, life had not given me much experience with love letters. I have gazed into the eyes of very dear women, talked on a balcony in the wee hours, walked silently in a cold fall rain, slept by the sea all afternoon, a girlfriend at my side, waking after nine on an empty beach, the tide rising, waves lapping the pines, a distant ship on the horizon, but I have never gotten a love letter. And her letter had a subtle musical quality, too, like a simple song, strong enough to lift us briefly, all too briefly, and express the inexpressible truth of our hearts. It had a kind of melody, pretty, and moved at a nice tempo, steady, with some ups and downs, of course, little details that could be passed over, like some song in Norwegian—I didn't speak Norwegian, and I never would, but it could touch my heart anyway. Her letter colored those morning hours, and every day that week, with a clear light tone, so that I often smiled during the day, the way you sometimes feel bad, for no apparent reason, and I finally located the source of this joy, after I subjected it to analysis: could it be the day dawning so bright and sunny? No, that wasn't it. The film I stayed up to watch? No, that wasn't it either. No, it sprang from her letter, and the light was composed of its words.

I now saw that the simple cut of the cotton dress she'd bought herself in Odessa, the broad shoulder straps, the three big white buttons, revealed much of what now left me breathless, her figures of speech, her turns of phrase, the smooth way she had of introducing speech after speech, developing a thought, grasping an idea from every side, quickly connecting it to another, like someone sewing, someone darning a hole in a sock, stretching it out with her fingers, holding it at arm's length, giving a sigh of satisfaction, and picking up another, or maybe a wool sweater, with a hole at the elbow, biting the thread with her teeth, spitting on the end, and picking up her idea where she left off, at the last stitch. Quite a contrast between this woman, in a dressing gown open to the thigh, sitting down to write me this letter, in her peaceful home in some tiny village (almost a hamlet)—and the cold, hard, tough woman I had met in Istanbul.

That woman hadn't come to me in Livadia, I realized. Reading this letter was a surprise, like cutting into a fruit and discovering ripe flesh. I had not seen her soften up, I thought; it had happened since she disappeared that afternoon, shortly after I (foolishly) sat down to read Chase, after admiring the fresh intelligence of her arms with their golden down, unshaved. I had appreciated her intelligence my first morning in Istanbul; I had taken her for the very model of intelligence at first sight (those white teeth chewing lettuce at breakfast), the organic intelligence of shapely ankles, deep blue eyes, pale blond hair, falling to her shoulders. She had a few bumps, but luscious ones, like the plump—bare—arms bursting from the sleeves of her blouse, the ones I had squeezed as if testing the softness of a pillow, good for laying your head on, imagining the days on the beach, the dips in the sea we could enjoy in Livadia.

Before I got the first letter, during the three days I had waited at the Yalta dock, in a downpour that lasted just as long, I thought

(wrongly) that I should have treated her rough, the way I saw her treat
Leilah, the other girl from the Saray (the way you pound a peach or a
mango to tenderize the flesh). But V. had ripened on her own, bedded
down in the hay, in the loft of her hut, staring out the blue slot of the
window, watching the leaves on the trees changing color, the flocks
of wild ducks crossing the sky in perfect formation. She woke up dazed,
her mouth thick with saliva, her ears tuned to new sounds, the cheep-
ing of chicks just out of their shells, the clanking of the bucket against
the lip of the well. She had guessed the hour from the faint glow around
the apple trees in the garden and slipped downstairs, sliding her hands
over the ladder rails; or maybe she had leapt down and thrown on her
clothes, a simple percale smock (or her bathrobe), and then went into
the kitchen and sat down to write me this letter, surrounded by jars of
preserves. In the same soft light of that hour, the same silence, the same
sense of peace, reinforced by the rattle of the bucket against the side
of the well, the creaking of the rope in the pulley. She had gotten up
way before me, with this amazing handwriting and this letter full of
truths I hadn't suspected she knew. It came to seven sheets covered
with her small but well-formed writing, saying things I had always
imagined could be said in letters, but that I had never seen spelled out
so nicely, with never a false step. It was written at one sitting, I now
felt sure, but by whom? How could it have been written by the same
girl I rescued from Istanbul, by the same V. who told me those lies
about working as a figure skater, tracing endless circles on the ice? I
had seen her behave coarsely, yelling at her friend Leilah, almost coming to blows; but then, I had also heard her claim she'd studied art,
drawing or painting, I can't recall. (I do remember: it was at lunch in
a Chinese restaurant in Istanbul. While we waited for our order, I made
some comment—out of place—about the painting that was hanging
on the wall in front of us, its vertical perspective. Immediately realiz-

ing the absurdity of my remark, I turned to the glazed duck, praising the dish we'd been served. But she had stopped my move toward my plate, saying that she had studied painting and had never heard that term, vertical perspective. I assumed she was lying—she had never studied drawing (or painting)!—and so I joked that I'd just made it up. But she was bent over her plate again, carrying a piece of bread to her mouth, taking a bite without lifting her eyes. I hastily abandoned vertical perspective, and we finished eating in silence. V. waited almost two months to break that silence, without showing any impatience, like those people who won't talk about complex subjects, can't say such things out loud. Who write treatises instead, books that are rarely complex, just the reverse, quite simple. Her letter wasn't complex either, not in and of itself, but it created an unbearable complex within me, as the fine thread of her handwriting unreeled our days together in Istanbul, the difficulties of our flight, the drama in the Russian merchant ship, ending in a disappearance in Odessa. Her letter's real subject (I realized after several rereadings) was friendship, love if you like, but a love that had waited for days to pass, for the great Russian rivers to start to rise, the trees to sprout, the afternoons in Livadia to grow longer, for her pen to break the ice of those days of screams and shouted orders, of fear, suspicion, and danger.

A brief description of V. may help explain my confusion, the uncertain state in which I found myself. After I went to meet Stockis at the Istanbul club, while I was standing there at loose ends, I saw the girls from the Saray (among them V. and Leilah) at the sidewalk café across the street, having what I later learned was breakfast—it was already lunchtime. I saw V. that morning, sitting at a nearby table (as if posed), and my eye was drawn to her. She shone in the sun! That's it exactly, the only way I can describe my impression. She was not in direct light, it was filtered through the umbrella over her table and fell gently around her like a halo (no exaggeration)—like a photo shoot, with a model lit by floodlights, which are softened by umbrellas, and a life-size picture for a backdrop, (for example) an Istanbul street scene. But this background was real and changing. A crowd flowed by—looking almost European, but unmistakably Turkish, when you slowed it down and looked carefully: a butcher in a leather apron, indistinguishable from the stream at one moment, then moving into focus; Turkish women, many in headscarves; their husbands in sports coats that barely meet across their bellies, wearing two vests, one on top of the other— and in front, set off against this backdrop, the splendid woman who had caught my eye. I could not see her legs, which are generally the first things I check in the women carried my way by the river of humanity in a busy street. With some sixth sense I register a sort of overall perception of a beautiful woman—face, eyebrows, cheekbones—and immediately, even before I confirm this strong and virtually foolproof first impression, I form another impression (again, always or almost always right, at least in some crowds, some cities, some countries) of legs that are absolutely outstanding. Confident, steady, onward come those legs, and above them, borne aloft like figures in a holy procession, the faces that I study like a part from which I can reconstruct the whole. I submitted the young woman who was sitting (or posing) at the next table to this procedure. Since I could not see her legs from where I was, her arms had to fill that role: firm fresh arms exuding frankness. They spread out slightly from elbow to shoulder (she was in a sleeveless blouse), then joined to form a perfect arch, a shrine to the patron saint of arms, to be kissed reverently. Her shoulders, deep anatomical soap dishes, appeared from under the loose cut of her beige, nearly white blouse. She was not looking at me, her eyes were fixed on her plate, and she was eating her breakfast hungrily. The skin of her neck reacted promptly to the first movements of her jaws, which were working furiously. An earring dangled from her earlobe, and with my eyes on the soft curl of her ear I whispered: "Turn around and look," and she turned and looked but did not linger on me since it was the waiter she wanted, and he was at the table behind me. Seeing her this way, head on, hardly inspired painful thoughts. She did have a pretty stiff spine, it's true, like the water-seller in the print, walking away from the the fountain without spilling a drop. And the friendly look in her eyes was undercut, belied by a perennial scornful smile, tight-lipped.

During our week together in Istanbul some real feeling, a real look, a real spark sometimes flashed between us (in the space between our physical bodies), but she would try to hide her feelings, afraid of losing this real chance of escape, of staying trapped in the Saray (the nightclub with dancers and strippers—prostitutes really—where we met). Like a bean sprout shooting up through layer after layer of clouds, this letter had opened a path to me—passed from sack to sack, tumbling around inside mail trucks, eventually coming to me in Livadia. It was no angel, as I had imagined in the Post Office, no, it was a plant, a bean sprout, that had slowly germinated and finally got to me.

...

It was growing lighter every moment. I slumped forward, put my head on the table, and fell into an uncomfortable sleep. I had not written a single line. I woke up in misery. Out the window was the deep blue of daybreak. I picked up her letter, held the pages to the window, watched them turn as red as the glass. I had moved the table near the window, wanting to shed more light on the butterflies, the bottles holding the butterflies, and Stuart's illustrated guide. Now the light was shining through the layers of papers, and I sought in them a sliver of strontium, some chemical element radiating brilliantly, like a technician scanning an X ray, deducing from its shadows the healthy functioning of your kidneys, the oiled mechanism of your internal body—or (readjusting my focus) my own anxious eyes in the glass.

I went out into the world.

I didn't head straight for the gravel path, like I did most mornings at eleven (with less apprehension), no, I did what I had intended from the first: I turned right and walked to the wall behind the house, which looked out to sea. The garden in front of the pension stretched for ten or fifteen feet to a double row of beech trees, with the road to Yalta beyond. At the end of the row—if you turned left, not through the garden—was the path to the veranda. I usually cut through the garden to go to town, and there were signs in the wet grass that others did too. Only the oldest boarders, I noticed, took the path, which circled too far away from town. But you could take it to the beach, going out to the road and then through the woods, coming out a few yards away.

The pension had six windows on the first floor, seven on the second, all painted (in about, say, 1935) pale green like the downspouts. My room's was the first one, at the corner, and I had a second on the other side (two windows, lots of light). The building was set on a foundation of solid stone, its mortar white behind the acacias. There were rusted tin cans, cigarette butts, and old newspapers in the grass. It was a great place to sunbathe: I could lower a chair right out the window or spread a blanket on the lawn. The women who rented rooms in the house, most of them single, tanned themselves on this strip of grass. I walked through the shadows to the other end of the house, as far as the path, but I didn't take it. Instead, I cut through the garden and went to town.

I sent a telegram to Vladimir Vladimirovich in St. Petersburg. I just dashed it off, using the model letters, the samples under the glass on the desk, copying word for word, my hand not shaking at all. I merged one wishing a happy new year with another announcing: "Tanya and the girls. Coach five. July 7. Moscow at 17:00. Kisses." I skipped easily between the two telegrams, finding all the right words, the proper expressions. I had planned to ask him to send me a list of collections of letters to consult in writing my answer to V., but instead I asked him to send everything he could find, to general delivery in Livadia. The books started arriving that week, brown-paper packages, tied up with string, sealed with wax: letters, mainly in Russian, French, English, and in Spanish, my own language.

Among the first he sent was one that was not much use to me, except here, as an example. Its title: *A Treasury of the World's Great Letters from Ancient Days to Our Time, Containing the Characteristic and Crucial Communications and Intimate Exchanges and Cycles of Correspondence of Many of the Outstanding Figures of World History, and Some Notable Contemporaries, Selected, Edited, and Integrated with Biographical Backgrounds and Historical Settings and Consequences.*

SECOND LETTER

I

LIVADIA

The girl in the Post Office handed me a second letter from V. She watched with a smile as I turned it over in my hands, incredulous. Out in the street, a cloud of children swirled around me, Greeks, Armenians, Tartars with biblical curls. A youthful chorus asked the time, but I opened the envelope, oblivious to their cries, as if I had jumped up to close a door, shutting out music that was too loud. V.'s greeting resounded in my ear, like in those movies where the offscreen voice descends on a character, getting too close for comfort. Or like that old tapestry (in the north wing of the Hermitage?), an angel unrolling a parchment for a boy in a saffron toga and sandals, his bowed lips at the ear of the rapt youth. When my eyes had made their way to her name on the last page, after reading a letter perhaps more beautiful than the first, I stood stunned for a moment, scarcely aware of my surroundings, immersed in absolute silence, her words of farewell ringing in my ear like a glass bead bouncing around the walls of a seashell, speeding through the spiral chambers. My eyes lifted from the page, darting around, where was I? where had my walk taken me? not really a walk, a glide past walls, entrances, standing at the crossroads, watching two cars go by, then a wagon, pulled slowly by a Percheron (its flanks and feet covered with long hair), as if I was running on automatic pilot, like ships use on the high seas, functioning only enough to move forward, to get around without bumping into things. I blinked and my eyes were caught by something vertical, which got bigger and bigger; then I was hit by a wave of images, breaking over me in a dizzying flood, indistinguishably. They were clear signals of where I was, but only images, no sounds, and they slid past my retina so fast my head spun, each vision of the place rushing past before a single thing, any detail, could pull up on my memory bank. I knew that I must order my ears to reconnect to the exterior if I were to have any hope of grasping some part of the tide of images coming at me, so I went back to open that door and was struck by bursts of sentences, the music (a Greek melopoeia) of the place, and heard clearly: "Two octopus in ink for table five," and there in front of me stood the person who had turned to shout (I had seen it a second before: the mouth appearing over the shoulder, opening, yelling, the vein in the neck distending—all of which was captured by my ears after a slight delay and subsequently deciphered by my speech centers as an order that this man, the waiter, was shouting to the kitchen).

The crystal bead crashed against the nacreous shell one last time. As if awakening from a dream, I saw the mocking face of Diodore (Diodo), the Greek, and knew I was in the restaurant with the bay window, and I ordered: "A beer. Dark. Draft."

I had stopped at this restaurant many times. I had spent hours reading letters, copying sentences, whole paragraphs, with the secret hope that if I repeated those words written one, two hundred years ago (and more), my hand would acquire the skill of the ancients. I hoped, for example, to acquire a sense of freedom by copying a passage from Petrarch, describing the ascent of Mount Ventoux, from a letter dated April 26, 1351, into the reply I was starting to draft, sitting in the bay

window of the restaurant, looking down on Livadia. The Faustian
impulse, the craving for travel of this "first modern man": "Inspired
only by a desire to contemplate the lofty elevation of the place, I have
today climbed the highest mount in the region, known, not without
cause, as Windy . . . I stood astonished and overwhelmed by the vast
panorama and by the unusual breeze that was blowing . . ."

I too was "astonished and overwhelmed by the vast panorama" from
the Greek restaurant high above Livadia, the spot on the globe I had
chosen to see. V.'s letters completely altered this setting. Instead of a
simple nature preserve (for *yazikus* butterflies) I now saw beeches, oaks,
cypresses—a row of tall cypresses marking the end of the gentle slope
on my left—and the harbor in Yalta, boats anchored there, boulevards
running down toward the sea. The octopus I impaled on a broad fork
with large tines and raised to my lips came from this very sea. I chewed
it slowly, its thick sauce spreading an oily cloak over my taste buds.

With my back to the little restaurant where Diodo was moving
between the tables, I leaned over the balustrade and studied the afternoon light, just a hint of the shadow of the hour floating in it: the rays
of sun slanting through the clouds and growing shorter, the pyramids
of poplars growing less sharp, withdrawing slowly into a larger darkness in which it was impossible to distinguish the branches, their foli-
age dissolving into a green-blue mass. It wasn't that everything had
become obscured (it was far from totally obscured), no, the initial
change here was just as fast as a nightfall farther south, but then a
brighter twilight lingered as long as another five hours, with the sun
hanging a few meters above the sea.

I rested in my room for a few hours. It was already dark, but for
me a good night began at midnight, when no light at all filtered through
the curtains. I surveyed the garden in front of the pension, leaning over

the rail around the veranda, toward the beech trees in the distance, my eyes wide open, pupils dilated in the low frequency light, infrared. In the painfully harsh light of day, I could not help noting the differences between Crimea and the outskirts of Stockholm, for one example. During the day I registered every detail with my eyes half-closed, hidden like some bird's behind a double eyelid (or the lace-curtain shutter of a camera), the disk of the sun suspended in a deep blue sky, the bright colors of the bikinis on the beach. I had lived in the north for years, traveling in geographic zones, regions that received less light for most of the year, but more rain and snow, often visiting cities where it snowed as late as May, Stockholm, for example; if I was going there in May, I would certainly take my warmest overcoat, wear it when I left St. Petersburg, to board the train in the Finland Station, and then keep it near me in the luggage rack, so I could put it back on in Helsinki, to board the ferry to Stockholm. I would open it when I got inside, in the glassed-in cabin, pulling the zipper down without taking my eyes off the black rocks along the coast, the dark cold water, the gray sky, good indications of a northern country, no palm trees, no yellow orb throwing thousands of watts on them. A breath of cold air, at last. Yes, I should turn up the collar on my overcoat.

A trip should be traced beforehand in a traveler's soul, in a tiny polygon like a Wilson camera, where you can follow the trajectory of an atomic particle, to arrive at the state of satisfaction that awaits on the other shore, the water boiling in the kettle, the sun hidden behind the trees, the *bashkir* guides chatting quietly a few steps away, in their makeshift stores. Because of the importance of the *physical*, of skin exposed to the wind and sun through the eyelids. But the mental and spiritual are just as important, the heightened experience that allows us to watch entranced as bubbles rise through liquid, to see the universes contained within their narrow walls. An idea that is elusive and fragile, the wings of a butterfly, a dream. Two dreams winged my feet, speeding my descent from the platform. The first, a Chinese parable, I will not repeat, as it is commonplace; the second, maybe less so. (I felt so alive throwing my knapsack onto the luggage rack, drinking homemade liquor with the chance companions on my trip, some Cossacks from Zaporoshets, wrapped in red kerchiefs, just a masquerade for the weekend; it's true, but so what?)

A man travels to the past like a light ray, cutting through time as easily as a hot knife though butter, as cleanly as night-vision goggles penetrate the darkness. That ray lights the part of the Jurassic forest he is moving through. The traveler can't leave the path, can't join the flutter of birds and butterflies on either side, it is forbidden. But he happens to stumble and accidentally steps on a butterfly. That's all he does. Returning to the present he discovers that his momentary interruption has not only had unfortunate consequences for the trampled butterfly—its death—but he has come back to a very different world, which has spun far off its previous orbit. We cannot know the position and spin of an electron (or a butterfly, in this case) at any given moment—I knew that when I decided to go to Astrakhan. I trampled on the order in my life more and more often, straying farther from the path each time: the Caspian Basin, for example, was almost on the complete opposite side of the earth from my birthplace. Even if nothing had made me think I would wake up someday believing I were a butterfly dreaming it was a man, I still have to worry about breaking some law and getting stuck here, alone on the delta of the Volga River, on an island swamped by a rising tide, slipping and sliding into outer space, penetrating the night like a sounding device that was sent out to photograph Venus, or a few hundred kilometers of its surface, the Venusian seas, obtaining images of unsurpassed beauty and then going too far, and unable to correct its course, flying over Saturn, beyond all hope, to discover more heaps of dust, new rings, all useless, all destined to be lost to the world and its people, to be swallowed up forever in the galactic night. As I passed across Istanbul, V. saw my solitude, and I was saved, caught by the heavy mass of a woman who drew me with the full gravitational force of her belly dance, her omphalic wisdom. The letters she sent me were like new directions, page after page, the binary sequence I needed to correct my course.

...

Why had I traveled to Stockholm (and then later to Istanbul)? To get rich. Inspired by base instincts yet again—I should write that down, to explain to V., and to myself, how I had arrived at that table in the café in Istanbul. The account I gave of my travels at that time was quite brief and largely false. Now I could describe them in detail, scrupulously, like an eye following the sinuous Cufic writing on the doors of some Tartar houses (the Tartars from Khanato in Crimea) here in Livadia. In her second letter she told me about her trip back: how she traveled across Russia to get home, how her mother clapped her hands to her cheeks, speechless with amazement. I should begin with the trip that brought me to Istanbul, the chain of purchases (and sales); list the transactions that eventually led me to that café by the Saray, the night-club with exotic dancers and strippers.

Because before the butterfly business, I had sold glasses for seeing at night (*natt kikare,* in Swedish). And before that—just to give her a sense of the turbulent atmosphere in Russia at the time—I told her I had laid eyes (and hands) on the skins of Amur tigers, on the endangered species list; the tusks and teeth of mammoths, preserved in the permafrost on the banks of the Liena, in Yakutiya; new antlers from young reindeer (for months my refrigerator held a bottle of blood obtained when the horns were sawed off, blood that had medicinal properties, scientifically proven); also snake venom (from the Karakorum desert in central Asia); and red mercury, a mineral no one had seen before, worth hundreds of times its weight in gold. On one occasion I was contacted in Tallinn by a potential buyer, a Scotsman, redheaded and red-blooded, with a dagger in the bag he wore over his kilt, not a knife, but a dirk, which he pulled to intimidate me: he wasn't going to fall into a trap in Russia, so far from Scotland. It's not so much whether you deal (obey the laws) as *what* you deal (maximum gain with minimum risk).

My list—the preceding one—is considerably shorter than Amerigo Vespucci's. Did V. know (no, of course not, I'd just learned it myself) that the continent where I was born owed its name to a letter, one Amerigo Vespucci sent to Lorenzo de Medici in 1501? I'll copy his list, Amerigo's merchandise, for the sake of comparison. Here is what the Italian wrote, his mouth watering: "The aforementioned ships carry the following: They are laden with immeasurable cinnamon, fresh and dried ginger, abundant pepper and cloves, nutmeg, mace, musk, civet, liquidambar, benjamin, purslane, mastic, incense, myrrh, red and white sandalwood, aloe wood, camphor, ambergris, sugar cane, much lacquer-gum, mumia, indigo, tutty, opium, aloe hepatica, cassia and many other drugs that would take too much time to record . . . I do not wish to go on because the ship does not allow me to write." You see, behind every voyage of discovery is hidden (that's it! hidden!) some low motive, a little spice and "immeasurable cinnamon!" All I had wanted was to make a little money, a small fortune, just enough for a modest palace, a couple of balconies, some grandly appointed rooms, where I could live in style. At night, as I passed through my billiards room, I would pick up the cue, idly run a few balls, then go out to the balcony and stare off at the horizon, penetrating the darkness, cutting through it smoothly, like a warm knife through butter, or those night-vision goggles, the kind helicopter pilots use, with a thousand-meter range, which would also come in handy for observing the flight of certain nocturnal butterflies, their iridescent wings.

...

"In total darkness, *Herren*, the lenses in these goggles pick up the very lowest rays, invisible to the naked eye, a wavelength below infrared. Behind the lens the photons are focused and then accelerated by a high-voltage current. Hear that faint buzzing? Same principle as a television, cathode ray tubes. The photons are propelled onto a phosphorescent screen, agitating it, creating the image on it. Like this. You look through here, through this opening. No, you can't see anything, because it's not dark yet. It's turned off. No. Impossible. It would burn out. The photon current is very strong this time of day, bright as it is. Your eyes would be burned out, permanently damaged, like a man who's been in prison for years. Gets blinded when he's let out, his retinas ruined. Actually, that's what I just explained . . . A steal like this and you stand here trying to make up your mind!"

"With these goggles you could go out on the Baltic, the high seas, in the dark of night, keep watch for the coast guard, sail to some designated spot, some buoys marked with paint, only visible through these goggles, my cargo floating safe and sound in a watertight container . . ." He was thinking out loud, the smuggler who bought the first pair from me, a Pole, pushing a lock of blond hair off his face, a gesture that would allow me to identify him later, in case of trouble, a grilling from customs agents.

"Or you could spend as much time as you like spinning the dial on a safe, again in perfect darkness, your ears tuned to the click of the correct combination, or else stand and watch your prey, man or animal, through this scope, attached to a high-powered rifle, using this silent lantern to light the scene with infrared rays, invisible to the naked eye . . ."

I was pointing at a battery of gunsights made for the assault troops of the Russian army. But the Red Army was now completely bankrupt, infantry, motorized, aerotransport units all liquidated, selling their *privori nochnovo videnia* (night-vision equipment), top quality but ten times cheaper than Western stuff, a price difference that gave me a nice profit margin.

I lost count of the trips I made carrying this illegal military equipment, traveling to Hamburg, Vienna, Amsterdam, Stockholm, so many other northern European cities, feigning sleep during customs checks at 3 A.M., enduring dozens of searches that didn't get to the bottom of my deep bags. I had passed through the smoking ruins of the Eastern Empire, from Varsovia to Cracovia, from Buda to Pest. And in the best plazas of those capitals, I had learned how to spot a buyer a long way off, to pick one out of the slow parade of passersby inspecting the merchandise suspiciously. The Swede I saw come around the corner one afternoon, walking toward me, smoothly slicing through the sea of heads—his walk, his bearing, gave him away. I broke off my pitch, wasting no more time on cash-poor gawkers, I practically pushed them aside, clearing the ground for this man with a pile of crowns in the bank, a BMW owner, but not flashy, dressed in a worn overcoat and cloth cap. After just a couple of questions, he picked up the

goggles to take a look (but didn't get one), a ring inexplicably dancing on his finger (thick as a Viennese sausage), which told me right
away that his overcoat held a checkbook, and that he was going to
buy them.

He took his eyes off the goggles and raised his eyebrows, sure my
answer would be close to the sum he was secretly willing to pay. No
fear of a trick: the price I asked for the goggles eliminated that possibility. I told him how the goggles worked, in no hurry—not pres-
sured like those hawkers who tell nothing but lies—explaining it in
detail (sometimes I even draw a diagram if I suspect the buyer knows
anything about the Second Industrial Revolution). I told him about
their military origins and brought up the problem of darkness, the
very problem the goggles were designed to solve. The man in the
cap, a large heavy gentleman (like a Viking), interrupted me: "Will
you take a check?" and before I said yes—with no doubt in my mind
he could cover it—he started to reach toward the inside pocket of
his overcoat, only to have his hand pulled away, by two mastiffs tugging on a leash. No problem, the deal was far enough along. I was
feeling relaxed, almost friendly toward him—he had shown confidence
in me and I in him. How sweet it is to close a deal, watching the
fountain pen smoothly inscribing the specified amount (no small sum,
that's all I'll say) and figuring how much more it is than the price I
paid just a few weeks ago, not too far from here, at the dark edge
of that garrison, at the hour I had chosen for testing the goggles,
quickly focusing them on a little patch of woods across the highway,
afraid of getting collared, and then ripped off, by second lieutenant
Vinogradov, an official who was making a killing on the illegal sale
of Red Army equipment. A man with a pack was coming toward me
through the woods. Suddenly I saw him stop and look up, staring
right at me, standing outside the garrison wall. I lowered the goggles

and couldn't see a thing; it was pitch black; the man couldn't have seen me either.

The Swede, Stockis was his name, wrote his phone number on the back of the check, so I could call if I had problems at the bank, if the teller pressed the alarm button surreptitiously because of the incongruence between the clarity of the figure stamped on it and the opacity of my non-Nordic eyes. It may have been a mistake, but I trusted this man who was walking off with my goggles under his arm, pulled along by his dogs. So I brushed off a curious guy, one of those browsers with nothing but questions: "Could you do me a favor and keep your hands off?" I bellowed. Tyrannical as any Moscow shopkeeper, I was already gathering up my merchandise, sure there'd be no more buyers today. One more lesson: always leave after a big sale, there's never more than one a day.

I still hadn't cashed the check two days later. The paper lent a certain immateriality to my sale, a certain flash of intellectual effort that would fade when it was exchanged for cash, reduced to the singularity of a few bank notes, the biggest ones they have in Sweden, it's true, the same bills, I thought, that King Gustav got paid in, if a king would bother . . . Well, haven't we all learned the surprising fact that Olof Palme goes to the movies just like any ordinary citizen? Those bills with Selma Lagerlöf on them—Gustav could well have held them in his hands.

Five days later, when he came back to the same spot on the plaza, I showed him the check. He liked that.

. . .

I had decided suddenly to change the course of my life, to take to the sea. I had spent nights in railway stations, covered thousands of kilometers by train, made five plane trips in a week. Now I found myself steering a yacht through the maze of islands around Stockholm, at the invitation of this great big man, a Viking with a gold hoop dangling from his ear. We were headed to his house to discuss a subject that needed a place like this, covered with pines and completely surrounded by water: an island.

We docked off a narrow pebble beach: water quietly lapping against the rocks, wind whispering in the pines. I jumped down from the yacht. Stockis had a proposal, he had said, something that might interest me. And while we went up some wooden steps to a terrace overlooking the beach:

"On dark nights I come out here and keep an eye on my yacht with the goggles you sold me . . ."

"Are the dogs yours?" I shot back quickly, because my English wasn't up to the circumlocutions of normal conversation, forcing me to latch on to a subject directly, like a mute. The blunt question stood for this long speech: "You have two mastiffs, don't you, the spotted ones you had in the plaza, so why do you need night-vision goggles to guard your property? You may be fabulously wealthy, you certainly seem it, but isn't that rather extravagant?"

Stockis had been to China (and in China, to Manchuria); I mean, he'd been around, all over the world, and he obviously knew how to carry on a conversation, however rudimentary the English. He came back with an explanation.

"You can't even see your hand in front of your face some nights here in Stockholm. It's dark by three in the afternoon in the winter. I don't think you could have picked a better place to sell these goggles. I have a yacht and don't sleep well. Sometimes I get up early and watch the sunrise from this terrace. But come, we're not here to talk about that . . ."

We went into the house. Through a service door in the back. On the kitchen table I saw food-caked dishes, a half-eaten box of chocolates, candy wrappers all over, as if there'd been an explosion. We went to the study, down a hallway littered with beer cartons, stepping over ads for pizza parlors with Swedish names, with the mastiffs (which did belong to Stockis) nipping at my heels. The mess suited me fine, I'm the same when I'm home alone and end up drowning in magazines, pants, shirts I can wear one more day, clean enough, hung on the backs of chairs, glasses still holding the dregs of tea, but on top of it all anyway. I know what it's like to let myself go, to slide down that slippery slope of slovenliness. Between trips I often find myself watching television, which I detest, until four in the morning, a book open in my lap, bored by whatever's on, knowing the bad cop will betray the good one several dull speeches before it happens. And never anything about smuggling, there's almost never a show with anything about smuggling, much less smuggling bugs or butterflies.

"Russia has several rare butterflies, extinct in the West . . ." he began. "There is one type in particular, the *yazikus*, which lives only from the end of May to mid-September. I would give everything to possess it."

"Everything is not anything," I replied, and then, to his broad chest, "How much?" because I do not believe in a numerical infinity, which I consider an intellectual concept, nothing more.

"Stockis is also a trade name," he said, as if confident this would add some weight to his proposal, but not explaining why. I had followed him into the study, preceded by the panes of the plaid lumberjack shirt stretched across his broad back. When he turned to see what effect this revelation had on me, I climbed up on tiptoes and peered over his shoulder, to expand my field of vision. My gaze slid along glass display cases hung from every wall. There was just one window, in the north wall, and, on both sides of it, innumerable cases full of butterflies, glowing with a soft light.

Sure, we were here to look at butterflies, and for him to propose some deal with butterflies, I knew that, but he could still have some other field, and I said, "So, you have a business . . . that sells . . . ?"

He stopped in front of a case and tapped the glass, answering me without saying the word "butterflies."

"I will be sailing to Istanbul at the end of May, on the *Vaza*. I have clients in the Middle East who are going to meet me on an island, on Crete, but before that we can look around Istanbul, you and I. Have you ever been to Istanbul?"

I had not been to Istanbul.

From floor to ceiling, up to the rafters, the study walls were covered with cases full of butterflies, which were held down, I noted, with round-headed pins, easy to get hold of. I did not know a thing about butterflies at the time, on that day near the end of winter.

"No questions until they make the first offer," he lectured. "That way, you'll know what kind of number: tens, thousands, tens of thousands. There are innumerable orders of butterflies. If a collection has specimens from a single order, it's no good. It's worth much more if it contains examples from various orders, organized lowest to highest. . . . By the way, there's a forest in Finland, near Carelia, planted by the Russian army for the production of masts. A friend of mine got the mast for his yacht, a sailboat, there . . . I don't know Russia. But they say it still has some *yazikus*, butterflies that are worth a lot of money" (or did he say "a fortune"? I don't remember). "And they say Czar Nicholas II was the last person to capture one. He was the last czar, too, right?"

(*Who* says? I felt like asking Stockis, *who* told you that?)

He was thinking, about to add something, maybe about the offices the Nobel brothers had in Baku and St. Petersburg, but out came:

"Wait," he struck the arm of his chair, worried, and asked me: "How will you recognize it?" like in some detective novel, so that I pictured myself waiting in some nightclub or restaurant, with a copy of *Botanic World Illustrated* spread out on my table. But I wouldn't have any trouble identifying the insect: it would show up for our meeting with a green umbrella tucked under its right-front leg, in outsize boots that rattled around on its last pair of tiny legs. And it would have its wings folded, so that if not for its skinny thorax it could have been some flashy cowboy in a sunflower overcoat.

2

For a reader of Conrad, the passage across the Baltic, the Gulf of Finland, can be as charged with mystery as journeying to the South Seas. I was skimming over it on a fine ferry, almost a hundred meters long, with twelve decks. Standing on the aft deck (the captain's deck), I imagined myself the hero in a storm, warning the captain of danger, an approaching iceberg. At nightfall I saw the carnival lights of another ferry passing me by, looking lovelier, more luxurious than mine, with more pleasures for their passengers. The other ship disappeared in the fog and I turned my back on the picture window, trying to get in shape for this trip, which was no less of an adventure. I had abandoned a normal life, apprentice writer with occasional weekends on the loading dock at a meat-packing plant in St. Petersburg. It's easy enough, anyone could see my main motive, what made me jump into the cold water of dealing (a euphemism, to avoid "smuggling"), fully aware what I was getting into. Like that captain in Conrad, in full command of his seafaring faculties, with a successful career in the English navy, who listens to Lord Jim's disturbing tale—the disgrace, the loss of honor—and then makes some careful annotations in the binnacle log, winds his watch, and throws himself into the water. I wanted to be converted, to become something more than a novelist, more than a storyteller, and so I jumped into the cold water of dealing, I learned all the numbers and "How much does it cost?" and "I'll give it to you for half price, since you're my friend" in more than seven of the languages of eastern and northern Europe.

I relived those trips in my dreams, as if my bed kept moving all night, just as if I was in a sleeping car or a ship's cabin, below sea level. Yesterday, asleep, I thought I heard the wings of a helicopter over my head, an asthmatic gasp, a slow crackling, syncopated, as if it was about to crash, and the next morning I stood at the newsstand, in a trance, staring at a photo of a ferry tilted up on its side, listing, half submerged. I felt sure that a dream of shipwreck had been about to take off from that sound of wings, but had mutated into a peremptory summons, an open hand slapping on my door, knocking. It had wanted to be a rescue helicopter, a long ladder unrolling slowly toward our raft tossing in the waves, wind and cold eating into our bones, women screaming. In fact, I did hear screams eventually, Kuzmovna yelling at Petrovich, and from the same direction, a flurry of slaps, like the stuttering wings. I leapt out of bed and into the hall as if propelled by the force of those blows, transmitted to my body through the air. A step ahead of me, in a floral bathrobe, with one hand on her belt and the other raised over her head, swinging back to pound on the door, the arm exposed, soft flesh slowly sliding toward the impact. "Petrovich!" Kuzmovna shrieked before her palm slammed once more against the blank of the door. "Petrovich!" she yelled again, pulling it back into launch position, winding up for a new attack. "Maria Kuzmovna!" I yelled. And then again, quietly, "Maria Kuzmovna." Meaning, the time, a good place to start, it's six in the morning, for one thing, and then there's the knocking and the letter, the answer I had been writing, trying to write, to V., up, wide awake, till all hours. And also the completely tasteless soup she had served yesterday, the quivering of her fleshy arms, that sort of thing. Petrovich finally half-opened the door, and I heard them whispering furiously about something, who knows what, as if it was terribly urgent, which it surely wasn't.

I had made many trips in the ship that sank yesterday between Helsinki and Stockholm. That's what the wings were trying to say, the knocking and the open door I saw before going back to sleep, the light of the sea at the end of the passage. Kuzmovna was talking to Petrovich outside his room. I was puzzled by the unusual brightness of the water and the cold air pouring in through the door. I moved toward it, walking past Kuzmovna, catching her in mid-reply, motionless, like a wax figure. There was another long hallway that I had to walk down, past the doors of many rooms that I hadn't noticed before, full of unknown people that Kuzmovna must have let in, new tenants who must have moved in recently, but when? The wall at the end of the passage had disappeared and the water came right up to it, like in a house on stilts: I was dreaming again.

I thought I hadn't slept at all, but when I finally woke up, the sun was bright: it was late and so was I, later than usual leaving the pension.

"Shipwreck" I read on the front page of the paper at the newsstand by the Post Office, in such a rush I went right past. It hadn't been a dream, I managed to tell myself, but the transmission of images in real time: the tangible heaviness of a helicopter about to crash, blades spinning desperately. I doubled back anxiously. My God! Hundreds of people had been trapped in the cabins of the *Baltic*. (The long hallway, the door, the cold wind of my dream.) I broke out in a sweat and the system securing my joints fell to pieces, like when there's a warning signal in a dream, emergency lights flash, and the whole crew rushes to the engine room to pump out the water, abandoning less important systems.

I had just enough strength to turn, trembling, to the shipwreck article, after a brief glance at the weather report for Crimea and southern Russia. Nice all weekend: as if I could believe that. Cold water had awakened many of the passengers in their cabins, the article began. Screaming in terror, they ran down the flooded hallway in the dark, trying to reach the stairs before the sirens suddenly stopped wailing, and the ferry sank. I had imagined it dozens of times falling asleep in my cabin, but thought it would never happen with me onboard. With no desire to read the details, I put the newspaper back in the rack. I made a futile effort to straighten my back, then dragged myself limply to a bench near the Post Office door. But I would have been saved, I thought, half-closing my eyes to see better. I never went to bed early on those trips, and that would have saved me from dying trapped in my cabin, drowned. I would have had plenty of time to run from the salon to the darkened discotheque, pull open the glass door, out to the deck, to get a seat in a lifeboat. A bit calmer, I managed to pull my feet under the bench, raise my head. I sat staring at the sea, the horizon, through the tops of the pines. The same sea, in fact, but a bit warmer.

It is possible to reconstruct sensations and states of mind from experiences and states of mind that are infinitely more minor, on another scale entirely. Resting on that bench, overcome, I knew what it was to be lifted by a flimsy flying machine, the deafening noise onboard the helicopter, the blind confidence that we have, in spite of everything, in mechanical devices that sail through the water and fly through the air. I was able to reconstruct the satisfaction of a narrow escape from insignificant pieces of information, unrelated incidents, last-minute rescues, anxieties that were similar, but on a smaller scale. Like not having a place to spend the night in a cold city, very far north, Helsinki, in this case. I knew more about this shipwreck, my shock, my horror were greater than that of someone who just read about it over breakfast: in some way, I too had been there. This prostration thanks to my last trip. I had missed the last train when I got back to Helsinki. Arriving at the station only to watch it pull away from the platform was like being lost at sea. The sea: a cold city like Helsinki was similar; the mast, that was my knapsack; the punishing sun, the snow sliding down the neck of my overcoat; the despairing castaway, me with my sopping shoes and cold feet; the distant shore, the coastline, and the glossolalic mission.

I had the phone numbers of a few acquaintances in Helsinki, but when I dialed them, I got answering-machine messages or the recorded music that tells you the person you wanted, who should have been there to give you a place to stay, isn't home, he's off in Oslo or Copenhagen or God knows where. It was nine at night and the snow hadn't let up since I left the ferry. I listened to one after another of these devastating messages, and I stood in the phone booth watching the Finns saunter by, all of them with homes, and beds to lie down in, with the easy manner of people with keys in their pockets. Of course, it wasn't the first time: I had watched—trying to keep from freezing in a telephone booth, or in some clean well-lighted American fast-food place—as merry Viennese waltzed by, and happy Krakovians, and the fine folks of chilly Stockholm, looking forward to a hot cup of tea in their kitchens at home, while I was strolling around the great outdoors, looking for a spot to throw down my backpack and if I was lucky (in Prague) a cardboard box to shield my shoulders from the cold, sleeping on the ground.

Someone had told me about a couple of priests who provided lodging for travelers. Would I still have the number? Yes, fortunately. One of them—I first greeted him in Finnish and then described my situation ("I'm in . . . distress, quite honestly")—was kind enough to say he'd pick me up at the station. An excellent beginning: tomorrow at this hour, I would be home in St. Petersburg. "My name is Peckas," he told me. Peckas? Perfect (great, terrific, whatever).

He looked like a priest on a pirate ship. With his sleeves rolled up you could see he-man arms covered with tattoos, anchors and sayings in Finnish. I imagined his past with the fleet, the tough chaplain who forced the refractory cabinboy to his knees, putting a hand on his neck and pushing him down onto the polished boards of the deck, in Jakarta or some other South Seas port. Seeing him come toward me, rocked by the swaying of his muscular legs, his thick finger between the pages of a Bible, I felt like I'd been shipwrecked.

Many wandering souls had taken shelter in the church, so the tongue-speakers couldn't keep track of which of their guests had been baptized (they baptized them all; that was the price you paid for your lodging: letting them baptize you). Peckas put his arm around me good-humoredly and asked if I had been baptized at his hands. Two Nigerians and a Kurd, who were also spending the night in the church, piped up that they'd never seen me before. I explained that it had been another time, when they weren't around. Peckas, speaker in tongues, let me lie, to use up my supply of lies for the day. The Kurd pulled me aside and asked me to say yes. Baptism would put the priests in a good mood, they'd slice up the salami for supper. Did I like the bland sausage in Helsinki? And the whipped cream? They wouldn't leave without eating. They were devout Christians, but there'd be no mortadella or nut butter for me. I'd already taken a shower on the boat, I told them. So what did another bath matter? Should we go to the North-Nautic? Sure, the North-Nautic is a nice little place, at a hundred eighty dollars a night. . . . He had let them baptize him many times . . . I agreed, what else could I do? Peckas called to his companion with a big loud speech in Finnish—more than ten grammatical cases—and a second tongue-speaking priest appeared, also smiling and rosy as a baby.

To talk to God, they told me, you don't have to know any particular language; you can address him in any language whatsoever, because at the peak of your communion with him, you'll be possessed by "the gift of tongues"—by glossolalia. To most ears they may be unintelligible sounds, but to God they are sounds that come from the deepest part of your soul and transmit all your love for him. I couldn't stop staring at Peckas's forearms, the play of the tattooed anchor and the siren, fascinated; he had even opened my shirt and pulled out the money I had hidden against my heart, dearer to me than my feelings for God. I didn't have time to think, to ask any questions. They read some passages from Peter's Epistle to the Romans, put their hands on my head, and from either side I received an imperious order, they shouted in unison, "Speak," and my mouth opened and out came a mad rush of inarticulate sounds, blending with the incoherent phonemes of a speaker in tongues, and for I don't know how long, I talked to God in words from my heart because onto me, too, had descended the Gift of Tongues.

Shaken to the bottom of my soul, deafened by everything they had shouted in my ears, I thought I was waking from a dream when there was a sudden silence and Peckas asked something that made me think my program for deciphering human language had gone completely haywire. That getting converted, becoming a glossolal, too, had overwhelmed me, and with the many languages I would understand from now on, I had lost the ability to understand my own. Peckas asked me in Spanish, "Do you have clean underpants?" And since I just stared at him (unable to believe my ears) he realized how ridiculous his question sounded and explained: "to use as a bathing suit for your baptism. You have to get wet."

I still have the photo: I'm emerging from an Erickson bath that they had filled with running water from the fountain, supplied by the many lakes and glaciers of Lapland. I'm shivering with cold, in a well-worn bathing suit (no clean underwear) and an ill-fitting alb, which was supposed to symbolize the purity of the newly baptized, my sins running off into the gutter and to the Gulf of Finland, my heart cleansed of the stigma of the dollars hanging around my neck, between the glacial waters of Lapland and the pure water of the sea.

And then to capture the moment for eternity. Next to me in the photo, Peckas, smiling slightly. It's just possible to make out a faint filigree on the forearms piously crossed over his belly. In this holy gesture I have always thought I could see—examining the photo so many times—the many innocent throats those hairy hands had forced into silence in his shady past, long before he had decided, perhaps to atone for his guilt, to make as many others speak in garbled profusion. I could not send this photo to V. I looked, quite properly, like a hungry person, waiting for dinner. The end of the ritual consisted in recording my name, which would be included in an annual report, a missive they sent to His Holiness in Rome, as testament to the good works of their temple in this remote province of Christianity. The next morning, before leaving, I received a tape of sermons recorded in Spanish, English, and every Scandinavian language (glossolalia), all delivered in the same voice, the stentorous Peckas, speaker in tongues.

3

ST. PETERSBURG

It was raining in St. Petersburg. The city was suspended from the sky by dark gray threads that melted onto its sidewalks and zinc-covered roofs. I caught a cab at the metro entrance, and we drove down Nevski, through raindrops spattering on the asphalt. I told the driver to let me out on Liteinaya, the booksellers' street. I wanted to visit Vladimir Vladimirovich, an elderly gentleman always bent over a book, his back to the bookstore's main room. Which was in a small cellar beyond the sound of the rumbling streetcars; you got to it through an arch that opened onto a patio with crude bars on the first-floor windows and drain pipes whose ends were cemented to the ground by silver icicles. The basement was in a second patio—there was also a third, through which you could exit, escape to the next street if necessary—behind a door covered with layers of pasted-up signs. They were the work of the girl who watched the cashbox, the girl I had discovered one afternoon passing a colored pencil over a plastic stencil of the alphabet. They ran because of the constant humidity in St. Petersburg, which soaked right through them and even dampened the pages of books that sat too long in unheated basements. Like the copy of *Diurnal and Nocturnal Butterflies of the Russian Empire,* for example, which I found on a shelf near the door. In the same room one afternoon I found a book that I didn't dare return to the shelf once I held it in my hands and leafed through it, that I kept clutched to my chest, exultantly. I remember it perfectly well but won't say what it was. This had to be the best bookstore in St. Petersburg, which at the time was called Leningrad, an ugly name. So when my new business interests forced me to embark on a preliminary study, following the trail of the *yaƶikus* through the Public Library and the used bookstores, I remembered this man, who spent hours—the time I lost sniffing around the shelves—bent over a book, like any other customer, even though he was actually the owner, the principal investor, so to speak, in the bookstore, and Liena, the girl with the cashbox, who colored a new sign for the door every few months, always switching the store hours. Later I learned that these changes reflected the hours she closed to meet her lovers, with their various occupations. She took me, for example, to her house, which was close by, in the Fontanka, from 1:30 to 2:25, and then closed at 6:00, even though it was spring, and the days were getting longer, so there were still customers at 7:00. The old man, I remembered as the door opened with a jerk and warm basement air hit me in the face, was named Vladimir Vladimirovich. I had never spoken to him, but Liena often complained about him after the short midday break in her room, half dressed, throwing on her clothes, pulling up her stockings, putting on makeup at the mirror, bra straps cutting into her back: "Vladimir Vladimirovich is going to kill me. I can't go on like this, always getting back late, changing the hours. You know though?"—and she sought my eyes in the mirror—"He doesn't even notice. He has tea and biscuits in his office, never comes out till closing time. God, he must be eighty years old."

I found him in his office sipping tea from a discolored cup that could have come from an imperial service.

"Vladimir Vladimirovich! I don't know if you . . . Look, I have a job. A Swede, a rich man, has hired me to capture a butterfly, a rare specimen. I'll tell you the whole story if you have the time . . . Do you know that in Finland they still have stands of pine grown for masts, with thick trunks, no twists? Of course you know that: I've read it, too, actually, wait . . . Right, in a book I bought here a few months ago. Peter had them planted, but by the time they were big enough, fifty years later, there was no use for them. But no, that's not true. They were still making ships with masts. Even today there are a few left, old-time ships . . . No, I had some before I left home . . . Okay, one cup . . . I was just considering a catalog of butterflies that you have. But maybe you know a better one. Yes, you're right, a butterfly that's almost extinct, what book would that be in? Thanks, Vladimir Vladimirovich. It seems I'm going to the Caspian Basin and from there to Istanbul. I have some books I'd like to leave on consignment, for you to sell. I'll stop by before I go."

Talking to Vladimir Vladimirovich, into his big octogenarian ears, made me nervous. We had never had a real conversation. One day he told me that he was planning to write a book about Nevski Avenue, about a house on Nevski, number 55. The one that has some dancing birds, griffins, a pattern, you know, from Scythia. That's right, was all he said. He never lingered on the salient points in my remarks, like he did on the winged griffin, the animal motifs of Scythia. I hadn't told him what I did (at the time I was moving sides of beef in a packing plant on the edge of town, awful, terrible pay). I had never seen him outside this store, behind his stands. One afternoon, it's true, I saw a very old man, in a moth-eaten greatcoat, crossing Liteinaya, just about caught between the tracks as two streetcars went by. He managed to get through first. Vladimir Vladimirovich had never asked me, like the police, for example: "And you, young man, where are you from?" That was a subject completely immaterial, irrelevant to him.

. . .

On the same thin stiff translucent paper that he used for labels (writing the names of his butterflies on narrow strips in India ink) Stockis had copied down the distinguishing marks of the *yazikus*, in English, in the neat hand of a professional clerk. Wingspan: 30 to 40 millimeters. Wing pattern: dorsal, pale yellow background with a pattern of angry eyes, a defense mechanism, inspiring the concept of danger in its predators (this unnecessary explanation and the ticklish term "concept" puzzled me). The description I found in *Diurnal and Nocturnal Butterflies of the Russian Empire*, by V. V. Sirin, was less "psychological," more nineteenth century (St. Petersburg, 1895). It agreed for the most part, but the ink drawing by Rodionov, S. V., illustrator, was clearly superior to the photographs in modern catalogues, like *Stuart's*.

He used the same paper to explain how to preserve the specimen if I should capture it. First I should kill it by putting it into a wide-mouthed bottle full of ether, being careful not to touch the wings and spoil their fine iridescent powder. Once it was dead, I should pick it up by the thorax, the top part, and fasten it horizontally, somewhat loosely, so it could be moved when it was in the collection . . . He broke off in the middle of the instruction. Put two thick lines through it. Resumed more confidently, taking a different approach, from the word *bottle*. Use it to carry the captured specimens (now plural), so they would not get dislodged and damaged during transport. From where to where? I thought. We had spoken of only one point: Istanbul. He would prefer that the sale occur there, rather than somewhere too dangerous, like Russia, since the violent explosion of the mafia, or too safe, like Sweden, where the cops could not be bribed: forget Sweden.

I bought a *Handbook for the Young Insect Collector*, too, for a thirtieth of what I paid for *Diurnal and Nocturnal Butterflies of the Russian Empire*. I thumbed through it right there in the bookstore. How

to prepare a mount. Materials needed. The insect or butterfly net . . .
It's better to make your own net . . . I didn't have time for that. I bought
one with an adjustable handle, the kind they sell in Yuni naturalist
stores (for "The Young Naturalist": me, for one).

At last I had my hands on a detailed description: it lived in sunny
open spaces, border areas, its wings deeply cut on the outside edge,
two series of submarginal spots, bright yellow. A verbal portrait com-
plementing the photos from Stockis and the beautiful illustration in
Diurnal Butterflies, a full-page vellum sheet, behind which pen-and-
ink butterflies seemed to be flying in the morning mist, or just the way
I saw them now, through half-closed eyes, lying on my back in a field
in Livadia, only half-looking, sure that *yaẓikus* were long gone: whether
killed by DDT, intensive farming, or seventy years of Soviet rule.

The Natural History Museum would probably have one on display.
I had studied every detail of the *yaẓikus* picture: the tiny legs that
the illustrator must have painted with a fine sable-hair paintbrush,
the antennae . . . they were engraved in my mind all the way there
in the cab.

Still inside, I stared out at the streetcar landing by the Winter
Palace, at the women with raincoats and umbrellas rushing to board
the trolleys. I began the climb, my black shoes glistening from the rain
against the horizontal gray lines of the stairs going up to the museum.

Leaving behind the moth-eaten bones of mammoths, their skeletons
clumsily resting on bony feet, unable to take flight, I began the dizzying descent to the winged simplicity of the *lepidoptera.* Right at the
door, eye-catching, a huge example of *Lepidoptera fenestra.* I drew
closer to look, pinning it down in the middle of the multicolored flutter in the other glass cases, the silent flapping of the *vanessas.*

There were no *yaẓikus* on display. I carefully checked all the little
labels, straining to bend over them. I seemed to see a reflection of

myself in a low genuflection, but quickly realized it was a live specimen of the local fauna, a little old attendant, slowly shifting in her chair
in the corner, her soft cheeks puffed out by the gob of caramel she was
sucking placidly. I stepped forward to look at her face. Her eyes were
shut and she seemed asleep, but her jaws kept working automatically.
She did not open them when she heard me talking to her. Just stopped
sucking since the interior roar from that activity isolated her sonically
from the room: *Ya slushayu Vas* (I hear you). I asked to see the *yazikus:*
she was as slow to answer as if a team of stagehands had to roll back
the tarpaulins and pick up the instruments that an orchestra had left in
the rain at a summer concert. She blinked, opening just one eye, and
studied me for a moment: "There is no such thing. I have never heard
of such a butterfly. Who said we had one here? Konstantin Pavlovich
. . . Well, he is not here today . . . Our *nauchni* (scientific) *konsultant*
could explain it better, but he has Sundays off. He gave me strict
orders . . . I mean, there is no such . . . If there was one, wouldn't we
have it here, in the best museum of entomology in Russia?"

The whole time she spoke she was darting back and forth in her
chair, peering around, trying to watch the corners behind me, since I
could be part of a gang, the one who keeps the guard busy with friendly
chatter while his accomplices ransack the display cases. After all, museum robberies were on the rise in Russia. But it never even crossed
my mind to steal the *yazikus* from the Natural History Museum, even
though it would be a lot less work and a much shorter trip—a few
trolley stops from my home—than organizing an expedition to the
Volga delta.

That trip held the opposite appeal: tramping around in my tarred
boots, hiking through the trees. If the Russian state, in the person of
some anonymous hunter, had gone ahead and bagged a couple of specimens of *yazikus* for its collection, then I don't see why I should have

to get them by force, stealing them instead of winning them honestly, playing by the rules. I had had no plans to use a handkerchief soaked in ether on the old lady who had been so slow to open her blue eyes, eyes that were strangely bright, probably in mint condition from how little work she gave them. But she was sure I was a foreign occupier, she'd seen plenty of movies about partisans, and during my interrogation she had to lie at any cost, even her life; so she just kept talking, that is, *zagoborit menia*, misleading me with aimless remarks, denying any knowledge of where the weapons were hidden, or the *yazikus*, those were her instructions, she had gotten them from Konstantin Pavlovich, the *konsultant*: "Nadieshda Ivanovna, you know that this is a terrible time for our country. We have been hit by a crime wave, youthful crooks attracted by our wealth, anxious to enrich themselves, as you well know. This new tide comes from the West. They will ask about certain specimens from our collection. I will mention no names because then you can't remember them. This is all you need to know: deny everything. You know nothing. The specimen they want does not exist; you have never heard of it. There is one butterfly in particular . . . But no. You only have to say (playing dumb, you know): No, I don't know what you're talking about. Yazi? Kuz? Well, no, never . . ."

It was obvious she was lying. She was agitated, like a person not used to it. She kept rocking in her chair, as if an accomplice behind me was busy filling his sacks. Not too long ago, some thieves—very polite, attentive young people, eager for knowledge, like so many previous generations of pioneering youth who had toured the museum in big groups, totally innocent in appearance—had come into one of these rooms and stolen some mammoth teeth. I had read it in the newspaper before I left for Helsinki. I did not, however, draw any practical conclusions from that item in the *Sankt Petersburkie Vedomosti*. True, there was no reason for such considerations at the time, when I was at the station, waiting to board the train to Helsinki, but when Stockis gave me a list of the butterflies he wanted, and I decided to visit the Natural History Museum, back in Petersburg, it had not yet dawned on me that the Volga expedition was completely unnecessary, since the specimens Stockis wanted were all in that museum, caught by the long arm of the state, conveyed from their far-flung confines to the former capital of the empire and confided to the feeble custody of a frail old lady, easy to knock out with a handkerchief soaked in ether. Instead of knocking out dozens of butterflies, that is, moving tortuously across the irregularities of the map, burned brown by the sun, breaking ground in my hob-nailed boots, I could reduce my ether overhead to the few drops it would take to put this old crone to sleep and then board the trolley outside the museum, blending in with the raincoats, and cross the city on the bus. Much shorter, and much safer, than a trip to the Caspian Basin.

4

CASPIAN BASIN

We would land somewhere between the mouths of the Volga and the Astrakhan. Traveling through the tangle of the delta's canals in a coastal steamer, I saw the Caspian as an empty wineskin, with the steamboat dropping down into it through the narrow neck. I would leap ashore, into a patch of reeds in some spot not marked on the map, and a week later I would be at some other beach waiting for the same steamer, which would take me home, fabulously wealthy, my saddle-bags stuffed with rare specimens.

But first I had boarded the boat in Astrakhan, at a dock so full of barges that it looked to me—viewing the countryside from the heights of the city—like it would be possible to walk across the Volga without ever touching the water. I began my descent to the dock down a poorly paved street, positive I was headed in the right direction because a thin stream of water was running down-street, too, trickling along the edge of the sidewalk. That water could hardly be wrong about the way to the Volga, from which it had so recently ascended to heaven, then fallen to earth again and been dammed. Deep in a cold storage room someone had opened the tap, I thought, like releasing a bird to return to the woods, and the water now led me to the Volga: flowing along, following the course of gravity. I stopped in the middle. Water swirled around my heels and I felt a chill from deep in the Volga through my leather boots. In a shed near the shore, some workers were stacking barrels of pickled fish. I got within twenty meters of it and was about to ask how to get to pier no. 5, where the steamer was docked. I had already taken a big breath and picked out one of the workers—the man standing in the doorway of the shed cupping his hands to shield the flame of a match, who would raise an arm when he caught my question and point either to the right, fifty meters beyond the shed, or to the left, past the building with the barred windows—when I saw the sign myself, nailed to the top of a post, over the head of the worker, almost scraping it: "River dock no. 5," written in rust-proof paint. The man finished lighting his filter-tip and went back in the shed.

...

The low light at that hour made me look even more like a criminal, a sturgeon poacher, a member of one of the huge gangs trafficking in Caspian caviar. The steamer let off dozens of silent men who tossed their packs ashore and then jumped after them surefootedly and took off without a backward glance, their sights already on the banknotes snaking through the reeds. I didn't turn back either. I moved toward the riverbank feeling the eyes of the captain on my back. My equipment differed considerably from that of a sturgeon fisherman, but I chose not to disillusion him. He would not have believed me anyway, even if I spread the contents of my pack on the cabin floor: no clubs to stun the poor sturgeons, nor curved knives to slit their bellies: just flasks of ether, two butterfly nets with adjustable handles, an acetylene torch for night hunting, and an inflatable rubber boat, to cross the delta's numerous waterways. V. V. Sirin's *Diurnal and Nocturnal Butterflies of the Russian Empire* says two *yazikus* were captured in one of the fields in this delta, in the Caspian Basin, in 1893.

Standing in the reeds, I saw the steamboat move away. I watched it back up, testing the depth of the river with its propellers, then straightening its course and continuing its trip.

By eleven that morning I was on the edge of a field, dark green with hundreds of butterflies floating above it, but no *yazikus* in sight. The heat kept intensifying, rising gradually, like the sounds from the orchestra pit at the opera. Without daring to leave the protection offered by the trees, I opened *Diurnal Butterflies* and flipped through it like a conductor glancing over the score one last time before striking the music stand with his baton. None of the butterflies paid any attention to the stick (of my net), which I slowly drew out after five minutes scanning the book, trying to match a butterfly from the page with the one that landed a few inches from my eyes, on a branch. When I found it at last, a common *colias*, I waved my net, desperately hoping that the butterflies would synchronize their flight across the field, get into formation, glide along the ground, rise in a loop-the-loop, pair up to waltz past me, prettily, then get in line and drop into the bottles of ether, one per bottle, with me cavorting joyfully, like a faun, blowing a panpipe, sealing the bottles, holding them up to the light, admiring each specimen before setting it in the bottom of my pack.

The music (Disney) disappeared as soon as I swung the net, missing completely, and started racing around the field, in giant strides (Chaplin), scaring off the *colias*, streaming with sweat, and getting stung by mosquitoes—they were nowhere to be found during the waltz of the butterflies, but when I stepped into the grass, breaking the luminous skin of my field of dreams, they swarmed up and rushed toward me like a group of ugly actresses, with no talent, mobbing the producer at a casting call, hoping to win the role of Sleeping Beauty. Dying to go to an eternal sleep at the bottom of my ether bottles. I had to postpone my career, start hunting mosquitoes, an easy job, slapping. They died without having sucked my blood, empty, insensible. The *colias*, more peaceful, came back and landed on some nearby flowers, to tempt me.

The Volga was shining through the trees: I could always leave this island, throw my rubber boat in the water, let the current carry me along. I thought of Stockis. Not cursing him, simply thinking he was the only person who could make sense of the mosquito bites and sweat running down my spine. To me they were just butterflies: I had no idea how to exchange them for holidays on Niza, books or oil paintings. The design on their wings held no interest for me—unless it earned some real interest. I needed an expert in the field, an experienced hunter, but then I'd have to split the profit.

I saw one right next to me, exploring a flower with its delicate feet. Not a *yaẓikus*, but I hoped that focusing on a single specimen might save me from despair. I followed it all over the field, past lots of other butterflies that I could easily have had, ignoring them because if I lost sight of it, if I wandered for a moment, I'd be doomed to chaos, the dozens of *colias* flying over the grass sipping nectar from the flowers. I took my time, trailing it like a hunter after a hare, matching its zigzags step-for-step in an attempt to wear it out. I saw only the shifting backdrops that framed the desperate beating of its wings, small squares of sky, grass, trees. Sweat dripped from my eyelashes, but I didn't raise a hand to wipe it away, obsessively wielding my net, moving forward. I caught a glimpse of the steel belt of the river. Refreshed by the breeze, I cut through the trees, the flashing point of its flight leading me on.

I had seen too many movies to not see myself, running forward exhausted, sawed-off Colt in hand, ignoring the small-time crooks, pursuing the arch-villain, who'd given me a deadly look before the chase, before fleeing the scene of the crime, police cars closing in,

sirens wailing. The sand slowed my pace, the breeze checked its flight: a gust of wind forced it to fold itself against a tree trunk. I pounced with the butterfly net, pulled tweezers from my pocket, and seized it: the glint of the steel, the enormous hand, gigantic, it threw me one last terrified look and hid its head between its wings, its fear reflected in the thousand octahedrons of its eyes. Glazed over.

I raised the flask and held it to the light. The breeze blowing off the river finally dried me off and I called it quits, staring at the silhouette of the other island covered with pines, which seemed to be floating past, carried along by the current.

...

Studied more closely, through my waterproof binoculars, the island looked no more solid. The pieces of beach, of woods, the fallen trees hollowed out by the water, their roots in the air, all jumped about in the eyepiece, too silent, the birds songless on the branches. It would take an hour's hard work to get there—through the branches I could not see the river, just the sky and the pine trees that grew very straight, upright like pins in a pincushion.

It did not see me arrive, I thought, looking at that island. Standing on the shore, the wind drying my back, I felt like a sleepwalker awakening on the edge of a tiled roof, horrified, nine stories up, the ground tiny below. Through my binoculars I saw a bird on a branch—on a tree on that island—and I was bewildered because it was not chirping. I studied its red maw for a long time; I saw it take a breath, pause, and start to warble. I lowered the binoculars. I could see the tree, the branch, but not the bird. I put my feet apart, dug in my heels, bent my knees, and dropped backward onto the sand. I wound up sitting on the riverbank; finding that bird was more important to me than the butterfly in the bottle. Still, I wasn't getting paid for birds. But I wasn't

enjoying this butterfly hunt. So why had I agreed to it? I put the binoculars back in their case and thought nostalgically of the days when I sold ten pairs of binoculars like these, 20 x 60 magnification, waterproof, in a single day, with a net profit of fifty percent. It's true, completely and absolutely, I wouldn't lie to you, or else, like Amerigo Vespucci (in that same letter), "Believe, Lorenzo, that what I have written here is true."

The past two weeks in St. Petersburg, the train trip to Astrakhan, the crossing in the steamer, all seemed to have gone up in smoke, as if my appearance here—on the delta of the Volga, a bird singing on the island across from me—had been both swift and direct, as if no time had elapsed between that trip to Sweden to sell military equipment and my landing this morning. My stay in Stockholm, my fortunes sunk and then baptized into new life in Helsinki, all that was gone. I'd just arrived and taken a look at myself from that other island, standing on the bank, studying the landscape, a sight that surprised and scared me. I'd heard that butterflies fly along at ground level, sit on flowers to drink their nectar; it's easy to trap them under a hat, even easier than in a butterfly net with an adjustable handle. They were thick in the Caspian Basin, flying over the fields. It didn't take a big investment to chase butterflies and all you had to do was inventory the specimens you'd caught, on a good day, cheerfully checking them off your list. You wouldn't have to invest much money to chase butterflies, nor would you face so many problems getting home, even before setting out on the return trip. I always have money—ten times as much as at the start of any deal—before I enter that tunnel, but I'm in the dark from then on, feeling my way along walls oozing water, shivering with fear and cold. I almost never see where I'll land, I follow such a long arc, seven gleaming colors lighting up the treasure. And arrayed between me and that treasure are customs sheds, customs inspections,

crooked sellers, crooked buyers, swindlers of every stripe, shady manu-
facturers who supply the army with shoddy equipment (imagine the
fate of a soldier left blind in night combat, his viewer broken in the
heat of the battle), counterfeit checks, counterfeit dollars, the double,
triple fence I have to cross on my way home, the motorcycle gangs on
the access roads to St. Petersburg, the lights out in the reception area
in my building, the elevator stuck on one of the top floors, the red
button glowing in the dark like the flame of a votive candle, a slam
behind me, the car descending, a deafening squeak, so I don't hear the
steps of the person coming toward me. Why go back and look? I go
back and look. The old woman from Apartment 2. No, an unknown
person in a raincoat. Another coming out of the foyer, smiling strangely.
I go up dagger in hand (it's true, I have a Finnish knife up my sleeve,
strapped to my arm, so if I put my hand in my jacket in a pious pose,
I can grip its handle, ready to pull it out, stabbing and slashing). The
keys. Open the door without delay, without betraying the cash I have
hanging round my neck, enough to buy . . . okay, everything has gone
up nowadays. At last the door's open, then closed. Turn on the lights,
fast, close the latch, drop my backpack, throw myself on the sofa.
Think how nice these steel doors are, bulletproof. Keep my eyes on
the window, watching the snow fall.

Catching butterflies had to be easier than that, I'd thought before
sitting down at the kitchen table to study Stockis's list and plan my
fruitless visit to the Natural History Museum.

I stopped and listened, stopped staring at the bird. Something was
coming upriver. A buzzing, like a far-off motor, very faint, wavering, getting weaker, getting lost in a cloud of other noises. A minute
later it reappeared, a strip of sound, thin but well-defined; first, an
electric mower (perhaps some farmworkers cutting forage in a field
not far from here?), and then getting louder, steadily moving toward

me, the propeller of an outboard motor whipping the water, churning the air. A pair of farmers in a launch, a man with a pasty white torso and dark sunburned arms and neck, and his wife, spitting sunflower seeds into the water. I watched through my binoculars till they were out of sight. They seemed harmless enough, hauling hay, the woman sitting in the prow to counterbalance the load. Long before they appeared, the knowledge that a boat with a big engine was coming upstream made me look for a hiding place, back from the river, behind a fallen log, on the pine needles. Running up the bank and dodging behind a tree trunk, my heart almost jumping from my mouth, I justified my panic: *Must watch out for sturgeon poachers.* They wouldn't want to see strangers on the riverside, someone who might inform the river police: "Yes, there were four men in the launch, two in black raincoats, all in tar-boots." "Like the ones you're wearing?" I would lower my eyes, study my shoes for a moment. "Yes, just like mine. . . . But what are you getting at?" "Nothing. No one's insinuating anything." That kind of question. The police would be in on the poachers' racket. They'd have to be, here, in a place like this. I'd ask to spend the night in the station, in the log hut they have at police stations sometimes. "What? Do you think we're running a hotel here? Get out, go spend the night outside . . ." I—their you—had done everything I'd come to do . . . and I was leaving. Slam. Eleven at night. The interrogation over. One of the leather-jackets would lead me to an encounter next to the shed, piles of wood, fresh cuts, under cover of darkness; he would ask for a light . . . that type of business, then the beating.

Hidden high on the bank, I watched the pair of locals pass, relaxing as the wake of their boat rocked the logs along the shore. People lived here. It wasn't just a stomping ground for illegal fishermen and illegal hunters, for smugglers, the dregs of society.

"That's it. You're right. But how can you know in advance? Do you know how many sturgeon fishermen go by here every day? Dozens. You must excuse me for not opening up right away."

It was almost dark when I got to the log cabin. A few meters from shore, in an open field at a bend in the river, it could have been put there just to keep an eye on the launches and boats that went by. The couple's motorboat was on the beach, still loaded with hay. I knocked on the wrought-iron gate, getting up on tiptoe to yell over it, but no one came to open up. I walked around the house, the shed filled with wood stacked high for the winter, the stable for the animals, the bog at the far end, the big garden with sunflowers, the raised bed for cucumbers. The man, the farmer, had installed a pump in the river to water the cucumbers and the melon beds. Clearly no sign of danger, clearly a Russian farm, although it was in the Caspian Basin. When I went back to the gate, I saw a toy truck on the patio, loaded with new cars, red and blue, plastic, knocked over in the mud by the well. I put my hand through a hole in the gate and raised the iron latch. They were home, I realized immediately, but did not want to let me in. Behind me, on the opposite shore, the pine trees formed a horizon a few degrees above the natural one, and the sun was about to drop behind it. The light did not let me see the face of the person who was approaching. I bent toward the windowpane, shading my eyes with my hand. They were here. The shutters were open, who would leave an isolated cabin without closing the shutters? A silent man pointed at me through the glass. I blocked out most of the last rays of the sun, so they didn't hit the bronzed steel of the barrel, the two chambers of his gun, but I could still see its dull shine. I stood motionless, my hands on the glass. Then started to back up, looking him in the eye, keeping my face toward him, getting farther away from the window frame, the shutters, the log wall, the smoke pouring from the chimney. I hadn't noticed it had smoke coming out before. Or I wouldn't have approached this home in the Caspian Basin without taking precautions. It was obvious they were here and were preparing a bath after a hard day foraging. I was about to open the gate when the little boy got to me. He grabbed me so low, around my pants legs, I thought at first they'd set their dog on me.

...

"Butterflies?" the man said in an astonished voice, not taking his eyes from the soup; but at the far end of the table the blond head of the little boy turned to examine me more frankly; he stood his spoon on end as if asking for the floor: they all come here looking for caviar, he wanted to say, how come you're looking for butterflies? He too had suspected that the world had some other organizing principle, that life did not have to revolve around caviar and the river. He stopped, indecisive, with the brilliant blush of this discovery.

"Not just any kind of butterfly. I'm supposed to catch a special one. Some are worth lots of money . . ."

I had wanted to buy them milk, a kilo of bread, to ask them about other butterfly hunters, if any had happened along, and how they did. They had let me in when the boy caught the bottom of my pants leg and I thought I had a dog bite. The man invited me to take a bath, I could spread out my sleeping bag on the hay in the shed. I preferred to sleep outside. The next day, before the little boy got up (the adults were up two hours before me, they had already unloaded the hay), we breakfasted on milk (I bought them a liter) and bread (I bought two kilos of rye). I followed the river down to the beach where the steamer would land. I spent another two nights there, out in the elements, with no success (or sense). On the last night before the steamer's arrival, I lit a fire on the beach, in the sand, and I must admit that I was feeling somewhat sad and lonely.

There were living forces in the logs that refused to burn, protesting, throwing off snaps that mounted in a rapid staccato, with the rhythm slowing briefly before launching into frantic calls for help. It was the moaning of the souls that had been held captive in the trees, dryads martyred by the fire, or else, I thought at once, it was shouts of joy they raised toward heaven, free at last. Before joining the huge mob of other souls, they should have said something to the other me, my errant other half, buttonholing him for a second in some bar in Linz, in Austria: "We ran into J. a while back sitting on the banks of the Volga. He looked kind of blue. Don't you ever think about him?" My double would splutter, annoyed, and return to his glass of beer, but for one moment, he would have given me a thought, and in that instant I would recover my integrity, some earlier quality would exist again, if only briefly, like those ephemeral atoms synthesized in laboratories, which break down immediately, nanoseconds later, into their primary elements. In that brief period, I discovered a scrap of newspaper with a big spot of oil in the middle, it must have been wrapped around some greasy food, maybe a herring. I stretched out my arm, picked up the paper, and started reading. That was the only way to explain my relapse, this reflexive movement toward the piece of paper, which I attributed to a momentary connection with my double. "'Excellent!' Nicholas II seems to have exclaimed that morning in 1912 while walking through the English garden of the Palace in Livadia" . . . I moved the paper closer to my eyes, the red glow of the fire coloring the yellow oil stain. Two columns of an article in *Bolshoi Livaditski Dvorets* on the Grand Palace of Livadia, which the Russian imperial family had had constructed in the subtropical region of Crimea, five kilometers from Yalta. Although I hardly stirred after reading it, sitting there quietly with the paper in my hands, I was making preparations to go; staring into the fire hypnotized, I saw myself unrolling my sleeping bag, traveling to the station, taking the train to Odessa or Jerson, flying from there to Istanbul. Why hadn't I thought of it before? Why had I gone to the Caspian (the habitat listed by Sirin in *Diurnal and Nocturnal Butterflies of the Russian Empire*) rather than Livadia, the Grand Palace of Livadia, with its gardens by the sea, the soft winds of Crimea, Nicholas's high boots gleaming, treading softly on the gravel path, the bright eyes of an amateur entomologist (as he was described by the *Kaspiski Rabochi*)? I rolled the paper in a ball and tossed it into the fire. It flared and was gone, with no cry for help. There was nothing I could do this time of night but store up some energy for my leap, so I fluffed up my sleeping bag carefully and snuggled down inside. I closed my eyes contentedly. Five thousand dollars? Fifty thousand dollars? A hundred thousand dollars? I slept soundly.

THIRD LETTER

I

ISTANBUL

A beam of light threw my shadow onto the pavement, and a sharp whistle made me jump back onto the sidewalk. An electric van flashed by without a sound. The close call heightened my awareness of where I was, the narrowness of the street or alley I'd come down. I spread my arms to keep from falling, my sandals arching over the hard curb. When I had my balance back, I took a step forward, and anyone sitting at the deserted café across the street would have seen my outline in the lighted doorway before I instinctively retreated to the shadows.

I was in front of the wall, standing by a dimly-lit niche lined with photographs. Of the women offered by the establishment, I thought, until I took a closer look and realized they were close-ups of a single woman, different parts of her, arranged vertically, to form a body. I walked past the collage again, from the feet to the head, lingering on the legs, the torso, the bust, hypnotized. The head was missing, unnecessary, as on a stone Venus.

While I was looking, the disk jockey in the bar picked out a song and pushed the button on his console to start it. I'd heard music when I turned down this alley, the last notes of a song, my favorite that year. I recognized the new one, too, and glanced up in surprise at the red-coated doorman, who was bowing toward me, tilting his fez, also red, inviting me in. Even though it was early: I could be any tourist, lost in the maze of streets in this city. The doorman had stood there, unmoved, observing the incident with the van, my reaction to the dissected woman, only reacting when I turned toward him, drawn by the song. He was wrong taking me for a lost traveler: I had an appointment in this bar. I stepped back to check the raised letters over the door, a brilliant gold: SARAY. I was meeting Stockis here, I would have gone in anyway. Only the song that broke in waves out the door, pounding against my chest, helped to pull the shadowy veil from Istanbul, an unknown city, tugging it back into Europe, since the same song had been playing in Helsinki, I had danced to it skimming over the Baltic just a few days ago. I could have heard it anywhere, I thought, already crossing the threshhold, passing through the hum of the bass as if it were a beaded curtain, the same sense of a heavy mass.

The Saray was run by Turks, with a mostly Turkish clientele. Dark, with spotlights tracing a few faint yellow lines that almost disappeared among the tapestries on all sides. I found Stockis, his broad shoulders blocking out a big chunk of wall and wall hangings. He was like a black hole against the club's fabric of kilims and copper plates. I had never thought of him as a fat man, "the fat man, the Swede." He may not have been fat, I now realized, but he was big. His frame could carry another fifty pounds easily and it wouldn't even slow him down.

He greeted me, languidly raising his glass of beer, not that he was tired at nine at night, at the end of a long day: he (and this gesture) had assurance and dignity, that's what got him an island in Stockholm, and all his money. And while I was walking toward his table, past the other tables, which were still empty, I kept revising my asking price, the little red ball bouncing jubilantly, stopping at his yacht, on the island, in the BMW purring toward the door in Stockholm. Later I learned that he had a house on the Costa del Sol, a collection of prewar Hispano-Suizas; he was always telling me about something else, yet another possession, rubbing in the measly fee I'd settled on.

I stopped at the final combination of numbers, the highest one. The music had stopped. Stockis took the glass from his lips: "One for my friend, too," he told a man, an employee who'd come over without my noticing.

Now, from where I sat, leaning back against the kilim, I saw some legs emerge from the shadows by the stage, interminably; then some arms, the body, the head of a woman appeared in the narrow red spotlight, moving forward, along a path that almost took her out of sight. I followed the woman like one of those migratory birds with a tracker in its brain, keeping it oriented to the lines of force in the earth's magnetic field; I could not steer my eyes away from her half-naked body, gradually swiveling my head, because of the sharpness of the angle, without missing a curve of her knees, a fold of her harem pants, glued to my chair, it all seemed so unreal. Because I saw her ask the doorman a question, stare into his eyes for a moment—which seemed to reverse the polarity, switching the dynamo that propelled her so smoothly she could have been running on rails—and then come back along the same circular route, returning to the darkness from which she'd emerged.

I'd waited so long—I'd rubbernecked till it hurt, I'd peeped through curtains, all steamed up, watching some unknown woman get undressed in the next apartment, a loose young blonde I'd seen from my room several times: coolly dancing with an older man, wiggling around one morning, headphones on, five afternoons fully dressed—and tonight, at last, boots were being tossed aside, clothes stripped off, piece by piece, down to pink panties. Everything that made it all worthwhile—craning my neck, sneaking around behind the drapes, holding my breath, dimming the lights, etcetera, so I wouldn't give myself away—was finally passing a few meters away from me, but now some mental defense mechanism seemed to distance her from me, so that, paradoxically, the naked breasts and glowing navel made her seem less substantial, less present in some way, like an animated cartoon. The head man, a little guy, so cheap and flashy he could have been dipped in gilt, sent the woman over to our table and as she got closer I could smell her perfume and see the fine grain of her belly. My alarm grew so I lowered my eyes, but the magnet or something hidden in my brain was irresistibly drawn to the iron of her eyes, and I slowly began rais- ing my sights, first peeking at her navel, then at the bare breasts show- ing through a jacket studded with fake jewels, and finally landing safe and sound at her eyes, like the view from the beaches of Marmara, clear and blue. I was about to give a good hard kick, like a skindiver trying to swim away, but I was held by those eyes, magnified by astonish- ment, "eyes as big as dinner plates" (the plates spilling from a sunken ship), and stared back, into eyes haloed by bright red hair, a band of light playing around it, strangely familiar, but I didn't know her. She quickly composed herself, identified Stockis as a big man, important, said something to him in Turkish, and moved off to another table. I avoided following her. Stockis said: "You seem to know that woman."

"No, how could I know her?"

"Hey!" Stockis called her, pulling a chair over with his foot. "Sit down. Look harder, don't you know each other?"

The girl approached, giving Stockis a hard look she'd perfected on customers just as big as the Swede. She pointed at me, as if he could be talking about somebody else at our table. Since Stockis had intro- duced me to the woman, I could now surrender openly and at length to her gravitational pull, come out from behind my little curtain. I took in harem pants, tight-fitting over opulent hips, held up by a belt of hammered silver, under the rhinestone-studded jacket, bare breasts peeking out . . . Better yet, for a clearer sense of the impression her costume made on me, I'll insert a fragment from the Turkish letters of

Lady Mary Wortley Montagu, wife of the English ambassador to the court of Ahmed III (1716), a description of the "surprisingly rich" attire of the Sultana Hafitén:

"She wore a vest called *donalma* . . . of purple cloth, straight to her shape, and thick set, on each side, down to her feet, and round the sleeves, with pearls of the best water, of the same size as their buttons commonly are . . . and to these buttons large loops of diamonds, in the form of those gold loops so common on birthday coats. This habit was tied, at the waist, with two large tassels of smaller pearl, and round the arms embroidered with large diamonds: her shift fastened at the bottom with a great diamond, shaped like a lozenge; her girdle as broad as the broadest English ribbon, entirely covered with diamonds. Round her neck she wore three chains, which reached to her knees: one of large pearl, at the bottom of which hung a fine coloured emerald, as big as a turkey-egg; another, consisting of two hundred emeralds, close joined together, of the most lively green, perfectly matched, every one as large as a half-crown piece, and as thick as three-crown pieces; and another of small emeralds, perfectly round. But her earrings eclipsed all the rest. They were two diamonds, shaped exactly like pears, as large as a big hazel-nut. Round her *talpoche* she had four strings of pearls, the whitest and most perfect in the world, at least enough to make four necklaces, every one as large as the Duchess of Marlborough's, and of the same size, fastened with two roses, consisting of a large ruby for the middle stone, and round them twenty drops of clean diamonds to each. Besides this, her head-dress was covered with bodkins of emeralds and diamonds. She wore large diamond bracelets and had five rings on her fingers, all single diamonds, (except Mr. Pitt's), the largest I ever saw in my life."

Stockis told the girl to have a seat, she refused, and he reached up to grab her. She stepped back to duck him, jerking her arms away, lifting and bending them, hands flying: the right, fluttering near my eyes, a gold ring on each finger, on fine chains leading to a bracelet. She finally sat down by me, with a scornful glance at Stockis, resentful. Turning her whole body toward me, she looked deep into my eyes. I didn't know her, I wasn't a bit worried by the scene. Stockis was big and fat, but not dangerous. I knew that. She didn't, and her chin and throat were trembling. She said: "We met each other this morning." Perfect English. Fake sounding. She meant: "Sure, we've known each other since we were kids, we grew up together." Making it a joke, ridiculous. Stockis laughed, satisfied. He opened his fist, let her go.

"It's my first time in Istanbul, Stockis. How could I know the girl?"

. . .

"Livadia?" Stockis asked, surprised.

"It will be necessary to organize an expedition to Livadia," I explained as if we were talking about some lost city, ruins on the steppes, circular structures reduced to rubble, footprints disappearing in layers of dust. A place I would never consider visiting without elaborate preparations, a city by the sea, on a bay of the Taurico Peninsula—it sounded wild when I used the Greek name, instead of Crimea, a name domesticated by common usage and a war between Alexander I and the Turks. A war that was set off—I didn't say this at the time—by a spirited exchange of letters between the military representatives of both nations in Istanbul. Nicholas II, the last emperor, had had his summer palace there, the Grand Palace of Livadia. Moving the Russian imperial family there, a spot milder than that of the steppe kingdom of Khorezm, I understood completely. But before Stockis could get the idea it was a nice place, I told him about Mithridates, Sovereign of the Euxinio Sea and the Bosporus from to 63 B.C. That date was the coup de grâce. He was hanging on every word when I got to Mithridates, describing the way he avoided death by poison: taking tiny doses—homeopathy—to build up his immunity. A much more dangerous place, Livadia, I warned, than the Caspian Basin. Finally I launched into my main theme, really playing it up and pounding it home: how much this butterfly hunt would cost, the price of the trip, three meals a day, a room in the town where I'd stay. I insisted on Livadia, citing the article in *Kaspiski Rabochi*. Stockis was so excited he wanted me to live on his boat, the *Vaza*, while we were in Istanbul: he would gladly pay for my expedition.

. . .

Before the part of the show with naked women—maybe to get around some Islamic law, like when you have to order a plate of food if you want to get a drink—there was a magic act. But to eliminate confusion among the customers, the girls came out first, showing off their belly-dancing outfits, and when I saw them all onstage, they reminded me of the illustrations in *Diurnal Butterflies* or of a row of butterflies in a collection. They thrust their legs out (harem pants billowing) and came up to the edge of the stage. One of the girls raised an arm, pretending to lift the corner of a curtain, and that's how they glided off, with a turn of the shoulder, like they were slipping behind a curtain, going into an unlit part of the stage (again like butterflies, when you're sitting in the park, under a streetlamp, and see them fly into the circle of light, flutter around for a while, and then return to darkness).

They left the brilliant space vibrating, the bright blue backdrop. And immediately, out of that blue sky, slithering into the space where the girls had danced so awkwardly (not being Turkish), slipping in softly as if not seeking attention, were the thin legs, the blue star-spangled jacket, the red fez of a magician. Center stage, a beam of white light hit him, and he recoiled from its icy circle, beating a hasty retreat to the spot he'd come on, a trapdoor, rocking on his heels, his long legs, his whole body arched back. Waiting for the light, which hadn't kept up with his flight, to find him again, and then standing within its cylindrical walls like he was trapped in a test tube. He tiptoed away finally and began an elaborate zigzag, ending up center stage. He straightened up then and peered into the wings, his left hand shielding his eyes, and his right—well, he put two fingers together, stuck them in his mouth, and gave a loud whistle. (I threw Stockis a look.) A second beam of light, not as cold as the first, a warmer yellow, revealed two people, also in comical getups, kitty-corner from us, at the far end of the stage, two dervishes, but he must have expected them to come from the other side; they gave him an awful fright and then hit him, too, with the edge of an enormous trunk, before dropping it on his feet. The tips of his pointy slippers were trapped under the heavy trunk. When he tried to take a step, to approach the audience to say something, the magician discovered that he was rooted to the spot and yanked off his fez, soundly thrashing the dervishes, who made a huge show of horror, running off, palms pressed to their heads, shrieking in Turkish. Then the magician sprang lightly from his pointy slippers—because he was wearing another pair just like the ones that were stuck, stuffed inside them—and landed on top of the trunk.

"Ladies and gentlemen," he addressed the crowd in English and Turkish. "You can see what a mess those rascals have gotten me into. I may have an extra pair, but I still want the others back" (and he pointed at them). "An excellent pair, as you may have noticed. I'll show them to you . . . What's more . . ."—and he leapt off the trunk—"I

will move this trunk" (one of the show girls, the one with the deep
blue eyes, had appeared below him, next to the platform, looking up
at the magician, smiling). "This heavy trunk . . . but no"—he wrestled
with it, tackling it from all sides. "There, see, without those two scoundrels . . ." He whistled again, this time in both directions. He put his
cupped hand to his ear, heard the girls laughing in the shadows. Then
the light flashed on for an instant, in the background, and we saw one
of the dervishes tickling one of the dancers. The magician took
advantage of the apparition; he saw his chance, yelled "Ibrahim!"
and took off. But the light went out and he stopped dead, lurching
violently. "Somebody"—he wailed—"somebody help me. Some
muscleman . . . A strong man . . . But"—he added quickly, as if
recovering—"I still have a couple of tricks up my sleeve. I can still
do a few things." He placed his fez on a small table, ripped the tassle
right off, miraculously stiffened it into a wand, and tapped the brim,
twice. On the first tap, he pulled a rabbit out by its ears, on the second, a big bundle of silk handkerchiefs—"That kind of thing"—he
said and then returned to his howling—"Somebody help me, some
muscleman . . . A strong man . . . You!"

I didn't look at Stockis, pretending not to realize the magician was
pointing at him. As if there could be another person seven feet tall sitting at one of these tables. I sat there paralyzed, like when a blast of
air from a bus you didn't see coming informs you of a narrow escape,
the danger that missed you by a few centimeters.

Everyone applauded. There were lots of customers in the bar by
now. A fine hangout for sailors and Turks. Stockis, the man (also a
trade name), accepted the challenge, leaned his big body forward, and
said to me: "They didn't have this act a year ago. No magician." But
while he was talking and taking off his jacket, rolling up his sleeves,
and striding toward the runway, the spotlight focused on the trunk

again, and a dervish materialized in its beam, casually lifting the trunk with one hand—one of the girls was tugging at the other, laughing, trying to pull him out of the light—and picking up the magician's slippers, tucking them under his chin, raising the trunk a little higher—as if making sure he wasn't missing something, so no one would come pestering him again—and inspecting the bottom, then tipping it over, lifting the lid, and showing the audience the inside, which was empty. He set the slippers down on the lid and suddenly out went the light, and so did he. The magician, who had gone to meet Stockis on the runway, talking all the while (in Turkish and English), turned to direct our attention to the trunk, raising his arms, palms in the air. Spotted his green slippers and shrieked like he'd been struck:

"Oh! Oh!" he rushed over to the trunk, abandoning Stockis. "My shoes!" He put them on. He skipped around joyfully. "My apologies, sir. You can see for yourself, they're right here. An excellent pair. Marvelous. Soft. Flexible. I know who made them . . ." He pretended to search through his pockets, looking for the shoemaker's address, and then made a show of remembering Stockis, standing there not sure what to do. "Although if you . . . But if you . . . if you still want to prove your strength, why not? Not that it's necessary now, more as a sporting event, you could say, a feat of strength . . . Gentlemen, I wish I possessed the strength of this man . . ."

A new light, lilac-colored, settled over Stockis on the runway, accompanying him to the trunk. Stockis lifted the iron latch, letting it drop, with a loud sound, tested one side with a knee, tapped the top with his knuckles (a woody sound), and then—since he was a man of the world, with a yacht tied up in the harbor—sat down on it with all the coolness in the world, leaning toward me, outside the light, to ask for his beer. He drank it down in one gulp so that everyone could see it move down his throat, filling every vessel in his enormous body, giving him strength. The audience clapped and the magician did too, with the rabbit jiggling under his arm.

...

In her letter V. took great pleasure in reminding me of that night, how I didn't recognize her when I had met her that very morning, even gone out with her (maybe gone as far as falling for her). It just proved what a splitting effect the Saray had on its audience. The night Stockis was wrestling and losing—brow tightening and neck veins bulging—and one of the dancers—the girl with red hair and blue eyes—came out and stood by the stage, so we were sure to see her, glancing from Stockis to me, his companion. It was V. Making sure I didn't recognize her. She twisted her body each time she turned, not just her head, her whole body, so that the ends of her red mane whipped her shoulders. But she was standing still, her back toward me, when I reached toward the stage, stretching to hand Stockis the glass, lowering my head from the effort. My eyes lighted on her toenails, painted different colors. Astonishing.

And when Stockis was slow to admit defeat, I stared at the reflections in her red hair—not real. V. knew her game had gone too far: she was wishing she could go back and rejoin the other girls, when my ejaculation escaped—"It's her!"—and my whisper must have reached her, because she turned to meet my eyes, and now it was easy, I saw that the features on this dancer—actually a blonde—belonged to V., the Russian girl I had met that morning. I was speechless, breathless, all shook up. Carbon dioxide was boiling in my blood. I couldn't pretend, as she had earlier, that we didn't know each other. In the applause that followed Stockis's failed effort, V. came over to my table, and that was what we talked about. How I hadn't recognized her.

Stockis lingered on the stage a bit longer: the magician, cordial, patted his shoulder; the dervishes, kidding, gave him a hand.

All I said to V.'s "You? What are you doing here?" was "Nothing, I came with a friend," something she already knew. As if it was the most natural thing in the world, which it wasn't, hardly satisfactory. And then brought up the *Vaza* and regretted it immediately. How could I not have known her? How could I not have known she would leave me in Odessa?

2

ISTANBUL

I had arrived in Istanbul just that morning. Stockis had sent me a note (by fax—an alarming machine that sends a letter instantaneously) saying that he would be several hours, nearly a day late. He changed our meeting to the Saray, the nightclub across the street, at ten that night. It was his message I was reading on the terrace of the café, a sea of Turks flowing past in the street, when I spied her at the next table devouring her breakfast. Over her shoulder I could see the waiter, who had already brought her a huge salad, coming out of the kitchen with more food—fried eggs, oatmeal, a cup of coffee with cream, toast, strawberry jam, and a carton of yogurt all ended up on her table. The girl looked over the order, still chewing the lettuce with her beautiful teeth, nodded her satisfaction, and then stopped eating and said something to the Turk, a sentence that I couldn't hear but took for an affirmative. Watching her eat, I remembered my own hunger and signaled the waiter.

When he approached, I was rehearsing my order mentally, frantically searching for the English word *oatmeal*, a dish I loathe: "the same as the young lady, but without the porridge of . . . ?" I stammered out, pointing at the girl's breakfast. I stood up, went to her table, looked into her eyes for a moment, and then delivered my order again: all but the oatmeal. And the waiter's posture, head held so stiff that the tassel of his fez swung back and forth, told me he had no clue what I'd said. I pointed at the oatmeal and spit out a robust *nyet,* through that mental quirk, thinking any language I knew well, he must too. Thinking: he may be as ignorant of English as I am, but a simple *nyet,* in Russian, so close to Russia. . . . The cashier spoke English, I recalled, when he delivered the fax, the message from Stockis, but finally the waiter got it, decided I was Russian, smiled, and asked: "Vodka?" For breakfast, to whet my appetite. Which told me the voracious girl was Russian and I asked if I could join her. "No, no vodka, coffee." (To the waiter.)

"Russian, everywhere, Russian. It's terrible. Everyone in the world speaks Russian, I sometimes think. Even you . . ."

And she was about to add: ". . . you're not Russian, but you speak it; what a drag," but she took a bite of toast instead and chewed it, staring at me. I watched her swallow hastily, as if eager to ask me something, and I easily guessed the question. "A few hours ago," I answered. "By plane. How about you?"

She'd come by train. She shook her head no. She gestured with her hand, pressing her fingers together to imitate a train pulling in.

Then asked, "Do you want tea?"

I said yes and she gave the waiter's sleeve a tug. "Çay," she said. (And got immediate results.)

"Huh"—my surprised reaction, it sounds so much like the Russian, *chai* . . . I liked the airport, it wasn't bad at all. In the taxi, I felt like I was in a modern city, perfectly normal. I was expecting much worse, I must say.

(It felt like any other city, except different music in the cab, but every country's different. I wasn't too keen on the minarets I saw en route, their lettered tiles. I was happier when I spotted one of those giant housing blocks, with tiny apartments, just off the freeway. It made me feel better, made the city seem normal, plus the car was Japanese, not some old junker.)

I was a smuggler even though I was sitting in a café in Istanbul concentrating on the yogurt the woman had given me from her breakfast, scraping the bottom of the carton, turning it in my left hand when I put the spoon into it, not looking much like a smuggler. The idea of describing myself as such, actually using the word—though it was an accurate term—made me uncomfortable. I kept my eyes on the starched tablecloth, setting the carton down after making sure I'd gotten out the last of the cool gelatinous substance. I hadn't sent a note to Stockis, a fax, not even a couple of lines about my failure to capture the *yazikus*. I'd come to Istanbul to tell him in person, to try to talk him into fronting me money for a second expedition.

I'd landed in Istanbul that morning and come straight to the café to meet him. Thinking of having some more yogurt, I picked up the carton with labels in Turkish and English. Carefully read the "Nutrition Facts," ignoring the Russian girl so I wouldn't lose her. If I didn't look, I wouldn't look too interested in her, though, in fact, I was, way too interested. I would be—not cold, no—genuinely disinterested. I was thinking of breakfast, of eating this marvelous breakfast, before inquiring sincerely: "But do you really like oatmeal?" or something slightly more formal and polite. At that moment I was sincerely interested, free of any evil designs, defenseless as a child, light as a feather. Some women inspire this state of genuine innocence in me, and when I eventually found the nutritional value per single serving of yogurt, delighted at the discovery, I raised my eyes to hers without faltering or falseness.

We chatted away in Russian, enjoying ourselves. We were both lying, making up explanations for being in Istanbul that day, at ten in the morning. I was here for an important business conference; she for an ice show, with skaters from all over eastern Europe, mainly Russians. She was a figure skater, the girl said. . . . I waited for details, but she didn't offer any, just set down the little spoon she'd been using to draw circles at shoulder height—threatening me with short thrusts toward my chest—and looked down at her plate, fingering an earring. Istanbul is a big city. Maybe not as big as Moscow, but still big. So, the chances of our running into each other again were low, minute, not even worth considering.

She got up to leave. Lovely legs, sheathed in jeans, were outlined against the Turkish market stalls across the street and against the Saray, too, no neon halo around its entrance this time of day, and I should have let her walk away, but just then I happened to notice a man across the way, struggling along with a side of beef, bent under its weight, and I said: "That man, over there, across the street . . ." She turned to look. "You know, I've done that, carried a side of beef . . . but in this sun . . ."

"It's terrible," she agreed, "you wouldn't believe how many events we've had to cancel because of the heat. Fifteen minutes and the rink is impossible . . ." (Which means, there's a rink, and skaters, and she's one of them.)

"Nice talking to you," she said. "*Poovshalis I jvatit.*" And to make it look good, she added to the yarn about figure skating. She invited me to that night's show, coming up with a phony address, thinking we'd never see each other again. I asked her to spell it, not laying a trap for her, just so I'd remember it, but she'd already forgotten the chance combination of words and said: "I have a better idea. Do you like museums?"

. . .

I never go to museums in the cities I visit on business. Other places hold more interest for me; more interesting things occur when I stop to look, or carefully linger over merchandise; I pick up things I can ponder for weeks, even months. Like the time I went to a perfume plant on the outskirts of Berlin with the sac—the musk gland—of a musk deer from Altai, procured from an acquaintance, cheap. I was playing pool, I recall; I'd set up the deal a few days before, with a down payment, and my friend came over just as I was aiming at a scuffed cue ball and dropped the musk sac on the edge of the table. I knew what it was, I'd asked for it, but I was still surprised when it was right in front of me—I'd never seen one before and had no idea it would smell so strong. It was covered with fur, as if it had been torn from the animal, or cut out—this was the case, I learned later—from the animal's belly. I snatched it up, poked at it, and, naturally, lifted it to my nose. Amazed. But not as amazed as the manager of the perfume factory on the edge of East Berlin. I wanted to become its musk supplier and needed an appointment with its head. I gave the sac to the secretary and Herr Direktor must have picked up the scent, because his office door popped open and he invited me in. Highly interested. He asked, "If you were to sell me a load, a lot, how would I get the musk? Like this, in its natural state, sacs covered with belly fur, or duly processed?"

The abrupt shift in his attitude mystified me. I had waited outside for a long time, but he looked right past me when he came in (I saw him arrive, knew it was him). It was cold, I remember, the end of April, because the snow had melted, but the trees were still bare, the soil around them still dark and wet. I didn't have a good overcoat, I'd bought a black jacket made out of some material so cheap the sleeves squeaked. The factory manager in East Berlin was wearing one just like it, only shabbier; he couldn't be doing very well. Why should he want to meet a young man waiting for him in the same jacket—something he'd probably rather forget? The secretary followed him into his office and came out to say: "No, he can't see you today"—when the

Herr Direktor stuck his head out the door, obviously agitated, maybe smelling the musk. He said, "Come right in, *Herr*."

I said nothing (nearly) on my way home from the factory. The manager's metamorphosis occupied my mind for two weeks, and I was still thinking about it months later. Terribly important things like that don't leave room for thoughts about museum visits. How can I enjoy historical displays when I need to make sense of this sort of behavior; it keeps me up nights, dreaming of a nice steady 10 percent growth rate, no risking my capital on shipments of hot merchandise? I have to stay ahead of things—I should rush right out of this café, hop on an express to the suburbs, visit the stores—I need to think. Always running as fast as I can, a rush of activity. Alongside me is a much slower track, a walkway, an automatic people-mover gliding past museums, but it's not my speed, my frequency, I'd have to cut my RPMs to even think of visiting them, or wandering around, stopping to gape at the galleon from the Swedish armada that was recently salvaged, the *Vaṣa* (the original), like any tourist lost in the crowd, interesting myself in things as uninteresting as the year it sank (1628). How can that be worth a thing to me? Really, what would sell better here, in this country: musk from the musk deer of Altai or snake venom from the Karakorum desert? I'll stick with things like the sudden transformation of the manager of that East Berlin perfume factory. I'll get more out of that, I'm sure, though I can't say how.

But the merchandise I had here in Istanbul was for Stockis alone, and any money I might get would come from him. That helped me to loosen up. I knew I could have been lurking around the bazaar in Laleli right now, trying to sell something really heavy, like a telescope or a batch of night-vision goggles.

Going along with the Russian girl, since I wanted a better look at her, that was a legitimate activity, even though it meant seeing a museum, the Hagia Sophia, which, she informed me, "all Russians should visit." Still, I'd better be careful not to stray too far from my routine, the places I usually go on business: airport, ferry or rail station, train or boat trips, long-distance calls.

She didn't skate in the morning, she explained, which made sense to me. They probably practiced all afternoon, going round and round on the ice. She'd had enough of that furious spinning, she told me, she wanted to do something more peaceful, climb up to the gallery of the Hagia Sophia and look down at the ships in the harbor, the tankers on the Bosporus.

We set out under the same sun that was punishing the Turk with the beef on his shoulder. Her third letter, two full pages, reminded me of that first walk, when I—happy and unsuspecting, just glad to have met her in the café, unaware that her profession was anything more nocturnal than figure skating—agreed to go to the Hagia Sophia with her, even though I never (I repeat) visit museums in the cities I go to on business.

I studied her hairdo, blond hair parted down the middle and pulled back in a simple ponytail, her blue eyes with an intelligent look that (I now believe) contained the embryo of all of her letters. "For me, it's not a museum," she said, lightly climbing the stone stairway in the Hagia Sophia, lifting her head, which had been on my shoulder, tilting it for emphasis, taking my hand and putting it on her hip, "I come here to pray." We were alone on this flight of stairs, on a landing cooled by cold stone. Then she said something I didn't quite catch, something Turkish I thought, looking down at the next step. But my eyes came up once my brain started to decipher what she'd said, identifying it as Russian: *ty takoi joroshi . . . Ya by tebe I tak dala,* meeting her moist eyes, and finally understanding: "You're so nice . . . I'd sleep with you for nothing," and I was completely at a loss. She saw her mistake and turned pale, seeming to shrink into the stone wall, to melt into it . . .

. . .

Something, a noise in the bushes, made me look up from her letter and stare off into the garden, the shadows opposite the pension. When I turned back to the letter, it was as if her voice, the same voice that uttered those words that noon, had been raised again: I heard her perfectly clearly in the deserted patio, telling me, "it was a joke."

I saw her emerge from the stone wall, like a figure in bas-relief, a vestal virgin holding a horse by the bridle, and met her eyes of stone. The long months she'd spent in Turkey had readied her to tune in to that little lapse, to pick up and interpret the time lag before I caught her invitation. Even before I transmitted a response, she could see that I didn't present a polished surface like a reflective screen, that the waves were lost in me, curve after curve entering my chest, the words lost in the convolutions of a tortuous internal structure, and she knew that I was not a potential customer, a man she could reward with a bonus night, in exchange for generosity, to thank me for coming with her— that is what had caused her sudden transformation, that and the fact that she decided immediately (I now believe) to use me to get out, to escape from Istanbul.

It was fear of losing her chance that drained the blood from her cheeks, that left her paralyzed, afraid she'd made an irreparable mistake. She regained her color when she saw how changed, how correct, her words appeared without their negative side, the obscene invitation, removed.

She had unintentionally revealed her secret. At that moment, I felt utter dismay and also an ulterior elation, because "More than anything in the world I fear honest women and high-flown sentiments. Hooray for grisettes, fast and easy . . . ," as Pushkin says in an 1827 letter to Zinaida Bukovski (his lover, we have to assume).

Here in Livadia I came across a description, in a letter, of a fear I might have felt, but didn't. It was a letter from James Joyce to Nora, his wife, and he really went to extremes (the poor man). A letter dated September 2, 1909, and postmarked 44 Fontenoy Street, Dublin: "I have *enormous* belief in the power of a simple honourable soul. You are that, are you not, Nora?" The pathetic tone, the tremendous desire to believe the opposite. Nora Barnacle? My God! The whole world knows. Someone should have warned the unhappy writer. Less madness, less experimention in *Ulysses*, I'm sure.

When we were on top, on the circular balcony, I looked down at the floor to admire the mosaic and saw her manicured toenails, painted different shades. If I hadn't happened to see her again in the Saray that same night, and recognized her by this tiny detail, the painted toenails, I probably would have wound up rescuing her as an ice-skater. Maybe later, once we got to Russia, she would have confessed her secret, faking tears. (But when I found her belly dancing in a nightclub, dressed like an odalisque, she was quick to turn it to her advantage, I must say.)

Starting to get leery, I asked:

"You're not a skater, are you?"—and then—"Why don't you come with me to Livadia, to the Black Sea?"

My rude invitation pulled her yarn to pieces, but she didn't react violently, just disentangled herself slowly and sweetly. I sure wanted to say: "Look, instead of staying here in Istanbul, ice-skating . . . or whatever . . . why not come to Crimea and stay with me for a few months?" V. had on a pair of jeans that day with geometric trim, like guiding rays, an optical trick that kept drawing my eyes toward her pelvis. She caught my look, which was not too hard to recognize, and answered without lingering for a moment on my Black Sea beaches:

"Why should I go there? With the fabulous beaches here!"—she'd come to Turkey for its beaches, too. The phony talent agency had sent her brochures full of pictures: hotels by the sea with nightly ice shows. And when I asked her to go to Livadia that day, she still hadn't figured out how to connect my invitation to Crimea with her desire to escape from Istanbul.

3

LIVADIA

I had two passports in my name; not two passports with different names, like a secret agent, but two official passports in my name. I got the second from my embassy, pretending the first was lost, stolen by some teenagers outside the metro, on Nevski. Having two passports let me pass through the same border station several times without arousing suspicion. I alternated them so that neither the customs agents nor the border guards would notice that the date stamped was Monday when it was actually Thursday. Very convenient. I looked a year older in the second, because I applied for it a year later, when I figured out the advantages of having not two personalities but two valid passports with the same name. If I happened to get held up by cops, or by robbers, some unexpected problem like that, I would have had to wait for six months until the consulate of my country—a slow country—had a new one ready. I'd lose out on deals, discounts, fire sales in the neighboring barracks. Or if they fined me when they discovered my suitcases full of American cigarettes stolen in Russia (I didn't steal them, just delivered them, to a Panamanian in Stockholm, a real sharp kid) and restricted one passport (which happened one time), I could use the other with impunity, until the stamp on the first—its dates of No Entry—had expired. No way—just to take another example—could I have found myself in a situation like V.'s, when Tiran held hers against her will. She could have broken into his office in the Saray, it's true, and forced the lock on his desk, but easier to pull a second passport from your pocket, tell them, *pliunut na vsio* (go to hell), and you're out of there. I told V. about it one day, something to keep in mind for future trips. It was just as if there were two of the same person: you could see one in Tallinn; the other, in the market of the Old City in Krakovia—at the same time.

And all of a sudden one afternoon, in a packed elevator, way in the back, I was amazed to catch sight of so many fair heads, so many Russians in front of me. A violent transposition occurred in me that day. I asked myself, if I considered them foreigners, what was I? And since this was in St. Petersburg—the wet trunks of the birches, the moisture fogging the lobby window—I had to change the way I saw things, reminding myself that I was the foreigner, not they.

Or this better example: here in Livadia I was looking over the *Epistola Obscurum Viborum,* and my eye was caught by a word (I might be able to use it in my reply), and I stared at it without recognizing the language. I got stuck on *veleta* (angel) and had to ignore the text and study the letters, one by one, for a long time, before I managed to figure out that Vladimir Vladimirovich had sent me a Spanish book.

And the other day I was going to say something against *kisel,* the scalding jelly we'd had for lunch, but Petrovich shut me up: "You shouldn't talk. You're a foreigner." I hadn't grown up with glasses of *kisel* for breakfast, it's true, but how about the liters, the hundreds of liters I'd swallowed—in big gulps when it was cold, downing solid clots, or else in tiny sips, like the other day, when it was over a hundred degrees, because being viscous, it boiled hotter than water—didn't any of those count? The Moldavian who cooked for Kuzmovna, Nina

("Nina!" everyone would shout), would chill glasses of red-hot *kisel* on the window ledge. But that only allowed a deceptive skin to form over the molten lava of the jelly—it actually cooled down only when it came into contact with the esophagus, which lowered the temperature from 100 degrees to 36, normal body heat. Petrovich always talked during meals. One time I saw him gesturing madly, waving his arms wildly, embroiled—I thought—in a heated argument with his neighbor at the table. He was speechless with emotion, I thought. Two tears welled up in the old man's eyes, a film covering them. "Nina!" he finally managed to articulate, a shriek, because in the heat of discussion he had forgotten to let his *kisel* cool down. I, a foreigner, was the first to catch on and hand him a glass of water.

I have experienced, on several occasions, the strange sensation of a divided life (aggravated, no doubt, by the fact of having two passports). I suspected this was because I had gone so far, to put it one way, in these last few years: I'd flown over so many cities, touching down briefly, buying and selling, reduced to tatters, torn by the fierce crosswinds roused by my hasty passage. I still lived in the air of all those cities, and although somebody was here, now—my body: my back crushing the daisies in a field in Livadia, my eyes gathering the blues from the sky—I also saw myself in those cities, rushing down streets, in and out of markets, buying and selling.

I must tell my soul, explain as clearly as I can in my divided state, why I behaved so irrationally in Istanbul. Putting it down on paper, perhaps I can arrive at a full understanding of the motives for my conduct in that city. And I'll start even earlier, to explain why I took the commission for *yazikus,* how I came to plan a trip to the Caspian Basin—as if it were the most natural thing in the world. Only someone with a divided soul is capable of such things, someone who believes (and detects signs) that he is also somewhere else—let's say

Vienna—at the same time. One morning as I passed the Czar's Summer Palace, I experienced this sensation—for an instant I was sure that I was in some other place. And it wasn't that I remembered the other place, no, it was that when I walked past a statue in the English garden, I felt as if a curtain had been drawn aside, or rather, as if a portion of my brain had been energized, allowing communication—in real time (that is, simultaneously)—between my self and my double, who at that very moment was walking past a (Viennese) sausage shop.

I didn't understand the essence of this phenomenon—bilocation, the simultaneous appearance of one person in two different places—until I read a book by Jamblico, the Alexandrian philosopher. When I got it, I thought there'd been a mistake, since the title was *On the Egyptian Mysteries,* but the frontispiece said it was his answer to a letter: "Response by Master Abamon to the letter from Porfirio to Anebo and solutions to the problems it raises."

This is what Jamblico says, in brief: that a certain divine cause can temporarily sever the real quantitative connection that a person's body has to a particular place, spiritualizing it (modulating it, I'd say, but explanations later) in a certain way so that the body can be seen in far-off places. *There is no contradiction in this.* The existence and nonexistence of a body in the same place would be contradictory, but that's not what he's talking about. His is a different relation: the existence of corporeal substance in one place and extensions in another, simultaneously, a phenomenon common to the gods.

I was not a god. Nor was I an exile, I don't like that word (I prefer an older one, from before 1917 and even 1789). I was just a traveler. But the state of a traveler emulates that of a god, because it goes everywhere. Therefore: what is true of a divine body is also true of a traveler's.

Okay then, I won't attempt a formal refutation, just advance my argument ex cathedra: the root of this phenomenon lies in the redundancy of the body—there's high-grade redundancy in the physical frame and the fluids running it. And technically, it's perfectly feasible to cut the atomic unit in half without decreasing physical or spatial presence.

And I'd left bits of my consciousness, bits of myself on so many customs' screens, a copy of me could easily have been formed from those samples, a me composed of fifty percent of my person. Not a clone, but the same signal divided in two. Along the same lines as frequency modulation, the process by which a radio signal is divided into two packages of waves, one for the left canal (or ear) and one for the right canal (or ear). Reading about demons in Jamblico, or about densified spirits, or astral doubles, I said to myself: no, that's not it, I'll never go along with that stuff . . .

Still, in bilocation I can find a plausible—forget about plausible, scientific—explanation for my strange visions. I'm not talking about Dr. Jekyll and Mr. Hyde, turning from good to evil, but of two J.s, basically good (why else would I have decided to rescue her?), acting in different places, bilocated. But don't start talking about a soul divided, it's actually a statistical sample; it's not a soul separating from its body, but two simultaneous bodies and souls, oscillating (flip-flop) at high speeds.

I had doubted the reality of those visions, of those connections with remote cities: seeing myself peacefully strolling in Vienna, having a beer or getting onto a water-bus in Amsterdam. But I was in those places, literally; I could be like a television signal that travels around the world and is reincorporated (or made visible) in a receiving device. I was the original, or One, no question, but I'd crossed over some cities (again and again) and formed chance connections, and at last I *saw.*

And so I knew—with thanks to this treatise letter—that I have a double (it's an old saw); but what happened to me on the Stockholm-Petersburg-Istanbul axis (not to mention Astrakhan and the Caspian Sea) can be explained by my half-existence, split in two. It was another reason to stay in Livadia. Here I would live with the hope that my double—left behind, by virtue of too-speedy displacements (trains, boats, and planes)—would rejoin me and I would regain my former fullness. The fullness, you could say, that had given me the strength and resolve to leap into smuggling without fear, with the confidence of a man able—thanks to his amazing physical and mental powers— to bend an iron bar with his bare hands.

Then I found the very same feeling (not to mention the disintegration of the soul, evident to a psychologist in this case) described in a letter that Karen Blixen wrote her mother on February 26, 1919. The identical sense of being in two places at once: "I have the feeling that wherever I may be in the future, I will be wondering whether there is rain at Ngong."

And after reading Jamblico (the phenomenon goes by the name *Jamblic bilocation*) I said to myself: while waiting for my soul to get here, what could be better than answering V.? Back in Istanbul I already knew that I would not spend my time in Livadia frenziedly pursuing the *yaẕikus,* nor any other butterfly. In the first days after V.'s disappearance, I had fallen back on my original plan, ascending Ai-Petri and posting myself on its grassy slopes—but that was before I got her letter. Then I discovered a higher purpose and spent days in taking notes and sleepless nights preparing the first draft of my response, bringing leaves of paper to life in the lamplight, only to find them dead in the morning, because no longer warmed by my hands their edges have curled and dimmed like the wings of butterflies.

I was writing this letter to him as well, to that other me (or my half-frequency). My detailed account of these last few months would be addressed to him as well.

4

LIVADIA

I climbed the mountain in my white Panama hat, the butterfly net with the collapsible handle over my shoulder, going directly into the woods from the beach, like a peninsula, a point of trees that reached almost to the water. I could feel the sea at my back for the entire ascent. At one point, in a meadow full of flowers, with heat rising from the grass, the tapping of a woodpecker on a rotten tree made me forget the beach, but when I turned—my eyes sweeping the clearing with a machine-like efficiency, rejecting useless butterflies, comparing the various butterflies to a single standard (the *Yazikus euxinus*)—I saw the sea (Pontus Euxino). Had Czar Nicholas ever climbed up here? Had he gazed down at the horizon and dreamed of a liberated Zargrad (Istanbul), of making his pan-Slavic dream a reality? The view was beautiful; the boats seemed to float on the pyramidal poplars and pines of the coast . . .

On the way back to my pension, a woman called out to me from the market some Abkhazi had set up in front of the Grand Palace. They sat along the esplanade leading from its cast-iron gate, waiting for customers behind boxes of last year's oranges and melons. A few tourists—people from the north, pale, with gums bleeding after the long winter—made a quick stop on their way to the beach to buy a couple of peaches, a melon, a paper sack of the bitter oranges from Abkhazian. Standing there with a split watermelon, testing its weight, I could see people kicking balls on the beach, slowly wading into the water, or running up and jumping in.

I had gone by the Post Office earlier, but it was closed. There could be a letter waiting for me at general delivery, in one of the little boxes. I had passed the Post Office every day for a while, so it gradually blended with the others I'd visited in Russia. But it was unique now, different from all the others, like it was the first day. Like it was pre-served in sepia ink—the image, I mean—so that it held a separate at-traction in my memory, even though I came again and again, hoping for a daily or weekly letter.

The girl from the first day—the one who had rapped on the glass with the handle of the postmark stamp—was there whenever I went. I watched her smile become less ambiguous, as if it were emerging dot by dot on photographic paper. Most days her head swiveled from side to side, on the same plane as her body, like a wooden doll, to indicate: "No, nothing for you." Sometimes she smiled broadly and held out a hand, letting me come up to the window to read the handwriting, giving me an envelope (a letter from V.) or a receipt for a shipment from Vladimir Vladimirovich. In the latter case, I'd go to a different window, next to a scale and a conveyor belt that would bring me bouncing books of letters, collections of corre-spondence. For this, the woman who worked the conveyor—and also told people how to label their packages, which she closed with seal-ing wax—made the belt run backward, and I finally realized one day that it was her voice—she was young, too—I had heard calling me that first time, from the general delivery window, saying: "*Gospodin* (Sir), I think you have a letter." Without attaching any particular im-portance to this detail, I had unconsciously attributed this voice to the dark-haired young woman at the general delivery window. The voice certainly fit those Tartar cheekbones, the straight black hair, the invariably smiling eyes, which had drawn me closer with each visit.

I saw her, the girl from the Post Office, two or three Abkhazi ahead, trying a slice of melon the vendor was holding out to her on the end of a sharp knife. She took it between her thumb and index finger. She brought it to her lips, pretending to enjoy its flavor for a moment, as if she were actually intending to buy it, then glanced over at one of the villager's peaches and left *without a word*. She was wearing a white linen dress, with sateen bows, also white. In front of the peaches, she quickly pushed her hair back with her thumb, parting the blue-black hair loose on her shoulders. I watched unnoticed as she finally bought three peaches, then went back to the melons, picked one out (no, not that one, this one, nodding vigorously), and bought it, cleverly resting it on her hip. I decided to follow her. I followed her.

There were parts of Livadia that I didn't frequent. Groups of houses, dirt sidestreets, with flagstone ditches on the edge for rainfall, but in the middle, the street itself, raw, rough. To get to Ai-Petri I skirted that neighborhood—the closest I got in my daily wanderings was crossing the little plaza in front of the Post Office, which jutted out from that cluster of houses. Following the girl from the Post Office I took a shortcut through a narrow passage between two pensions and came out onto the highway. Before, I had had to walk three extra blocks, unnecessarily making my way around two fenced-off sanatoriums. We came to a street without a sign—she was twenty steps ahead. I stood undecided at its mouth, wondering if she knew her way out. The girl stopped and waited for me on the opposite side. She'd thought for a moment that I just wanted to ask her something about the mail, whether they'd gotten a letter for me before they closed, she told me later. When I came up to her, she took a letter from her purse, smiling so jubilantly that I thought she was going to ask me to dance, to pretend I was doing a few steps, like they do in Russia—they often say "Dance" as a joke, commanding you to slowly lift one leg and then the other, like a circus bear, to get the letter they're holding. I took it and when she saw I wasn't going to open it right away, nor leave to look for somewhere to read it, she moved as if to make a space for me in the three or four meters of the street and let me walk at her side, smiling to herself, looking down the whole time. She wasn't so innocent, I realized later, as to think I'd followed her here just for a letter. When we got to the middle of the block, she stopped and handed me the melon, which I balanced on my hip as I'd seen her do, and we continued on till we got to a house enclosed by an adobe wall. *Without exchanging a word.* Can you believe that at that moment, after that walk, I still did not realize that the girl, the young Tartar from the general delivery window, was a mute? At that moment, I still expected—when I put my hand through a slit in the door and lifted the latch—to hear her say, "Would you like to come in?" or "Come in." But she left the door ajar, propping it open with her foot for me to enter, her lips forming no word of welcome.

That didn't surprise me. I attributed her silence to the peculiar intelligence of some women, a certain temperament or mental disposition, that allows them to skip the customary empty phrases of an introduction. The smile that first appeared in her eyes and that swiftly moved to her lips, the way she'd allowed me to walk by her side, and then done me the honor of handing me the melon, these gestures were more eloquent than words. I've known women to move past the ordinary introductory phrases in this way, avoiding their intolerable conventionality, and then talk for hours. To the point that, with some, that's all I've done, talk, from two in the afternoon, meeting outside a St. Petersburg department store, until 1 A.M., sitting in the Admiralty Gardens.

But with Alfiá the silence lasted. A silence we maintained as we walked down a path, mortared bricks set in the soil, between the pear and apple trees of a kitchen garden.

I sat down on a *takhtá,* a Turkish (or Ottoman) bed, waiting for the girl to say something, but she went out without opening her mouth. I pulled my legs up, pillowing my head on my arm, lying there curled up, contemplating the afternoon light, without the energy to get up and close the window. I didn't feel cold at the moment, but I don't like a draft when I'm sleeping.

I woke up before the sun had set, still in the fetal position. For a long while—a stretch of time that felt like this, say you were standing on a beach as the solar disk dropped toward the horizon and you saw a seagull appear on the far right, more than a kilometer and a half away, and it flew past in a full arc, and disappeared at the opposite end of the beach, while the sun sank lower, for a stretch of time like that, the same duration—I didn't know where I was. What woke me up was the fear of sleeping through the sunset, a fear I'd picked up at some point, in a different house, because between the historic time of a life and the mythic time of meeting your destiny, you pick up things—houses, acquaintances, beliefs, fears. I couldn't figure out where, in what part of the world, the sun was setting. While it slid down its celestial grooves, I came fully awake and studied the divergent lines of the floorboards, the glassed-in veranda, the other trees in the garden, relieved I was no longer being subjected to a torment of electrons in the defenselessness of sleep. I saw a kilim on the wall behind me and tried to identify this place. I quickly sorted through various locations from the last five or six months. For a fraction of a second, I paused in Paris. Then I thought: Turkey, because of the kilim and the brilliant matte finish on a fretted brass vase, an Oriental style, and in the split second the delusion lasted I thought, "In that case, V. has not yet left me in Odessa, and I still have time to work things out." The sun sank into the sea, the dying light faded on the limed trunks of the pear trees. Without raising my head from my swollen arm, I cast a glance at the far end of the room, at some bookshelves behind glass. I have to see what those books are, what the Post Office girl reads, I told myself, because now I knew that I was in her house, that I'd fallen asleep on her *takhtá*. Then the rest of the electronic disturbance from the sunset hit me, and I was attacked by an awful anxiety. What was I doing here, lying on this low bed, in a strange woman's house? Shouldn't I be doing something, getting something, achieving something? I was wasting the best years of my life in this country. And I told myself all this so that I could cope with my anxiety in some rational way, this nameless fear, inexplicable, which was really a cosmic anxiety, insufflated by the solar wind. In this moment of awakening I felt my cosmic insignficance, a dread as if foreseeing the waters of the Great Flood. I concentrated all my forces on a beam that I sent to the muscles of my arm and managed a first movement, almost imperceptible. Gradually widening the revolutions, I pulled fragments of myself toward my nucleus, with the force of gravity, centripetal. I achieved a certain atomic solidity, the particles flying close enough to one another, cohering to form an effective entity, molecular, palpable. I didn't pull myself together and leap up ready for action. I lay low even though I was completely certain, convinced that I was functional, that I had restored the connection with the self I had misplaced in my sleep. What had I been thinking about before I fell asleep? The *Yaẓikus euxinus*? No, the letters, the art of letter writing, writing back to V. I brought my hand to my shirt pocket and pulled out her third letter—the one the girl from the Post Office had given me in the street—and began reading in the little light that remained.

When I got to the last page, I noticed a man sitting in front of the window, an old man. He had been invisible against the light from the patio, but as this backdrop grew darker, he stood out, grew larger, jumped out at me.

Then the girl from the Post Office appeared in the doorway, leaning against the frame. I set the letter aside and pushed myself up with my fists. I rested on my elbows a moment and then used a foot to slide myself back against the kilim. Sitting like that, I looked at the woman, and the man by the window, too. I couldn't read anymore, it was too dark. I had to get up, light a lamp, prepare tea. The woman raised an arm so that her hand was outlined against the weak glow of the patio and her fingers traced successive points in space, as if it was a remote control for turning on the voice of the old man who'd watched over my sleep. The voice of whom came from such a sharp angle that only my left ear heard it, as if it was a recording used to check the balance of a stereo. The old man told me the young woman had said, "I couldn't come earlier because I had to feed the animals, water the garden," and then he spoke to me directly, in his own voice: "I saw you reading a letter . . ."

The girl stretched her arm even farther, touched the wall by the doorframe, and flicked the switch. The light hurt my eyes. Alfiá—that was her name, a Tartar name—turned the dimmer and softened the glare.

FOURTH LETTER

I

LIVADIA

"May I?" The old man put on his glasses and examined the letter, running the pages past his eyes without moving his head, as if the rose-rimmed glasses were the beam of a scanner. He went back to the first page, lingering briefly on the letterhead, then returned to the end, looking for the signature. His inspection took less than a minute. Refolding the letter, he apologized as he handed it back: "It's just a habit, that's all."

He didn't speak English, he hastily informed me, thinking I did. (Why? The letter from V. was not in English.) He had worked as a handwriting analyst at the Allied conference in 1945. The Yalta Conference—as everyone knew—had been held in the Palace of Livadia. (No, everyone did not know.) It had been April, a fairly warm month here, with none of the freak snowstorms that sometimes hit as late as May farther north, ruining the crops. Before the general demobilization of 1946, he had gone—still in uniform—to visit Bajchiarai, the old residence of the Tartar Khans of Crimea. He learned from the tour guide that the last Khan had married at the age of seventy-three, and then he went back to his hotel and dashed off a letter to a Tartar woman he had known before the war. The future grandmother of Alfiá.

He proceeded to tell me what he had seen (not read, as I had), what he had learned from V.'s handwriting:

Graphology, he explained, is about moving through *levels of character* to discover its architecture, about reconstructing the writer's personality, building from written to psychological "character." With no more than a letter discovered under a suspect's bed, a graphologist can create a *character study*, a sketch of the suspect's dossier. It should come as no surprise, he informed me, that handwriting reveals things, certain inclinations that the person herself does not suspect, just waiting for a propitious moment to display their prejudicial effects. From his analysis we learned that V.'s spirit of ambition, while modest in scale, was strong enough to allow her to take off from the pelagic depths of a Russian village and fly south. She was *freethinking, broad-minded*— besides having picked up a tolerance in moral affairs from her mother (who had several lovers, tractor drivers, workers at the grain elevator)—*temperamental*, and *quite gifted, spiritually and emotionally*. Exactly! I knew it, her many spiritual gifts had swayed me. No question! If she had been able to go as far as persuading me—or, anyway, if I went as far as agreeing—to rescue her in such a short time, less than a week, it was her gift, she really knew how to do it, and that's the truth. There was no crude effort to force me into it, because she was counting on—the graphological report of the ex-captain corroborated this— the subtle intelligence that had trained her hand to produce this *rounded, curvilinear writing*, a reflection of her *flexible attitude*. And that's how it was: for three straight days she had made strategic advances on several fronts, pulling away when she felt she was putting too much pressure on me or not paying enough attention to certain areas, because while she focused on rescue, she did not want to lose sight of love, the feelings she pretended to have for me, and since she had a full grasp of each development in our friendship, she knew that once it had reached a certain point, she had to make me jealous, to create some sort of little break between us, but without driving us so far apart that she couldn't relaunch the pontoons of reconciliation when the time was ripe. She was like a retreating army blowing up bridges, but trying to leave the piers standing, because the high command has plans to re-take the territory and has given orders to preserve as much as possible, even though the enemy . . . And when I was ready to quit and told her, "I'm leaving," and then ran into her at the Saray, it was all part of a much larger plan, I now believe, a giant maze with her looking down at me as I kicked at every slight barrier, in my blindness, my jealousy and rage—maybe in my love, though it is painful to admit—unaware of how close I'd come to the exit, two turns to the right and one to the left. Her handwriting was calligraphic, Alfiá's grandfather went on, all the letters followed an easily recognizable pattern based on precise forms, with sizes set by the letter *m*—not that it copied schoolboy pen-manship models exactly . . . Obviously, these were a woman's tricks, and the crying, the tears the day she found me talking to Leilah outside the Saray, were all the tricks of a woman who knew how to give things a personal touch. You can see it in her letter, the personality that had transformed the graphic model so elegantly . . . Alfiá's grandfather paused as if he didn't think I would understand his technical terms: V.'s handwriting was *clear* (he cocked his little finger), *controlled* (he cocked his ring finger), *deliberate, grouped, homogenous* (having finished with his left hand, he began counting on the little finger of his right), *rectilinear*. Then, allowing me to appreciate the basis for these dazzling judgments, he explained that elementary calligraphic distortions betray the author's character and disposition: people with delusions of grandeur, for ex-ample, leave large margins and add flourishes, while sensuality is shown by a *fusiform* handwriting. There is a lot to be learned even from a mark that seems insignificant, such as a tilde: slanting up, it reveals the writer is stubborn; touching the letter, willful; drawn as a long, thin bar, ener-getic, impatient; forming sharp points, aggressive . . .

V. was everything he said, too; truly, she was broad-minded, free-thinking, temperamental, and impulsive. As for her heart: warm, sympathetic, understanding, altruistic; and her spirit: a practical streak, organizational skills, above all, a masculine ambition, and as I said before, youth. This type of person needs a large playing field to express herself fully. She's not used to being tied down in a tight situation and won't accept too many limits. She needs space—all kinds—to follow her fate coolly and decisively, the way it should be followed, so careless and unthinking that it could almost be stupid. She has what it takes, the impulsive energy and painstaking thought for plotting and planning. This person is sometimes restless, constantly craving new ventures, without deriving any lasting satisfaction from them.

And a few final notes: love and the ability to give it, adaptability in handling projects, but *shrewd* and *devious*, artistic talent, mystical tendencies. He based this last observation on the ink V. used to write me this letter and the previous ones: a violet ink, watery, *sedative*, with a mystical quality . . .

. . .

Vladimir Vladimirovich soon sent some useless *pismoviki* (old secretarial letters, pre-1917) as well as an account of the first advances, the first documented successes, of the Russians in the Ottoman Empire. That afternoon in Istanbul, when we left the Hagia Sophia, we saw some very fair women—whom we took for Russians (which they were). V. pretended not to see them and they did the same. I cannot remember, or picture, those women—the one hanging from the arm of a man with white sideburns and wire-rimmed glasses, the other, a tall woman, like a hussar officer, in knee-high boots—without thinking of the letters of Ghislain de Busbecq, even though Roxana's story did not color my perception of them (or V., as a matter of fact) at the time. The tale of a Russian, "La Rossa," they called her, a name that turned into Roxolana, or Roxana. A story authenticating and illuminating the picture Alfiá's grandfather had painted of V., who had a much more modest design. Roxana's had been grand: to marry Suleiman II, the Turkish sultan.

Busbecq, it seems, saw her himself in 1555. I imagine Roxana stretched out on an ottoman, two harem slaves fanning her "alabaster thighs." One particularly torrid afternoon, when not the slightest breeze was stirring the Gulf of Nicomedia, Busbecq reports, Roxana came up with an astounding ploy: she feigned a tremendous longing to build a mosque and a hospice for foreigners. Suleiman, who was more enamored of her, of her beauty and talent, with each passing day, provided the building materials. But the work could not be carried out while Roxana was a slave, declared the Mufti—obviously in league with the Russian girl. At which she fell into such a terrible melancholy that Suleiman (the Magnificent, the emperor of the Turks), terrified of losing her, raised her to the throne and married her. Once enthroned, Roxana—looking at things from a new angle, a more elevated position—began to persecute all her former enemies. She schemed, she plotted, she organized a revolt—against Suleiman himself!

Imagine how Suleiman felt about this woman, as completely bewildered as de Maupassant was by Maria Barkishev when she first wrote to him. Barkishev, a young genius—or *wunderkind*—initiated the correspondence in Paris in 1882, sending him a letter without revealing her identity, without telling him that she was Russian— and a woman. Her letter confounded the writer; his astonishment at her complex design must have been like Suleiman the Magnificent's at Roxana, and mine at V. In a single letter, and what's more in a single paragraph, the young woman had bombarded him with names: ". . . you gave me quite a start, madame. Without any warning, you launched a volley of quotes from G. Sand, Flaubert, Balzac, Montesquieu, the Jew Baahron, Job, Spitzbube, the Berlin scholar, and Moses," De Maupassant guesses that the, "mystery lady" must be "a sixth grade teacher at Louis le-Grand."

But let's get back to Suleiman, who had made an appointment to meet his son in a hostelry a few miles from Constantinople, because according to Turkish law—Busbecq relates—no child of the sultan can set foot in Constantinople while his father is alive. Suleiman's slaves were waiting for him and confiscated his sword and dagger. Roxana hadn't missed a trick: "foreseeing how frightened the boy would be about presenting himself to his father," she had slipped past the walls of Constantinople and "was hiding inside a house that Bazajet, the son, would have to pass. As he went by, his mother called out from behind a linen-draped window, telling him: 'Corcoma, oglan, corcoma' (Courage, my son, courage)." What a trick! This made her even more appealing to Busbecq, incidentally, since he was sort of a smuggler himself. Someone who brought (as contraband, I'm convinced) the tulip, the Angora goat, and the horse chestnut tree to Europe way back in 1551. I mean, he never came back from a trip empty-handed, something I too try to avoid.

And if Suleiman, a sultan, was ensnared by Roxana, how could I, a simple smuggler, not fall into the trap set for me by that other Russian woman—V.

Those Russian women thought of themselves as more than just streetwalkers, and so they ended up as less, to speak plainly. New careers had mushroomed in Russia, the circle of prospective professions expanding prodigiously. A person could turn himself into a stockbroker, a real estate agent, a banker, with equal success. A nice-looking woman—and there were plenty of beautiful women in Russia—could use the natural talent of her long legs, the luster of her blond hair, her blue eyes, to make some fast money in Turkey or the Arab Emirates. As a result, you could run into country girls with awful manners—villagers from Riazan, from Omsk (in western Siberia)—in department stores, yelling across the counters, holding up pink panties for their friends' approval. These, naturally, didn't interest me. I'd never stopped or even slowed my rapid course through the streets of a strange city in order to contemplate them, to appraise them thoroughly. But I also met beautiful girls with wonderful manners, like the one I approached in Brussels one afternoon—asking her size as my pretext (a sister, a sweetheart, about the same height, similar proportions)—as she shopped for boots. I advised her not to buy a pair with fur cuffs around the ankle, quickly shifting to a familiar tone, someone who knew all about the depths of Russia, the muddy streets of whatever provincial Russian town: "They'll be ruined the first time it snows. I swear. Believe me, with all the mud you get when it thaws. They're mid-season, won't give much protection. It's the weather for boots, I suppose, but this strip of fur . . ." And at my sincere words of warning, friendly sounding, and in Russian besides, she turned a worried face toward me, looking deep into my eyes—a stranger, but one who had been able to read her most intimate thoughts—letting a small sad "Do you think so?" escape, a question already evident in her turquoise eyes, like a warning system with two signals, a flashing light followed by a redundant sound. Foolproof. Like this woman, in fact. She smiled then and slowly turned away, her eyes fixed on another pair of shoes, the next rack. She smiled because it had been foolish, falling for my feigned interest. Moving beyond one display case, she looked at me from behind it and walked off without a word, obviously thinking about something—my origins, perhaps. I saw her a bit later, wandering among the shelves, and then lost sight of her. That woman. She suddenly burst upon my memory a few days later, while I was still in

Brussels: tripping over one of the colored images from that day, I took a closer look, recognized the woman with the boots, and realized that I had not classified her correctly, that I had done her a disservice with that label, which had left nagging thoughts, successive images restlessly swirling around my brain. I had taken her for a student from Moscow or Petersburg, on a shopping spree in Brussels. There had been enough intelligence in the look she turned on me, the same one she had been giving the boots. But the blocks forming this memory must have shifted somehow, and the new arrangement made me pull up short and ask myself: *"Was she there to make money? Selling herself? Selling her body?"* Without the least hint of condemnation or moral censure; it was her business, not mine. My curiosity was aroused, that's all. I sold night-vision goggles, and this woman with whom I'd exchanged a few words in Brussels, maybe she sold herself. At a profit? That's what I wanted to know. I paid for each of my trips with cartridges of fired nerves; wouldn't her expenditures be even higher? If I had seen her again I would have made conversation, asked her about things like that. How she manages her beauty, her intelligent gaze, about her sense of herself, the high idea she surely has of herself, about whether it's paying off, this business of hers, making money at the expense of her body. Why this and not some other job? It made me sad to think about it: I was afraid she was making a mistake, throwing away her beauty, but if we had had a chance to talk, she might have convinced me of the opposite.

V. was one of these women.

. . .

Two days after that walk, I talked to a small-time smuggler, a *chelnok*, in the Grand Bazaar in Istanbul, while V. waited in the interminable line to use the women's bathroom, her flowered dress a break in the vast sea of Turkish ladies in headscarves. Never, I said to myself, when I saw him lugging an enormous sack made of some synthetic material, Never again, thank God, would I tote a sack like that or a backpack bursting at the seams. I felt sorry for him, seeing him in the Grand Bazaar, trying to peddle that heavy stuff, several kilos of merchandise. With no way out. I was living proof that this life of his, as beast of burden, wouldn't last forever. We spoke fast, like two ants exchanging information on a tree trunk. His sidelong glance took in my clothes—soft-soled sandals, linen shirt, loose jacket, well-cut but unstructured. We were veterans, we had carried contraband to the same European capitals, and we talked as if we had fought on the same fronts, been in the same decisive battles. But I had been on a strict campaign for a year, always increasing the density of my merchandise, trying to find the optimum ratio between its weight and that of an ounce of gold on the New York markets. He had been fooled, I realized, by how easily he could carry that many-kilo bag on his back. He was tall and broad-shouldered enough, he didn't have to pull it behind him in a luggage cart, like so many people. He wanted to find out what I had done that I could afford to just stand around the Grand Bazaar, leaning on the wall of this little hallway, idly watching the Turks. But no drugs, he said, he had a college degree from Kiev. He knew higher math, "Algebra I and II," and he had it all figured: take the Russian life expectancy, subtract the jail sentence for drugs—the yield was too small.

. . .

Did V. actually fall in love with me during our first walk? Maybe she noticed a certain regularity in my conduct, like the way I gave her a hand to help her down the steps at the Hagia Sophia. And fell for me right away. Or else she was pretending, and her cheeks glowed like a woman in love due to a highly developed mimetic mechanism, which made it look like we shared the same stripes, like certain patterns of her character matched mine, the same insecurity and anxious introspection. So that the most thorough ocular examination could not discover any difference between her and a woman truly in love. And since her thorax was more complex, far more complex than an insect's, the transformation affected her interior, too, so that she ended up thinking she really loved me. We had talked on and on, jumping from subject to subject, hours passing. Even Castaneda—an author I've never read and don't intend to—we had even talked about him that first day. She stood with me while I waited for the streetcar to the yacht harbor. I let fifteen, twenty, thirty go by, heard their bells ringing, watched them jolt around the corner and pull up at the stop, saw the doors shudder, first sticking, then sliding open, the passengers swarming in and out, Turks who live in Istanbul, who travel by streetcar all the time. V. just kept talking, her mouth always going, wiping it with the corner of a tiny handkerchief between one sentence and the next, holding onto my arm when the folding doors of a streetcar slammed shut, standing so close to me, her back to the street. After a start like that, why should I have had any doubts?

2

LIVADIA

Within three days my door was covered with several of those awful little self-adhesive tags—*Post-its*, they're called—that I refused to read. One morning, while I was putting my key in the lock, they fluttered, moved by an air current, like yellow eyelids: a terrible vision of eyes winking at me. On the fourth day I found a small note that had been folded into a triangle and slipped under the door. It was from Maria Kuzmovna. She asked me to come see her when I had a free moment.

Kuzmovna had two rooms in the left wing of the pension, next to the stairs. I hadn't ventured to that end of the house since my first days, when during a furtive inspection of the notes the renters wrote, someone gave a sharp cough behind a door. I wasn't alarmed. Just stopped doing it. Reading them had been a major effort anyway, overcoming my antipathy for those yellow eyelashes that couldn't hold more than a few words, a directive, an order, something simple. From Kuzmovna's tiny note, I learned that my visit was to "air a subject of some importance."

I found her seated at the table in her room, identical to mine, but embellished with doilies on the TV set and the wardrobe. She was sitting motionless, staring at a blank sheet of paper, with the expression of someone about to pen another announcement, or a short message (what other sort could Kuzmovna be writing?).

"Ah, it's you!" she greeted me coldly, since parents, headmasters, even middle-management executives had picked up the style of the government that ran this country. Maria Kuzmovna had seen plenty of films with scenes of wayward party members being interrogated and she could do a perfect imitation of the inflections, the voice of the little bald guy who could inspire fear with a single question, in a tone that might seem friendly and well-intentioned to an outsider, someone not in the know, but that held hints—special frequencies only revealed by spectral analysis—of the final allocution of the fanatical local leader. Maria Kuzmovna's voice contained another substratum: fossilized bands, tinges of the dominant attitude of the thirties, which colored her greeting with feigned pity: "It's you behaving this way, you're forcing us to resort to these measures. Nothing I can do, it's out of my power. And to think that we trusted you . . ."

"I know you've had women in your room . . ." she said, looking me in the eye and blowing the smoke from her filter-tip toward the ceiling. The filter cigarette, the fake velvet shade on the lamp, the flowery housedress were from the same period, Stalin's first Five-Year Plan. She stood up from the table as if coming out from behind an oak desk and searched through her dresser as solemnly as if it was a file holding the fates of several prisoners. "Here it is, I received a letter, an accusation . . ."

She came back and sat down across from me.

"It says here that you are violating one of the strictest clauses in our contract and entertaining women in your room . . ." (Alfiá, laughing her head off, climbing in the window.) "I confess that I hadn't seen anything, I didn't know, but I received a letter . . . anonymous, as you'd expect—" I reached for the letter, a natural reflex, to see if it actually held this accusation, but she waved me away.

"No. It's real. Do you think I could make up something like this?"

"Who?"

"I can't tell you that."

But we both knew who had written it. She looked me in the eye, giving me the information off the record, because she was a good woman—only her chilly greeting had the tough style of an interrogation. Now she made a little mental run toward the backdrop, threw off the official costume she'd had on, and returned wearing a smile, gleefully smoothing her dress.

"Is it the Tartar from the Post Office?"

She launched a roar at the ceiling.

"Nu ty daiosh!" (An untranslatable phrase; but she seemed to mean: with all the girls around here, in all of Russia, how did you get mixed up with the mute from the Post Office?)

She looked at me intently, breast heaving, carried away by the scene: the nails tapping on the windowpane, the lips pursed for a kiss, the entry, body lifted into the room.

She tore up the letter and threw the pieces on a plate of appleseeds.

"I had to summon you because he knows everything. He spies on all of us. I haven't thrown him out because he always pays on time . . ." And she broke off, because suddenly she was whispering, she was thirty years younger, and she felt arms around her in the darkness as she groped her way along the back of the chair, and fell into bed, holding her breath.

She pressed her hand down on the table to dismiss that vision; she had put on too many pounds in the past twenty years, she would never be lifted through a window like I lifted Alfiá, kissing her while she was still in the air, holding tight to her wrists, without telling her to be quiet, without whispering "please don't talk" or "don't make any noise, okay?"—because Alfiá didn't talk. Kuzmovna ran a business and I suspect she dreamed of a partner, a man to go over the figures with, up till three in the morning.

"I know you're doing research on letters. Why didn't you tell me you came to write your doctoral thesis . . .Yes, of course, the same person. . . . Certainly, did you know that Moscow is the only city in Russia that won't publish marriage ads? They're afraid people would answer them just to go live there. It never crossed my mind. They run the ads in all the smaller cities—Simferopol, Kiev, Kostroma. Why would I even want a boyfriend from Moscow? Aren't I sick enough of having them here, knocking at my door at all hours of the morning, asking me to 'sew on a button'? Look . . ."

She got up to open the drawer that had held the informer's letter, and it was full of registered letters. "I've seen you waiting for the Tartar, I go to the Post Office almost every day. All from a single ad in *Chernomorskie Viesti*. Lots of people do it. But no one told me I'd get so many letters. Should I answer them all or pick a couple out at random? And what if the love of my life is one I don't answer? Are you writing about anything like this?"

. . .

On Monday I had noticed a certain alteration in the disorder in my room. As if someone—unable to imagine a mess of the same magnitude after moving my things—had tried to put them back "as they were" (how were they?): the books, the pages of my first draft on the table, the pile of shirts over the chair. The hint of order alarmed me because it meant someone had been in my room . . .

"V.!" I thought. She had been here Monday, come into my room, examined my things, run her hand caressingly down the lapel of the jacket hanging in the wardrobe. She had sat down to read the draft of my response, smiling at the many little things she didn't know. This very day, I thought, going back out into the street, I might return to find my room clean and tidy and V. sitting at the table with a cup of tea. I was happy, I wouldn't have to write anymore. I would tell her the whole story in my own voice, live, naked, both of us, on the bed, watching the ships go by.

I imagined still more: the many ways that V. could arrive, the many ways she could surprise me. She might, for example, sneak up behind me in the little restaurant with the bay window while I read the *Cartas Morales a Lucilio* by Seneca, covering my eyes with long thin fingers, which I would mistake for Alfiá's. V. would burst out laughing, delighted to have caught me: "So it's Alfiá, eh?" Not angry, not a bit angry. "You abandoned me in Odessa," I would say in my defense, "so I looked for a woman who was mute"—aware that I was betraying the very nice Alfiá—"and lent her your voice, V., from your letters." Pretentious, a little pretentious, but pretty.

And as soon as I thought that, I realized one of her letters was missing; I had been robbed, and by Petrovich, I was sure. But I couldn't prove it—I had nothing to go on but the way Kuzmovna had alluded to V. and Istanbul: "I don't get it. Don't you have a girlfriend in Istanbul?" Petrovich hadn't been able to make out much of the story, but I was a foreigner, so he figured the letters must be from another foreigner, a Turk.

The theft must have occurred in the last two days, since I had decided Saturday to put the letters in a box that had held halvah or some sweet. A cigar box would have served just as well, made of cedar, with decorated vellum. My mother, in Havana, kept her letters in a box like that, I remembered it well. The lid closed tight so I hadn't tied them with a ribbon. Nor had I had the sense to put a lock on it, because I thought no one ever came into my room. Now I imagined Petrovich lurking in his room, waiting till he saw me go out, ready for work, in the boots I wore for the sharp crags of Ai-Petri. As I walked off with my butterfly net on my shoulder, he was watching from his window, thinking he had three or four hours at his disposal. He hurried to my room, opened the door—with the master key that I later found in his nightstand—and glanced out my window, watching me from another angle. Just then I turned, throwing a last look toward the pension, without seeing him. A scare! Petrovich took a hasty step back in his felt slippers, recoiling in a stagy gesture of shock, raising one hand to his mouth, fanning the fingers of the other, touching the blue box of halvah or candy, and accidentally discovering the letters.

Petrovich wanted one of my letters to incriminate me. The day they came for me, police agents shining flashlights in my face, pulling me from my bed, half-asleep, he would be outside the door, waiting to hand over the letter, to fatten up the file for the proceedings against me: thanks to his zeal, conclusive evidence of my illicit activity. He had not had a very clear idea of my objective in Livadia, but now, with the letter in his possession, he could imagine a case against me, if not for spying (not to rule out that charge), then at least for poaching, hunting endangered deer. The butterfly net, the flasks he found in my wardrobe? Red herrings to throw off the examining magistrate.

He had taken the fourth letter, the most recent. I had numbered the envelopes for convenience, having read this advice in a letter Madame du Deffand wrote Horace Walpole in April of 1767: "I will number my letters, you number yours," the shrewd technique of an experienced letter-writer. I could tell which letter had disappeared immediately without having to decipher the blurred postmarks from V.'s village. In fact, they all contained incriminating material, enough to arrest me for smuggling, for selling the surpluses of the shrinking Red Army. Now—discovering the robbery, feeling my danger—I wished I had kept some of the equipment I auctioned off when I couldn't find a better buyer. An underwater pistol, for example, a silent air gun—I wouldn't mind training one of those on Petrovich. The only things I had kept were some goggles still in their cases, night-vision glasses, which were hardly necessary here, since it was clear as day where I'd find the stolen letter.

In Petrovich's room, a woman's voice was wearily spouting the news of the day, most of it lies. Petrovich could sleep lulled by the monotonous voice of the announcer, without losing contact with Moscow for a moment, acoustically or mentally. Before forcing the lock—careful that no shadow was passing between the light from the window at the end of the hallway and the shiny parquet floor—I heard the weather report for the Caspian Basin and the Crimean peninsula. Tomorrow the high would be thirty-one degrees centigrade, an excellent day to chase butterflies.

I often saw Petrovich outside the pension, prowling around all over. Last week, for example, he was on the Yalta pier, hanging around a group of Georgian swindlers. The whole bunch gambling, pooling their bets, waving their arms in the air, pretending to have lost all the rubles one of them had piled in front of a marked card. I suppose Petrovich traveled around the city, going into all the stores, noting which bookshops were authorized to sell Turkish merchandise, which big halls had been rented to Libyan businessmen, which kiosks were selling pure alcohol by the liter, enough to make six bottles of watered-down vodka, registering his outrage at the exorbitant price of milk, the decline in sales of the local filter-tips with the introduction of Greek cigarettes . . .

I didn't test the wallpaper nor did I unscrew the mirror on the armoire—good places to hide letters, with room for several sheets of paper behind them—it didn't seem necessary. Nor did I feel I had to divide this room, furnished almost the same as mine, into twenty-inch-square sections. All I did was sit down in the swivel chair by the window, which Petrovich used for spying on boarders headed to the beach, me for example, coming and going with suspicious frequency, butter-fly net in hand. In this comfortable perch at the windowsill, he wrote the letters that covered the table, filed according to subject: reports on the decline of the Russian monetary system, on the child prostitutes who accosted passengers in train stations (with resulting profit to their Armenian *souteners*) . . . Whether standing a few meters from the card players or sitting on a park bench on the boulevard, next to an adul-terous pair on their yearly jaunt to Yalta, Petrovich was indistinguish-able from the other retirees, wearing a shapeless hat of some synthetic material, which had been worn too many summers, and which he con-tinually molded with his hands, so that its brim was arched like a quiz-zical eyebrow when he turned back toward the couple to make a mental note, the first point in his report on the "the high incidence of adulter-ous couples vacationing in Yalta. You might say: 'already back in Chekhov's time, the lady with the lapdog' . . . but what you see today is quite different . . ." One section of his file contained reports on the alarming growth of the foreign presence in Crimea, in all of southern Russia (reports on his trips to Odessa and Sochi). The day I saw Petro-vich observing the Georgians at their tricks, he swung around at a particularly bad moment—when a miner from Donetsk, clearly an honest man, lost his wedding ring on a bet—and swept the gathering with the question mark of his twisted hat brim. Would no one put a stop to those scoundrels? He was a retiree, a little old man (his skinny arms hugged his newspaper: he would dash off a letter to the *Cherno-morskie Viesti* deploring the incident), but the young people, the cabin boys laughing at the miner and gesturing at the girls, no more than children, watching the scene from across the circle . . . And you didn't even have to look that far, why right here, in this very rooming house, renting a room, a foreigner staying on indefinitely. Couldn't tell what country he was from, a skinny foreigner, maybe Moroccan, or from

Tunisia, an Italian? Not very likely. Maybe Spain; well, it was some (abominable) equatorial place.

I went over to the window. I half opened the horrible green curtains that Petrovich must have gotten from some Yalta sweatshop. No one was coming up the road that ran by the beech trees. A woman, maybe the one who brought the mail, was pedaling away on her bicycle.

I found the letter and quickly stuffed it in my pocket. V. sent her letters in large envelopes, so she didn't have to fold them. Now this one was in two small envelopes, standard size, decorated with pictures of May Day celebrations, the kind you can buy at any newsstand in Russia. Petrovich left them out by the window, hidden in plain sight, two letters ready to be mailed, stamped and addressed to a newspaper in the capital. . . . I heard someone open the door—too late to jump out the window, so I stood perfectly still: camouflage, another defense tactic.

Petrovich set his briefcase by the door, rocked onto his heels to slip out of his worn sandals, mentally whistled to a nonexistent dog, asking it to fetch his slippers, carrying them gently and wagging its tail. Leaning back so it couldn't lick his face, he patted its head, petting it, again mentally. Petrovich did not have a home anywhere in Russia. I had moved out of my Petersburg apartment, too, before going to Istanbul. On my way to the station I'd taken some books to Vladimir Vladimirovich, leaving them on consignment, a couple of Chase novels, an excellent translation of Genzi Monogotari, five volumes, in Russian (this had nothing to do with the epistolary question; he had wanted to buy it for a long time, and I had read it). I may not have had a place to call my own either, but I was sure that I would get one, a house where I wouldn't have to hang hideous green curtains to make it look homey, cozy. The lamps with their ugly green lampshades, the broken-down chairs, the cheap wardrobe—I didn't care about any of those things. I would be leaving at the end of butterfly season, with the first cold days.

It would never be a real home, not this place, a room in a pension. Petrovich didn't even look angry at finding me there. Things like that happen all the time in places like that. The same with me, it was a drag sharing the bathroom at the end of the hall: I couldn't even leave my toothbrush out on the shelf, or the next time I put it in my mouth, I'd worry what my neighbors had been doing with it. I had forced the lock to get into his room. Maybe he planned to change it, get one that was more secure. Too late. He had been in my room when I wasn't there and now I was in his. No sense protesting. He blamed himself for not hiding my letter someplace else. He never dreamed I'd find it so fast— perhaps he'd read about a similar ploy used to hide stolen letters, some story that made a big impression on him when he was a kid ("The Purloined Letter," no doubt).

"Have you been reading my letters?" he asked.

"I haven't had time," I lied. "I'd barely come in when you got here. I was about to start this one when you walked in on me."

His arm dropped to his side, fingers tightening around the grip of his briefcase. He wanted to throw himself on the bed, lie there staring up at the ceiling for a while, prostrated by the heat and the theft of state property in Crimea, where such cases were on the rise, but my presence stopped him. His eyes fell on the carafe of water on the night-stand. He went over to it, then turned to say:

"It doesn't bother me: they're open letters; anyone can read them." (Making them epistles, strictly speaking. That's the difference between a letter and an epistle: a letter is a private communication, an epistle is for a broader public. Though I didn't interrupt to tell him that.) He drank some water and sat down on the bed. "I'm sure you read them, but that's all right. I've been curious about your frequent visits to the

Post Office, I've seen you there several times. One day you left an open book on the patio. I took the opportunity to see what you were reading: it was the letters of Azef, the agent provocateur. Kuzmovna thought you were writing a study of letters, a sort of encyclopedia—or maybe it's an epistolary handbook, an instruction manual for letter-writers? But then, why the butterfly net?—it didn't seem to fit. Unless it was a cover. But a cover for what? What were you really doing in our pension, in Livadia? Maybe you were helping the Turks plan a second invasion of Crimea, now it's so weak. Reading your letter seemed to confirm my suspicions. Yes, a violation of your privacy. I would never let a consideration like that stop me, that kind of scruple . . . after all, didn't Hamlet violate the confidentiality of a letter when the king sent him to England with sealed instructions for Rosencrantz and Guildenstern, the two bums who were supposed to kill him? I saw the play a while back, in Simferopol, put on by a company from Perm. A real travesty—they might just as well have come out in bathing suits. It wasn't theater season and it was no secret they were only in Crimea for the beaches. The first time I saw it, the fall of fifty-one—I was already over forty—I had an excellent excuse for taking the day off. It would never stop me, such a simple barrier, I'm beyond that.

"And so you can see . . ." he continued. "Do you know about the letter hidden by the Bolsheviks? A letter, I tell you, at the very root of the Russian tragedy. In 1881 Vera Zassulich, you've probably heard of her, wrote a letter to Marx . . ."

(The short version, in my own words: In 1881 Vera Zassulich—the terrorist who had tried to murder Trepov, St. Petersburg's chief of police, and been let off after a huge public outcry—decided to put a stop to arguments among the first Russian Marxists about whether or not Marx's doctrine applied to Russia. And she thought of the most efficient way to do it: by writing a letter to Marx himself. I asked

Vladimir Vladimirovich for a copy of this letter, a long and rambling letter, a real treat: "Honorable citizen . . ." it starts. Not comrade Marx, oh no, all quite formal. She fired off her question on February 16, 1881, with the same steady hand that had taken a shot at Trepov. "A matter of life and death" occasioned by "the excessive timidity of your disciples." A very dry subject: historical necessity, whether every nation in the world must pass through a phase of capitalist production before constructing a socialist state. And because her school had taught her well, she added, please: "If you do not have time to develop your thoughts on this subject in sufficient detail, at least write me a letter and authorize me to translate and publish it in Russia."

"At least write a letter." Marx [Karl] was staggered by this woman, taken by surprise in the solitude of his study. He wrote a drawn-out draft, a true treatise, and then decided not to send it. A masterpiece of ambivalence. Looking into his eyes, suffering like Dimitri Karamazov, Russia had asked him, through Vera Zassulich, "Do you want me, Marx[ovich]?" and he, too much of a graybeard, gave this cool rejoinder, "I regret that I cannot offer you a concise statement . . ." A few lines later, declaring the truth: "The 'historical inevitability' of this movement is thus expressly confined to the countries of Western Europe . . . Russian peasants, on the contrary, must transform their communal property into private property." A statement equivalent to a round *no*. Russia was not the best country for the Marxist experiment. The Russian Marxists—Plejanov, Lenin, and Co.—hid the letter. It cost Russia almost a century of trouble.)

"Seventy years, almost a century, millions of deaths . . ." the indignant Petrovich concluded. "Can you imagine? All for a letter, if it had been made public . . ."

I opened the window to leap into the garden. If I crossed the room and went to the door, I would turn with a "So long, Mikhail Petrovich," as I turned the knob. Mechanically, by the mechanism that makes a person ending a visit conclude with a phrase like "Thanks a lot," or "See you later," all wrong under the circumstances, since I sure didn't want to see him again. Still, if I jumped out the window, I would break the thread of the visit, its continuity, and introduce a furtive element, the agility of a cat burglar, to the tone of the events. Petrovich would find me gone when he opened his eyes, but he wouldn't have heard the doorknob turn. My letter would be gone, but had he ever had it? I lowered my feet, heard him say something, already fading away, with the wind whistling in my ears.

3

"I've got it!" I shouted at Stockis, springing to my feet. "They switched on an electromagnet under the stage! That's why you couldn't lift it, the trunk. It must have a metal plate on the bottom: connect the electromagnet, and it's pulled tight, stuck to the ground. Ten men as big as you couldn't budge the thing, an electromagnet's stronger than the strongest Swede. Hadn't you seen the trick before? And the magician? That Jewish guy—or maybe Spanish?"

I hadn't been thinking about it, trying to solve the mystery. It just came to me out of the blue, as if the seagulls circling above us, in the cabin of the *Vaʒa,* had squawked it in my ear. Stockis had struggled with the trunk for quite a long time, his arms wrapped tight around it, neck swelling and turning red, forehead bulging, eyes focused off in space as he marshaled his strength, gathered it into him like electrons charging a battery. The whole room, all Turks, some of them pretty sturdy, were bolstering the charge with their sympathy, their full solidarity. They were shouting, cheering him on, chanting in Turkish, which Stockis couldn't understand, although he picked up the physical energy vibrating their vocal cords so thunderously. Then, to make sure he was really hooked, they cut the current to the magnet for a minute—actually the tiniest fraction of a second—and it was like a miracle: Stockis managed to pick up one corner of the trunk, which immediately snapped back down, thump, pulled toward the big magnet. Which made Stockis think he could lift the trunk just like the magician's assistants, move it as easily as the dervishes, and win the contest. "Have you seen"—of course he had—"how much scrap iron a tow-truck magnet can lift, a car's frame, its axles, they all stick to the magnetic disk . . ."

Stockis leaned back in the flimsy folding chair, stretched till he hit the lid of the ice chest, and pulled out another beer, which he held up to the light. Someone was shouting my name, a woman stopping at every yacht along the dock. She pronounced it the Russian way—with the "o" open like an "a"—so Stockis didn't realize she wanted me. He almost never used my name. Except right after we talked in Petersburg, that morning way back when, at his house in Stockholm or on his yacht on the fiords, then he had said, "Oh, J.," pronouncing it correctly, because he took that yacht to a harbor on Majorca twice a year. Unless you'd heard a Russian say it, you would never guess the woman was calling my name. Stockis had listened to my lecture on electromagnetism without much surprise, muttering "Ah" a couple of times, pleased each time a piece of my speech filled a little gap, satisfied it all fit together. Then with one motion he had reached over the arm of the folding chair—leaning away from its canvas back long enough for me to catch a glimpse of a man getting into a motorboat alongside the yacht a few meters from the *Vaʒa*—stretched out over the plastic ice chest, and grabbed a pale beer—it might have been a Pripps, I don't recall—which he held up to the light. Then he spoke to Lars, machinist on the *Vaʒa*, making a melodious Swedish request (an order, apparently) for a bottle opener. Before Lars could stick his head out the door to give the opener a friendly toss toward Stockis, the woman who had been shouting her way down the dock finally drew alongside the *Vaʒa*, once more shouting a name—mine. From below Lars warned, "I'm going to throw it!" or "Here it comes!"—also melo-

diously, in Swedish—and launched the opener in a soft curving trajectory, making it easy for Stockis to calculate its flight and put out a
hand so it landed in his palm. I had to get up and answer. It was V.
She would be gone in a minute. She repeated her cry and was ready to
move to the next yacht. If I didn't catch her now, I would have to call
after her. I said my name to Stockis twice, once pronouncing it correctly, as he did, and the second time, imitating V. I pointed at my
chest. Stockis said, "Go ahead, answer her!"

"I'm here! Come on up!" I shouted, bending over the rail.

I gave her my hand, helping her up the ramp. It was almost one in
the afternoon. V. had on a nice outfit, matching linen jacket and shorts,
a popular look, I thought, everyone was wearing it lately.

"V.?" Stockis asked, glancing over at Lars. "That's a Russian name,
isn't it?"

In the sense that Lars, for example, was a Swedish name, since it
sounded like one, then V. was definitely a Russian name.

V. looked over my shoulder and saw Lars knitting. I had been surprised too, a moment ago, to see him making socks. When I first saw
them, when Stockis asked for the opener, I thought they must be
nets—after all, we were in a boat and in Turkey besides. When Lars
got back to Crete, I thought, he would string his nets between trees
to trap ducks from Anatolia (which couldn't see the nets, so that
whole flocks, thick as shoals of fish, flew into them each autumn).
That's how they catch ducks in southern Russia, I had seen it and I
had read that they do the same thing in Turkey, its canneries snar-
ing ducks en route to Africa in the off-season. But by that time, the
first cold days of fall, Lars would be migrating himself, only in the
opposite direction, toward the north. He had four needles arranged
in a square and growing from it was a blue and red striped cuff, the
thick wool socks he was knitting.

With socks like that she would not have felt the cold in her village, V. must have been thinking. Her mother combed her two collies all year, V. wrote, and then spun wool to make mittens and warm socks for the winter. It had been a shock to see a man knitting socks like that so far south, so far from Russia. "They could be Russian," I said to myself, "they're so nice. They look Russian." She was a bit apprehensive about coming aboard. She had been on yachts before, known two or three yacht owners, all of them Turks. But now, in the cabin of the *Vaza,* she felt at home. A motorboat took off from a neighboring yacht, and its foamy wake reminded her of fishing with her father when she was young, the little lake she had gone back to visit recently. She too thought she saw nets taking shape in Lars's hands, from his needles, but quickly realized the truth, and kept watching as he reeled all the stitches in, to one side, over one needle, and then cast off, quickly, skillfully, freeing the yarn. She threw a fleeting glance at Stockis and looked into my eyes, starting to tell me what she had been thinking, "This Swede, this . . ." but her voice trailed off, changing tack now that she had seen the knitting man, Lars. She hadn't been happy to see me with Stockis last night in the Saray. I have to confess, I was put off by him at first, too, the plaid shirts he wore with the sleeves rolled up to the elbow, the pale straight hair pulled back into a ponytail, four inches long, hanging down past the nape of his neck. Plus, they have a very odd way of smiling in Sweden when they want to appear sly or suspicious. But with him it was more of a half-smile, a grimace affecting half of his face: he would purse his mouth on one side, wrinkling all the muscles around it. I saw this expression while proposing that he finance an expedition to capture a specimen of the *yazikus,* the one butterfly missing from his collection. About halfway through the discussion, half of his face had been mobilized, with the muscles assembled around the right corner of his mouth and one eye half-shut. A wry look that was so dramatic it had to be a national trait, codified, with the same meaning all over Sweden. He had used it again the night before to tell me that I couldn't fool him: I knew the woman. Now he wasn't even fazed watching her come aboard the *Vaʒa*. Her Russian name, which I called out to her, that was the key. No way the girl and I could be in league, planning to attack him and steal his money. He was satisfied, it explained everything, the urgency of her approach, searching for me along the wharf, shouting my name more or less correctly, her visit to his yacht.

I was the one put on guard when V. came aboard the *Vaʒa*. She had not appeared previously in my mental picture of the yacht, when I'd sailed it through the maze of islands around Stockholm. There's no denying, it was good to see her, but the reason was a mystery, and I picked up all the anxiety Stockis had shrugged off. Because I could not accept his solution, I did not think she had come to the *Vaʒa* just to talk to me.

...

After she searched me out that afternoon, as if she desperately needed to see me, we had talked in the stern of the *Vaʒa,* away from Stockis and Lars, so they couldn't hear us. The motorboat finished delivering provisions to the neighboring yacht, noisily departing, stirring the gray Bosporus water, aerating it. (There was a lake near her village, about five kilometers away by the new highway. When it froze over in winter, the fishermen—including her father—would cut holes in the ice and idle their motorboats for hours to keep the fish from dying of oxygen deprivation.) "Why me?" I wondered. "Isn't there some sailor who can help, a *chelnoki* if you can't get anyone else?" That was my first reaction, it didn't take long to see how odd her request was, how odd her coming to me. I stared deep into her eyes for a moment. No shadows tiptoed past in the depths of her pupils. Her eyes were still perfectly transparent—it seemed I could look clear to the bottom of her soul. "Why me," I asked, "a foreigner?" She regarded me in silence, without answering.

"Why me?" I asked.

"Haven't you brought things across borders before? You're a pro, right?"

I had told her about my smuggling, without going into detail. It had been a mistake.

She had made a mistake, too, and she told me about it. Coming to Istanbul had proven a big waste of time and money. We leaned against the rail of the *Vaza,* appraising the situation. Like accomplices planning a holdup, we held a serious conversation with few words. No need to ask directly, what are you capable of doing? (And how are you capable of doing it, selling yourself?) etcetera. As for me, I had once picked up some binoculars, tiny field glasses for races, which I thought would sell like hotcakes in Lillehammer, at the Winter Olympics, and which had turned out to be a total loss. You never knew in advance whether you'd find a buyer for something like that, like the musk I'd ended up liquidating, practically giving it away to a Palestinian in Berlin. But there was a ready market for V.'s merchandise and she wanted to earn money, was willing to pay the price. Not that she was squeamish. Nor was I. But the reality did not match the estimates she'd made in her Siberian village.

There had been no prostitution in Russia (much less Siberia) for more than seventy years. Now newspapers wrote about it a lot, but in a superficial style dictated by the reporters' ignorance of their subject, and always with hints, glimmers of adventure. V. watched her mother at home, going out to pump water, carrying back two buckets on a pole, and thought she'd get herself some money the easy way, in Istanbul.

It was a relief that she didn't want me to redeem her, save her from sin. I would have fled—throwing myself over the rail of the *Vaza* and swimming away—if she'd asked me to do that. But her angle—the truest and most intelligent, the only approach she could take—allowed me to stay right there, leaning over the rail of the *Vaza*, listening to her case, hearing her plea. Which wasn't to be rescued from sin. Her mother, for example, slept with truck drivers from the grain elevator, absolutely free. And she was no sinner, just a single woman. She outlined her request and I listened to her reasons, and the bright sun on the dark gray water hurt our eyes, so we got out our sunglasses and put them on, looking up at each other from time to time. The glasses were like masks, reducing the intimacy of our conversation. You must have noticed how safe and easy it is to talk in sunglasses, even more so if you're both wearing them. A chance meeting on the street, on a sunny day, you can talk without getting too involved, without worrying about where you're laying your eyes, hidden behind dark glasses. I listened to her talk, noticed her free arm, naked to the shoulder, and I watched her—in some pause, or the opposite, a rush of speech, delivering a long argument in a single burst—not on the sly, but turning my whole face toward her, looking at her, seeing myself, wearing an expression of perfect comprehension, reflected in her dark glasses. A nice pair, definitely, excellent taste.

And in the interest of achieving mutual understanding, and obtaining my completely disinterested help, we were now *reprogramming*, deleting the previous day's nasty error in the gallery of the Hagia Sophia, and reestablishing our relationship as a friendship (even though her bare arms still disturbed me, and the shimmering down that short blouse allowed me to glimpse at her waist): we had to agree that nothing could happen between us. We wanted to make that perfectly clear. Now we would share a camaraderie, like strangers on a train, with nothing in common, who discover they're from the same neighborhood and talk for hours, exchanging eager reminiscences: "Do you know Yuri K.?" No, I know a guy named K., but no, his name isn't Yuri, but . . . Hey, what's the difference?" I had been to Siberia often enough, I knew what her hometown was like. She told me about her mother and the truckers; about the studio, the painting school she attended for eight years. Risk-free topics, low in sodium. I could help that kind of woman, why not? We had been set in motion around the same time. She two years after me, galactically speaking. We had been propelled, sent into outer space, by the explosion of 1991, the enormous collision of East and West that produced stars, planets, asteroids. But the two of us were not even asteroids. Just motes of cosmic dust . . . (No, scratch that.)

"Look," I said, "I just don't know. What is it you need? Some help? From me? But how can I help you? Get you out of here? Back to Russia? There's no work there. Anyway, you're not stuck in Istanbul, there's Cyprus, Crete . . . That's a great idea! You can go with Stockis. Sail to Crete. Leave with him. We can talk to him right now. Me, I've never been there, but he has Arab clients, rolling in money. Oil: Need I say more?" I could look her straight in the eye (in her dark glasses) and pretend sympathy, but under that smooth face my legs were twitching, carrying me away at top speed: "Not me, I don't have the time, and, even if I did, I don't have the money. Come on, we'll talk it over later . . . Tiran?" He was the man she'd told me about, the club manager. "You must have seen him, the head guy." Yes, I'd seen him, the Armenian, flashy, like he was covered with glitter, like a statue, a mascot to entice customers.

"How much do you owe Tiran?"

"A lot."

"But how much?"

"If I tell you how much . . ."

She took off her glasses without a word, giving me a bitter look. It seemed to say, After all our talk about my hometown, about Siberia, about Russia! I stood up to that look without imitating it, keeping my glasses on. I wouldn't return her fire—a heroic gesture in war novels. It was safer this way, like a battalion with a seventy-five-inch cannon sustaining enemy fire behind a sixty-inch bunker.

I crawled away from the stern with a fake smile. And a little pat on the back, like a friend. Just one because she snapped like elastic, betrayed: her shoulder blades clenched like she was going to bite my hand off if I tried it again. "Maybe you'd like a beer," I said. Instead of: "Stop being so silly; you're going overboard. I'll think about it. I promise. You're rushing me, don't you see? There are a couple of things I need to take care of. And besides, I have to visit some stores, see what I can take back to Russia to pay for the trip. What do you expect me to do, anyway?" (She had made it pretty clear: get her across the border. Without her passport. Which was the real problem. She had only been dancing—a euphemism—in Istanbul for six months; she had hardly saved a thing, not enough to bribe the guards at the airport. Again, it came down to money.)

...

I had no idea she was deceiving me, not the slightest clue, nothing, because we're not as quick in real life as in the movies, where we have 120 minutes to look at every angle, add up the evidence, and catch the villains. And V. wasn't even a villain, not by a long shot. She was a good girl. I want to say that here to prevent any misconceptions, to eliminate any confusion. She wasn't a bad woman, or mixed-up, not at all. It was a bad decision, that's all; she just needed someone like me to set her straight, give her some friendly advice, like "no, don't go there, they're awful in that store; sure, I bought them there before, but I got some on the corner of Liteinaya and Nevski a few months ago. Right, from those Armenians or Georgians or whatever they are, and you know what, they're fine, you hear me." There are easier ways to earn money, other ways to make an—honest? Does it matter?—living. V. could rely on my help in this respect.

4

ISTANBUL

I no longer heard the Arab litanies here in Livadia. I noticed this at the bakery when I stepped aside to let a customer go in and he pushed the door open, and I suddenly heard the voice of a woman, a Fatima or a Zulema, singing as if from deep in a cave full of pain and regret. In Istanbul I had always seemed to move under a cupola of music, with Turkish and Arabic songs continually pouring out of the speakers in the Grand Bazaar or blaring from the market stall of some young vendor. The singing seemed to create a vault, voices echoing in the hollow space of a dome. Did that fit in with what Spengler says about the vault, about Arabic as a culture of the dome and the cave? Here in Livadia, I was no longer covered, sheltered by melodies. I would walk to the Post Office, for example, or even farther, to the Palace or to Yalta, without this musical accompaniment, without feeling I was at the bottom of a cave. I rarely heard music in Livadia. Only one night, on my way home from a movie, a melody came out of the darkness, the first bars, horns blaring, of a popular song from a far-off Caribbean island, and the lyrics really got to me. They went: "Dear lady dot dot (:), don't make me feel so blue, comma, I'm going to write you a sweet letter, so you'll know my love is true." A Dominican merengue, I recognized it right away. And with no one around to see, I glided smoothly down the street, doing the steps the way they should be done, joyfully. It was strange to hear this song, a merengue, here in Livadia.

A couple of adulterers were meeting in the woods—it was just background music, not important to them. But it was to me. I tried to find it later, in a record store, but was out of luck. (It was, after all, Crimea, southern Russia.)

I never listened to the lyrics of the lovely Arabic ballads, though. Still, I couldn't resist their charm—I would pick up the thread of some song and follow it hypnotized. The young and old men in fezes, in the stalls of the Grand Bazaar, didn't seem to listen to the words either, although something in their self-absorbed expressions said yes, they were tuned in perfectly.

...

Hearing that song—which a Turkmenistani peddler was playing while selling melons to the customers at the bakery—was like a flash, taking me back to the Grand Bazaar, the afternoon that V. searched me out on Stockis's yacht, desperate for my help, and I took her there, hoping to lessen the sting of my refusal by finding some merchandise she could resell in her village in Siberia.

What we found were heaps of figs piled on counters, dates swarming with bees, and a little clothing, too, shoddy stuff. Some Turkish creations that had already infested Russia, smuggled in, a veritable plague (I thought this a fair assessment). Nothing to her taste (or mine) until a red dress caught our eyes—we walked toward the rack without talking, both thinking this could be good. Needing to feel the fabric. I let her go first. She reached the hem to me, spitting a pistachio shell into her free hand, preparing for a more serious inspection. She rubbed her hand on her skirt and pretended she was going to rub it on my suit, too. I stepped back and said, "Hands off," with feigned annoyance, before we shifted our attention to the dress. She asked the shopkeeper to get it down; he handed it to her still on the hanger; she held it in front of her, chin on her chest, and said to me in a confidential tone, concealing her interest from him: "With all the *dermó* (shit) they've got here, this isn't too bad, don't you agree?" I did. Could she try it on? Just looking, she told the shopkeeper, who wasn't impatient, not pressuring us at all. Just the opposite: a Turkish trader behind his mound of merchandise, wielding the hook for getting down his dresses, and sweaters, too, the hideous acrylic sweaters hanging from the same rope. Only this dress was nice. She didn't necessarily believe the label, of course, Donna Karan, but if she could get a good price, considering that the seams were fairly straight, and the fabric, and the red looked colorfast . . . V. broke into rapid Turkish.

"Bu ne kadar?" How much is it? I gathered she asked, and I repeated in a low voice: *Bu ne kadar? Bu ne kadar?*

"Cok pahadi," Way too high, her scornful response. *Cok pahadi. Cok pahadi.* I, of course, would have added a few words: *"Cok pahadi.* Are you nuts? At that price, no way!" etcetera. That *Cok pahadi* of hers was just a start. Although the price actually wasn't high at all.

V. gave a snort and pulled the dress off the hanger. She looked it over carefully, the finish or seams, the darts, which should—and did, quite nicely, I soon saw—show off her shapely breasts.

"Too much, no way," she should have told the shop boy, but she decided to give him a little more line, to set the hook, which he took calmly, no extravagant display, no wailing—he looked young, but people caught here, at the crossroads of Europe and Asia, had been in the markets for centuries.

V. went to try on the dress behind a curtain. At least, I thought, they *have* a curtain. But I know V. wouldn't have hesitated to take off her blouse with me barely hiding her, saying: "Hold the dress, please, while I take off my blouse." Simply observing the form. I'd often seen Russian women standing around in their underwear in the makeshift markets in cities where I'd sold my merchandise, even in Petersburg itself—it didn't bother them. Some of the shopkeepers, in St. Petersburg and elsewhere, made no secret of watching them. And on one occasion, I heard, or thought I heard, a milky-skinned blonde saying to the friend who was warning her about this outrage: *"Pust padaviatsia."* Meaning "let them get their fill." What's the harm in looking?

She slung her blouse over the rope and came out in the red dress. Gorgeous.

"Gorgeous," I said. *Prielest.*

She stood in front of the mirror, moving her feet as if she was following a diagram, doing a dance step, maybe not as complicated as the ones I'd done down the street in Livadia that night, but enough that she needed arrows on the floor. She turned to the side. The dress fit perfectly, sliding over her hips like a slalom run, up and out. V. flexed her leg and lifted a heel, tossing a look over her shoulder: the standard pose in plenty of advertising campaigns. Elegant as a model, I told her, like a *maniquen*, I said in Russian. She stood out in this red dress. V. was glad she'd spotted it in this market, among all the *dermó.*

She pretended one last time she didn't want it. The shopkeeper, a Turk, did not fight her lie, but let go of his price a bit, so it suddenly plunged halfway down, where he'd probably hang on, V. thought, opening her purse, but not without trying to give him one last tug, casting a look at the hem, still dissatisfied. She finally paid and took the dress, which the boy wrapped up in due style.

I had thought it was possible to make a deal with a woman like that, I recalled, listening to the song in the bakery. The music reminded me of that, because the previous scene (and the ones in the Saray, too) really should have had background music—zithers, hands clapping, a drawn-out song in a guttural voice. "Aren't you going to buy anything?" V. asked me. "Okay," she relented, "I wouldn't have gotten anything either if I hadn't seen this dress, because it's so rare, you see. There are girls here . . . (she meant Russian girls, table dancers and fake ice-skaters) who dress . . ." She broke off, thinking she saw some pumps she liked, making a sudden leap toward a shoe rack. I came over and saw they were not right for her at all. We went back to the aisle without going to the counter. "Who dress . . ." I prompted, returning to that subject, so she could pick up the thread, but she had already lost interest, and wouldn't say anymore. She meant "who dress like *shliuji* (whores)." I can finish it now, here in Livadia. It's plain that's what they were. *Shliuji.* But not her.

5

The day—that far-off day—when I'm ready to make a clean copy from my rough draft, I'll need some good paper, like the rice paper V. uses for her letters. She wrote that she had saved a bunch of this paper during her origami lessons and was using it now to send me—not "her soul" (as du Deffand had asked of Walpole), but a completely counterfeit version of herself.

I went to a store in Yalta to buy a ream of paper, reaching my hand between two thick belts that kept me away from the display on the counter, poking suspiciously at some glossy paper. It was hardly worth a glance, all dog-eared and soiled, pawed over by the customers who couldn't make up their minds. On my way to the bookstore, I had noticed paper for sale in the kiosk by the Post Office, hundred-sheet pads decorated with bunches of daisies and fluted columns, artistically divided in two. Under the picture the artist had added "Crimea," in an angular script, deliberately Greek-looking, because it was so far south, and so close to Greece (once its colony), and visiting tourists would be sending the paper far and wide, to every part of Russia. No wonder V.'s letters got to me here, I said to myself. There's always a brisk trade in correspondence in these seaside towns. . . . I had no interest in those writing pads, nor in the cheap paper, shiny and slick, that was stacked up behind the saleslady. But I used it to try out some of the pens for sale there. The Post Office in Livadia had fountain pens—the ink flowed along a channel to a metal nib—for customers to use. I always forgot and started using one, setting it down when I saw I was ripping the paper to shreds, like I had every other time. If you knew how to hold those pens, you could control the thickness of your stroke and write a really beautiful telegram, but the product of such incredible calligraphic care would just go to some indifferent telegraph operator and be transformed into teletype.

I got back from Yalta at noon and picked up Alfiá. We went to the original Greek ruins near Massandra. Fluted columns, just like on the stationery: she pointed with pride. While we swam in the sea and later, when we were lying in the sand, burned brown by the sun, dark as figures on a Minoan amphora, I couldn't stop thinking about a passage in Busbecq, one about paper: "The Turks hold paper in high esteem because the name of God can be written upon it . . . On one occasion my Turkish guide became furious at my servants because they had used paper to wipe their asses." This passage just kept running through my head. Where was I going to get my hands on the right paper for my letter?

"And the position of your body, that's very important, too, Alfiá. Picture yourself: back straight, using the left hand for support, to hold some of your weight as well as the paper. Keep both feet perfectly flat on the floor; grasp the pen loosely between your thumb and index finger, without exerting any pressure . . ."

I wouldn't write to V. about her. At one time, I had thought of including a fragment of a letter that de Musset wrote to George Sand, to explain why I had chosen Alfiá. This is the part, from a letter he sent her from Paris on April 30, 1834: "I will have other lovers yet; now the trees are bursting with greenery and the scent of lilacs fills the air, all is reborn and my heart leaps up in spite of myself. I am still young, the first woman I have will be young too, I won't place my trust in a *mature* woman. That is what I had in you, reason enough not to seek it again."

"And you know what? Ovid—An amazing find! I should use it— was exiled to Tomi, a small Roman garrison in the country of the *getas* (who were they?), only three hundred kilometers from here, on the Black Sea, too, but in Romania. The same town where he wrote the *Letters from the Pontus,* which I just read this morning. I found this lovely phrase: 'May my letter be enough like my voice / that when you read it, you see me before you.' Something that sounds like this, in Latin: '*Sit tibi credibilis sermo . . .*' Credibilis! That's it exactly, I've said it before. And to think that these columns we see in front of us are from the same era as Ovid, or rather, were knocked over by those same *getas,* who hated Rome.

" And a woman," I continued, "what a brain! Had an idea for a novel based on the letters that Julia, the daughter of Tiberius, wrote to Ovid. I saw it on a list Vladimir Vladimirovich sent me, but I wasn't interested, since it was a novel. I haven't read any for my reply, not *Les liaisons dangereuses,* not Richardson's *Pamela,* no novels. But one study of Laclos appealed to me. It turns out that he, too, was on an island, held in a fortress, when he got the idea for his novel . . . After I told you the name, I forgot it . . . And if Laclos, while in that prison, could conceive a work 'that is still explosive long after his death'—he was a top gunner, to judge from this image—what better way could I possibly spend my time here in Livadia? By the way, I've found out—I'm sure you didn't know, I'd bet anything—that Livadia means 'meadow' in Greek.

"Ovid boasted of having invented the epistolary genre, elevating it to an art, but that is a typically masculine mistake. The best letter-writers are women. Trying to answer V.'s letters has convinced me of that—it's so hard to sum up our week in Istanbul in a single letter.

Whereas V.—with a cool hand and all the paper in the world before her—has written not just about those days, but about her life in the village, her childhood, and many other things. I was really moved by some passages, I read them to you. And here's something else to think about: we're impressed by the letters Flaubert wrote to Louise Coulet, and Kafka wrote to Milena (and also Felice), fine, but weren't they inspired by letters from these women that could be even better? Only the letters of these authors, mainly men, are read, are considered publishable, but behind them—and behind my draft—are invisible letters from women, true works of art, sublime. Sublime, I can't think of a better word.

"Will you write to me, too, Alfiá? You have excellent handwriting. I've kept some of your notes, I've pored over them. I can't write any to you, though, my handwriting is awful, and besides I'm scared, what if your grandfather got his hands on one . . . Why, this trip we're on right now, if I sat down to write about it I wouldn't know where to start.

"I've found some nice little touches in Ovid—the fourteenth elegy, for example, from the first book: 'To a young woman who was going bald: "Stop dyeing your hair," I advised, "There's not enough left to matter."' A realistic note, a feminine tone. In Laclos, too, there is a lot of woman, even though he was a gunnery officer, the inventor of the hollow shell . . ."

. . .

The only thing I could write with perfect precision, without my hand trembling, was the date, because I know perfectly well, sometimes, what year it is, but not always the day, *much less* where I am. No problem recording the date, which I now write at the beginning, although V. wrote it at the end, a better idea, since it doesn't really matter when you start the letter, or else, of course, you could write the date in both places, to indicate that throughout that period, maybe a day or two, you'd been adding thoughts, speeches, to your letter; then, any explanations you tack on at the end would become *post data*, strictly speaking. The displacement of the date to the beginning—clearly a modern phenomenon, this obsession with days and hours and minutes—explained the term *postscriptum*. Only once, in her first letter, did V. add a *postscriptum*, which I didn't take seriously at the time. It said, Another letter follows, or, I will write you again soon, at greater length— just empty words, I thought, like saying, I've been so busy, I'll pen a few lines now and send a real letter later. And besides, why was she resorting to such a glib formula? Sure, I could sit right down and scribble: I hope this letter finds you well, but an opening like that would paralyze my hand, it's awful.

As for closings, I've examined a number of formulas for them. "All yours," Vincent van Gogh ends a letter to his brother Theo. This impressed me: I could hardly believe that a man, a genuine artist, would write it so lightly. Not "With best wishes" or "Sincerely" or even "Love." *All yours*. Obviously I could not use this formula with V. There was too much bitterness and suspicion between us. Other formulas really bother me. I couldn't believe my eyes when I came across a "yours trly," an appalling contraction of the no less appalling word "truly." I found that some closings—like Francis Xavier's habit of ending his letters from such far-flung spots as Goa, the Japanese Sea, or Japan, with "Your brother in Christ," "Your dearly beloved brother in Christ," or "All yours in Christ"—were quite powerful, but too much so for V. A passion, a devotion, I recognized, that must respond to a powerful interior impulse. But how could I make myself, my hand, write these words for me: "All yours," or—if I didn't want to go that far—just, "Hugs," or "Kisses." Maybe my best choice would be the dry "Regards." I wondered if I could write "Sincerely yours," surely an English expression. But "sincerely"? And "yours"? Too soon, it seemed to me, for that formula. And Mozart? "Your most obedient son," to his father. All his problems, the enmity of the Elector of Salzburg, the booing of *Mithridates, King of Pontus,* his first opera, all originating or contained in this formula: "Your most obedient son," his customary closing. Refusing to sign his letters that way created serious problems for Kafka, it seems; at least he wrote a long letter to his father to explain his rejection of that sort of formula, which I now feel is submissive. And "Love"? No, I don't love her, in any absolute sense, I want her to come here, to Livadia, but I can't put it that way: "I want you, here."

But I'm not just writing to V.—I'm writing this answer for my double too, and I need to get him into the picture, so it might not be a bad idea to end with a familiar "your." "Your J."—that was plausible, that was accurate. "Your J."—I was that to her. And my double?—I was "Your J." to him as well. And "Hoping to hold you in my arms soon"? . . . No. Far from it.

6

LIVADIA

Only yesterday, after going to the Post Office, I walked past a neighboring pension, on the corner of a street I never took, and caught sight of someone spying on me from behind the lace curtains. I glanced their way again today and the lights were on—a bright yellow bulb was shining through the curtain. Both times I thought I saw a woman silhouetted there, a flowered dressing gown. It's not easy to conceal a butterfly net, I thought, to hide the fact that I was here to do a job, to capture a rare specimen, a *yazikus*. I hardly looked like someone who would chase butterflies for fun, with the casual way I dressed, the baggy linen pants I wore at the beach after swimming in the afternoon, the comfy leather sandals, the flowered Hawaiian shirts (which had come back into style again this year). Nor did I have the solemn air of an amateur entomologist, Stockis, for example—no, my unenthusiastic grip on the handle of the net betrayed me as your basic fortune hunter. Maybe someone was staking out this pension, hoping to get a tip-off from my face—a pleased or satisfied look—the signal to follow me up the same path. But a woman? I had just gotten a package from Vladimir Vladimirovich, the correspondence of Tchaikovsky and Nadezhda von Meck, so that's what I was reading this afternoon on the veranda, when I re-read a letter written in Florence and dated November 21 that revived all my troubling suspicions. I looked over at that window again. Whoever was watching me turned out the light to make it easier.

Von Meck, the rich widow of a mining engineer—who made his fortune by an infallible route, building a railroad between Kiev and Moscow (and most likely between Kiev and Simferopol too, the line that still brought mail to Crimea, carrying my packages of books from Vladimir Vladimirovich)—was an ardent fan of Tchaikovsky's music, called it first class and him a "brilliant composer," in a letter on November 24, 1878 ("It is impossible to compare you to anyone else. All one can say is that you possess the best of the best composers . . . I do not have the slightest doubt, you are a brilliant composer," was what she wrote). Once they had exchanged their first letters of admiration and appreciation, the widow bestowed an annual pension on the composer, six thousand rubles with only one condition, that they never meet, hardly a problem. But in 1878 when von Meck and Tchaikovsky had been corresponding for two years, they found themselves in Florence at the same time. He was staying in the Villa Oppenheim, she in the Villa Bonciani, a few blocks from Peter Ilyich, neighbors. It was pure chance that they were both in Florence, and von Meck's presence put Tchaikovsky in a panic. They might run into each other at any moment, out for a stroll. Frantic, he wrote to his brother: "Nadezhna Filaretevna was at the theater too and this limited my movements, which have been limited by her proximity anyway. I constantly have the feeling that she wants to see me. Every day I think I see her walk by my villa, stopping to try and catch sight of me."

I imagine that V. is the woman spying on me. She hadn't gone to Siberia. She had hidden in the crowd in the Maritime Terminal in Odessa, and later watched me board the ferry. A plane or train had taken her to Simferopol, and from there to Livadia. Then she had started watching me go out each morning, and writing me letters. She had invented the story of the trip home—it was just a form of punishment that she was imposing. None of her letters had a return address in the lower right-hand corner of the envelope, where it is usually written in Russia. Instead, there was a big bold capital *Z* covering that space, the red stamp used when someone leaves it blank, someone passing through a city, with no permanent address. Hiding in the house next door was a strange way to atone for her guilt. She would live so close, a few steps away, from the person who had rescued her from captivity, from the Turks, but she would not approach him until she was sure her letters had produced the desired effect, when I had formed a completely false impression of her. I was positive that V. had come. Four letters were enough to prepare me.

The next day I went to the neighboring pension. I stood under that window, staring intently at her curtains, lilies worked in tulle. No one seemed to be home. I asked Kuzmovna who lived there, in that room, in the other pension: "a divorcée," she said, "an older woman." Who I finally saw, coming out with a bicycle, gripping the handlebar. She must have lost her honor long ago (a summer romance) and decided to stay on, for the pleasant climate and closeness to Kazan and Ekaterimburgo.

V. could arrive at any moment, I had to be ready to meet her.

FIFTH LETTER

I

ISTANBUL

She cut her right off. V. cut Leilah off without the slightest hesitation. She must have seen us from across the street—she came rushing over, glaring at Leilah, another girl from the Saray. Leilah must have seen us the day before, returning from the Grand Bazaar, and had come up to me like she knew me while I was waiting for V. at the outdoor café. I had been flipping through a Turkish *Bazaar,* trying to figure out a photo caption in Turkish, the price in liras of a dazzling Versace ensemble. Leilah stood in front of me and I tore my eyes off of the glossy page, glancing up at the short skirt of a pretty dress, purple with shiny piping on the black satin cuffs. Instantly bringing me back to Istanbul. It couldn't be V., I knew that from the purple and the hips, at least five inches wider than hers. I cursed Stockis and looked down again, feeling no desire to widen my circle—to admit another name, new territory, new eyes, black hair—to extend myself further. The stranger in the purple dress bent her knees, slid smoothly into the other chair at my table. "Stop reading," she said, offering her hand. "Didn't I see you with V. yesterday? Leilah." Hand and name came out with surprising ease. I was feeling the wear of my long trip: I had only planned to spend a day in this city—an afternoon, actually—and to fly out at night. I snapped the magazine shut like a man in a dentist's office hearing his name called from the end of the hall. Seeing Leilah's hand reach toward me, I felt as if the girl in the photo—dark glasses, bright scarf tied under her chin, arm on the door of a convertible—had materialized in front of me, straight from the glossy magazine.

We were discussing the Versace ensemble when we heard a loud: "Leilah!"

Now it's her turn: her name has been called, and she's going to disappear through that same door at the end of the hall. I'm sorry to see her go, like a lady in the waiting room who shares an anxious half hour with you outside the dentist's office and then walks off without a backward glance, her cheek bulging with cotton balls, yanked back to reality. Leilah jumped at V.'s voice, pushing me away in a panic, like she was trying to ditch the evidence, the compromising bundle. I had moved closer to her as we talked, bending over the table like a man poking around in somebody's purse—cool, because I had honest intentions, curious, not about to take anything. V. was my woman in Istanbul (Stockis's late arrival left room for a woman in Istanbul). We automatically drew apart, then tried to resume our previous pose, leaning over the table, but where we had been natural, now we were stiff as wax dolls, which have to be molded quickly, before they cool. We "froze" (as the English say) in that position. I had no reason to be afraid: I had been gazing into her eyes, listening to her talk about fashion (telling me she wanted to be a model). But her face clouded with fear: those liquid eyes hardened, crystallizing, dropping like snowflakes.

Leilah seemed younger than V., a couple of years maybe. She kept her head down, trying on a smile, then a number of others, before deciding the last would do, and looking up at V. wearing that one. We were talking about fashion, she told V. in Russian, her voice thin and distant, like a long-distance operator hundreds of miles off. She turned back to me, saying, *"Excuse me. One moment."* Because we had been speaking English (hers was fluent and faultless). I had taken her for a Turk, with those gray eyes and her black mane, more than I could handle on my third day in Istanbul, so I didn't even try. I didn't have the energy to take on a Turkish woman right now. V. was Russian. As was Leilah (that name and her translucent skin came from someplace in southern Russia), which, if I'd learned sooner, might have tempted me to switch to her before she got away. (I once saw a man with the dirty face of a farmworker leap from the bed of one pickup truck to another traveling at the same speed. I was watching this from a train, which was also moving, like one of those problems they use to illustrate relativity. The man landed on both feet, swaying a little before he regained his balance, and then hung onto the slats of the second truckbed, laughing.) I would let the furious V. go right past me, with no more than a farewell wave. Or so I imagine now—since she left me without saying good-bye. Daring to run off—not like Leilah, who was a lot steadier, staying right with me, trembling, the wind ruffling her hair.

"*Ty govorí yemú po russki, dúra. On goborit po russki!*" (Say it in Russian, stupid, he speaks Russian!) Leilah swung around surprised, looking into my eyes for a moment to see if I had understood V., to read the swirling traces of Cyrillic script on the liquid-crystal display. Seeing, *reading* the truth there, she turned back to V. and said: "We were talking about fashion," this time breathlessly, shocked speechless, she opened her mouth to add something, but sat motionless, her eyes slowly dimming, suffering a brownout. Their light was nearly gone and she was about to rise, but V. held her in place with a steely "you," which fell heavily on the table, thudding like a briefcase full of weapons.

"*Ty suka,*" V. told her, "*esly ya bizhu tibia izhio raz rasgobaribaya s nim morgala bykaliu!*" ("You bitch, if I see you talking to him again

I'll scratch your eyes out!") Something simple like that. She twisted toward her and shouted in her ear, *"Ponial, Masha?"* pulling her lips back to spell it out, a slow drawl like in some gangster movie, black and white, set in Istanbul. *"Ponial?"* she screamed, meaning, "Got it?" eliminating the feminine final *a* from *Poniala,* deliberately making it a masculine address. A gender change conveying the gravity of the threat. Like, "Got it, Bud? We're talking man to man. No fooling around. You know the consequences." Plus, she called her Masha, a name so common it was like saying Jane Doe, or maybe Mary (Masha) Smith. All the Russians at the Saray addressed each other that way in private, I found out later that day, to show how far they were from home, the leveling power of their common trade. Then, too, it made it a direct threat, V. informing Leilah that she would act like any peasant, any Mary, the town Masha, shrieking, tearing her hair, killing the faithless lover with a kitchen knife, resigned to her fate, five years in prison embroidering kerchiefs and singing local folk songs.

I had put that incident out of mind by the time V. brought out her full arsenal, a case packed with shiny weapons, later that afternoon. It had taught me nothing: I had not grabbed V. by the hair (pretending to lose control), tossed her to the floor, picked up the briefcase, tossed it after her, barely missing her head, and shouting: "You asked for it, *súka . . .* or *ponial.*" Something simple, manly, like that. I'd been too soft on her, that's where I went wrong.

My attraction to Leilah? It was as if it had never even happened; I forgot it as soon as I was with V. again, when we left the café and went out to the street where there was a view of the Bosporus and its ships with their huge smokestacks. I walked alongside V. for five or six blocks, studying her. She had maintained an offended silence, after breaking off in the middle of a sentence. Her hair was pulled back in a ponytail, blonde with bright highlights.

She had left herself open in that moment: had I drawn a bit closer, I could have peeked behind her curtain, caught her crouching there unawares, rehearsing her roles in different voices, weaving the fine net in which she planned to trap me. Some things were almost obvious, it's true, visible knots, tangles of falseness and falsehoods, which I now think she wanted me to catch, knowing I would dwell on them, with justifiable suspicion. But I only saw her in this false light, tripped up in the snarl of her terrible acting—the fake warmth in her eyes, which she accentuated by half-closing them, a trick she had learned at fifteen, at a crude pier in her hometown; the broad gestures she used to indicate anger, jerking to a stop, slapping her thighs, propping her hands on her hips, things like that—but a net is not visible lines or the knots tying them together, empty spaces are the real trap, and although she seemed unreal to me, as if my arms could slip right through her, I found that I was caught the moment that I tried to pull away, like an Indian elephant held fast by ropes woven from the slender strands of a woman's hair. Weeks later, with a sort of false courtesy, a mockery—like an evil king visiting the noble knight in his dungeon, taunting him with the truth and roaring with laughter—V. sent me another letter, the fifth, in which I was able to recognize not just the knotty lies she let my fingers grasp in Istanbul, but the real her. Again I say I should have spotted her game earlier, I had the chance, during that exchange with Leilah, her best friend, her only friend. I could have disarmed her as easily as she had Leilah. A couple of *súkas,* that's all she needed, in a cool steady voice, keeping my composure, not breaking my stance, but letting her know I had "sunk my teeth into her game," as they say in Russia. Clear to the bone, the hard part, the truth behind that show of anger. Her fear had been real, though; she had accurately gauged my volatile spirit—thanks to her familiarity with the unfathomable practices of customers from Anatolia and the Asiatic parts of Turkey—and calculated that she could use me to power her flight, the way you would grab ahold of a helium balloon and get carried away. When she saw me talking to Leilah (totally immersed, as was obvious from my position, the way I leaned across the table, elbows on my thighs, hands interlaced before my chest), she was afraid her friend's beauty would drive her flight off course, that Leilah's gray-green eyes were darkening the picture, creating a disturbance in her plans. Those eyes meant threatening skies, so she shouted out a storm warning.

We had stopped in front of a shop with philatelic supplies in its window, stamps and albums, tweezers lying artfully atop them. Seems symbolic now, foreshadowing the letters to come, in which she tried to soften the effect of her furious outburst, her merciless manipulation. While at this store, she went so far as to put on a display of jealousy, hoping I would attribute the flare-up, the fierce words of a few moments ago, to simple jealousy. But I already knew that she was no figure skater, she wasn't here to skate, and I was unmoved by this act of hers, stepping back mentally to give her—as well as the long pendulum on one of those executive desk toys in the shop window—an appraising look. But she had her eyes on me, watching through a veil of tears. She broke off in mid-sniff and pulled herself together, taking out a hankie to pat her lips.

The incredible thing (I can hardly believe it myself) is that I would even think of rescuing a woman (and a whore) that I had never even kissed.

I approached her like a young customer who wanted a date, but was afraid to ask, my eyes averted, palms sweating, fingers tingling with embarrassment. I slid my hand from her shoulder to the nape of her neck and left it there, feeling her muscles grow tense. V. sensed my attraction immediately. The mooring ropes holding her taut slackened suddenly, as if they had been slashed by an ax, a single blow that sent her head tumbling down, bobbing for a moment on her chest before it broke free from my grasp. A desperate farce, my pretense at ownership, that failed kiss—it took me several minutes to recover, standing there without moving, head turned away, staring across the street. Now the full absurdity of this story spread open before me like a fan, with question after question, red then black, written in its folds, which finally hinging on a single point. I had to turn my head on its side to read them, one by one, the way it was laid out. And managed to decipher: Why (in the first place) did I ever take the job from Stockis, the *yazikus* madness? How did I let it happen, that trip to Astrakhan? What was I doing in the Volga delta, on islands plagued—really plagued—by poachers? And then? The flight to Istanbul. I closed my eyes, I couldn't read any more, it just kept getting worse: the walk through the Grand Bazaar, the talk at the streetcar stop . . . the chain of propositions, the tree of decisions: Yes / No.

2

ISTANBUL

Saray may sound like *Serallo* or *Seraglio*, which is a corruption of the Italian word for "harem," but forget the scholarly explanations; whenever I mention the "Saray"—and when a Russian says it—it means "warehouse" or "woodshed." *Saray*, Russian: a big dumb soulless place; as in, *"chtó ʒa saray takoi!"* (What a horrid ugly building!) I'll say it again, the club was no *Serallo*, just a *saray*—a put-down, but a sly one, since the name attracted business (there were at least twenty *Saray*s or *Serallo*s in Istanbul). I saw a lot of them on my walks through the old city, all brothels or strip bars; but I had already seen V.'s and felt no desire to go in.

V.'s was different.

In the Saray with V., surrounded by beautiful women, I was inclined to repeat Nicholas I's lament: "How can I trust such a villain?"—referring to the Marquis de Custine, most likely after reading his letters. Most of the Saray women were Russian and it was them (or women like them) who had forced the Turkish prostitutes to go on strike protesting unfair competition from these beauties. It's all documented, *they wrote protest letters*. Anyone who was in Istanbul at the time knows it's the truth. About the Russians—have you ever heard such trickery?—Custine actually wrote: "What can I say about Russian women? The ones I have seen thus far have been repulsive . . . They are short and stout, with shapes cinched under the arms, above their bosoms, which spread loosely beneath their smocks! . . . These women couldn't be more hideous! . . ." I'm with Nicholas I: "How can I trust such a villain?" Leilah was gorgeous, Natalia, sitting at my side, was gorgeous, Maria, Galia, Irina. All Russian. Or eastern European, since V. said that some were Romanian, Croatian, even Serbian, and Macedonian.

All individuals, each with a different kind of charm, different hair, a different neck, different ears: dismissed as "Natashas" by their displaced competitors, christened with this generic term out of a confused jealousy. Any Russian or Slovak was a "Natasha." Fairly apt, though, since you could close your eyes and pick a girl that way, blind, any one of them, and you couldn't go wrong. Well, two might have been a little heavy, Miloslava, a Czech, and another girl, Romanian. I say to them: "Don't go away. I'll be right back. I'm just off to catch V. while she changes."

I went up to the rooms. In the hallway was a filthy sofa upholstered in some synthetic fabric covered with fuzzy pills—that's where I waited for V. She had written to a performance agency in Jerson, answering their ad for a ballet on ice making a Turkish tour. She laughed when she got home to Russia, she wrote, and found the clipping still tacked onto the wallpaper in her room. The agency had mailed her an illustrated brochure, with pictures of the portable ice rinks used for their shows. Turkey is so far south it never snows, and figure skating is a novelty. They would tour for several months. By the end she would have made enough to buy three fur coats, mink or sable, the finest.

When Tiran received letters from these silly country girls, I'm sure he observed an epistolary convention that "no longer reigns" in the West, as it was described in the prologue to one collection of letters. Each time he got a letter, the Armenian would touch it to his forehead before he opened it, to show his respect and gratitude, and when he was done with his reading, he most certainly would kiss it devoutly.

For the peoples of the Orient, the author of the prologue affirms, "each letter has the dignity that words have for Paul of Tarsis." It was the Turk within the Armenian who was responsible for these acts, working the gears and levers to raise his arms, bringing the letter to his head, the gestures of respect. After which he would copy the Russian name onto one of the fraudulent contracts he sent out. Some of the women who received them, like Leilah and Natalia, had no illusions, they knew what they were getting into, what kind of setup this was.

I sank into the sofa, lying with my knees up. In this position, I saw all the women who worked at the Saray, a blonde head appearing at the top of the stairs, then breasts, hips, pelvis, coming down the hallway toward me. This kept me entertained, while I twisted and picked at the little fuzz balls. Chorus girls, I thought, professional dancers, harp strummers. It helped me to think of V. as a chorus girl.

Many of them winked as they went by, glad to see a "boyfriend" there. One of them, Eva, the Serbian, gave me a really broad wink, offering her services, a free quickie, on the window seat. I was sure I could take her there, sweat it out with her for a while, our backs to the hall, she was fast and loose enough (and that wink). None of the women seemed to be pining for rescue. Which is not to say they didn't want out. V. herself told me about Miloslava, the Czech with the sad face. Miloslava wasn't among the women downstairs swarming around the bar, some of whom had strong scents—like a lot of the beautiful women you meet in Russia (not that it bothers me).

Miloslava's story takes place along the Turkey-Bulgaria frontier, in an atmosphere charged by the many conflicts there. By the Bulgarian weight-lifting team, the athletes defecting to Turkey. There was a lot of talk about one guy—small and brawny like everyone in this sport—who got into Turkey, became a citizen, and now competes for them. It was an atmosphere heavy with free-floating hostility that Miloslava got stuck in, and she was shot through with this hatred—like a pizza zapped in a microwave, or a bird fried in midair by a high-voltage radar dish. Miloslava took a chance, hoping she'd get lucky at the border station, that her story would fly: claiming to have lost the passport that was actually in Tiran's safe. (This was a key point for V.—since Tiran had hers, too—and she kept repeating it, making sure I got it.) Miloslava was staying in a local hotel. Many Bulgarian and Russian women worked there, she discovered, because of all the truckers with long hauls. Probably a good sign, she thought: having women there might relax tensions in this border town. (It was hard for me to imagine this problem with visas and borders. I used to get in fixes like that, but not lately. Nowadays, thanks to my two passports, I can travel from Denmark to Helsinki, or from Brussels to Milan, and I never get stopped, not even once. Then again, I hadn't tried to cross the border between Turkey and Bulgaria, or between Turkey and Iran—trouble zones, since the Kurdish dispute.) But no, when she got into the line of cars leaving Turkey, Miloslava realized that there was strict control at this checkpoint.

V. always got upset at this point (she told me the story three times): the border guards were trying to speed things up, so they didn't wait for Miloslava to reach the station, they came up to her car—she wanted to turn and bolt, but could not reenter Turkish territory—and knocked on her window (still friendly), asking for her passport. They waited as she pretended to look in her purse, in the glove compartment, under the seat, and then—instead of letting her go, like they would have if she'd been a man (well, maybe not, the Turks are complete pigs)— they forced her out of the car and took her to the police station, where they had something in store for her. Horrible, *slushaesh!* (Do you hear me?) Horrible. She wasn't the first prostitute without papers caught at that post. At midnight they changed shifts and another eight guards came in. Six before midnight and all of the second shift, it seemed. "Attempting to leave the country without proper documents." I don't know what the fine was in liras, some astronomical sum, with the exchange rate. She must have robbed and killed a customer, they claimed, something like that, and was on the run.

"Boobshe, dúra" (what an idiot), V. said in a low voice, like a child telling a horror story: "They took her money, her clothes, and you know . . ."

3

ISTANBUL

I watched Tiran greeting customers at the door. V. was dancing at the Saray tonight and I was on the phone to Stockis on the *Vaza* while waiting for her. From the telephone booth I could observe the Armenian without his knowledge—just like Dalmas (a detective) in *Too Clever by Half* (a novella) by Chandler, a real writer, not some letter-writer.

The Armenian looked like he was run by a heavy flywheel that was slow to crank up and turn over, to shift the torque and push the connecting rods of his motor, that hard heart of his. The command to raise his eyes and scrutinize each new arrival seemed to come from a creaky control mechanism—Tiran's was a World War II model using cogs and gears, a crude ancestor of the modern computer. It was actually quite a sophisticated model, I learned later, but his clients, mainly fussy Arab princes, wanted a traditional look, old enough to seem respectable. It came equipped with the last word in wireless communications—a superior intelligence (in production since before the time of Christ) camouflaged by the fez on his head. For example, sensitive microphones—very acute hearing—allowed him to follow the conversations of customers anywhere in the room. Thanks to the sensitive spectrometers in his eyes, a mere glance could analyze the personal chemistry, the inner processes, of any man. He identified the streak of amorous disturbance in me long before I did, before I confessed to my image in the mirror of the *Vaʒa's* cabin—aloud in my native tongue, glad the truth was out at last, but transfixed by a thousand qualms and pangs of conscience—"this woman could make any man lose his head," to fall back on a Spanish cliché, which was somewhat overblown, but described my condition to a tee. He had even foreseen its consequences and predicted our flight—while I still thought that mine went straight back to Russia—determining our escape route by factoring sense data (a conversation I had with V. in which we mentioned the *Vaʒa*) with information (every way that we could get away), just as he figured every possible play at each table, calculating infinite combinations, using his advanced programs and huge memory. He gave quite a performance as guardian of the Saray. He didn't just watch over the girls, no, his acting skill created the image of an ideal guardian, not naturalistic, but highly stylized, and utterly convincing. Oriental-style, not attempting a realistic impression, just a caricature, the broad outlines of a character. "That stooge!" I said to myself—with reason to hate him, after what V. had told me—watching as he moved around the room, my perceptions constantly shifting, seeing him within different traditions. At first he looked to me like the villain (gold watch chain, scarlet waistcoat, pointy boots, like buskins) in a comic opera, but this was Istanbul, so it turned into the Peking Opera, with me a regular patron, exquisitely attuned to the Oriental aesthetic, the refined symbolism of his costume. I would find it all terribly convincing then—the painted-on eyebrows, the studied actions, the theatrical gestures indicating his disapproval, the threatening stares, "looking daggers" at some girl, a perfect expression of the real danger that he represented.

In the original libretto of *Abduction from a Seraglio,* this character played a minor role, Mozart told his father in a letter dated September 26, 1781. Osmin, the Seraglio guardian "sang only one song," Mozart wrote, "no more, except for a trio and the finale." (After the opera's premiere, a Leipzig newspaper received an angry letter from Bretzner, the minor poet who penned the original libretto, who now complained that "a certain person by the name of Mozart has taken undue liberties with my drama 'Belmont und Konstanza' to make his operatical text . . .") It was artistic genius—according to his biographer—that made Mozart expand this role, one of Germany's best-loved characters, one of the high points of Mozart's operatic career. Needless to say, I would have preferred the first version, the *singspiel* "Belmont und Konstanza," in which the harem guardian plays a marginal role, harmless and amusing.

Underestimating him, I found out shortly, was a mistake that could cost me my life, could have sent me "to feed the fishes"—certainly a threat familiar enough to Pródomo (another Byzantine distinguished for his hand- and letter-writing), whose plays became popular years after his death, after the fall of Constantinople in 1453, in the Turkish puppet theater, the Karagöz.

Exactly! He was like a doll, a puppet, not a bit frightening. V. and the other girls called him Tiran, even though his real name was Tigran, an Armenian name: "Come right in, you will get a warm welcome here . . . I am entirely at your service: your every wish is my command . . ." Mellifluous. He spoke English, but mainly the words you hear at airports, in those announcements of international departures intoned by computerized voices, in several languages, with each word rising or falling. And Swedish too, that's how he greeted Stockis, I recalled; in fact, while we were talking, Stockis had ordered two beers, first asking for them in English, then repeating his request in Swedish, with a smile: a *birra*. "Bier, Bière, Beer, Birra," he recited toward Tiran, who was already moving away.

And I laughed, still naively thinking it was a make-believe harem, like in Montesquieu's *Persian Letters*.

I was surprised to find that V. had made a real effort to master belly (or belly-button) dancing. With her choreographic expertise—she'd studied ballet as a child—she could simulate the real contortionism of the chorus girls. All these exertions would end up as internal knowledge, a secret measure of self-confidence, she thought, since she wanted to go home, get married, buy a little house, raise pigs and chickens, cultivate her garden. Once she was married, there would be no more flashing her belly button. Her faithful husband—a trucker coming home tired after a long day hanging around the silos playing cards with the other drivers while the wheat was unloaded—would see no demonstrations of the omphalic skills she had acquired during her youth in an Istanbul "harem." Nevertheless, she had made a real effort to learn, mimicking the group's Turkish girls, who were quite lovely, too, as I saw that night.

They wriggled fiercely, like caterpillars stretching to their full height, the kind without ventral feet that advance by humping up, casting their forebodies out, and inching their tails forward, coming toward you slowly, blindly, toward some spot where you are, bent over a branch watching them. Seen up close, parts of some of the women were disturbing, they had hips that were too narrow—I verified against my will, trying to remain detached—and buttocks too white. I couldn't help feeling alarmed when I saw them run toward me from the backdrop, springing to the edge of the platform, tigerish, feline looks, heads rolling wildly, hair swirling. A collar, yes, trained but still feral.

What a contrast to the woman I saw sunbathing here in Livadia just yesterday. Her breasts pressed softly against the plush towel, swelling out on each side near the remote region of her shaved armpits. I moved closer with a tremendous effort, digging my nails into the sand. This woman—and the book she had been reading, which was lying open by her head (I couldn't make out the title, but it looked like the letters of Madame de Sévigné)—interested me more than the half-naked girls in the Saray. I preferred the style of her bikini, homemade, kind of a generous cut; preferred the waist of this woman discovered—you might say—by chance on a beach.

The one that the girl in the Saray wore was cut high on her hips, revealing her hip bones. She was clinging to a shiny pole, lowering herself on it and not letting go, attempting to excite me—because the girl is doing what novice actors are supposed to do: pick out a single member of the audience and perform for him, and at the moment, it's the one in the combed linen jacket. She moves down, wiggling her hips, swinging her rump from side to side, two handwidths from my face. Depressing. I was profoundly depressed, and it took an act of will to keep from jumping up and leaving. I tried returning to the show, to the present, from an artistic angle. Impossible. There was nothing artistic in a woman hooking the waist of her panties, rolling them down with her thumbs, letting them drop in a tangle around her ankles. She would have to give her leg a good shake so those panties would go flying and land near Stockis, who would pick them up and bring them to his nose, sniffing their fragrance. This girl, too big and awkward for my taste, was she a clean woman? She sat down on the floor, opening her legs, clumsily displaying a shaved mound of Venus, and took off a *Wonderbra* (whose advertisements, fittingly, made a supermodel of a Czech peasant with a farmgirl chest), cupping her breasts modestly. Who was going to buy that? I wasn't letting it get to me, this obvious pandering to the lowest voyeuristic instincts of these customers who came from far and wide—places like the Arab Emirate Republic or Sweden—to exploit her subhuman condition (or some such feminist argument). The women seemed satisfied enough dancing in the void of a deplorable melody, a saxophone solo; they never stop smiling, not openly, no, insinuatingly, secretively, without the Dionysian frankness that I found in a letter by Alciphrón, an author from the third century A.D., representative of the Second Sophists, about whom nothing is known but his name, according to the guy who comments on this compilation: "The most enjoyable part was the competition between Thryallis and Myrrhina, to see which had the softer, the better ass. First, Myrrhina undid the belt—of her silken tunic—and began swinging her buttocks, which quivered like twin custards. She cocked an eye back at this shimmying and a few sweet moans escaped her, like in the throes of love, so that—by Aphrodite!—I was thunderstruck . . . But then she gave herself a shake and set those hips in motion, jiggling side to side and all around, and that was when we all burst into applause and said she was the champ." None of that here, among the Saray girls, none of the pagan frankness I liked in this letter. These women should arise from the depths of their Judeo-Christian guilt, a feeling that is Western but deriving from an Eastern rite, because a Byzantine touch has certainly been added: the proverbial corruption of the Byzantine woman detailed in the correspondence of Elios Penestrino.

I felt ill at ease, not pleased—I'd never asked to have such a large fleshy woman dance a few steps away from me, assaulting me. The sort of experience Stockis must like. And I thought: V. would be another thing, looking at V. wouldn't disgust me, and just then it got dark and some black lights came on and a smoke machine sent a plume jetting along the floor, as if (we imagine) a catacomb had been opened. I thought they had dropped some foam or fake snow from the ceiling, and little flakes had landed on the sleeve of my black jacket—I rubbed them repeatedly without getting them off—but it was just the fiber, the flaws in the fabric were phosphorescent, glowing in black light. There were only a few such fibers in my suit, a minimal percentage of impurities. But someone had imagined the effect a blacklight would have on a bikini made entirely from synthetic material, 100 percent impurities, a fabric designed to glow in the dark. And now two bikinis appeared at the end of the platform, tops and bottoms floating in the air, intertwined like a double star (Beta Gamma, in the constellation Cassiopeia), then swaying apart, in separate orbits. One of the girls moved off to the far end. The shapes were barely distinguishable, their flesh very dark, like shadow puppets, and I told myself: now I could reach out and feel her if I wanted, like a blind man identifying the inner face of her thighs. The bra and bikini rising and falling as if they had acquired a life of their own from the blacklight. I guessed she was bent at the waist, torso thrown way back, top and bottom on the same level, rotating. I glanced over at the other girl, on the other pole. They were gyrating in unison. Then I spotted a smile floating in the air by the stage, a set of dentures. I don't think it was deliberate—more like my suit, the way a few fibers, some impurities in my nature, lit up in this vicious black light—but Tiran's false teeth were a mixed polymer, and phosphorescent, like an oversize row of square teeth in a mask. I'd better watch out for those teeth; if anything could block an escape attempt it would be those teeth looming up in the darkness like the bars of a prison window, impassable. The woman, the shadow dancer, removed her bikini and threw it to a neighboring table. I would have liked to have caught it, to get a closer look at its phosphorescent fibers, its chemical makeup. The dancer was now a dark shadow, a spirit. But there was one difference, hers was a form we could divine. When the lights came up, what I saw first were painted toenails, in all colors. Whenever I took a new step toward recognizing V., her "I," there were those toenails—which were beginning to seem like a portal, taking me to another level of complexity and comprehension. Then, since this dancing in the dark hadn't had enough sex or appeal for the customers, there was a second part, a colophon, no cheating, under white light, so all the men could poke them deliberately with their gaze. I wish I hadn't been there. I wasn't interested in observing V. this close, turning her back and bending over as a special favor, fanning my face with a rapid movement of her rear end. I felt bad, I must have changed color like Alyosha Karamazov. And I felt their shame, inflamed with a sense of infinite pity for these women (not just V.) forced to undress in public, sit down in a scissors, legs spread wide, stroking their chests, pulling an earlobe, feigning pleasure . . . But, who was forcing them? It was their decision, their own gratification . . . Okay, let's not get into this right now.

When he saw the look on my face, the Armenian was ready for action, like the captain of a ship who'd been watching the maneuvers of an enemy squadron from the bridge and, when he'd seen enough, lowered his spyglass, uncapped his megaphone, put his lips to its mouth, and gave the order: "Battle stations! Man the engines! Full speed ahead!"

. . .

I pretended the glow-in-the-dark dentures attracted me, going over to Tiran as if drawn to his magnificent plastic teeth, and then told him about my goggles. I had taken them to the Caspian Basin, to a tributary of the Volga, and had hiked along its banks watching bats and owls, seeing trees and rushes, the radiance of the river, with perfect ease, my goggles picking up and amplifying the photon flow from distant stars—the ideal light for the glasses, since the luminous scale of the stars, the astral spectrum, contains the full range of infrared light.

Tiran could be a buyer; men like him, with no scruples at all, used to working in the dark, were my best customers. Why should I pass up this chance to screw a nice profit out of him? He seemed interested at the start, but in a childish way. He wanted to see "how it works." And since it wasn't dark enough inside the club and the street was too bright, with neon lights and the sign saying "Sa-ray, Night Club, Saray, Night Club," I said maybe we should try under the stage. It would be pretty dusty, I realized immediately, but that wouldn't bother me, I must admit, if Tiran bought the goggles, but he wasn't going to, I could already tell from the infantile gleam in his eye, because he could not begin to imagine their uses. He entered skeptically, poking a dubious head through the trapdoor. I was inside, squatting down, waiting for him. Shutting the door made it pitch-dark, except for a few shafts of light that slipped through the cracks between the planks. The stainless steel poles on which the girls wriggled—up and down (like caterpillars)—came through the stage, where they were bolted to the floor. I helped adjust the goggles; I switched them on; I asked, "Do you see anything?" knowing his answer: "No, nothing." Which is what I got. Partly because he didn't want to buy them and partly because, with these goggles on, you don't see the way you do in daylight, quite naturally, when you're aware of the amazing coloration on the wings of a butterfly. These goggles allow you to see full well, obviously, but they're specially designed so they don't tire your eyes: you can make out everything, but it all looks green. Near the edge of the stage, for example, I spied the electromagnet they used in the trick with the trunk. Sure enough, I noted automatically. I didn't bother with it—so what? — I'd already deduced its existence.

He said scornfully, "a plaything for children." And it wouldn't have done any good to tell him: "neither the 81st Airborne of the United States, nor the Spetnaz of the Russian Ministry of the Interior, nor the Mossad agree with you." I just shrugged and got out of there, my jacket covered with dust and spiderwebs.

4

LIVADIA

I opened the *Chernomorskie Viesti* to see if Petrovich had sent a letter denouncing me. Someone had written "To the Editor" complaining about bad service on the trains. Surely, the *gospodin* director sometimes travels by train. Pray God it's nothing like the Kiev-Simferopol! For one thing, they don't serve tea at all, and the waiters in the restaurant car take the cake. The porter brought damp bedclothes, we had to hang them out in the upper berth. And to top it all off, there was a robbery, a real novelty. The first since Baron Wrangel's troops were expelled from Crimea. A gang stopped the train on the steppes and went through each car, robbing the passengers. The letter-writer had been prepared, he had locked and bolted his door, but what about his neighbors? Etcetera, etcetera. A string of complaints like in all Russian newspapers, which have a special department for analyzing and filing correspondence. I have read beautiful letters in this paper—in this very issue, one about a girl and a prisoner. The girl had waited all of one winter day for his train to pass through a tiny station, no more than a whistle-stop, so she could see him for just fifteen minutes and kiss him between the bars of the prisoner-transport car . . .

Tears welled in my eyes. I looked up from my reading, touched. Diodo came over.

"An interesting article?"

"A letter, Diodo; it's just a letter, but beautifully written. It made me cry, as you can see."

V. was just as good. Ah, the Russian soul!—I thought—with its immense reserve of goodness! And other primitive souls, too. Francis Xavier makes the exact same point in one of his letters, about the natural goodness of the Japanese. Here it is: "We prove to them (the Japanese) that the law of God is the first law, telling them that before the laws of China came to Japan, the Japanese knew that killing, stealing, bearing false witness, and other actions against the Ten Commandments were evil, and as proof they suffered pangs of conscience for these acts, since shunning evil and doing good are inscribed in the hearts of all men." And with this fine argument, which he wrote to "his brothers in Europe on January 29, 1552," he succeeded in converting many Japanese—and in convincing me, almost five centuries later, of the innate goodness of V.

The innate goodness of V. And of the human race: "shunning evil and doing good are inscribed in the hearts of all men." I would like to write to a Moscow newspaper, "A Letter to the Editor," with that sentence as a heading. It would tell of a young girl—almost a child really—who was hired to ice-skate and ended up in a brothel in Istanbul. There would be a reporter here within days. First, just the local stringer, but then, since it looked important, reflecting a "national trend," a big-city reporter would fly to L., a small city in the southern part of our country, in Crimea, where our special correspondent talked to J., a young alien (names have been changed to protect the privacy of the people in this article). They would take some pictures and run a big article, maybe a feature, and they would get it all wrong.

One thing would be missing from their story—rejected as an odd twist, a detail not worth the readers' attention—V.'s original plan to con me. I didn't fit into her initial scheme. She had intended to empty

the money pouch I wear around my neck, bribe the guards at the border station, and get on a plane to Odessa in a black wig and dark
glasses. To ditch me in Istanbul—leave me stuck there, staring stu-
pidly at the seagulls swooping across the Bosporus, the ferries sailing
from shore to shore, Turks hanging over their railings, the pewter-
colored water.

I chanced on the letters of Evno Azef: more evidence of her evil and
perfidy. Who was Evno Azef? I knew his mind from his letters and
quickly lent him a body, that of Mikhail Petrovich, transferred to the
beginning of the century without losing a speck of evil in the process.
Azef was a Russian double agent, a brilliant one. He was the best secret agent in the best police force of the era—at the same time he was
the top leader of the top opposition party. And he left a volume of
letters, of denunciations, carefully collected in the police archives of
Petersburg.

Azef was a genius, considered a "superior man" by the police—and
by his party. Naturally, he had to plan and carry out some real attacks—an attempt on a high official, for example, in his box at the
opera, a bomb under the seat—and to turn in his co-conspirators. He
demonstrated boundless loyalty to both groups, as he said in a letter
on June 14, 1909: "No one wants to believe that, for many years, I gave
my all to the revolution," and also—he added—to the police. Without him, without Evno Azef, the Russian Revolution might never have
happened. He was behind such important events as Bloody Sunday of
1905, when demonstrators gathered in front of the Winter Palace, and
Nicholas II—before he captured the *yazikus,* and with a much harder
heart—ordered police to shoot into the crowd. The police and the
revolutionary forces owed equal debts to Azef. And he loved his two
roles with equal passion, without seeing anything wrong in this: "Some
say I'm a blackguard, and behaved heinously, but wasn't it to help

others?" What duplicity! I said to myself. What perfect treachery! Incomparable! And this all took place in Russia! Not some other country! So there was a certain evil innate in V., and she hadn't hesitated to turn it on me.

I have to thank this double agent for helping me see how V. had fooled me, just as Evno Azef had fooled his comrades in the party; him for years, V. for days that felt like years to me. She acted as coldbloodedly as Azef, who, when he was unmasked, convinced his comrades to let him go, promising to return the next day with proof of his innocence! Just like V., with me. He never blushed when caught out, no, he was unflappable, completely poker-faced when he switched gears and, not missing a beat, hopped onto a story going in the opposite direction, contradicting himself without a blush. For example, when I asked if she hadn't suspected the true spin of Tiran's figure-skating operation (or the spin events would take) as soon as she'd read the ad, she said no, even though she had admitted earlier, quite cynically, that she figured a few extra services might be required, but it hadn't upset her too much.

And since I was angry and felt horrible today, really awful, I started to copy whole passages from the letters of the Marquis de Custine, on the medieval morality of the Russians, their essentially faithless nature. This, of course: "Russia is a very filthy country . . ." And another, beginning: "And when your son complains of France, follow my example; tell him: 'Go to Russia.' It is a very salutary trip: anyone who has seen this country will be happy to live anywhere else."

5

ISTANBUL

I don't want to get involved in anything sordid. Even though I've spent a few nights on cardboard boxes in airports and train stations. By the elevator shaft, too, in the Central Station in Prague. Before dawn, a freight elevator rose at least three times, loaded with sacks from the Central Bank of the Czech Republic. Soldiers in camouflage uniforms, combat boots, seated on the sacks. Two soldiers on each side, hands on the grooved grips of automatic rifles. Half asleep, I saw the boots passing before my eyes, the sacks containing several million crowns, and then dreamt of stealing some money, the dream of a petty dealer, a smuggler. All that day I figured how to get it, the haul, the pay for all of Bohemia. I could plan my attack with the band of Gypsies camped by me in the basement of the station, or else with my Russian friends. We would stay wide-eyed till morning, watching for the freight elevators (which didn't run at night), waiting for those doors to open. I had an appointment the next day, a buyer just visiting Prague, a Viennese ornithologist interested in my binoculars, the ones for night vision. I was dead tired at the end of the day. I needed all the sleep I could get, but was awakened when a soldier came in, and then another, covering him, both headed for the freight elevators, clearing a path to the shaft. And then the elevators arrived, their doors silently sliding open, the frigid air inside from someplace deep in the vaults of the Central Bank turning the atmosphere into billows of steam. These soldiers were ruthless killers, I would be gunned down right there, among the boxes. I'd have to pretend I was asleep, then spring up and spray them with nerve gas, my only weapon, the one I would be sure to procure before tomorrow morning. I was thinking this as I watched them walk away, down the platform, before going back to sleep. I woke up with a new plan to steal the money, but I had to rush off to meet my last customer, the Viennese ornithologist, and by the time I left his hotel I had money, enough to rent a suite in one of the most luxurious hotels in Prague, the Gustav II, not that I did, I just got two nights in a room with hot water, central heating, and a view of a beautiful bridge. I rested, relaxed enough to take a few strolls, but did not tour any museums. Only philatelic shops, which I was studying because I had tried to sell postage stamps once, rare stamps from the twenties, and my failure whetted my interest. Nothing sordid or sleazy, never.

Nor had I dreamt that V. had anything sordid about her; I had not imagined any such thing. Maybe I would agree to rescue her, and help her return to Russia, but not by working out some sleazy plan or scheme.

By writing to me, V. was trying to create a better image of herself. But she did not need to consult any models for her letters, she already knew several by heart: the ones from Viera to Pechorin in *A Hero of Our Times*, by Mikhail Lermontov, from Natasha Rostova in *War and Peace*, and, of course, from Tatiana Larina to Onegin, in Pushkin's *Eugene Onegin*. Only the fifth letter she sent struck a false chord. Blame it on Turgenev, Lermontov, even Pushkin.

V. would have done better to look at the letter Natasha Filipovna sent to Mishkin, the idiot prince. Behind that letter it's easy to read the real ruin of a lost soul. The inevitable end. What else could be expected from an ex-convict, a gambler? And friend of a prostitute, it's well documented: the real attraction Fyodor Mikhaylovich (Dostoyevsky) felt toward Marfa Brown, the prostitute with whom he corresponded, imagining Sonia Marmeladova, Nastasia Filipovna, and Grushenka.

Marfa, the "world wanderer," always held that "life is for enjoying strong emotions." She lived in England for four years until an "unforeseen event" forced her to seek refuge in Turkey. But she never got to Istanbul. As she says in a letter she sent Dostoyevsky from a hospital, on December 24, 1864: "I traveled through Austria and Prussia like a whirlwind, with a certain Hungarian as my companion; much later I traveled with an English adventurer for six months; I traveled through Switzerland, all of Italy, and all of Spain, and finally, the South of France, never knowing a moment's rest, traveling from morning till night, sometimes on foot, sometimes on horseback. In Marseille I separated from my Englishman and went to stay on Gibraltar, and from there to Burdeos, and then to Paris. In that city a person who was not an adventure-seeker, but a foolish glory-seeker—a Frenchman—took me to Belgium, in exchange for a certain payment, fetching me directly from a masked ball. From there we traveled to Holland. We were forced to leave the first country and deported from the second. After a house arrest by the military in Amsterdam, I went to live in England with no means of support, without knowing the language. I stayed in a police station for two days after a suicide attempt; then I spent two weeks under the bridges and aqueducts of the Thames, with the tramps of London . . ."

It was enough, more than enough, for a 500-page novel, in octavo. Marfa (what a beautiful name, women aren't called that anymore) and Fyodor (you don't see many men named Fyodor either). We don't know, the introduction to this letter says, the culmination of this friendship between Marfa and Fyodor because "his letters to Marfa were not preserved." What hypocrisy, my God! I certainly know how it culminated. How else could it culminate with Marfa healthy, out of the hospital? The first evidence, I'd say, is Prince Mishkin's affection for Nastasia Filipovna, as well as his sweet, redemptive looks; and Rodion Raskolnikov's plans to save Sonia Marmeladova; and Aloysha's agitated sermons to Grushenka. Presumably Dostoyevsky's second wife, Anna Grigorievna, purged the archives, removing the letters he wrote to a prostitute. And not a common prostitute, but a woman who could write such dazzling letters. Marfa was even better than Grushenka. She spoke perfect English, wrote elegant Russian, and apparently knew other languages, too. "Before Dostoyevsky"—I read in the introduction to the letters—"Marfa had fallen into the hands of Fleming, an elderly editor, from whom she passed to Gorski, the journalist who introduced her to the novelist." With a heavy toll on his conscience, Dostoyevsky made her a proposition, deviously suggesting that they do translations together, with a much less spiritual exchange in mind. The year 1864 was a hard one for Dostoyevsky: his first wife died, making it easier—the intro suggests—for the writer to approach the prostitute. Pure speculation, or rationalization. Why not admit Marfa was ravishingly beautiful, like V.? It must certainly have been the case.

Thank God I didn't have to convince V. that there was nothing bad about being a prostitute or considering herself one. Even a holy woman like Heloise (this testament to her sanctity: when she was laid in the crypt, Abelard, who had been dead eleven years, welcomed her with open arms) announced that she preferred—no beating around the bush—the word *whore*. As she says in one bloodcurdling letter: ". . . although the name wife may seem more holy and binding, another will always feel sweeter to me, that of lover, or even, may I say, concubine, or whore . . ."

Heloise writes a better letter than the pedantic Abelard. She knows that prostitution can be a holy calling. In that sense, V. was not as blessed as her friend Leilah, for one. Like when you're gossiping about a woman and you say, "She's no saint"—well neither was V. And a good thing, too, come to think of it. Leilah didn't see herself as some sort of Ancient Egyptian priestess with an inexhaustible power supply between her legs, and lines of men—Egyptian in this case—plugging in for energy.

(Men are "energy vampires"—V. explained, when we were talking about Castañeda—who will pursue a woman relentlessly for seven years, because the woman gives up energy during the act. Every time he starts to droop, the man will seek a new contact with the woman— with her uterus, V. insisted—to renew his vigor. She had heard her companions talk about this sometimes, getting out of bed at noon. Apparently she had spent many afternoons meditating on this, staring up at the ceiling, the cracks in the roof, the chips in the plaster.)

V. was not truly called to her vocation, though she didn't know it at the time. And as for mystical qualities, they weren't obvious in the Turks or Romanians I noticed either, bored-looking women leaning against walls or in doorways, wearily shifting their weight from foot to foot. It would be impossible to find any proof or even evidence supporting this Babylonian or Egyptian thesis of holy prostitution on their aging thighs, completely covered—if you looked at them close-up, through a magnifying glass—with men's fingerprints. Leilah didn't believe in it either, and I'm sure she didn't want to talk about it, and yet she didn't lack holiness (nor did Natalia, or Marina).

I needed some argument to sanctify my rescue plan, something to make a convert of Stockis; to give him a nice immaculate conception of the girl. Retouching the image, which is always possible however murky or damaged the negative. And as van Gogh says in a letter to his brother Theo, it's something the Old Masters did. The delicious anecdote I found in one of his letters confirmed it: "Delacroix took his customary two steps backward, squinting: It's perfectly true, he said.

Take this, for instance (and he pointed at a dirty gray flagstone). With this drab color Paolo Veronese could paint a nude, and she would look fair and blonde in his picture."

V. was no saint, almost the opposite: her conduct was as low and filthy as a flagstone, but from that base I had to build up a portrait of a saint to give to Stockis, an ivory beauty held by swarthy Turks, a captive needing a rescue.

I could glimpse this benediction, but did not know how to say it, so I would just have to improvise. There's a saying: "Every prostitute is also a saint." . . . A little too strong, but it had a nice ring. That was more or less what I told Stockis, to see if he would swallow it. Ha!

6

ISTANBUL

I followed Stockis down the ramp of the *Vaȝa* and we walked along the dock, past the yachts anchored there. Stockis looked imperturbable, holding his briefcase like a man who owned a secret business in Göteborg (import-export of insects), the plates of his armor rippling, well-oiled, overlapping without a chink, not the slightest opening for my plea for aid. He had invited me to the baths (Turkish), and I could have simply followed him, popping up at his right (or left) side now and then, never catching up to walk beside him; instead I hurried along, telling him my plan to rescue V., glancing up at him occasionally, plucking at his elbow to catch his eye, either the milky iris of his left (or right) eye. It flowed out smoothly, deep and mellow, like a bassoon solo, with phenomenal phrasing and fingering, note after brilliant note. We caught a taxi when we left the docks, and he spent a good part of our trip clutching a cell phone, his chubby fingers on the minuscule buttons, miraculously reaching his number—his fleshy fingertips looked like they were flattening three buttons at a time, but he pressed the series of numbers into the tiny keypad, and confidently put the receiver to his ear, sure he'd got the right person. He sang (or seemed to sing) several melodies in Swedish and then listened briefly to a weather report for the North Sea, learning that some platform had been ripped loose by the maelstrom. He responded to that news, his lips swimming close to the holes over the microphone, closing an

antediluvian eye and winking, as if he was talking about me. I even
thought I heard him say my name, and he might have been complaining about my poor work, coming to Istanbul without a *yaʒikus*. I would
have preferred to float the subject of abduction somewhere other than
the baths.

Stockis had not returned to the *Vaʒa* the night before. I had planned
on talking to him then, but he slept someplace else. He didn't say
where. When he got back to the yacht at ten in the morning, he didn't
just talk about going to the bathhouse, he did it. The blows the mas-
seur was giving to the Swede's big damp shoulders were hurting my
ears. I had to make a huge effort to hold his shifting mass and pin it
down long enough to pour out my rescue plan.

"Constantinople," I said to him when we were both up to our waists
in warm water, "remains captive." Under the skylights a primitive
picture emerged, a Russian *lubok* unfolded in the air, dozens of tiny
figures, everyone involved in the plot, in various scenes: in the distance a Russian village, V. at home, the newspaper ad, "Girls who can
dance—Come to Istanbul," her village soft and hazy, drawn by an
Impressionist, in contrast to the stony bulk of the Hagia Sophia; the
top floor of the Saray, the Armenian in his office, holding her letter—
his eyes immobile behind an iron mask—touching it to his forehead
before locking it away with all the others; V. boarding the train in
Russia; the Saray sign, sketched by an artist, in delicate strokes; V.
standing under it, when she first arrived, looking up at the other girls,
all the Russians leaning out of the second-story windows: they may
be ice-skaters, but those necklines sure are low, she can't help noticing. And finally, Czar Nicholas II on his throne in St. Petersburg—
you can see the Cross of Saint George on the collar of his military
jacket—pointing at Constantinople, the final objective of the Russian
troops in the 1914 war. The Russians plan to storm the Dardanelles,

to recover Constantinople for Christianity. Which is the reason, I told Stockis, that the provisional government decided to continue the struggle in 1917, after the czar was overthrown. Giving my plan a strong historical precedent. But first the Turk in my panorama must be defeated, his heart pierced, a pin stuck in him. Then the happy ending—I showed it to Stockis—V. and I (her savior), behind the battlements of a Christian tower, safe at last, our cross-covered banners snapping in the breeze . . . No mention of the terrible end met by Nicholas II himself. On November 5, 1917, while in captivity, he sent a letter that really struck me, especially this (premonitory) passage: "There are innumerable processions for the holidays in March and April, bands marching in the streets playing the Marseillaise, and very often the sound of Chopin's Funeral March. This insufferable Funeral March haunts us long afterward; we whistle it hardly thinking and hum it until our heads ache."

Stockis snorted and submerged, sliding underwater like some prehistoric beast that had surfaced momentarily to snatch its victim from among the denizens of a seaside shantytown. The water closed over his broad back, and for a while I sat there amazed, staring at the calm surface that gave no hint of the body below.

He came up and started to say something. "Oh!" I broke in, I'd remembered a vital detail, so I unrolled the canvas again and pointed at the Armenian—in this panel he was bringing a small red notebook to his lips, licking them with pleasure, perfidiously. "He steals their passports! She can't leave: it will take months, even years, to scrape up enough money to buy her passport, plus her passage."

That was the actual reason, an actual fact. When V. told me that, I believed her: a concrete detail! not something she could make up. Tiran had bought her some of those skimpy dresses, those saris, for example. And he had paid her fare from Russia; she owed him several thousand

Turkish liras, a debt that never got smaller—just the reverse. To the initial costs that had welcomed her to Istanbul were added others, day by day, room and board, bribes to the police. The night we got back late, for example, after our walk through the Grand Bazaar, she lost some customers, a Turkish group, who wanted her, plus Nastasha and Leilah, for a yacht trip to Prinpiko Island.

Stockis leaned toward the painting, in search of himself—and found that he was depicted as a Flemish merchant, a generous man providing a young lover (an understandable mistake) the money he needed for the rescue. He was dressed in a slashed doublet and cloth beret, his muscular calves encased in green stockings. He was satisfied. He motioned to the bath boy to throw a sheet over his shoulders and advanced across the sun-splotched floor, treading like an emperor (Justinian, who built the Hagia Sophia, or Suleiman the Magnificent) holding court in the Termes, hearing a magician's tale of the pearl beaches of Ophir.

Or like a naturalist, Linnaeus (also a Swede), seeing through the variety and apparent dissimilarity the number and position of the flower's stamens, to arrive at a taxonomic classification, just as Stockis did with the superficial confusion of my explanation, my muddled rescue plan, everything I'd told him, simplifying it as quickly as he had disposed of the worthless specimens I had caught in the Caspian Basin, the night I first came onboard. *"Papillon de nuit,"* he murmured from the shadow by a patch of light on the checkerboard floor. Seized with taxonomic zeal, he interrupted my story to introduce this term. Too abstract, he meant, it won't work, this talk about a woman trapped in Istanbul; let's speak of a night butterfly, or, more precisely, a prostitute.

(I had chased nocturnal butterflies. The white splotch of a sheet spread out, shining like an urgent summons, an inexplicable source of light attracting butterflies from the depths of the steppe, from its inhospitable darkness, with the hope of living a bit longer, of adding to the few days of their ephemeral existence. Flying over the arid field, the clay beds, echoing the hills undulating below, they turned toward the white square shining like the sun, growing like an open door in the wall of the night, as if waiting on the other side were flowers dripping nectar, the breeze of a new day, empty and meaningless, but a new day. They must pass through this rectangle of light, this Sublime Door. Myriad butterflies, flying from the four points of the compass, drawn great distances toward the tiny breach of light, which grew larger with each wing beat. I stayed under the stretched sheet, like a new author hiding behind the scenes, watching in amazement as the first play he staged met an unexpected success, hundreds of butterflies approaching to bump their antennae against the rough fabric, strangely, suddenly, transformed into the thin ethereal air of an imagined morning, the butterflies blindly testing its surface, bravely beating their fragile wings against it, when it would take steel blades to tear a hole in it, to slice it open, my eyes huge with amazement, watching them escape back into the darkness.)

"Abduct her?" he asked like a patron raising objections, correcting a passage in the libretto an author is reading to him. And adding, on a whim, another scene, set at a racetrack. He explained it while dressing: he would lend me some money, an advance on payment for the butterflies I would capture for him in Livadia—not the full fee, just a small part, but I had to put it on a horse, make a bet at the track. If I won, the purse was mine (for V.); if I lost, he picked up the tab. Here's how I figured it: I'd never see him again. I wasn't going to spend my time in Livadia chasing butterflies (especially not *yazikus*) and I wasn't going to pay back his money.

7

ISTANBUL

Stockis's vulgarity generated more vulgarity, in ever-widening waves—and sordidness as well. The way he gave me the money was just one more example of his bad taste, but it all had been in hopelessly bad taste right from the start: the meeting in the strip club, when we could have had an interview in the Divan, in the hotel restaurant, with a pianist, maybe a Russian, playing "Autumn Leaves" with an anguished air. I would not forgive him for making me bet on the races, nor for christening V. with that name, *papillon de nuit*, so tacky, but also tempting, I must confess, since it was short and suggestive.

We went up into the stands to get a place. I had been *chernieye tuchi* (a black cloud) according to V., when we picked her up at the corner where Stockis—somehow—knew she was waiting. We had stopped outside a café, and I had seen her move toward its glass door, come out to the street, and walk over to meet us, placing one foot directly in front of the other and swinging her hips provocatively. How could I save this woman? I asked myself. I was the one who needed saving. Pretty suspicious, the dress I'd helped her pick out—a lot like Leilah's, I see now, minus the black satin piping—blatantly red, no doubt about that.

Her dress bothered me—that and the fact that I had never been to a racetrack. I much preferred investing in merchandise, in glasses or laser range finders for airborne artillery. (The "Varo," the American model, cost six grand, so I was sure of a nice profit.) That way, I thought, I could be both horse and rider. And wagerer, too—right?—when I was sitting home in St. Petersburg and said to myself: "I'll go out and take a chance on the market for stolen goods." "Stolen goods" overstates the case, it was hardly assault or armed robbery, just chaos and the spontaneous privatization of state or army property. I had taken a long time over the laser range finder, aiming its ray at the blue cupola of a church, over the roofs of the houses, and then telling the seller: "It doesn't work," when it really did, perfectly, the distance in meters registered clearly and accurately in the sight. I just wanted to let him know I wasn't going to take his first price, he was dealing with a pro. I also asked for the technical manual and looked it over carefully, standing in the snow, barely feeling the cold. "Do you know these batteries are hard to get? How's my customer supposed to buy them?" "Your customer? Where? Who's going to get them?" he asked curiously, because a lot of these soldiers took equipment from their barracks without any idea as to what it was for or how much it was worth. It was a mystery to them why some people (foreigners, obviously, they're all idiots) would want to buy this stuff: military equipment, night-vision goggles, laser range finders, gyroscopic binoculars, and even, if you didn't mind risking your life, earth-air missile launchers, fifty thousand bucks apiece. The information was all he wanted. We each had our place in the market. He would never board an airplane, never bribe a customs agent to pass a briefcase holding fifteen automatic rifle scopes. I was going to buy his laser range finder, but after testing its cold-resistance. I came back an hour later, picked it up, and tried it again, focusing on the same blue cupola and speaking up my sleeve: "I bet I can sell this for ten times his price, whatever he asks." And that's a fact. That's a safe bet: you don't have to know a thing about the jockey and how he spent last night, about oats or enriched horse

feed. But now, without a bit of knowledge or confidence, I had to bet
on the bay. How? Why?

I decided to watch a few races before placing my bet. Stockis wasn't
afraid to cool his heels in the stands, his hair still damp from the baths.
He watched the track, relaxed. He got up two or three times, not worried about the money he was going to bet for me, running a comb
through his wet hair.

I would have liked more time to prepare for this race. Like that London tout, a man with incredible knowledge of technique, who had come
up with an infallible method of winning at the track. I don't remember
if the jockey was in on the scam. His binoculars (this detail got my attention) had been fitted with a powerful transmitter, which he would
point at the front-runner as it rounded the turn—straight in its eye, which
looked distant to the naked eye, but close through the binoculars—before pressing a button that activated a signal, a high-pitched whistle that
incapacitated the horse, so that its legs gave out, suddenly going weak,
as if it had heard a train whistle, as if an archangel floating above it on a
fluffy cloud, propped up in an easy ride, had blown a thin copper trum-
pet and *psssst!,* that horse was out of the race, its legs, which had been
beating steady time, *in crescendo,* got tied in knots mid-stride, taking this
whistle as a command (obviously ill-timed) to slow to an amble, a complicated step: moving its two right feet, and then its two left feet, in
unison, the gait used in parades. And lost the race.

There was nothing I could do without the necessary technical cov-
erage—for betting savvy, I could look only to V., who was excited,
and Stockis, whose head was circling gently, eyes glued to the track.
The Englishman—that man I read about in some newspaper article, I
don't remember where, in what country—made a fortune on the Derby
before he finally got caught, either turned in by some eagle-eyed neighbor in the stands or a routine investigation by the betting office, who

banned him from the sport. I couldn't remember the details. Technical stuff, like the ultrasonic whistle, I wasn't too sure about that, or I would have told V. the story, while we watched the race. Anyway, the man ought to try his luck at other tracks, he could get on the circuit: a month in Paris, then back to England, or someplace else, some city like Istanbul.

V. and Stockis decided to go down to the stables. I stayed in the stands with no desire to see the horses close-up. It wouldn't do me any good. It took me a while to find the two of them with my binoculars: having a lively discussion, like they were really hitting it off, how strange! Very strange! I aimed at Stockis's ear and pressed an invisible button to start my imaginary transmitter and send him the signal: "*You*, give me the money, no hassles!" But Stockis, who was at the gate of the training ground, didn't even put his hand to his ear. Above, in a glassed-in box, some rich Turks—they probably already had mansions on the Gulf of Nicomedia—were filling out race cards between forkfuls, with perfect confidence, the kind of security that comes from good information whispered softly in your ear, no shrill urgency, no sharp notes, no headaches, oh no, marking sure things, triples and doubles. Naming the first three horses, I mean, betting a hundred to one, on the money. It could be a business, that's for sure, but I didn't have time to get into it, to learn it the way that I had mastered customs stations, which ones were weakest, and at those stations, the weakest agents, and their shifts, figuring it all out in advance, when to make my move. I was horse and jockey. Just one person. And not one about to waste time on the races. When they got back, I asked V.: "What was it like down there? Did you see the horses?" and told Stockis, "This is it . . .

"This is it, bet on this gate. Any horse . . . This one . . ." The horse I had spotted, number five, finger running down the list.

V. burst out:

"I saw it! I saw it! It's a good horse!" (I felt like shouting, "What do you know about horses?," *begging* her to shut up. Felt like it but didn't.) We went down to place our bets before the window closed. V. stopped trying to stir me up, but maybe she really had seen something in the horse: *That day, V., when you told me it was good, were you just talking or did you know? Grigory Rasputin, born in Siberia like you, was a horse thief, did you have dealings with horses as a child?* No, better not, she had already forgotten the name of the horse. Mine.

"All the money, Stockis, on this horse." And I heard a voice, an angel with expert binoculars trained on me from up in the heavens, speaking to me, in my own voice: "Bet on it to place." I grabbed Stockis's sleeve and passed on the message: "To place, Stockis," and added: "Just half."

This message, that final "half," came from my deepest darkest days of poverty. I couldn't bet all of it, not even on second place! my other last-minute inspiration. I shouldn't bet at all! Stockis! I started to reach for his arm, but let it go: I would only lose half the advance. But I'd been put off racing forever.

V. was pacing around by the window, really excited. Don't forget: "We're playing with her future," which is none too rosy. When Stockis went out for a soda I told her about the ridiculous deal I had made with the Swede—and she might well worry, since it all depended on her luck, whether she'd be leaving Istanbul with me. But it was the thrill of the race and the betting, too. Which left Stockis unmoved. While V. screamed and jumped up and down. The race, a mile and a half, went by in the blink of two eyes. Mine, since I closed them when I heard the gun, amplified by the loudspeakers, and followed the race at a distance, as if it was coming to me over the radio, in the nervous calm and expectant hush of a hotel room, through V.'s screams and tugs at my arm. *Davai! Davai!* (Go! Go!), V. yelled, directing her shouts at the ear of our horse, number five. Without cracking my eyes, I pictured the race, a few opening shots, close-ups, horses' hooves striking the clay, clods flying, caking the camera lens, the jockey's whip beating a rhythm on the flanks of my horse, or somebody's—go, go! . . . Did it go? I opened my eyes, got to my feet, focused on the pack, calm as could be, no interest at all in the lead horse. Not the leader of the pack! Who cares? The second, the second one! Unflappable. Just like preparing for a customs inspection, disconnecting my nerve endings one by one, with studied calm.

An eternity later, V. was still knocking at my door (my *Doors of Perception*, a book I once read). It was like when you have a friend who's high up a hill, waving her arms and shouting for your attention, making hand signals to tell you something happened. She came down to me, leaned over and put her arms around me: "We won! We won!"

How much exactly? I began to calculate, but the answer came to me in a flash—I didn't have to do the multiplication—the number in a flickery green, like the read out on a laser range finder. V. arrived at the same figure, I recall, and then Stockis quickly got it, too. I wasn't particularly happy; not like I felt after the risky first leg of a trip, the night my first customer, a Mr. Erikson, phoned in his confirmation, yes, he wanted some goggles: I should come to his office the next day. A miracle! I was speechless that night, staring at a white sky lit by the aurora borealis above a dark border of forest. It was below zero, at least fifteen degrees, and I took deep breaths of this cold air. I couldn't believe it. That horse had come in second: some horse has to come in second. But nothing had forced Erikson, my customer, to buy those goggles and at that price.

I had won unexpectedly, putting my money on a horse named Smuggler. That's how I chose it, I liked the name. I actually forgot about V. walking alongside me, she was completely out of sight for long stretches, receding like some woman I had happened to meet in Istanbul and known for a few days, so she might cross my mind occasionally. I was surprised to see her whenever she drew into sight, and I would make a superhuman effort, trying hard to concentrate on her, on the back that was glowing brighter in the darkness, seeking out her hand, struggling to hold on, and still it would slip away, and I would pass clear through this moment of solidity, of walking down an Istanbul street—with this woman!—to a beautiful memory, a leather album with gilt edges, worth a fortune, that I had leafed through in Vladimir Vladimirovich's shop; and all the other books I had leafed through, feeling glad they existed, standing by the rack, because I hadn't wanted to travel, visit museums, see new cities. I'd just like to go somewhere I could assemble a little library, or even better, where there was a library I could visit each afternoon, after spending the morning practicing my writing (letters, perhaps). I explained this to V.: *It's the life,* I said, *I've always wanted to lead.* For a year or two. Then I would see. At that V. collapsed, legs suddenly doubling under her red dress, slack as if the tendons had been slashed, like a wounded gazelle crumpling to the ground, feet swiftly folding. She sat on the curb, legs out, motionless, torso tilted back, shrouded in that dress. That swoon was also the delicate snare she had woven for me, so that I too would fall, as softly as the blouse of a woman undressing at the sink in a (Turkish) bath. I held out my arms, perplexed. It was so logical, so obvious—there was a lot of money, why should I share it? To invest in arranging her flight? I wasn't thinking of that. I stood staring at the part that divided her hair, the thin line of her white cranium, so far from me. I had no doubt I was behaving correctly, but still went over my reasoning, checking for errors, muttering in Spanish. I reverted to Spanish for personal use and now added a fierce oath, one I used only in a strange land, in the dead of winter, shouting it as if to wake myself from a dream, or to restore my harmony, like a musician pulling a pitch pipe from his pocket in the middle of a performance, quickly breathing a *la*, retuning his strings, then strumming confidently, his song set long before this trip to Istanbul, the walk in the Grand Bazaar, this horse race. I did not have to "play tough," to force myself to deny her entry. It was simple. She should be grateful I'd let her get this close to my stroke of luck, just seeing the cashier count out the money, push it to me through the window. Stockis, who had more experience, wider experience, supervised the transfer. V. said, "Stockis is good," without any rancor, but I knew she should thank the money, not the man. Money in the world is like water vapor in the atmosphere; it falls on one person or another, on cold surfaces, silver salts. All you have to do is imagine yourself as a favorable particle, and let your body temperature drop. Do you understand? I shouted back at her, speaking to the white line on her scalp. I showed her how artificial rain worked, and my second point soon formed around it—once we are saturated, charged, we must precipitate . . . run. Each body, each crystal has a specific dew point. I had to hang around a while, to float in space until I reached it, and then I would fall upon—and fertilize—a life with no obligations, no daily trips to work. I won't pretend I won the jackpot; there wasn't all that much money. Just enough so I wouldn't have to work for a few years. God was my witness, I had tried hard enough. Getting it on a bet, that didn't change anything. It took essentially the same effort on my part—why should I share the fruit of my labor with some stranger?

I had frozen. My negative derived from the same physical process, the same icy solution I had used in my explanation. I looked at both sides of the street. What was I doing here in Istanbul so late at night, ten o'clock? V. had fallen a few meters from a streetcar stop. The tracks, shining between the cobblestones, disappeared around a curve.

SIXTH LETTER

I

ISTANBUL

I crossed the bay to see the captain of a Russian merchant ship docked on the far shore. I had been eyeing the prow sticking out from this stretch of the pier since the day before. Russian customs would be a snap, I was thinking. A woman without a passport? No big deal. At a price, of course; I'd have to slip the agents some money. In a Russian ship, I realized, it would be a cinch.

I had already decided to abandon my illegal trafficking across borders, back when I was talking with the *chelnok* and saw myself through his eyes, still a smuggler, no matter how successful and well-dressed. I was fed up with the black market without knowing it; at bottom, that was why I had taken the job with Stockis. I had enjoyed it for years—crossing borders, taking advantage of the diffusion of value between one cell (nation) and another. And after a few days' idleness, taking off charged with oxygen, maximum payoff with a minimal toll on my nerves. When Stockis approached me in that plaza in Stockholm, I was making good money, but my bags were starting to feel too full. If I wanted to do better, to expand—as I had tried to explain to that *chelnok* in the Grand Bazaar in Istanbul, without any success—I could increase either the volume of my merchandise (which meant container shipping—and a longer jail term) or else its density, the specific gravity of the smuggled goods. Traveling with suitcases that are nearly empty but fabulously dense, with a few grams of stellar matter that are like a ton of gold. That was why I was drawn to the Swede's proposal. A butterfly weighing far less than a gram could bring more than ten thousand petrodollars from a Cretan oil sheikh, a collector. But not just any butterfly. I had to capture the right specimen, the *yaʒikus,* the imperial butterfly.

Turning away from huge volume and density, I went to the other extreme, as if traveling through a dark woods to reach a clearing, moving beyond butterflies with their meager but still measurable weight to arrive at the imponderable lightness of a soul, V.'s. Bringing out an illegal soul was the ultimate challenge, the coup de grâce to my years of heavy smuggling. It would be the finishing touch, the high point of my career, to transport a soul—so what if it happened to be enclosed in a corporeal envelope, "captive in a body." From my cabin in the *Vaʒa* I stared at the writing on the Russian merchant ship, until I was able to make out its name: *Mikhail Svetlov.*

In fact, I just came across an ideal explanation of this challenge. Karen Blixen summed up my feelings exactly in one of her letters; I can always reread that sentence to understand my actions, should I want to remember the real motive for my rescue. Karen Blixen said: "Regarding lions . . . I can only say that I do not believe that any normal person can live in lion country without trying to shoot them."

Just so: I would try to take V. with me.

And the dangers that must be faced: Blixen described them in the same letter, written December 3, 1914, changing the point of view to see herself (as I now saw myself) as a young lion: "Perhaps it is wrong from the moral point of view, but seen in relation to the lion itself I must say that if someone should come and shoot me in the full vigor of youth, so that I died in five minutes, without having any suspicion of it in advance, I would be *sincerely* grateful to them . . . (*Letters from Africa,* Karen Blixen).

I get her point: obviously I must be prepared, ready to fight, to engage in combat. Ready, but not very happy about what might occur. In these situations, I'm carried along the inevitable route: a hollow in the pit of my stomach and suddenly, inexplicably (and by the standards of ordinary life, it is totally incomprehensible), I find myself kicking furiously, or being kicked, drenched in sweat, forced to pull a knife. Once I was bound, and had to break the telephone cord around my wrists and ankles, and stand up still dizzy from a beating, rising and moving in a fog, to jump out the window. Into the vortex, thrown right into the vortex. I had looked at Tiran's hairy forearms on more than one occasion, sizing them up from the primitive perspective of brawling with him and breaking them. And this sort of thinking just confirmed the abnormality of these trips. Here in Livadia, for example, when the waiter in the Greek restaurant (Diodo, another muscleman) sets a glass of beer on the table where I'm sitting and reading (today it's *Eight or Nine Wise Words about Letter-Writing*, by Lewis Carroll), as his forearm enters my field of vision, I have never once taken a surreptitious look and said to myself, "Watch out for those arms!" I never saw them attacking me, strangling me; never pictured myself slashing through the thickest muscle, loosening his deadly embrace. In Turkey, yes, and Vienna, too, and even in Luxembourg, where I once found myself.

I thought of several ways to escape. We could drive to one of the beaches in east Istanbul, get a room in a hotel, and wait for Stockis to dock nearby, among the midsized yachts. Then we could gather up our belongings, turning out the lights in the room, virtuously leaving the manager a note, as well as the keys to the rental car and the address of the agency that owned it. We could run down the dock, jump aboard the *Vaƶa* . . . But a successful escape had to end with our leaping out onto a Russian beach, in Russian territory, a risk that Stockis was not prepared to take. After all, they could pepper him with machine-gun fire off the Russian shore or subject him to a fine-tooth customs inspection that would turn up the tiny fauna, a pair of insects from each species, and clearly not en route to Mount Ararat.

On the other hand, if we tried to get past customs at the Istanbul airport by bribing the guards, we could end up bouncing right back to the Saray with a stop in between at some dimly lit police station underneath a forty-watt bulb, swinging indifferently. Which left the *Mikhail Svetlov,* the Russian merchant ship.

2

ISTANBUL

I boarded one of the motorboats tied up near the yachts and went across to the Russian merchant ship on the opposite shore. Mooring ropes, thick as a man's arm, seemed to hang slack over its sides, growing larger as I approached. Looking at those ropes, I thought with apprehension about climbing them and scrambling aboard, like in some children's pirate story. There had to be some easier way to scale those imposing iron walls, rising from the sea as if cemented to the harbor floor, white water stains on the prow. This immobility was an illusion: two nights from now, three at the most, those ropes would be yanked up and the ship would lift anchor, chain clanking, and start moving, setting sail with me and V. hidden in its hold.

The captain was not on board. *Kapitana niet na bortú,* a gruff shout, the second in command or the official watchman. I had called to the cabin boy standing guard above, by the gangway, that I wanted to come up and talk to the captain. He pretended not to hear me, staring at the space where I was standing at the bottom of the gangway, with my hand on the rope. As if he did not notice me, just another inanimate object within his visual field. Then I heard a man without seeing him, a voice yelling over the cabin boy's shoulder: *Kapitana niet na bortú.* It could be the captain himself, I thought, he could have been on the bridge of his ship and seen me leave the *Vaza,* watching me through high-powered marine binoculars, and known my motorboat was heading toward the gangway of his ship, using the trail of gray foam in the wake of the launch to calculate its trajectory across the bay. Maybe the cabin boy had managed to exchange a few words with his superior before I shouted up my question and he assumed his vacant expression, that look focused on the far distance. They must have been surprised by the way I addressed them, in Russian. But I could be a sales agent, a new supplier (ship chandlers also used motorboats; plenty of them went around the harbor selling sausage or salt pork). The gangway had been painted white, but why had they decided to paint the handrail too? It was made of new rope, and its fibers, stiff with paint, stuck to my hand. The gangway rose above me, one section running to a support halfway up the ship, and the second going upward from there. I felt like yelling: "I have to talk to him about contraband," but it was too far to yell, and the only answer would be another yell, the same gruff voice: *"nikakij kontrabandov my nie ʒnaem y ʒnat nie jotim"* (We're not interested). Seeing that I wasn't leaving, his superior must have whispered something in the ear of the boy, who repeated it to me. But shakily, shyly, with no practice shouting orders from one end of the ship to the other, unlike the other man, who had a trained throat, so that he could project several leagues without even straining. At first the cabin boy talked far too loud, as if I was twice as far away as I was. But when he saw how easily I caught his words, he adjusted his volume: the captain was at a party, the mayor's office had invited the captains of all the ships docked in Istanbul. I could tell from the tone of voice he was surprised I didn't already know about it, a ship chandler ought to know about tonight's banquet. (But of course I wasn't a chandler and I didn't know.) It was almost seven at night. The ship's captain would have been back in his cabin by now if it hadn't been for this invitation from the mayor. On a day like this, fairly cool, he might have picked up a few things at the Grand Bazaar, taken a little stroll, eyes half-closed in the sun, gone into the Mariners' Club, enjoyed an ice on the terrace. And since he must have visited the old city, the murals, Topkapi Palace, many times, he would have returned to his cabin to resume his reading of Chadaev's *Philosophical Letters*. Nothing could alter the rhythm of a life that may have been confined (you could say) to cabin or officers' mess, but was no less normal than that of any fifty-year-old with graying though abundant hair, in a white shirt ironed by Niura, waitress in the officers' mess, and his secret lover. The banquet was just starting. I could bid adieu to the boy in the motorboat and catch a cab to the *ratusha*, city hall, or whatever it was called in Turkish. (It was *ratusha* somewhere in Europe, I don't recall where.) I could pass for the first mate of a merchant ship from my country. But to get dressed for the event, to present myself at the door of the mayor's office, I would have to return to the *Vaza*—that is, not dismiss the boy in the motorboat until he had taken me back across the bay. I had a sports jacket in my pack to change into so I could show up for an appointment dressing the part, like I did my first night in Istanbul, at the Saray, dressed as a businessman—a young businessman, because it was not a full three-piece suit, just a linen jacket that I wore without a tie, changing my sandals for a pair of flexible shoes, a casual style that went with the jacket. Tonight I'd dress up and get into the *ratusha*, where I'd go up to an unmistakably Slavic-looking man who would be tormenting his companions with English even worse than mine, unintelligible. I would address him in Russian, speak Russian to him, but the man, the captain of the *Mikhail Svetlov*, would insist on his English, the universal language, after all, it was an international party with captains from all over the world, sailing under many different flags. I would launch into my story (about the size of Tiran, the pimp, the guardian of the Saray) and then hear a fork tapped against a glass: "Ek-ius-me, van móment," the captain would say, automatically, unconsciously, and unjustifiably relapsing into docking-maneuver English, interrupting our talk to hear the no more reliable or intelligible English of His Honor the Mayor, Mustafá Afendí (let's say). Under those circumstances, we would never manage to discuss a matter as delicate as the one that had brought me to the *Mikhail Svetlov*.

Better head for the Saray first, come back here later and try again.

...

And this is what I saw when I arrived at the Saray. I saw V. with her arm around a young man who had his arm around her, too, the fingers of his left hand peeking out at her waist, under her elbow. Like an old couple who have reached a certain level of familiarity, a stable binomial relationship, and aren't afraid that a third element, a conversation, some mixing, would affect their union, loosen their bond, weaken the strength of their embrace. V. was leaning on the young man a little bit, comfortably, relying on him, her head resting on his shoulder, not listening to the conversation he was having with Tiran, either she couldn't hear or wasn't interested. V. seemed so happy, she was definitely not looking around, to the side, searching for something, an escape route, some rescue, no, even her eyes were laughing, and her legs, lively, just waiting for an order to start moving, pulling her hair to one side, bent so far that for a split second she was suspended at a right angle from his temple, tangentially attached to his shoulder, as delighted as Catherine Deneuve in *Belle de Jour* when this Japanese man, hugely corpulent, shows her a little lacquered box with a bee or a wasp, some insect, buzzing inside, and she's amused, another embrace, wraps her arms around him, but they don't reach, he's a sumo wrestler, her hands stick out at his waist. Now it's all clear! It's perfectly clear to me now, it's useless, I see I've been wasting my money on a woman who offered so little security, her reserves seeming to vanish right before my eyes, like the currency of some weak country, flimsy paper money—there's no way a man would convert his savings into this stuff with no watermark, no magnetic bands, no minuscule printing on the frock coat of some notable figure, nothing that would let a man rest easy, avoid the nightmare of the cashier saying, wait a minute, and calling the manager over to the register to check out the phony bills. I could not, I told myself, invest in such a risky business. Her thighs—I was thinking about them—her eyebrows, her neck, the soft hair at the nape, could all be purchased time-share, if you wanted to put it that way, for a considerably smaller sum, a negligible amount, and charged to Stockis as an incidental expense, like cab fares and breakfasts. The air wasn't knocked out of me, but I felt lighter: the net V. had woven around me was still shaped to a certain form (mine), encasing it, sealing my volume, but now I could ditch this ballast (V.) , and take off. I decided to go to the *ratusha*, not back to the *Vaʒa*, and check out the effects of this new look at V., a happy V., in love with some Turk. A good-looking one, that's for sure— probably (I decided after studying him a minute) just what V. had pictured in her room in Russia, writing her reply to the agency that wanted ice-skaters—with measurements: 90-60-90—when the shadow of anticipation moved from the dark corners of her house, falling across her page in the halo of lamplight on the table. So that she looked up expectantly and bit her lip, since she had seen many Indian melodramas with dark-skinned heros, and molded the shadow to form a young man with bronze skin, an elegant build, thick eyebrows, an aquiline nose. A gold cap glinted behind his lower lip when he smiled scornfully, feeling nothing but contempt for those men—he was telling the Armenian—who could fall in love with prostitutes, feel any pity for them, see them as women, in disgrace! Ha! he laughed, and he glanced over at me, a customer standing by the door, deciding whether to come in. He didn't recognize me, naturally. But it's easy to dismiss a dupe like me. He could brush me aside with a single blow, if need be, or scare me off with a switchblade, flicked out on the wharf. V. looked over, too, but claimed the next day she hadn't seen me. A lie! It had to be a lie! Although it is true that she can't see very well and squints to focus better. A habit that will eventually give her crow's feet, I had lectured. Stupid! I thought of going to the *ratusha* to end the evening at the multilingual party. By this time they would have abandoned all pretense of speaking English and would be mercilessly flogging their own tongues, completely indifferent to the blank looks on their neighbors' faces, just happy to be drinking the free Vat 69 and watching out for their second mates, who would be escorting them back to their ships, assisting all the swaying captains up the swaying gangways. I would meet the captain of the *Mikhail Svetlov*, telling him, *Gospodin* Captain, I practically rescued a *bliad*, a *súka*, a whore. He would die laughing! My God! We would get drunk, we would get drunk together, lucky that Turkey was a lay state. The two of us would try to remember the name of the founder of the Turkish republic, I would talk all night, diluting my misery with cheap Turkish wine, pouring more and more down my throat, one part pain per two parts *kagort*, one to five, one to twenty, practically gone, with so much wine, my tongue really loosened, talking, laughing. I would go to the *ratusha* (or whatever it's called in Turkish). "I'm off to the *ratusha*," I said in a loud voice in my native Spanish, and then the disc jockey gave me a nice exit (pretty smart, I thought, even though we never met or talked about his music, which was syncopated, with a complicated base line, interesting to follow), putting on another of that year's hits, so that I straightened up when I heard the beat and walked out of the Saray swinging, smooth. Not dragging my arms like an awkward albatross on a deck (what a bender!), no flailing and flopping, no, swinging along the street, confident that if I didn't end up at the *ratusha,* with its old-sters and old-time Turkish and Greek tunes, I would simply go somewhere else, where they would be playing (a Swedish song, too, what a coincidence) *"Roll down the rubber, man."* Ad hoc, a perfect anthem for the occasion. Some other place with whores, without V., whores in the abstract, the same white breasts, the same smooth bellies. It was cool outside. At the corner I saw the streetcar tracks, their steel polished from so many wheels, and they said to me: "We warned you, we warned you yesterday!"

3

ISTANBUL

I was startled to see a lapdog heading my way, straight toward me. What is she doing with that dog? I wondered, but what I had taken for a leash stretched tight by a yippy, high-strung little dog that would ruin our escape, giving us away with its barking, turned out to be the leather strap on the heavy suitcase V. was pushing ahead of her with her foot, hanging onto it with her right hand, steering it between the tables.

We had agreed to meet on the terrace of the Chinese restaurant, far from the Saray. When she made it over to my table, the song on the radio stopped, suddenly switching to a Turkish or Arabic one.

"How annoying!" she muttered. "That's a good song." And went on:

"Vanessa Paradis. Don't you think I look a little like her?"

"No, V., frankly I don't. You don't look like her. You don't need to look like somebody."

She didn't like that. She'd left home over disillusionments like that, unbearable insults, so mean. And I hadn't just said that she didn't have to look like anybody, but added that Vanessa Paradis was ugly, that she couldn't sing.

The restaurant had red-lacquered beams jutting out at the top of the wall, buttressing the overhanging tiled roof, and I thought, why not go in and eat? It was not a good idea. It was hot inside and, while they were getting our order, we had an argument, a taste of a disagreement about vertical perspective. Which now makes me want to hit myself on the head with a stick that says: "vertical perspective." Pretty stupid getting into such a conversation, but last night's irritation had turned into various localized pains, like a man with psychosomatic pains in five parts of his body, shifting from arm to chest, elbow to knee, all fixed by going to a doctor who massages a pressure point in his neck.

I suggested we have our ice cream on the terrace, where there was a breeze. We went out with a heavy feeling from the Imperial Duck. I thought about taking off without a word, abandoning her in Istanbul. It would have been better. But I could not control myself. I told her. That I had seen her. I said: "Forget Vanessa Paradis. Don't give me that stuff. I saw you yesterday . . ."

She gave me a perfectly innocent look, as if not understanding what I could ever be talking about. Finally, an expression of comprehension. Oh, that!

She had to act that way, she explained. And I had been there and hadn't come over to say hello? Why? No, she hadn't seen me, but why should that have changed anything. She would have gone with Ahmed anyway . . .

This name, Ahmed. Humanizing her customer.

"But if you know him so well . . ." There was still time for me to get up, walk away. She knew him. Much as she would like to claim otherwise, she was too smart:

"Sure I do, he's been a big help to me. You probably can't appreciate that."

"Well then, why don't you get him to help you?" I actually said that, how embarrassing. A stupid, ridiculous fit of jealousy over a woman I had never even kissed. How could I?

"You don't understand at all. He's a customer. A good customer and a Turk besides."

She didn't say: "If you don't want to help me, you can just leave.
I'll find someone who will." Oh no, she declared: "You're the only
one I've trusted." So, she was being irrational, too. She had no reason
to trust me. It was just a feeling. Like a couple that doesn't get along
but stays together for years. If she had tried to explain her motives just
then, for coming to Istanbul, for choosing me as her savior, I would
not have been taken in. But she just gazed into my eyes without a word.
Bewildered by the turn events had taken, and also by the fact that (actually) *she had revealed nothing*. She could not explain it to me.

"Don't you see?" she said finally. "That is the very reason I want
to leave," taken aback at having to explain something so obvious and
compelling. Even though you saw me laughing, with my arms around
him, I actually despise him, I have to force myself to pretend otherwise. (As I recall, she actually said: "I feel like cats are scratching my
soul," literally, in Russian.)

"You sure looked like you got along, when I saw you yesterday.
You looked very comfortable."

She was quiet, her eyes on me. No tears, no trembling nostrils. Her
surprise, her dismay, arose from one fact, the simple truth, which she
could not yet tell me. It was her job, she had been doing it for months.
She had developed certain techniques, professional indifference covered by a smiling mask, a pleasant manner easily assumed. Now she
was expressionless, no emotion at all showing in her face, blank as a
photograph developing under the red lights in a darkroom, and it meant
that she did not want to act, she wanted to be completely open with
me. I too had just one argument:

"But I saw you."

"So you didn't know I was a whore?"

I reached out, trying to touch her hand and defuse the terrible word,
but I stopped myself midway. I meant to convey: "How can you say

such a thing? That's not it." Like you do with any girlfriend accusing herself falsely, exaggerating, your gesture implying: "That's ridiculous!" But true in this case. V. had cut right to the heart of the matter. The bitter truth—I can't say she didn't warn me—and now I have no choice but to swallow it or spit it out on my plate. But I don't have to swallow anything. A whore and a good one! Fine! I spit on your mother's grave . . . (Spewed out in rapid Spanish, so she wouldn't catch a word.)

"A whore and a damn good one! And I'm a fool for being here with you, even giving you a chance to explain. Damn it all to hell!"

I glared at her, *my face as dark as a thousand demons* and—I would add now—*sunk in the blackest of thoughts*. But gradually, as if coming to me from a great distance, a great tenderness for this woman broke over me (or dawned on me), as if a great light had been shed on her desperate situation by this one thing becoming clear. I felt as if a valve had been opened, letting the air out of my anger, and I shrank back to the dimensions of a nice, understanding man. It was true, she was right, she hadn't tried to deceive me. I imagined that we would have a lot to talk about in some little restaurant in Livadia (who would have guessed there would be one as good as Diodo's, with Greek food?). I did not suspect any treachery: she just sat there the whole time, not leaning forward, cool and distant, hands in her lap.

"You can take rugs out of Turkey, you know, worth up to three thousand dollars," I told her. "I read that while riding here, in the customs regulations, in the cab. You're not worth quite that much, of course, you're not a carpet . . ."

We left laughing. Once more I knew that I would rescue her, that I would take her away with me, that we would go to Livadia. (This city, where I have loved no one, seems to recede, growing smaller, and the Istanbul of that hour to advance, its buildings inflating, acquiring a pneumatic quality. My eye is drawn to a house with a Byzantine capital and animal motifs on the lintel, evidence of the flowering of the art of the steppes in Europe. Nice.)

The same explosion of happiness, as if life had acquired meaning at last, in a letter that Nietzsche sent to Lou Andrea Salomé (another Russian woman—more on this later) in July of 1882: "The sky has brightened for me! Yesterday afternoon was like my birthday. You gave me your consent, the most beautiful gift anyone could have given me."

...

After leaving V., I went back to the *Mikhail Svetlov*. If I had gone to the *Vaʒa*, sat around relaxing in a deck chair a while, the wind might have gone out of my sails, but I acted immediately, impulsively, while I was still excited and the trip seemed urgent. I went to talk to Nicolai Ivanovich, the captain of the *Mikhail Svetlov*, and soon found myself in his cabin, sitting on the edge of my chair, balancing there, leaning toward him. At the end I anxiously offered my hand, to impress him with our desperation, how impossible it would be to plan a trip in any other merchant ship at this point. "I've already talked to her, Nicolai Ivanovich. Everything's ready."

"Yes," he answered, "but we're leaving tonight."

It's like the development of a drama (I could explain this to V. now), there's a certain rhythm within the dramatic structure, and we have to move at the right moment, not before and not after. The few hours left to us before our departure were the narrow strip of terra firma we had to race down if we wanted to save ourselves. That's how I saw it, and that's how I put it—in the note that I left in V.'s room, when I couldn't find her at the Saray. I left her a note with this news: "We're leaving! Today! Tonight!"

And when I went out to the street, following the streetcar tracks again, I remembered this: in Helsinki, that evening when I had missed the train, I had had time to buy myself a Finnish knife with a handle made of reindeer horn. I hadn't realized I needed a Finnish knife until I saw it displayed on the counter of a shop by the station. The rough reindeer-horn handle had attracted me immediately. I'd pulled it from its sheath and tested the blade with the tip of my thumb. There were many others, and I'd removed them from their sheaths, too, one by one, carefully studying each blade, feeling like I was far away, seeing the gleam of the steel, the three-millimeter-wide channel in the blade to direct the rush of blood. I'd seen a streetcar through the street windows, its lights approaching silently through air fluffy with snow, its passengers—all of whom had homes in Helsinki—seated like kids on a school bus. I had had nowhere to sleep, and when it stopped snowing the temperature would drop another five degrees at least. Faced with that eventuality, I had raced back to the station, scanning the arrival-departure board for the platform to get on the *Sibelius*, just as its last call was being announced in Finnish—which I hadn't known, how could I? I don't understand Finnish. (The *Sibelius* would travel past lakes and into woods, slip across the Mannheim line, and arrive in St. Petersburg without me, that very night, at eleven-fifteen.) Just then I saw the tiny red lights of a train; it could have been the *Sibelius*, to judge from the platform. *Faced with that eventuality,* my hands would think for me. That sharp Finnish knife could turn into a tangible center, a solid nucleus around which to organize a trip, the *yazikus* expedition. Somewhere, at some stopping place lost on the steppe, I could kneel down next to a box tied with thick cords, reach up my pant leg to pull the knife from its sheath, and slice through the cords with a single clean cut. Or if I should happen to run across some Astrakhan cossacks or

sturgeon poachers who tied me up, I could stick it into the ground beneath me and cut the ropes. It's called a *finka* in Russian, I remembered, a Finnish dagger like this. I put it back in the wooden cabinet
with the others; I had examined them all, and still liked the first one
best. I caressed a wolfskin hanging there, up on the wall. The bearded
gentleman behind the counter must have said something. I suppose it
was probably "wolf" in Finnish, naming the animal in case I had never
seen its hide. With a knife like that, I thought calmly—my distress at
having missed the train was rapidly diminishing—with a knife like that
I could defend myself, even against a wolf. In Lapland. The store
owner drew out the knife I liked, that he knew I liked since he'd been
selling them for years, and passed it along his thumbnail, shaving off
a thin strip, to show me how sharp it was. How many times did he do
this demonstration each day? I asked myself, leaving the store with the
knife in my backpack, thinking about his nail. Of course, not every
customer would be as difficult as me, so he would not have to give
this disgustingly vulgar proof to all of them. I bought the sheath right
there, with straps for securing it to an arm or a leg. I had found his
demonstration so revolting, I considered buying the sheath alone and
leaving without the knife. I pulled out another knife, this one with a
wide blade, for quartering reindeer. Putting it back, I finally made up
my mind to pay for the sheath as well as the knife that I had liked from
the start. A second streetcar stopped in front of the store. Someone had
told me about some priests who gave travelers a night's lodging. Had
I kept the phone number? I was already feeling relieved. Before paying, I tested the knobby handle of the knife, which fit in my hand perfectly, just right. I held the case in my left hand and practiced grabbing
the knife, wielding it with the blade forward, and low, thigh-high. I
would never strike from above, at shoulder height. I would have to
get into a tight corner, where I couldn't be seen, before I would make

an attack like that. When I was forced to use it, I thought, I would clutch it low, by my thigh.

(I stabbed without exposing myself, holding my body back. I was drenched with sweat, V. was behind me, clinging to my arm. We had run the whole length of the pier, along a brick wall, out of breath. A pillar, I was thinking, a doorway, a dark place where we can hide. The heat was incredible, we were like workers running between brick ovens, out of breath. My *finka!* I was thinking the whole time, my Finnish knife! To end it once and for all.)

4

ISTANBUL

The note with the escape plan was stolen. A hairy paw—Tiran's—intercepted it, and even though I had taken the precaution of writing it in Russian, the Armenian was able to decipher it. Armenians—as Flaubert wrote in a letter to Louise Colet on June 12, 1852—are "a race of dragomans." That is, translators. What would be impossible for any ordinary mortal was simply routine for Tiran, since he also came equipped with a universal translation program. Tiran was able to read any language with ease, like in those old films, where the hero gets a letter—in English, of course, during the U.S. Civil War—and a frame is inserted for the Spanish audience, with a convenient translation. And Tiran knew every detail of our plan.

I had returned to the yacht harbor. I knew there was a chance I wouldn't make it back to the *Vaza*—I had rushed around big cities like Petersburg often enough, with just a few hours to catch a train—so I packed my bags. "I may not have time to get here again," I said to myself. "I'd better pick up all my things right now." Like when you're on a trip and realize you won't have time to visit the store a man on the plane told you about, where they sell watches like his at a terrific price, because it's already three in the afternoon and it's just too far away, you know you'll never get to a store in the suburbs, somewhere you've never been, and still reach the airport on time, an hour and a half before boarding, so you resign yourself to the fact you'll never have a watch like that. But I had forgotten the suitcase V. gave me at the Chinese restaurant that morning—I'd left it on the *Vaza*.

I went to the Saray, rushing upstairs for V. She must have found the note by now; she should have been there, ready to flee. But she wasn't in her room. I ran back to the stairs, hitting the walls in my haste. The women called out to me from their rooms, the sound following me as if I was running a finger along the keyboard of a piano.

V. was below, on the bottom step. I saw her and shouted: "Let's go! Right now!" But she did not move any faster. She lowered her head and continued up the stairs at the same slow pace. Something unexpected, something real was happening, the machinery of the *Mikhail Svetlov* would start at nine o'clock, and there was no way she could stop it. And when the ship was gone, the pieces of her plan, assembled so slowly and carefully, would fall apart. Sooner or later she would leave Istanbul, but not with me. On the top step she spat out wearily, *"Nie sudva"*—a weak voice—"No luck," or "Bad luck."

"Nie sudva. I can't go out today."

"Why not? You always do. Whenever you want. What about your customers?"

"Yes, but Tiran read your note. I owe him money. He threatened me. And got me someone for the night, a man who owns some fighting camels. He's waiting for me downstairs. Thanks a lot for that little note," she added sarcastically.

I didn't respond with an incredulous "Fighting camels?"—that went right over my head. It only occurred to me later—what's a fighting camel? And how would it fight? Probably V. herself doesn't know.

It had been a stupid note, I had even attempted a joke at the end, some old Russian gag like *"Mikhail Svetlov tuu tuu!,"* imitating the ship's horn. Brilliant! Telling Tiran the name of the ship and its *kapitan*.

He had notified the police, a Turkish official, some crony, that a woman who owed him money (a considerable sum) was trying to skip out on her debt. She would be guaranteed a night in the police station, like Miloslava—*pustili yiyo pod tranvai*, "passed down the line," beaten and raped by everyone there.

Nie sudva. I was afraid to look her in the eye. There wasn't a thing I could do. I wasn't going to try something risky, that's for sure, I wasn't going to grab her hand and pull her out of the Saray, smash a bottle against the bar, wave it around to threaten Tiran, nothing like that. Any other night V. could have pretended she was going out with a customer—a smuggler, a young man with very unusual tastes: walking all over town, talking till all hours. Suddenly, I realized she must have been paying Tiran for all the time she spent with me, the fee she was supposed to have charged me, deducting her own licit (illicit) profit. So V. had made an investment, too, maybe a large part of her savings, depending on how many customers she usually had in a day, how much they usually paid. I wouldn't know; I never asked.

She walked toward her room. By this time, Tiran and his men would be watching all the doors. It wouldn't be necessary to deploy a huge force to keep one woman, V., from going out tonight. Just one night. Tomorrow there would be no Russian merchant ship ready to depart, no rescuer ready to help—then she could go anywhere she wanted, the beach at Kadiko, for example. At the door to her room, V. turned and asked: "How could you have been so naive?" I had sealed the envelope carefully, even drawn a pair of lines on the flap so she would know if it had been opened—a violation of private correspondence. I caught up with her and we went into her room together. The violated envelope was open on the table. Tiran had read it laughing through his teeth. "Trusting such an important message to a letter!" V. repeated. "How could you?"

"Look who's talking!" I would like to reply now. But that afternoon in Istanbul I was silent as a fish. I turned toward the door, intending to throw the bolt, but slipped out into the hall instead, again like a fish, soft and gelatinous. I closed the door softly: V. standing there, her back and hair, the harem pants of an odalisque. There was nothing I could do. "Damn!" I muttered. Writing it down, I'd make it that type of curse—more appropriate for a letter—but really I let it all out, in Spanish, outside her room. I can confide to this draft that I screamed, *"Manda pinga"* and even *"le ronca los cojones!"* Because I had ruined the whole plan with my little note. And I must say I was dying to put a neat end to this setup, maybe racing to the end of the hall, up to the top floor, whirling and firing off a shot at the monsters coming around the corner, down the other hallway, then standing there satisfied, the screen flickering: "You win!" and fading out. "The game is up!" I was walking away, downcast, but not dead yet—time for a last-minute reprieve, something unexpected, *magic,* literally.

I had been increasingly agitated in recent months; again and again I had felt nervous impulses racing down my lines of transmission, shifting my brain into high gear, driving my motor centers. Making me burst into Spanish. Again and again. I can't find the right words. I can be thinking in Russian, for instance, telling myself I ought to go back to the *Vaza* and pick up my things (my little bit of luggage, the unsold goggles), when suddenly I'll nearly be knocked over by a train of questions going in the opposite direction, speculations speeding by at top speed, headed right at me. I could not process it—or sort it all out—so I withdrew from Russian and curled up into Spanish, my first language, simple and familiar. I had serious relapses, like in those films where the hero suddenly regresses dramatically, curls into a ball, and starts sucking his thumb. Or like in Copenhagen, in the middle of a deal, and worried about the cops, when I stopped counting in Danish and went back to the first banknote, starting over from zero, reciting in Spanish, "uno, dos, tres . . ." schoolboy perfect, with no mistakes. And the mistress of the man with the illegal merchandise asked me: "What language are you speaking?" I finished the count (sure I had the right amount) and started to process the question—the calculating function closed, speech centers opened up—and then paused a minute because I could not say—and this is the absolute truth—I really did not know what language I'd used to count the crowns. I stuttered out: "Yes, right. It's all there . . ." and then, slowed down, "Oh, Spanish, I suppose . . ." And I held out my hand for a shake, still watching the corner for cops.

Earlier, when I went looking for V. on the second floor of the Saray, where the women sleep, but not with their customers, I had seen Elias, dressed and ready for his magic act. He came out of the tiny kitchenette at the end of the hall, where the girls fix food for themselves, and where the *efendi* fixed snacks for the customers when the Saray was a regular brothel. When I came back out to the hall—our plan ruined by my mistake, it's true, by the trust one tends to place in convention: how many letters, after all, pass through the hands of a concierge, of complete strangers, protected only by a narrow band of glue, in short, a convention?—I saw him again, this time near the window, standing by the parrot's cage, pushing bits of lettuce between the bars, feeding it.

I went downstairs.

That's where I bumped into him, near the bathrooms by the Saray entrance. He had his back to me, and I studied it involuntarily: the skinny back of a magician, covered by a red-and-white striped pullover. He had on a toupee, too, fake black hair above a wrinkled neck, which I peered at as I walked by, and I was almost out the door, when the parrot piped up: "Don't rush off, kid"; and I guess I was mum-

bling to myself, thinking that all was lost, I don't know, I don't remember, because the same rough stammering voice added, "Don't talk
so slow." Which I instantly understood, in a sense, by inverting it:
"Don't jump to conclusions," or "Don't be too hasty." It didn't take a
genius to realize that no parrot, however erudite (this bird knew the
first few verses of one of Sappho's odes), could have come up with this
advice, especially the second piece. But how had I managed to catch
that first sentence, to decipher its words? And it finally occurred to
me that although it had been some time since I'd been baptized by the
glossolalic priests in Helsinki, I must still possess the Gift of Tongues—
I could not only understand every language in Europe and Asia, but
also the squawks of a parrot. An illumination. I felt illuminated, but
for no reason. Paul of Tarsus, on one of his apostolic journeys to the
city of Corinth, must have meant to cure this same error among the
foolish inhabitants who practiced glossolalia or the Gift of Tongues.
In the Epistle to the Corinthians, 12:10, he tells them: To one is given
"the working of miracles, to another prophecy, to another the ability
to distinguish between spirits, to another various kinds of tongues, to
another the interpretation of tongues." That is, to each his own. . . .
Anyway, the mystery had a simple explanation: it was Elias who had
spoken, not turning around or moving a muscle of his striped back,
all the while pretending to be taking care of the parrot in the cage. I
had a rough time following the speech of the magician, it was like cutting a path through the jungle with a machete. I soon realized that I
was confronted by a Sephardic Jew, speaking a Castilian perverted and
plagued by foreign voices. I had to stop every step along the way to
extract roots and unearth whole trees of meanings, to decide among
related senses of a word, to replace terms and clear things up. Elias
had pressed his ear to the door, had heard my conversation with V.,
had recognized her despair. And had come up with a simple plan. V.

would disappear from the stage, he explained, as if it were the most natural thing in the world. "First she will be there, and then she won't," he declared with the simple power of the most primal language. He would open with "The Disappearing Woman" trick and follow that with "The Orange Tree." He explained them both to me, the second more carefully.

...

I had turned down the wrong street and gotten lost earlier on my way to the Saray, after I left the Russian merchant ship when I couldn't talk to the captain. I had known it couldn't be too far away, though. I'd heard shouts and music coming from a Turkish place, through a grated window that was almost on the street. Another bar, I thought, one of the many around here. First, I heard clapping, to a song from Anatolia or some other remote Asiatic region, and then I saw three young Turks jump up, then a few more, who put their arms around their neighbors' waists, and took two steps to the side, first clockwise, then counter-clockwise. From the song I figured I was behind the Saray, in an alley off its kitchen. A blind wall ran the whole length of the alley, which came out on a plaza with a sea breeze, off the Bosporus.

I would meet her there, on that corner. We would run down the alley toward the harbor, to the dock, and the *Mikhail Svetlov*, the Russian merchant ship. To confuse Tiran, I would sit in the bar and watch the women on stage, pretending to be entranced by Elias's sleight of hand and foot. After a while I would get up and stand in the door-way, like I was waiting for someone, for Stockis, and as soon as Elias made V. disappear, I would walk around the building and stand on that corner. A minute and a half.

Elias brought V. onstage for the disapppearing-woman act, pretend-ing to choose her at random. She had already made the Anatolian, the owner of the fighting camels, buy her a bottle of champagne (a down payment). He was in seventh heaven, winking at everyone, head swiveling, eyes glinting like a lighthouse. Before he could dazzle me with one of his flashes, I spun around toward the stage, like a celebrity ducking the cameras. V. climbed the three steps, looked to all sides, sat down in the chair the magician had set center stage, smiled back at the winks of the Anatolian, and I thought, she still doesn't know a thing, but then Elias bent over and whispered in her ear, filling her in on the escape plan, or so I thought. Wrong. I didn't know it, but when I was out at the corner store earlier, buying candy bars for the trip, V. came out of her room and Elias saw her and explained it all. I leaned in the doorway while the magician walked to the edge of the stage and hoisted his cape, displaying both sides. Leilah, sitting in a fat man's lap, caught my eye with a wink, her too. A pity. I would have liked to rescue them both, since V. was very fair, while Leilah's skin was a shade or two darker in the creases inside her knees and elbows, skin that could stand up to a lot of sun. We could go for long swims in the sea while V. waited under the pine trees . . .

The magic act did nothing to relieve the customers' usual tension: two young Turks were being quizzed by the breasts of a Yugoslavian girl in a very skimpy blouse; a nice place, I thought, now that I wouldn't have to come back to it. The kind of place—after five days there—that makes you seek out spots like it everywhere you go: you walk in and sit down at the bar, staring at the half-naked women, staring at yourself in the mirror, without ever finding what you're searching for, and you tell yourself: "No, the Saray was better. What a place! The women there were better, too!" V., for example, who kept smiling when Elias came over and covered her with the cape. I sensed her taking quick shallow breaths, the mental good-bye she was saying to everyone, to Tiran and the women; the whispered: *"Iditie vy vsie na jui"* or *"propaditie vy vsie propadom"* (or, even worse, *"Vas vsej v rot"*). Some awful curses in Russian, believe me. Without giving V. a second look, I left the room, my head and shoulders disappearing from the doorframe, exited to the street, and sprinted to the corner.

With me gone, running as fast as my legs would carry me, concentrating on moving my limbs, this is what happened: Elias had them all observe V.'s breasts—as I already had—rising and falling under the cape and had her lift her arms so that everyone could see she was still there, and then, pacing around as if he didn't know which way to turn, he stepped on a button that opened a trapdoor in the stage floor. Right under the spot where he had positioned the chair, which quickly tilted back—sliding V. out on her back into the space under the stage (full of dust and cobwebs)—before springing back into place, empty. No one in the audience saw the chair's movement: the cape retained the shape of the seated girl, so that Tiran, the camel-fighter, and the other girls (who were watching attentively, since this was the premiere performance) didn't catch the trick.

Elias raised his magic wand, touched what was supposedly V.'s head, in the cape covering her, and V. protested the blow—everyone in the room heard it—but it was actually Elias, or his gut, imitating her voice. No one saw V. crawl out from under the stage, because the lights were low, with just a narrow beam spotlighting the act.

Elias swept aside the cashmere cape with a tremendous flourish so that it undulated through the air like a floating jellyfish, propelled by the gasp of astonishment that rose simultaneously from the throats of everyone there. The cape landed on V.'s back, who pulled it tightly around herself and disappeared (as fast as she could) out the back door.

For his next act, to distract the Armenian, Elias did the orange-tree trick. He knew I wouldn't see it so he described it to me in detail and it really was quite good. He had never performed it there before. While V. ran out in his cast-off cape, the magician peeled an orange in four slow movements and then pretended to (or really did) taste it. He divided the fruit and brought the segments to his mouth, spitting out the seeds, so that you could see them in the palm of his hand. He even threw a few on the tables closest to him. Real seeds, monocotyledon, that he buried in the sand of a flowerpot, which his assistant—Leilah this time—handed to him. He watered the sand with blood dripped from a prick in his finger, and from this sand watered with blood, right before the astonished eyes of the audience, an orange tree began to grow: within seconds it was the size of a large shrub, but its branches kept on growing, and then leaves unfurled with a tiny bird perched on them, singing at the top of the tree, which soon flowered and sprouted oranges, round and yellow, real oranges, which Elias picked and peeled, again in four movements. Everyone applauded the miracle. But Tiran went to the door, and when he didn't see me there, he headed to the back of the stage. Leilah wrote that to V. She too was still marveling at this last magic trick, which was more amazing than the empty chair, V.'s disappearance. How could you explain that a tree grew, flowered, and bore fruit in such a short time, and in plain sight of everyone? V. also missed that miracle, and we didn't discuss it in the short day we were together afterward. It wouldn't make sense to write about it now, to explain that it was an old Persian trick: a folding rubber tree buried in the sand is quickly inflated, so that its leaves and branches burst open. And the bird they all heard singing? And the oranges, which were real and edible? I don't know about the bird. Elias hadn't told me about that. But the oranges—as he pretended to pluck them from the branches, he substituted real ones for the fakes, of course, with the skill of a prestidigitator.

...

V. reached the corner where I was waiting.

"Nobody saw you?"

She stared at me without answering, shaken by the getaway, unable to speak. She seemed taller to me. It was easier for me to look into her eyes, which were at the same level as mine. Had she grown before my eyes? I noticed she was running with particular awkwardness, lifting her feet very high, her heels resounding on the sidewalk. Before we took off at a run—even though no one was chasing us yet and we didn't know that they would pursue us relentlessly all the way to the dock, and then along the dock, and as far as the ship—I stared down at her feet, because I had discovered the secret of her height. She was wearing a pair of those platform shoes, the latest fashion, high as the cothurnus worn by classical Greek actors for the tragedy that would soon occur. With this title: *Harparte,* or *The Kidnapped Woman,* in Greek.

"But you're crazy! Those shoes!" I yelled, breaking into a run, looking from side to side, sure she wouldn't take them off at this point. What could I do? A lost cause. I heard her protests behind me: "I would hate to leave them behind." We ran. I pulled her down the street toward the lights of the Bosporus knowing that Tiran would soon be after us. How I would have liked a finale like Mozart's for *Abduction from a Seraglio,* which he described to his father in that same letter on September 26, 1781: "The Janizaries' chorus is everything one could ask of such a thing—short and amusing."

5

ON THE BOSPORUS

I had many ways to conceal merchandise at the bottom of my backpack. I tightened the cords cinching it, making each section harder to reach. I calculated the pack's depth and arranged my things so that very few customs agents ever touched bottom. An inspector would reach into the armpit, not sure what he might find, and then grope around blindly, without getting to the kernel of illegal merchandise. He would usually give up and pull his arm out slowly—as if from the maw of some giant mammal and he was a veterinarian finishing his exam—and then just poke the outside of the bottom halfheartedly, before giving up. I never smiled at the agents or acted concerned or cooperative, not at all, I was irate, in a hurry: someone was waiting for me outside, nothing illegal was in my bags—me? smuggle something into their country! There was only one way off a boat, you had to take the gangway. The customs agents would be lying in wait, lurking behind the tinted windows of their little guardhouse. The look on your face had to be perfectly ordinary—not perfectly innocent, which was always suspicious, but perfectly ordinary—so they would think you were just like everybody else, trying to bring in an extra carton of cigarettes, one too many liters of alcohol. Hardly worth stopping you, stepping out to talk to you. The worst thing was to get caught staring at some customs agent— He was about to let you pass, what business did you have looking over at him? Steroids, maybe? His gloved index finger would descend, like the barrier at a railroad crossing, halting you sharply, silently forcing you to empty your pack onto the counter. Sometimes the stuffed sausage technique, with the cords pulled tight "to avoid theft while asleep on the train," was all it took, since not many of them were as patient as you, to patiently extract item after inexplicable item from a stockpile typical of a traveler from Russia (and yet obviously not Russian): several chocolate bars, some soda crackers, lots of little snacks, the book you always carried but never had time to read, shirts that looked like they'd never seen an iron, well, then, yes, a cache of cigarettes, the regulation liter of alcohol, like everyone else, any honest citizen, someone from Scandinavia, from the fiords. Like the time I was entering Norway, and the agent stopped short in his inspection, figuring I was a waste of his time, and went out to pull in another passenger, a guilty type: a boy from Bangladesh, dark-skinned, kind of shifty. I waited dutifully as he brought back this new victim, a young man from Dacca—I had met him on the ship, we talked in the disco, he was anxious about border control. The customs agent saw I was still there—taking up the counter space he needed to lay out this new victim, tearing the steaming heart of illicit cargo from him—but wanted to forget about me: "Fine, that's good," he dismissed me with a nod, when I displayed the can of pickled tomatoes I had wiggled from the depths of my pack, holding it up for its return. As if asking, "Pickled tomatoes, good?" No special prohibition against the stuff? I would leave the can if necessary. But he was ignoring me by then, giving a close inspection to a flask of white powder from the suitcase of the boy from Bangladesh. I stood next to them a while, patiently repacking the belongings I had been forced to drag out of my luggage, thanks to the ridiculous zeal of the customs agent. Once I was past the barrier, I watched the growing panic of the young Bangladeshi, and, at another counter, the sad look of a Finnish drunk with quite a few too many liters of liquor in him. I closed up my pack, knotting all the cords, and went out into the street, a Norwegian street, under the mild Norwegian sun. It always seemed like a miracle to me. I would take a deep breath and sit down on a bench right there. Rest a few minutes, my thoughts slowly shifting from the customs inspection to the problems ahead of me in this country (It looked safe enough, but was dangerously expensive: I would have to get on the suburban train without a ticket, slip past those inspectors, and the ones in the metro, stuff like that.) and to the cargo I was carrying on this trip, way at the bottom of my pack.

...

I could tell we were moving. The ship's engines weren't operating, but it had started to move, pulled along slowly by the tugboats. We could speak in a normal voice, or even scream here, but instead we whispered in the pitch black, feeling the weight of so many cubic feet of darkness pressing upon us. We had run up and down too many ramps to have a very clear sense of where we were. Even before the sinking of the *Baltic*, I had always preferred to travel above the waterline. I could never figure out exactly how far it was down to the first deck, the lowest level of the ship. There were no portholes in the cabins at that level and riding down in the elevator a couple of times I had tried to calculate the depth, to get some sense of how far we were descending, as we went past all the other decks, two of which were full of cars and enormous trucks and buses. If there were a shipwreck, how would I be able to get back up to a lifeboat? I was sure that the captain of the Russian merchant ship would hide us below deck, in the lowest spot he could find. But we had not gone very far. When he had covered the money with his cap, he had assured me: "I know this ship better than its owner. They won't find you, even if they do a customs search, which they won't, because the cargo was checked when it came on board." So we would not be under the black waters as we crossed the Black Sea, a relief. Kolya the cabin boy opened a door and said: "Stay here and be quiet; I'll come and get you when we leave port," and I had glanced around at a kind of runway. A ramp high above the ship's cellar, I imagined, hanging in space behind that door. It could be the landing on a stairway for laborers unloading cargo from the bottom of the hold. We stepped onto the platform, which swayed like everything else on this ship, and didn't get another chance to look around; I turned to ask Kolya where we were, but the door was already closing behind us; he turned a handle and threw the bolt to seal the door, pressing a rubber gasket against the edge of the frame to make it watertight. We were left in total darkness.

It took me some time to realize that. I kept waiting for my pupils to dilate, kept asking V., "Are you all right?" clutching her arm. For a while, I thought that my eyes would gradually adjust to the lower level of light, so that I could see her face, her body, if only vaguely, divining her presence like I might have done at one in the morning, by the faint light that filtered through the curtains, illuminating the furniture in the room, a glow to which our eyes had become accustomed.

It was incredible—like one of those dreams where you want to run but can't lift your feet off the ground. I held my hands before my eyes, turned them, front, then back, closer to me, and still didn't see anything. Time went by and I held V.'s wrist, feeling her pulse, counting the beats. I could tell she was frightened, tense, but still, *you didn't have to fight off those two men. I did.*

I drew closer to speak to her, picturing her in front of me. I wasn't even sure I was facing her when I began my tirade, trembling from exhaustion, but trying to reach out, to find her. The awful tension! My God! The horrid darkness! Running down shadowy alleys to the dock.

"I had to cut him, V.!" I told her as if she hadn't seen it with her own eyes. I went back to the moment I struck, when I lunged at Tiran from the doorway. V. didn't interrupt to say, "Why are you telling me all this? I saw the whole thing! With my own eyes!" She was as excited as I when I talked about the fight, going over and over it, as fast as I could, unable to stop myself.

I had made a gash in the arm that was choking me. But no, first I drove my *finka* into his leg and he let out a terrible scream. I didn't expose my body when I stabbed, at thigh height, concentrating all my strength along that vector. The tip of the knife encountered something, tissue, muscle tissue, and I felt him slump, collapse. The shadow emitted a shriek and brought a hand to the wound. I didn't want to kill him, just get him out of the way, to clear the path between the doorway where we were stopped and the breakwater where the ship was docked.

He gave a shout in which I could hear embryonic words, embryonic curses, phonemes belonging to the group of Uralo-Altaic languages, with innumerable *r*'s sliding up and down the scale. Hissing like a serpent or like a teakettle you pull from the fire, he stood there for a moment, frightened, his shadow wavering—his accomplice, who was taller, held a light on him—as if he was hesitating, looking from side to side, but not actually moving. His wound was serious, I thought, he was probably losing lots of blood. I grabbed V. and we ran into the breach—false, I now realize—that opened when his shadow lurched sideways. But Tiran was too big for that: fear prompted him to run away, but when his wounded thigh contracted normally, which it must have, he flew toward me instead—and grabbed me. It was like crashing into the barrier at a railroad crossing. Tiran drew in his arm, pulling me to his chest. Putting all the strength in his body into that arm (which was around my neck). Her momentum had carried V. forward:

she shot ahead and just kept going, eluding our second pursuer, the tall man. I couldn't see her. "I knew it!" she told me. "I knew it!"

One odd detail: V. had cried out in Russian, skidded to the end like it was ice, and shouted again when she was safe. Desperate as I was, I couldn't trust my faltering English, doubly faltering since Tiran had a vise grip on my glottis. And with so little warm air to vibrate my vocal cords, I had cursed in Spanish. Then V. had cried out again, for the third time. In Russian, she had shouted at me in Russian. Once again I had cursed in Spanish, rasping something out in Spanish. Tiran was screaming in Turkish and the tall man rushed over to help him. I had noticed all that, I remember it perfectly.

"It was like this: I had kept my eye on the mouth of the alley while we ran down it, because I knew they would come that way. When we were still near the corner, I turned and saw them, first Tiran and then Ibrahim, his henchman. A taxi pulled up alongside us, stopping for some reason, so we got in. Did we look like we needed a cab? What do you think? No, really? The taxi had given us a big lead, but we'd had to pay fast. A ten-dollar bill—that had to be enough. We had gotten way ahead; they'd lost sight of us. He didn't expect me to jump him, didn't think we were that close, in the doorway. I took him by surprise. Our only luck. We could have let them pass us, get ahead of us. It was a mistake! It was a mistake!" ("No, J., we would have run into them anyway.") "You saw them, didn't you?" (Of course, she had seen them. Tiran was right in front of us, shifting his legs impatiently, dancing around like he wanted to bring on the rain of blows. Those legs were too bouncy, I had to cut them down to size, give them a little prick and let the air out of them.) "God, they would have given us a real beating if I hadn't had my *finka*. A last-minute purchase. I already told you that. And you? Imagine what they would have done to you! Same as Miloslava or worse. And what if we'd reached the pier, and the captain and Kolya had already left? Because they could have just kept our money and set sail. You know: lift anchor, set sail. But, *shhh!* Someone's coming. I hear footsteps. Quiet."

Someone came in. This is what had happened: Tiran had reached the *Mikhail Svetlov* as the crew was untying the last mooring rope— it was about to cast off. Despite the wound that made him limp like a pirate—or maybe because of it—Tiran didn't feel he had to dive into the water and climb up the anchor chain with a knife between his teeth. He had sent his henchman, Ibrahim, to notify the harbor police and soon several uniformed men showed up off the *Mikhail Svetlov*'s gunwale, forcing the captain to issue a counterorder to his crew in the rowboat and tie up at the dock again. They had the authority to delay his departure and that was what they did. The gangway went down again, and a group of ten men came up it, onto the ship.

V. was about to scream. Her frantic whispering rose higher and higher: "They're here, my God! They're here!" like a pendulum swinging farther and farther out of control. I reached for her neck blindly, my fingers feeling the cries rising in her throat, trying to clamp her mouth shut before any sound could escape, automatically pulling her down so we wouldn't be discovered. V. bent her knees just as automatically, as if protecting her belly from a blow, and felt around her feet for the cape that Elias had used to cover her on stage. Unconsciously. The reflex action of a woman surprised naked in bed. She covered herself with the cape and pulled it up farther, till it covered me too. We knelt together under the cape, still not warm. The iron door scraped open, creaking, and we saw Kolya followed by a couple of Turkish police with flashlights.

I could easily see them through the loosely woven cape. Kolya said: "There's nothing in here," cool as could be. And each of the policemen put one foot inside the doorframe, very tentatively, keeping the other outside, poking their heads in, extending an arm to sweep the landing with their flashlights. I could see them quite clearly. I moved my eyes in their sockets, rolling them from side to side, holding my breath, not moving a muscle in my neck, with fear gripping me. "What are those?" "Sacks, just sacks," answered Kolya. The cops felt around on the wall near the frame, like they were looking for a switch, and when they didn't find one, turned their flashlights up.

Their hobnailed boots rang against the grated floor. The first policeman stopped just inside the door, looking down over the railing, shining his light on the sacks, piled up in the depths of the hold. The second one came in farther, until he was standing right in front of us. The beam from his flashlight swept clear across the cape, shining in my eyes, so close I could see the wolfram filament glowing in the inert gas of its bulb. Kolya spoke again, "I already told you there's nothing here," which meant he didn't see anything either, and thought we had groped our way downstairs when we heard them coming and were hiding behind the sacks. None of them saw anything, neither Kolya nor the first or second policeman, who finished his aerial inspection of the sacks and then swept his light over the spot we were in, a cape-covered mass about the size and shape of two people kneeling, barely breathing. The first cop was so close I could see the shine on his high boots, laced up to his knees. How was this possible? Had we become invisible under Elias's cape? Was it a cape that made everyone it covered invisible? I can't believe that. I have one objection, and it's a big one: an invisible body must allow rays of light to pass through it, presenting absolutely no reflective surface to the light, so that no reflections are received by its viewers—the two policemen and Kolya, the cabin boy—and they can't see it. But, the same goes for the invisible man: if he can't be seen, he can't see either; by the same principle: if light goes clear through him, no images are reflected in his invisible eyes, formed upside down way back on his invisible retinas, no, every image passes right through him. And we certainly saw them, and what's more—although it's not actually relevant to my argument, which is an optical question—we heard them, too. Kolya waited for the pair of cops to return to the passageway. And shut the door without a single backward glance, without the slightest concern or confusion. We were back in the dark, but blinded even more by the wolfram filament that we saw as a sign floating in the air. I crept forward, leaning toward that sign, and buried my nose in V.'s neck. We tossed aside the cape with a single movement, but didn't feel any cooler, just the opposite, we felt warmer. I settled V. on my bent legs, and quickly took off her blouse, but again, we just got hotter.

I cupped my hands over her breasts and nibbled away at her neck as if I had caught her in prehensile forepaws and beheaded her with one bite, sucking the green lymph gushing and spurting from the open vessels. I wanted to believe that no one had kissed her like that in months, no one had held her so fast, so ferociously. The grating under us dug into my knees but she was younger and thinner, and I suppose she was holding on tight, with her fingers wrapped around the narrow bars. And then she was reaching out a hand that I couldn't see, and I could feel her, like someone squeezing a leather wineskin, groping blindly and clutching my soft and wrinkled container. Drops fell through the grille into the vast emptiness of the hold; we were dripping, but not onto the floor, because there was nothing beneath us, I realized, only a void. She and I, our mingled essences, fell in spherical drops on sacks of merchandise that would enter Odessa legally, that the stevedores would hoist to their shoulders without feeling disturbed or provoked by the odor of the drops that had been dispersed over those sacks, the odor losing its strength in the air, some of it escaping to the air in the hold, quickly drying up in that hot atmosphere. Sweat was pouring off us, our subcutaneous papillae flooding as if after a long winter, when it's so cold we hardly sweat, and we're amazed when it gets hot the first time and wake up drenched, drowning in sweat.

Far away, somewhere in the darkness, we finally heard the ship's motor starting. The pistons of the diesel were moving, in and out, dripping oil, two strokes up, two strokes down, effortlessly sliding inside the ignition chamber, which had been waiting—I would like to think—for them for so long, converting that embrace into the engine, or primary cause, of a story that would follow the north coast of the Black Sea, in Livadia. Moving forward, gaining speed, gaining momentum like someone running downhill in a hang glider, trying to take off, eyes closed, but not ignoring the indicators, tapping the altimeter dial with a fingernail, manipulating her breasts, kissing her, dipping a finger to check the oil on the connecting rods, gripping her again, and after a momentary pause, as if to change my speed, returning to my first stance, in which I was clutching her in my forepaws, and running along the last section of the hill to take off and begin a long glide, with V. letting out all the cries she had been repressing for fear of discovery.

…

We were lying nude under Elias's cape. This invisible body frightened me, like the bodies that visit men at night sometimes, always a beautiful, slender woman like this, and we embrace her without a moment's hesitation, and kiss her, and we feel her kissing us, even caressing, kissing our skin, and we take her head in our hands and press it downward, happy, and suddenly a barking dog, the refrigerator kicking in, some anxiety preceding the dream, wakes us up and we discover that we are alone, but we feel we have seen her, the sensation is so vivid that we stay in bed, sounding the darkness and asking ourselves: Was it a dream? Did I dream it? Instinctively closing my eyes, like I do when I shave without a mirror, considering the shape of her thighs, her waist, her spongy navel. I was afraid I would wake up and find no one there. But I must see her, I told myself, and pluck her from that tactile continuum, the constant body heat, of all those women in the dark.

I remembered the goggles, how Tiran had dismissed them the day of my demonstration under the stage, and how I hadn't thought it worth saying that: "Neither the 81st Airborne of the United States, nor the Spetnaz of the Russian Ministry of the Interior, nor the Mossad agree with you." But I hadn't known how to make use of the goggles either, how to turn them into an effective weapon in a dangerous situation. When we were running to the breakwater in the dark, between containers piled two and three high, it hadn't occurred to me that they could give us an advantage over our pursuers, a greater edge than our young legs. Nor had I thought of putting them on when we were hiding in the doorway watching Tiran dance about indecisively.

I reached over my head, opened my pack, and felt the plastic strap of the goggles. I pulled them out quietly. V. felt me poking around in the pack, but she didn't ask what I was doing. Lying beside her I raised my head a bit, pulled on the night-vision goggles, and switched on their tiny infrared lantern. I could see the cabling of the ship overhead, along the ceiling, very close to us. Then I turned over, propped myself on an elbow, and gazed upon her green thighs, green pubis.

She couldn't see me. She could only feel me above her, as I moved up to her face and began to examine it. Maybe she guessed what I was doing: my movements, the play of my muscles, my breathing, all belonged to a person who could see, inexplicably, examining something in the dark. She didn't say anything. The lantern was weak—the batteries had run down—and I had to view her in sections. First I looked at her legs to the knee, then a portion of her upper body and her breasts, I focused on her shoulders, her neck; I rolled her over and studied her back, her spinal column, and the paler flesh at its base, swelling, soft to the touch. I assembled all the parts just like a mapmaker after aerial reconnaissance of an unknown territory (unknown, not virgin), who takes the photos obtained from a low-flying plane, and puts all the pieces together to form a coherent map of the surface—or (this is better, much better!) like a predatory insect with compound eyes, which has to review the images it receives, so it won't think (figuratively speaking) that there are thousands of butterflies, when there's really only one—or else (and this may not be such an apt comparison) like the mental process I am using here in Livadia, reconstructing her from the fragmented image in her letters.

SEVENTH LETTER

I

LIVADIA

We weren't stopped when we left the ship in Odessa. Confusion at borders was at its height in Russia: it was possible to enter (and exit) without visas, without passports. You could tell the flustered customs agents, "Day before yesterday, the Duma passed a law eliminating visas for foreigners," denouncing them as no more than a dirty Stalinist practice, and since wave after wave of decrees were flying out of Moscow like bursts of energy during the Big Bang, that story, your lie, could easily slip in between one paroxysm and the next, and get you through. No need for that. We walked down the gangway with-out a hitch. I thought: it's just that we're still in the neutral zone, the customs agents, the border guards, will be up ahead. I stuffed some money into my shirt pocket. "My hands are full," I would say. "Our passports are in my pocket." They would find my passport—but what about hers? "Oh! It must have gotten lost!" The wad of bills would help the guard buy my story. But none of that happened. I couldn't believe it. There was a customs station about five hundred meters from the ship, at the end of the dock, with a mechanical gate to stop cars and cargo trucks, a turnstile for pedestrians. Here we go, I said to myself. Again, we got through. An Odessa crone was making tea in the hut, her back to the stile that spun right into Russia. We made quite a stir (she watched without a word) and then left. And entered Russia by a narrow street, an alley. We walked along a gray wall that came out on a broad avenue. A taxi drove by almost immediately, then stopped short and backed up toward us. Picked up again by a taxi we hadn't hailed. So easy. We climbed into the backseat. We were home, a few hours from Yalta and Livadia. All we had to do was buy V. some clothes, catch a steamer at the Maritime Terminal.

...

When I got off the ferry in Yalta three months ago, a hard rain was falling. It had started raining just out of Odessa and continued for the whole crossing; for all I knew, it could keep up for days. I imagined a weather pattern like St. Petersburg's: perpetual precipitation—rain, snow, or sleet.

I had gone to the dock in Yalta for three days straight, waiting for her, expecting her to get off the ferry. I still thought she would come. I kept seeing middle-aged men getting off with forty-year-old women, still young-looking. Deep in melancholy, I pictured one of Wrangel's white officers, and his sad fate in Turkey, evacuated to Istanbul by the English fleet. A survivor from that 125,000-man army. Who had also fled, I thought, with a young woman; washing up in Istanbul with hopes of continuing on to another country, to France, to drive a cab in Paris.

V. and I were repeating the tale of the White Army officers and the women who deserted them, I thought as I watched the passengers picking their way down the ship's gangway, glancing up with each careful step to note every detail of this landing in Yalta, looking around at the wharf, the umbrella-tables in the cafés, the blue mountains, and me looking back at them, at old men getting off with their women, some fat and over-the-hill, but others flashy in shorts, thighs still pale but working on a tan. I had taken a Russian working girl, *a camp follower* in Istanbul, and helped her escape to Russia—where she had abandoned me. It was the mirror-image of the White Army story—at least, in outline—the officer escaping to Istanbul with a woman who ended up in a whorehouse on the waterfront. I ought to write that to V., to be sure she appreciated the historical parallels, the similarity of our fates, mine and the unknown soldier.

I pressed up close to the people who were arriving, pushing in front of the ones waiting to depart, watching too steadily to be deceived, even momentarily, by the passing resemblance of any of the women getting off the ferry, into imagining V. was getting off the ship from Odessa. Three straight days I stood there, while the crew prepared to weigh anchor, and a hard rain fell on all three of them.

The officer must have written letters, surely, while sitting in an Istanbul café, in the Taksim Plaza in 1921. He would have had two important tales to relate: England's betrayal, only sending a few ships from its armada to the rescue of the army cornered by the Reds—averting a massacre, it's true—and Natalia's betrayal, even more painful and disconcerting. He was bringing a cup of very sweet tea to his lips one afternoon when he was struck by a terrible thought: he suddenly remembered their last month's rent. "Where did she get the money?" That did it. She had sold some jewelry, she claimed, but he had never seen her wear any. (He barely knew her, they had been married in Yalta, or Sebastopol, in 1920, while the front was quiet.) "I made a huge error in judgment," his letter must have begun. Back in Sebastopol, Natalia, his little wife, had seemed so . . . good.

Six months later, the man could have seen her in some cathouse or cabaret, lifting her leg in a crude imitation of a cancan. Oscar Wilde, another man who made a "huge error in judgment" and paid for it in prison, had taken another look at his ex-lover when he got out: the same long sad story, pathetic. Vladimir Vladimirovich quite wisely feared for my mental state—he had noticed the underlined passages in some of the collections of letters I returned to him (this, for example: "It seems to me that any man worth his shoe-leather would have done the same in my situation," in a letter van Gogh wrote to his brother Theo about Sien, the pregnant prostitute he had picked up on the street and provided with "fortifying baths")—and held off on sending me Wilde's diatribe until the very end. But I had found a model of lamentation no less awful in the—putative—love letters between Heloise and Abelard. Certain passages left me numb with horror. Abelard freely confessed that he had planned a seduction, an act of seduction (a game V. and I had played too, she more skillfully), but still complained bitterly when the trap he set for the young Heloise, which she had seemed to fall into, had closed around him as well, clanking tight shut—and through the diaphanous light of this passage I suddenly saw myself as victim to the same error in calculations. Well, in my case, it was only three days, three awful and agonizing days of waiting at the dock, but as the rain let up on the third and I saw the last person get off the ship—a young woman with a briefcase, wearing a green blouse (V. never would have owned a blouse of that color, she hated it)—I realized at last that V. wasn't coming. She had done her best to make me believe and trust her, all the while tricking me viciously, and now I knew that she was actually a *bliad*, a *shliuja*, and a *súka*, a bitch to the bone. Abelard did not have even that consolation. Not only that, the punishment he received—which he came to believe was self-inflicted, suffering pricks of conscience, as his reason (but not his faith) faltered—was enormously, immeasurably worse. He wrote a letter to a friend—secretly expecting it to become public—with the horrifying title *Historia Calamitatum*. And without a doubt the most horrifying part: "One night, while I was sleeping in a separate apartment in my house, they gave gold to one of my servants to admit them and inflicted the most barbarous and cruel revenge on me, revenge that would arouse pity in the entire world: they cut off the part of my body with which I had committed the crime for which they reproach me, and then took flight."

Before this quote, in the explanation preceding it, I've borrowed from Abelard—words and phrases I could use to deplore my behavior, my bad thoughts about V. (and then, here in Livadia, my bad writing), about her mimicry, her treachery, etcetera. But Abelard was much too long ago, and also too willing—strangely willing, given the magnitude of the affront—to forgive. Although I imagine he turned a blind eye—the perfect expression!—when his servants paid the traitors back in the same coin (or knife): "The two who were captured were deprived of their organs of sight and of generation . . ."

I needed some other model for my letter to V., a source to plumb for terms to describe the anguish of those days, the pangs I have felt for the last three months, the attacks of bitterness during those moments that should have been most sweet, the happy afternoons with Alfiá. A model that would allow me to transfer most of the guilt to V., to demonstrate her disregard for her savior and redeemer. Vladimir Vladimirovich finally felt that he could send me Wilde's *Epistola In Carcere Et Vinculis* (his *"De Profundis"*). De Profundis! Indeed! In it I found the perfect words for my own sad story, which would also be prolonged and pathetic, and the precise psychological portrait of a betrayer and his betrayal. In Wilde's case, this was a portrait of a young man—a minor detail, which doesn't change a thing—a portrait of Lord Alfred Douglas, who was Wilde's lover for many years, in fact, a few too many.

And a curious coincidence! About Wilde's imprisonment: the whole thing started with a letter, a little note, an accusation (which was not calumny, as Wilde and his lawyer tried to claim) of pederasty. So what? That didn't bother me a bit, it wouldn't have bothered me to be one, and I'm not, so help me God! Nor did it matter that V. worked in a brothel. What will it matter a hundred years from now? The tragedy ensued and Wilde ended up in prison—behind bars, as the saying goes—where he wrote his young lover a long letter reproaching him for his conduct. All I had to do was put "V." in each time he wrote the other name, his lover's. Try this, for example: "I made a huge error in judgment." Me too; an irreparable mistake! Or else: "You demanded without grace and received without thanks." Terrible! That's the way I felt when we were talking in the Chinese restaurant (Peking, that's it! Finally, the name came back to me!) and she didn't even deign to thank me for agreeing to get her out of Istanbul. V. was no boy, but she *was* quite a beauty, a real stunner. And one more similarity— the young Lord wrote a lot of letters. Wilde says: "You went sullenly after luncheon, leaving one of your most offensive letters behind with the butler to hand to me after your departure." And even lengthy telegrams! "Next morning I received in Tite Street a telegram of some ten or eleven pages in length from you."

(Now that was a revelation: I'd never heard of a telegram that size, just as big as any letter. Maybe I should send my reply that way. How many telegraph forms would I have to fill out?)

Wilde went even further: he filled twenty four-page folios, the longest known letter in history, the editor says, although mine—the one I'm going to write from this enormous draft—may well beat that. We'll see.

I'm indebted to Wilde—he has lent me just the right tone of injury, the perfect pitch. For example, he itemized expenses like a CPA, for boarding the Lord: "The week's expenses . . . ranged from 80 to 130 pounds. For our three months at Gorins my expenses were 1,340 pounds. Step by step with the Bankruptcy Receiver I had to go over every item of my life." The whole tab, what it all comes to. I could figure out how much I had invested in V., for example, what it had cost to bribe the captain of the *Mikhail Svetlov*, the pile of dollars I'd given him, on top of a bottle of the finest cognac, things like that. But the truth is that I spent it on a woman (not a man), and a beauty besides. And it's true I regretted—and still regret—being left in Odessa, but I have to admit, I wasn't left gelded like Abelard or jailed like Wilde. What more can I want? That's simple—to see her get off the ferry sometime, returning to me instead of disappearing.

My third day in Crimea, the day it stopped raining, I stood for a long time watching the waves break against the cliffs (like Ovidio Nasson in Tomi), halfway to Livadia, not wanting to return to my pension, to my room. I walked back to Yalta and went to a movie. I still did not imagine that V. would write to me, that I would stop seeing movies or reading anything not related to her letters for all these months. The film's title had a particular appeal for me. *When You Kiss a Stranger*. A beautiful and suggestive title, you'll agree.

2

LIVADIA

I could feel a switch in her seventh letter, feel her getting away from me, like when two trains run parallel for a while, and then suddenly one slips onto a new track, and its wheels start to move much faster, so that it's quickly lost to sight, it enters a new region, a land that is habitable—we can see that from the window of our coach: houses painted green, their roofs red, poplars edging a wheat field (a windbreak for the stalks)—a landscape where some people obviously feel at home, but not me. Mme. Blavatsky's *The Secret Doctrine*, for example.

This letter offered her explanation of the miracle that had occurred in the hold of the *Mikhail Svetlov:* Elias's cape was the veil of Isis. The goddess—through her intermediary, the magician—had protected us: covered by her veil we were removed from that other dimension of reality, the apparent reality of policemen in hobnailed boots, just dying to kick us in the ribs, to shove us, handcuffed and hangdog, down the gangway of the *Mikhail Svetlov,* to hoist us into their paddy-wagon and have at us right then and there, while we were bumping along, before we even made it off the wharf. Me they would have thrown from the moving car as we passed the harbor, so I would roll all the way down, scraping my hands and knees, smelling the diesel oil, because there were strict regulations governing the Bosporus, and yet there was always oil covering it in a thin slick, dancing on the surface of the harbor water at the same rhythm, never breaking up. While the police, at least ten of them, would take two hours with her. From all this horror Isis had saved us.

This was quite a mystery to me and I started scribbling on a napkin (I could recopy it later), outlining my arguments. Maybe it wasn't too late to get her back on the right track, slow down this impulse to break through the veil of Isis, which she saw stretched across the rails like a tape marking the finish line. She figured she would be crossing it soon, reading Mme. Blavatsky night and day. And once she crossed over to the other side and was floating in an immaterial world, she would look back at the months she had spent in Istanbul, in sin; and even further back, to the day her arrogance, her awareness that she was no ordinary girl, had led her to tempt fate and send the fateful letter that began a trip to Turkish captivity. I would be left on this other side, still in a fog, hazy because of the veil between us, but one thing was perfectly clear: I had saved her; she could hardly deny that, even if it was equally clear that all the assistance I had lent was not disinterested, that I had approached her in the café across from the Saray figuring on getting her into bed, exercising that "energy vampirism" of hers, gaining absolute dominion over her, so that she would listen to my demands, walking back and forth across the terrace, talking nonstop. (She wrote as if she had seen me, as if she had been present for the interminable speeches I directed at Alfiá, who naturally listened quietly.)

It was lucky the Tartar was my audience and not V., a woman with plenty of ideas of her own, who objected to everything, with whom I would have to argue, trying to convince her of the opposite, no matter what the subject, I have to say it was an ideal combination: Alfiá, who listened to me in silence, representing, you might say, the silent majority of Russia, and V., who offered her words from afar, to whom I could reply only in writing. I—and my interminable speeches—

belonged to the world of appearances, and so were not real. They had seemed brilliant on the false side of the veil, but V. was no longer a believer. She stressed that our waking consciousness, which we call rational, is only a special sort of consciousness: a more acute eye sees other potential forms of consciousness beyond this, separated by a transparent screen (the veil). I would begin my rebuttal by disputing this claim, with just cause.

All may be appearance, I would tell her, even the things that seem most real. But the charge that she had made would not overrule a single thing in my eyes. She may not have gone off to the Caspian on a butterfly hunt, but she must have admired butterflies on occasion, the beautiful pattern of their markings, the shimmer of their wings, the iridescent shadows they cast in flight, the vivid colors, rich and deep (*"physical colors,"* Johann Wolfgang Goethe, a German optician, would call them). All right then, all this is no more than a fabrication, caused by the interference of waves.

I would have to describe this very simply so that she could grasp it. Not an easy task. A discouraging lesson came to mind—the long-winded scientific explanation, in "Biological Letters to a Lady," clearly written by a very patient gentleman: J. Von Uexküll. I could not send her the whole thing, which would pain her, no, when I prepared my case, I would have to summarize, make it more accessible. Otherwise, I might get the same sort of dishearteningly silly reply as Von Uexküll: "Madam: I recall having asked you the other day: Exactly what did Newton notice for the first time when he saw the apple fall from the tree, since everyone knows an apple is heavy? And I recall that you gave me this answer: He saw invisible rubber bands tugging at the apple." Invisible rubber bands! My God!

I wouldn't mention Newton, I decided, nor his experiment with the diffraction of white light; no way to bring up wave and particle theory either. That would be going too far, it would get us off on the wrong foot. Best to begin with Fresnel lenses. That's closer to Optics I, in high school. An excellent place to start: two rays of light, with equal wavelengths, but out of phase—i.e., the sines and cosines do not coincide—create concentric circles when they're super-imposed on a screen, light and dark areas depending on whether the phases are added or subtracted. In the first case this produces an augmentation of brilliance (areas of light); the second a diminution (areas of darkness).

The wings of lepidoptera are covered with microscopic scales, at-tached with fine threads to the flat wing. Part of the white light falling on this scaly film—let's call it ray A—is reflected by the scales; the other part—let's call it ray B—goes through the film to be partially reflected from the wing itself, in a path parallel to ray A. Both rays A and B are weakened or amplified depending on whether the phases are added or subtracted. And that depends on the wavelength of the light, its thickness, and the reflective coefficient of the scales (or *lepis*, in Greek), as well as the angle at which the light is reflected from the wing (or *pteros*, also Greek).

Ergo: we should not forget that all is appearance on both sides of the veil of Isis, even the splendor of lepidoptera.

She advanced an even sorrier argument, the story of a fraud. I could easily find myself in the painful position of setting her straight, put-ting her in the right, since I had been in the know all along. My third day in Istanbul, V. had been reading my hand and had started talking about Elias in terms not usually applied to a conjurer, a vaudeville act. She was absolutely fascinated by the way he made rabbits appear and handkerchiefs disappear. They're more than just magic tricks, she had insisted, some of the things he does simply cannot be explained. Now, in this letter, she was blabbing on about Mme. Blavatsky.

Mme. Blavatsky's act was a scandal, big enough that an official commission was set up to investigate. It involved letters, and that's how I knew about it, from that angle. Like Marfa Brown, Dostoyevsky's friend, Mme. Blavatsky had traveled for twenty years, all around Europe, to Egypt, as far as Tibet. Near there, in Madras, India, she had established her Theosophy Society, and in its headquarters she had set up an "Ark," with magic properties: it repaired broken objects, and, even more amazing, answered questions—when letters full of questions for the *mahatma* were deposited inside, they received lengthy answers.

The *mahatma*, or great man, produced his answers in the wink of an eye, sending them back in fat letters almost instantaneously. This made a big impression on the believers—everybody knew how hard it was to write a letter—and thanks to the miracle of the express letters, the Doctrine gained many followers. Blavatsky lived with a couple, the Coulombs, who must have seen her spend many a wakeless night writing the *mahatma*'s answers; and when they had a falling out—no one knows why—they denounced her, presented evidence against her. They testified that they—along with two fakirs!—had been her assistants and that the "Ark" had a false wall wherein they put the *mahatma*'s answers. This is how it worked: when a visitor asked questions about immateriality, the possibility of astral travel, and jamblic bilocation, Mme. Blavatsky gave him paper and pencil and said: "Why not ask the *mahatma*?" The seeker of truth would chew his pencil, staring up at the ceiling from time to time, and wade into some pretty thorny topics, all kinds of doctrinal thickets, to write a letter that a fakir would deposit in the cupboard as if he was dropping it into an airmail postbox. Let me add—now that I've mentioned the ceiling and used the word *air*—that letters also rained down from above, as if by magic.

That's what the "London Society of Psychic Investigations" suspected: that the goings-on were magic, but white magic, and they sent their expert, a man named Hodgson, to India. He quickly determined that the "Ark" was simply a cupboard fashioned like a conjurer's trunk: the back wall slid away so a person could get into the cupboard from the next room. And most important, handwriting analysis revealed the *mahatma*'s letters had been written by the Russian's hand—Blavatsky's! It's perfectly true! Only a woman could have such confidence in letters, in the strength of her conviction, in her amazing sway over her congregation. (But no. Paul of Tarsus did, too, in his apostolic voyages.) But to get back to the letters falling from the ceiling: when new converts gathered to discuss the Doctrine, missives descended from on high to elucidate the topics in question. Pure genius!

I felt terrible about V.'s interest in this false doctrine, although it wasn't the most terrible thing in her letter: at the end she said that she had written to a prisoner, that she had started to correspond with a young man serving five years for robbery. I mention it here even though she didn't tell me what she said to him. His name was Artyom. She wrote nothing else: Artyom. All is lost.

3

LIVADIA

I noticed a very well dressed young man, who seemed to have gotten his clothes in some Black Sea town, maybe in Turkey, the Istanbul boutiques I hadn't had time to visit. I bought most of my clothes in Vienna, but my jacket was from a sale in Stockholm. I remember things like that; how could I forget? The young man raised his eyes—he had been reading a book, which looked to me like *Letters from Paris* by Annenski—and stared over at me, probably wondering where he could buy a linen shirt like mine. He reached under his chair and set a little case on the table, a laptop computer.

He excused himself. "I'm checking my mail," were his first words. I thought I must have heard him wrong. (I had been on my way to the Post Office myself, and had stopped in the Greek restaurant to have a beer.)

I might have heard right though, I realized. While I had been here in Livadia, a new form of correspondence had become available, just as fantastic, just as unimaginable as my devices for seeing at night. I could not verify the news till I got back to Petersburg. I could hardly believe it. Electronic mail? What's that all about? I mean, why? What would happen to all my work? All the circles I had drawn, the pages I had covered, exercises to improve my penmanship, to make it legible. And the soft paper I had finally found, after a long search, in an old store in Yalta?

I was carrying a package of letter collections—some of which I hadn't even opened (the letters of Ekaterina II to Voltaire, for example)—to mail back to Vladimir Vladimirovich. I ought to say good-bye to Alfiá, or maybe I would go to the English girl and just leave Alfiá the note I had written at Kuzmovna's request, when I was gone for a few days and she was curious about my absence and came knocking at my door, expecting me to cry out, "it's open, come in," as I so often did while working on this draft.

This new development, electronic mail, represented a real threat: the enshrinement of the telegram. I saw the young man write five letters in less time than it took me to copy out a paragraph of the Epistles of St. Jerome. He told me: "I've just sent off answers to several of my friends."

I immediately saw all the implications, pictured the dire consequences of this invention, the dangers inherent in such a devilishly easy way to correspond: with letters sent into orbit, zooming through the ionosphere, traveling around the world like papal bulls; the hoopla that would follow this innovation in adolescent countries, like the United States, where more than one person would object to my point: who, in this day and age, needs a letter-writing manual? I don't want to argue about the obsolescence of the traditional letter, or make pronouncements: "The invention of the telephone . . ." or "Just as television did not eliminate film . . ." His letters went into space, I could see that, so why worry? I had written too much, filling up too many pages. I was not blind to the advantage of a manuscript produced by hand (the uniqueness of the calligraphic work of art as opposed to the mechanical reproduction of print).

"What's your name?" I asked him. He gave a Russian name, common as any old Ivan. "Stay here a second," I told him. "I have something you're sure to like."

I went back to the pension for my goggles. I hadn't used them since that night in the boat. No problem that the lithium battery (guaranteed for three hours) didn't have much of a charge. Neither would I. No more than I had paid here in Russia. I didn't have the case, nor the technical documentation, the thick manual detailing how it worked, how long the phosphorescent screen would last. But I had caught on to this new electronic mail apparatus immediately and grasped its significance. I expected him to do the same and see the point of seeing at night. We could test it right there at the restaurant. The lights were already on inside, but down below, on the beach, it was perfectly dark. We went up to the balustrade and Ivan inspected the rocks, the water, and a man swimming in the sea.

"By the way," he said when he finished, "have you ever tried Bacardi?"

"No," I said, "never."

"But it's a rum, right?"

"Yes, I think so."

"Isn't that the national drink in your country?"

"What country would that be?"

"Well, I thought you were from one of those places where they drink it."

I had only heard it mentioned, maybe seen a bottle once or twice, but I still knew the accent was on the *i*, not the *a*. Not Ba-cár-di like he said, but Ba-car-dí. I was about to set him straight but thought better of it. I leaned on the railing.

"I'll let you have them for three hundred dollars," I said and regretted it immediately.

"Two-fifty."

"Three hundred."

"Where did you say you were from? God, you bargain like an Armenian."

There can be problems with this question of my country. I considered putting him off, saying, "I'm from Andorra," but I'd never been there, so the lie would lack an element of truth. I did not suggest exchanging the goggles for the computer either. I had suffered too much for my handwriting: I had bought some pens, I had studied the correct posture: back straight, feet flat on the floor, the whole sole. I didn't care for his questions. I was from another country, where it didn't matter.

I shot a quick glance at his ears. Not enough hair over them, a military haircut, not to be trusted.

4

LIVADIA

I had sent one last telegram to Vladimir Vladimirovich, asking him for Mme. Blavatsky's letters. Alfiá herself went to fetch the package and put it on the conveyor belt. An enormous box bounced toward me. I glanced at the return address as I was signing for it, and didn't recognize the writing—it wasn't from Vladimir Vladimirovich. That information was dispatched automatically, from the sort of memory cell that registers telephone poles along a road, freckles on a face in spring, the length of a helicoidal candle on a table for two.

Repetition and predictable patterns shape the soul and spirit, make things easy for you. You walk along, catching sight of the red face of the man at the kiosk, the grimy smock of the woman who sells *kvas*, the Assyrian shoeshine boy, who act as signposts on your route, so you don't get lost heading home. They're a reassuring part of the very comprehensible whole, the five thousand people who live here, counting police, dockworkers, and soldiers, a small garrison, all familiar, quite ordinary: the soldiers in green, the workers in orange, coming toward you, the guy from Morocco or Spain, the foreigner staying in Kuzmovna's pension. *Dobry dien! Kak pozhivaite?* Greeting them all, clutching your heavy package, listening to the growing ticktock of a stone in your shoe, a freshly dug hole where the lamppost should have been at the last corner. It wasn't Vladimir Vladimirovich's handwriting. Which is to say, in a small town, without the anonymity of the city, I was more exposed to attacks, to an outbreak of xenophobia! This foreigner, this young man without any set occupation, who goes to the Post Office every day, what can he be up to? Who can be writing to him? Who sends him the packages tied with twine, which he dangles from his forefinger, if they are not huge and heavy like the one today?

Or clasped to his chest if they are. I could try to hold the package away from me, but it would destroy my arms anyway, since it contained a bomb that would go off when I started to open it in my room. Oaths poured out of my mouth, a real blue streak, and my first, and very worst curses, were directed at freedom of expression, that miserable bourgeois value, which had given Russians the unprecedented opportunity to read full-page articles—like the one in the Sunday supplement of the *Chernomorskie Viesti*—about the Unabomber, the man who sent letter bombs, "murder by mail." It made me feel like mounting a protest, maybe dashing off something like: "Dear editor: With all due respect, I, a reader, must place the blame for many problems—organized crime, prostitution, drug abuse, just to name the most obvious—squarely on the press, which created them from nothing, mass hypnosis, spreading stories. . . . And the article about the Unabomber, look at the effect it had, when some local copycat tried to blow up an enemy, a foreigner. . . . What's worse, your reporter said that the Unabomber hasn't been caught and there's almost no chance of ever finding him . . ." I guess I'll have to work on the wording later. I was completely hysterical, set the package on the table very very carefully, cursing the newspaper—and then stared at it mesmerized, for a good half hour. I replayed that Sherlock Holmes film in my head, the one where Watson and Holmes get a package in the mail and there's a dagger inside, and Holmes cleverly lifts the lid with the tip of his walking stick and the dagger shoots out into thin air. My God! That

was easy! A dagger! I laughed till I practically cried. What about the
flying fingers of the Irish gentlemen who get letters from the IRA? Or
the clerk in Kuala Lumpur whose arm was torn off during a routine
customs inspection, despite the idyllic palm trees in the garden outside, their broad leaves trailing in the grass. And then there was the
Unabomber! Just look at the size of the box—and the timing! right after
the article—it had to be him. The Unabomber—"the mail-killer," as
the FBI christened him—struck for the first time in 1972. Then fifteen
more explosions in sixteen years. A million-dollar reward for his capture. Once, in a bomb that didn't go off, they found a note, and on it
a faint impression of an earlier note, on another sheet from the same
pad: "See Nathan," and the FBI investigated every Nathan in the
United States, and got nowhere. It's a fact: unless you use a fountain
pen, you press pretty hard on the paper . . .

If I had a seat in parliament, I'd be on my feet right now, up at the
podium proposing a law in favor of the violation of correspondence
in defense of the national security. With a good part of its budget going
to X-ray machines for every branch of the Post Office. Or I'd picket
outside the Assembly (since I was a foreign resident without much hope
of being elected), carrying a hand-painted sign: "Bring back the *black
bureau.*" Russia had a *black bureau* in the Azef era, even earlier. A police
department, a whole building, with inspectors who did nothing but
examine private correspondence. Like the one Louis XIV established
in France. With twenty-two employees picking letters to open, removing their wax seals, reading them, registering them, and then resealing
them. They perfected the art of opening a letter without a trace. Let's
say twenty-plus employees (picture them wearing frock coats); that
would cost the treasury fifty thousand gold francs per month, which
might seem high, but consider the benefits: aborted plots, unmasked
spies, etcetera. Excerpts from the letters were sent to the king, to the

deputy general of the police, and to the minister of foreign affairs. Wasn't that an excellent idea? A *cabinet noir* is what we need here in Livadia—and all over Russia. Of course, Russia used to have its own, even better ones, more sophisticated, with X-ray machines, but they were shut down in 1991. What a pity.

I felt a rush of fear: what if the young man who had bought the goggles was really a public prosecutor. Once I had taken the bus between two cities in Siberia with a guy who turned out to be an examining magistrate. He was thrilled to meet me, wanted me to change my plans and go to Minusinsk with him. (V. would know how far that is.) We had hardly talked, barely introduced ourselves. I told him where I was from when he asked, and he invited me to Minusinsk. I was so far from home, he figured, it would hardly be out of the way for me, not even much of a trip. I answered no, I was traveling for one express purpose—to buy mammoth tusks—going only one way at the moment. Our conversation turned to his job. He was an examining magistrate, fresh out of school, but he had a humorous anecdote, about hitting prisoners during interrogations, with the *Penal Code,* a book weighing at least five kilos in paperback. He would turn his back, pretending that he wasn't there, that he was taking a call, and his assistant, a sergeant, would pick up the *Code* and drop it on the prisoner's head, hard and fast enough that the head would be encrusted with the spirit of the laws, the minuscule letters of article number forty-five, which reads: "Beating the prisoner during questioning is punishable by five to ten years." And the violent discrepancy between the letter of the law and this barbaric treatment—incidentally, the Marquis de Custine's letters indicate he witnessed something similar—convinced the prisoner, a garden-variety thief, that he better confess, maybe plead guilty to a few old crimes he hadn't even committed, blemishes on the triannual report, a bloat in the statistics for unsolved cases. The magistrate, I've forgotten his name, repeated the invitation: "Let's go to Minusinsk. I have a lovely steam room . . ." And I wondered if maybe the guy who bought the goggles and told me about electronic mail went there too, because they had the same haircut, short above the ears . . . And he had been watching me, after Moscow sent him a *lettre de cachet*, a dispatch with the official seal, the order to arrest and deport me, but he couldn't resist the cheap goggles—and why should he? Or he could be the Unabomber's local competition, who had dared to make contact with his next victim in a café just a few days before mailing the letter-bomb—it was all part of an elaborate assassination plot.

I kept the box pretty close to my chest while opening it—not holding it at arm's length, in a ridiculous attempt to protect my body, to keep my distance from the blast—exposing myself to the shockwave. I cut the twine. A frenzy of unwrapping, a fierce crackling of paper: death meant nothing to me. It was a black leather suitcase. A black leather suitcase? I unzipped it, reached in a hand that could be blown to bits by an explosion so powerful it would mark the beginning of a new existence, tearing me apart, but putting a stop, once and for all . . . I'd better stop right now, before the explosion, and write a little farewell note to V., something short, to the point, not to say that I had loved her but that I had wanted to.

I pulled the paper aside, revealing a thin gauzy fabric, the sleeve of a yellow blouse, and knew at once what it was and who had sent it. V.'s suitcase, which I had left on the *Vaża*, full of the clothes she had bought, picked out of the heaps of Turkish *dermó*; and Stockis, who had mailed it to me—another general delivery—rather than its owner. It was Stockis's printing on the package. With this yellow blouse all the pieces of the puzzle magically fell into place, silently, softly, giving it the form, the shape, the manageable body of an oversight. It had slipped my mind entirely, the suitcase that I had left on the *Vaza*, that V. had brought to the Chinese restaurant, that I had taken for a lapdog at first. And suddenly, thanks to that yellow blouse—and the Chase novel, which I was reading again—I saw something that I had missed in Istanbul: V. and Stockis were in it together.

I had made a bad mistake: when I mentioned Crete, V. had gone right to work—sitting on the edge of her bed, barely awake, clipping her nails—and called on the big boss, exploring an alternative escape plan. I had seen her as Catherine Deneuve in the embrace of the enormous sumo wrestler, the Japanese guy, but she had actually thrown herself into the arms of another giant, the Norseman, like in one of those B movies where the Samurai takes on the Viking: the iron of Osaka versus a spike-studded mace. And Stockis would have wanted to inspect the merchandise personally, poke his thick fingers into her folds, appraise the goods . . .

It wasn't my fervor or the fancy speeches I made in the Turkish bath that convinced Stockis to lend me the money, no, it was another pair of perfectly simple (as well as strong, sensible, and elegant) arguments—V.'s legs. Getting the suitcase from Stockis was a stroke of luck for me, and all that I needed to clear up one mystery, the Swede's inexplicable generosity.

Stockis knew that V. would vanish as soon as she was out of the dark, in Odessa. It was no surprise to him. She must have settled herself on his broad chest (the image didn't bother me, it didn't matter, she had been on many other chests) and snatched a promise from him: to advance me part of the money for the second delivery of butterflies, enough to bribe the Russian captain and arrange the escape. And with Stockis such a big gambler, it turned into a bet on a racehorse. He would never have lent money to someone like V. Nor to me; at least, not directly. But if my horse won, I got the money for V. And she

knew it. Her jumping up and down on the bleachers in the grand-
stand showed that much.

It reminded me of the letter that George Sand sent de Musset on
April 15, 1834, from Venice where she was deceiving him with some
obscure doctor, which didn't stop her from making the following request: "Please send me twelve pairs of watered-silk gloves: six yellow
and six brown."

I fixated on those brown gloves; I couldn't get them out of my head.
V., on the other hand, had chosen dresses and skirts and blouses, lovely
colors, delicate fabrics, summer-weight, as if she were going to spend
many more months in Istanbul, a lengthy stay. Where could she have
worn those thin dresses in her village in Siberia, with September so
close? They were far too light for the north.

And she had left them all behind, like a caterpillar leaving its cocoon and spreading its wings in the sun. Those garments had shrouded
her during the metamorphosis from her previous life, while she went
through several stages, passed through several phases. Reading Sirin
and Stuart, I had learned about the four stages of butterfly development: egg, larva or caterpillar, pupa or chrysalis, and butterfly—but
it never would have occurred to me to see a woman this way. Somewhere (it could well be a letter) Dante Alighieri says: "Man is the
chrysalis of an angel." Which struck me, since I had read earlier, in
St. Thomas and in Pseudo-Dionysio, that angels are an intermediate
state between the human and the divine. Dante had a vision of a winged
creature emerging from the clumsy wrappings of the human body,
making angels the end-state of evolution, not an intermediate one. But
according to Thomas, angels are cast in a human mold and prefigure
the souls that remain captive in men's bodies until the moment of death.

I had thought of her as a butterfly—a butterfly of the night, in
Stockis's hasty identification—when I should have seen her as a cater-

pillar. Like when you lived close to the ground, when you were little, and you would hold a twig in a caterpillar's path, and it would rear up, rise on its hind legs, wiggle back and forth, and blindly move forward, with an enviable stubbornness. A many-legged caterpillar going every which way. Exactly: V. adopted this sinuous strategy to trick me, like the caterpillars you see in educational films showing their incredibly slippery footwork.

And like a caterpillar that finds a hole in a trunk and starts spinning its cocoon, she had covered herself with these dresses, these fabrics. But the Saray had been no sanctuary: there were low vibrations when she danced onstage, frequencies she picked up through the soles of her feet, suggesting that this was not a good place for her metamorphosis, that she would be permanantly deformed, so she latched onto the fur coat of a migratory animal to carry her across a wide body of water—the Pontus Euxino—releasing her grip on his hairy belly in Odessa. But her migration was not yet over: she had to return to her birthplace, to the village in Siberia, the featherbed, the eiderdown, which her mother had left unchanged in hopes she would return some day.

I had seen her as a butterfly because of Stockis's glib comparison. An understandable error. And how about me? A praying mantis? The trite image had not even occurred to me. Me lying in wait for the poor unfortunate butterfly? How tasteless! Completely sordid! And totally untrue—I had a feverish mobility, I stood out against the gold ground (Byzantine) of the Saray and adjacent streets, you could have seen me as far off as the dock, the track, the baths, the Hagia Sophia. And her? She had not flitted around gracefully, innocent as a butterfly, oh no, she had crept along, plotting deviously, twisting things deliberately, contorting things profoundly, to entice me, like the day she fanned my face with her buttocks and then assured me: "I had to do it, I was working."

And she had roused from her cocoon in the shed by her home in Siberia, waking up and watching the wild ducks cross the sky in a V formation, writing her first letter in one sitting, using the material she had been wrapped up in for so long, now dry and crisp as paper, leaning over the table to write, her shoulder blades trembling under the delicate wings that had grown there, translucent yellow wings quivering as she transferred their pattern to her letters, the submarginal stripes, the tiny, virtually invisible scales. She had entered another state. Frankly, I don't know if I would have wanted to see her changed into a butterfly. I had known her in her caterpillar form, a little twisted and bristly, fuzzy and soft to the touch, disturbing. What good is a caterpillar? That intermediate state, didn't it always point to an end? And then I remembered Stuart (which I had read a long time ago), and it was such an amazing coincidence that it felt like a revelation, because he had emphasized the importance of arriving at a state in which one returns a reflection of oneself . . . Stuart says: "In Entomology, the Imago, is the final or perfect state of an insect, usually with wings."

There is an exact correspondence between this final and perfect state—the imago—and her letters, which constitute an exact representation of her imagined self. V. had been growing, stretching her wings, into a mental image she had of herself, bringing it to life by force of will. Like a caterpillar, fully aware of its imago, as I read in a letter from Pavel Florenski: "The butterfly that emerges from the cocoon, which may live for only a few days, is the entelechy of the being that lived for months in the shape of a caterpillar. There is no similarity between the butterfly and the caterpillar, and a careful examination by a comparative anatomist or a histologist disproves any superficial similarities one might see between the caterpillar and the elongated body of the butterfly. In the butterfly everything is new, every organ, every tissue. And nevertheless the butterfly is the true image, the incarnation of the soul, the entelechy of the caterpillar, and in the butterfly, the caterpillar seems much more like itself than in its own vermiform state." (Pavel Florenski to Vasily Rozanov, September 15, 1915, St. Petersburg.)

I must communicate this discovery: the being that has reached its imago and lives in perfect harmony in this final and perfect state, and winged besides, has no interest in this type of reflection, I'm sure, even finds it abhorrent. It confines itself to flying. For a man who is condemned, according to Dante—and I'm starting to agree with him—to be the chrysalis of an angel, just knowing this can be a comfort, its own reward. For an angel—and V. was an angel, an angel of goodness, I must now confess, no longer afraid of repenting—it is no miracle, simply part of the angelic condition.

5

LIVADIA

I observed butterflies until the end. Walking lightly along the asphalt road through the woods on the way back from Massandra with the two bottles of wine I had bought in my mesh bag, looking around peacefully, gazing at the translucent wings of a *Hipolyte euxinius,* an iridescent satyr, not having touched my butterfly net in weeks. I would never have the patience to collect butterflies. Nabokov had donated his collection to a museum in Switzerland, in Lausanne—the butterflies in envelopes, according to his biographer, delicate paper covered with writing. And *nymphet,* the word he used to describe Lolita, is an entomological term. Like Stockis and his rather more vulgar *papillon de nuit.* We should see Humbert Humbert as a hunter—someday I must write this to someone, anyone but V.—pursuing a member of the nymphet group, captivated by its secretions, the perfume from its ventral glands.

There were still many things to tell V. This draft may seem exhaustive, but it is far from it. There was no hot water in the pension, for instance. Turning on the shower in the morning, I imagined cold water hitting me on the back long before I actually felt it. Kuzmovna held that it was invigorating, "and besides, this is the south, and the weather's been so warm recently." But nights were getting cooler, and days noticeably shorter. The leaves on the trees . . .

I must write more about those leaves, right now.

About the leaves. They had turned a red color and with each gust of wind fell softly onto the grass in the garden. The bushes went from green to red, the veins of the leaves turning a more intense color. V. was never going to come and my time was almost up. Nor would she ever send me another letter, even though she had not told me everything, nor I her—about the hot water, for example.

About the yaʒikus. I had gotten into the habit of noticing anything that flew, even toys, plastic helicopters, wind-up doves that soared straight out for five meters and fluttered silently to the gravel. Coming back from Massandra that afternoon, I suddenly thought I had seen a *yaʒikus.* At first I suspected I was only projecting the submarginal stripes of the *yaʒikus* onto the whitish wings of an ordinary *colias,* like a missing link falsified by soldering a primate jaw onto a Neanderthal skull. That the *yaʒikus* design that was dormant in me had been interposed between a simple butterfly and the light-dish in my eyes, so that I saw the image of a nonexistent insect, captured for the last time in 1914, on the eve of the war. Without getting up from the bench, not missing my net at all, since I could easily catch this one in my handkerchief, I took a good look at this specimen, as rare as a female mate for a plastic toy helicopter. I made no move toward it. I considered it a few moments. It had been a long time since I had thought about the *yaʒikus*—as you can see from this draft—and I had to get past the three cauldrons with boiling water, oil, and tar (and the brass trumpets), to get past Istanbul and the Saray and remember Sweden, that far-off land, and Stockis, its bad angel, before arriving in Livadia, returning to find myself sitting peacefully on this bench with two bottles of the best wine in Massandra, a town just west of Yalta.

Like the mental leap that gets you into cold water, or in the middle of a very long journey, when you feel like resting, but it starts getting dark, and you say: "No use stopping. I have to get moving if I want to make it. The fifth show starts at nine. I don't want to miss it." And before standing up, you picture yourself getting to your feet and walking to the end of the park, over to that tree (where you would be closer), and then you manage to get up.

The *yaʒikus*—or a butterfly that looked amazingly like it—was floating and bobbing around a boy's toy helicopter. I could see myself struggling along after it breathlessly, jumping over ditches, across a stony streambed, glimpsing its yellow wings in the film of water below, hanging in midair. Fine, I told myself again, what's the use. I leaned the bottles against the back of the bench, folded my hands in my lap, and sat perfectly still: I had a chase ahead of me and I wasn't looking forward to it. Then, it was off like a shot. A *yaʒikus*, that's for sure. It had been alive, asleep in its cocoon for all these years, since 1914, and my brainwaves, the power of my mind, had provided the heat it needed to mature, break out of its chrysalis and take flight. Could one see the *yaʒikus* as the symbol of Russian liberty, which only now, etcetera? Of course not, what rubbish. There it was, it was an insect, it was probably worth thousands of dollars, according to a Swedish collector, information that hadn't been verified, and I was supposed to catch it.

Only then did I realize that any butterfly at all could be a *yaʒikus;* the descriptions vary so much. Stuart doesn't mention it. And Sirin's portrait doesn't match the one I got from Stockis—although I didn't tell him that. This thought brought a brief surge of hope. Nothing was preventing me from conning Stockis, selling him this or any other specimen as a *yaʒikus,* and I could back up my story with the letter I'd been drafting if he should discover the fraud. I thought of letting it go. A gust of wind made it veer toward the woods, as sharply as a flock of seagulls obeying an urgent call to head inland. I saw it fly over the edge of the field, getting smaller before my eyes, and I thought again of letting it go. Stockis might have been deceived by some Russian, an insect smuggler—there might be lots of *yazikus* in the Caspian Basin, thousands of them flying around the Kashiria preserve, but since I thought they were extinct, I hadn't been able to see any. I became more convinced: some Russian had tricked Stockis, told him this enormous lie, and then departed the scene. The Swede had sat in Stockholm chewing his nails, getting more and more worked up (not about the overhead, like me, but from hunger, the craving to possess this rare specimen, to feel like a czar or emperor with his collection of rare treasures), and so he sent me, a vendor of night-vision goggles, on his quest. As soon as I gave up and admitted I couldn't find one, the Russian would show up with any old butterfly and claim it was a *yazikus*, charging Stockis some astronomical sum.

I speculated on all this in less than ten meters, the butterfly disappearing into the woods ahead. How could I verify my latest suspicions? Only by capturing this butterfly, which might be a *yazikus*. This was an emergency! I ran onto the grass in a panic. What about my bottles? I turned to see: they looked like they were waiting for me, leaning against the slats of the bench. I wanted to go back for them, hide them behind a tree, on the verge of the woods. But, my God! Ten thousand dollars (maybe more) was flying off into the woods. I kept my eyes on it and took off in pursuit.

Try sometime to chase a butterfly, to follow the plan or pattern of its flight. It's like tracing the score of a fugue with your finger, all those quavers and semiquavers, exhausting. I leaned forward, knees pumping at a steady beat, zigzagging over a steep hill. The thick tree trunks advanced toward me monotonously, grave and immutable, like a continuous bass undertone. It was getting late, the shadows were deepening under the trees, but it was still sunny higher up, along their crowns. I saw the *yazikus* alight, its wings vibrating rhythmically, as regular as a metronome, among the ferns. During a half-beat of silence—a full measure—I got closer, feeling the throb of its wings in my temples, taking out my handkerchief, ready to make my catch, but it glissandoed down the slope of an inverted chromatic scale, bounced off the double bar of a wall of air, and soared upward in flight. There was a sharp rise and I ran up on it, more hunched-over and breathless all the time, finally doubling over, panting with exhaustion, my eyes fixed on a patch of bark above the pine needles, a stitch in my side, the blood pounding in my ears, so that I wouldn't have been able to hear an organ if it was playing arpeggios right next to me. Like one time in Riga, in the Cathedral of the Dom, the night I slept through three movements of a concert under the influence of half a bottle of vodka. I vaguely remember waking up during the intermission. According to my companion, I staggered down to the lavatory, threw up, stared miserably into the mirror, went back up to my seat, and snored until the last chord. Through the mists of that lofty place I spotted the butterfly, its yellow flickering, because sounds have colors. This one, per Scriabin, was a "yellow" D in the fourth octave, very delicate, coming at me deliberately—giving me a chance to catch my breath—gradually slowing down, like a shepherd's flute. It flew toward a clearing. I followed. I ran into the clearing, past a log cabin on my left, and came to a lake.

Inside the band of trees, which extended only fifty meters, lay the green of a lake. The butterfly was nowhere in sight. This was not the "sunny, open clearing" that Sirin claimed was its usual habitat. The lake was ring-shaped, a circle with an island in the center, a few fir trees growing on it. My footprint on the shore quickly filled with water. Then there it was again (that's how it was—appearing and disappearing miraculously, as if "descending from heaven"), but going in the opposite direction, toward the cabin I'd just passed. I must have run around the little lake two or three times. Every time I went halfway around, I seemed to be back at the same log cabin. (Now that I'm writing this I realize there were two identical cabins, two ends of a secant across the lake, and I—luckily, if unwittingly—stopped at the first, the one I'd seen on my way up.)

I looked off to the horizon, over the treetops: not a glimpse of the sea. So the clearing must be in a hollow, and I had been going downhill without realizing it. It got darker. And started to drizzle, a light autumnal rain that made the lake seem far away, hidden behind a curtain of water. I was lost. I had been following the score, but when I took a rest, I couldn't come in again, I wasn't sure about the right passage, I had lost my place. I should be on the opposite slope by now; this lake, which I had never seen before, must lie to leeward, sheltered from the sea breeze, exposed to the cold winds off the Caucasus. I turned my eyes to the distant shore: it must be north. The water in the lake seemed to come from a spring, there were no streams feeding it. I decided to go south, toward the cabin.

Where do butterflies go when it rains? I took shelter on the cabin's tiny porch. I thought I would find the *yaʐikus* there, resting under the rough plank roof, but all I found was a metal hook for a lamp. A trickle of water ran down the eaves, flowing toward the edge, getting bigger as it went—like when the light at the corner turns red and cars line up, one after another until the light turns green—until the whole big round droplet plunged off the edge. The big bright drops were falling fast, at times in streams of water denser and more brilliant than the gray mist that filled the woods. It looked like it would rain at least an hour. I tried to open the lock on the door, and when I couldn't, went to the north end of the porch, to look through the window. A gravel wash surrounded the cabin; I jumped across it to look inside: a plank on sawhorses, a cast-iron stove with a woodpile, rolled-up mattresses against the wall for overnight stays. Nothing that made me want to force the padlock: I had no intention of spending the night here. I went back to the door, took off my shirt, and tried to break in, shivering from the cold. The pine tree by the porch rail had moss growing on all sides, not just the north one. I stuck my head out to look and in that short time, the downpour almost drilled through my skull. All right, I thought, I wouldn't be lost—I wouldn't be eaten by wolves—in these woods. I sat down to wait for the rain to stop. *Where do butterflies go when it rains?* I hadn't read anything about that in Stuart, or in Fabre, or in Sirin. I stared at the wall of rain and rested for half an hour. More or less. I didn't have a watch. I had stopped wearing it one morning when I checked the time and saw it said seven. In the morning? Yes, it was clearly morning, but certainly later than that. It didn't make sense, I had to stare at the second hand quite a while before I realized my watch had stopped. This must happen to many people. There was an impasse, a second, during which I didn't know how to explain that hour, that unfathomable reading. The answer was that the battery had died. Like now, realizing how long I had spent at this cabin and that I ought to get out of Livadia, not dragging along like an old-fashioned watch with a winding mechanism, but in one smooth leap like a new quartz watch, where the second hand simply jumps from one second to the next, discretely, sweeping away a whole second in a single move. First it's an hour and fifty-seven seconds and then suddenly it's an hour and fifty-eight. And the fragmentation caused by this new method of timekeeping, has anyone given it any thought? Today you can see time fly, its wing-beats are noticeable, measurable. A major change, that's for sure, a whole new attitude. You could stop dragging, start happily leaping, no more hanging suspended over a black void, tormented by the awful, infinitesimal passage from one second to the next. I would buy a watch that leapt from hour to hour if they made them. And if they didn't, I would write a letter to Mr. Swatch, of the Swatch company. It was a great idea, they might even pay me for it. (As I was saying earlier: money in the world is like water vapor in the air, just give off the proper—human—heat, get it to the right temperature, and it would shower down on you, golden drops flowing down your chest in a never-ending stream.) I would ask a modest sum, twenty thousand dollars. A bargain, considering the fabulous demand for this new watch, the relief it would provide, making it possible to compress time, the hand sweeping aside unbearable hours, whole days of waiting.

Great, I said to myself, quite a plan, a proposal for a watch without a minute hand, jumping from hour to hour, but it wasn't very practical, I saw that at once. I had been reading too many letters; they had affected me. Saint Augustine, an absolutely true story, was converted while reading in a garden in Milan—St. Paul's first Epistle. The passage that says: "Not in reveling and drunkenness, not in lust and wantonness, not in quarrels and rivalries. Rather, arm yourselves with the Lord Jesus Christ; spend no more thought on nature and nature's appetites." In short, "It's time to put smuggling aside." And I had read not just St. Paul's epistles, but so many others, too, both men's and women's, but primarily the latter. I was a changed man, exhausted, as if I had just listened to hundreds of years of confessions.

This was too heavy a load to bear, up there on the side of Ai-Petri— another Sacred Mount—so that I had no energy to write a letter to Mr. Swatch, with my new moneymaking scheme. Suddenly the rain stopped as if on command, and I started down the mountain without hesitating or looking back. Sure that I was going in the right direction. Glad that I had let the butterfly escape. Making giant strides like the new watch that Swatch could market without me, with great success, I chanted this military march:

Po sibiskim jolmam y dolynam
Partiẓanski otriad projodil.
(Over hill over dale,
the Partisans hike the dusty trail.)

I looked up and saw the steel-gray sea. I could see the lights of the Yalta harbor, the garlands on the swaying boats. From here, with a paraplane, one of those paragliders, I could get a running start, take off, and come down in the garden of the pension. I started that descent in my mind, in rapid flight without opening my eyes or moving a muscle, flying over the icy forests of Lapland, skimming the golden cupolas of the churches of St. Petersburg, the deep blue conifers and flower-filled meadows of the south, the lush wheat fields and snowy peaks of the Caucasus, to Livadia, the little town on the edge of the sea, and on a cliff above its shore, the little Greek restaurant with a narrow pseudo-Doric balustrade holding it back from the brink. Rapidly losing altitude I drew closer to my pension, its dark mass and bright windows, my window glowing with a special intensity under the blue-black sky. I glided parallel with the grass for a while, before plunging off the cliff, arms crossed, assured, like someone picking up a true melody at last—the rising current of air—and being carried along by it, to sail over the endless steel-gray surface of the Pontus.

Before I had gone too far out to sea, I turned back toward the shore and landed silently, like a bird or an angel, under the window of my room.

6

LIVADIA

The lights were on in my room. Strange because I had left early, going to Massandra for the wine. I stood quietly in the soft glow through the lace curtains, which were drawn back: someone had been in my room.

The same light flowed under my door, spilling out to illuminate the whole passage. I advanced slowly, my wings trailing heavily, feeling them scrape against the parquet floor, until they began to grow smaller, diminishing my great feeling of euphoria, expelling the air that had swelled my lungs as I floated above the couples making love in the sand, hearing the cries of the women, seeing them clearly though they could not see me. Like an angel or an enormous night bird soaring over sea and shore.

Standing beneath my window, I had been stunned by my profound inspiration, a profound apnea, like when a baby opens its mouth to burst into tears and the cry takes forever to emerge. It was V.! A profound aspiration, a burst of joy, and I started running, because this time I was sure. It was her. Seven letters. The magic number, with its esoteric significance. Reading these seven letters had been my initiation, my baptism, not the three cauldrons I had expected, the water, tar, and sulfur (with brass trumpets). Her unnerving intelligence (I took the steps at a single bound) had reversed the process of seduction, ensnaring me in the net of her letters. A trap that she had woven patiently, like Lars and his socks, so that I would have to proceed through its narrow tube like an explorer in the Great Pyramid descending through the tunnel, past the writing on the walls, to arrive at the principal chamber, the very heart of the pyramid. She would have had a bath while she waited. I would say, "Congratulations on the bath," like they do in Russia, or "I congratulate you on your bath!" What a crazy idea! Right? And when I got to the hallway I saw the white light, too white.

Which checked my flight. Had she lit my acetylene lamp? Why? She could explain everything. I rushed down the hall, past all the other doors until I reached my own at last, and pushed it open, imagining the way I'd be illuminated in the doorway, with darkness behind me, the tiny lights of the hall, a lighting effect right out of Georges de la Tour (I had thought of him before, nights hunting nocturnal butterflies in the Caspian Basin, and other nights, too, in clearings in the woods around here: the brilliant acetylene lamp shining on my hands and face, all the shades of light, the twinkling of the ether flasks on the ground, the shadows of the trees, the play of light and dark on the backs of the leaves, the quiet splendor of the starry sky above). I still had time to think about all this, to get in a thought about Georges de la Tour. But something terrible happened, I don't know how to write it, my hand trembles. I left it for the end.

I saw—how can I explain this?—I saw someone who was not V. A broad and muscular back, not a woman's back, which is narrow at the waist, nice and easy to clasp, no, it was the back of a man—attentively reading the draft of my letter! So absorbed he didn't notice me come in. Bathed in that light, perfectly white and even, not varying but not blinding. Not like in a photography session, no, another type of light. Celestial? Yes! It makes me nervous and embarrassed. It is a word I haven't used even once in this draft, but it is the right word.

My hand was still on the door, softly touching it. I remained on the threshold, staring at that man, an unknown man reading the draft of my letter, expecting him to say: "Come right in. We've been waiting for you." Like a public prosecutor who already has a case against you, such overwhelming evidence (about poaching, smuggling, despoiling the endangered species listed in the *Red Book of Russia*) that he is in no hurry, his weary voice displaying no eagerness, just boredom.

But he was still unaware of my presence. Opening the door to the hall had not affected the light inside my room. I stepped forward ever more slowly, moving at a speed that allowed me to conduct a mental survey of my room, the closed wardrobe, the apparent order, shaking like a leaf (yes, a leaf), feeling like an immeasurable time was passing, as long as two, three books or manuscripts like this one, or three just as lengthy letters or inventories, while I approached the back of the man, who finished setting a leaf of paper to one side with the utmost care, and started reading another. As I moved closer, I had time, too, to look over his head (oddly familiar, yes, it's true) out the window at the darkness of the night through which I had flown and to notice that the light, the celestial brilliance ceaselessly flowing, pouring like milk from an earthenware bowl, from the Milky Way, was radiating from him, from that man, passing smoothly through the fabric of his shirt and the pores of his skin and even through his hair, not maleficently but with infinite goodness.

I'm starting a new paragraph to convey the importance of this moment. I considered going beyond that "infinite goodness," but then decided there should be a separation after this preliminary examination, a break at this point: I was going to touch his shoulder and then he must have seen my reflection in the mirror and his head came up and he raised his eyes and we exchanged a look—a glance, I would clearly have to call it, given its brevity—and I recognized him. I began to scream (It was me, V.! Do you understand? It was me!), I began to scream, took a deep breath, and lost consciousness, falling to the floor.

I woke at the end of the night. The sounds of dawn surged through the pension, flowing from one end to the other, swelling and splashing occasionally, and very softly, an almost inaudible sound, the waves of the Black Sea crashing over the pebbles on the beach, one after another, again and again in regular intervals, washing out and back in.

Now that it was over I realized my danger. I had gotten too close to the light, getting more and more intense as I approached him, so that if he had not looked up and seen me, if we had not seen ourselves reflected in the mirror, it would have killed me. If we had made contact, if I had touched him, it would have meant annihilation. As Paul Dirac explains, in a letter I've lost, describing what happens when matter contacts antimatter. The two of us were material in this case—both my astral double and myself—but we were out of phase. Two perfectly functional collections of waves, essentially on the same wavelength, but out of sync: when I arrived in Istanbul, he was boarding the ferry in Helsinki; when I landed on an island in the Caspian Basin, he was just arriving in Sweden; and it went on like that. And combining the two—their fusion—required extreme caution, painstakingly fitting the wave-packets together tooth by tooth, pulse by pulse, heartbeat by heartbeat, an especially delicate task if the entity in question was as complex as a man (a butterfly hunter and smuggler, besides). And when I walked toward him before I recognized him—it makes my hair stand on end—the light grew brighter and brighter like when two halves of uranium 235 join together in a nuclear charge. Zero hour, deep within Alamogordo or Semipalatinsk, the two halves slide smoothly along the rails, combine and reach critical mass, then a chain reaction and an explosion. And when they get very close, but do not quite meet, electrons start to flow, an enormous emission, producing a white light, ineffable and unutterably deadly. Only one man ever saw it—a physicist who accidentally turned on the device and stopped it just in time, putting a screwdriver (!!) between the two halves, in the very epicenter of the nuclear explosion—and he died. I had come close.

While I lay there unconscious I had a dream, a beautiful dream. And when I woke, I knew I was not the butterfly looking down at me lying across the wood squares of the parquet floor, flying closer and closer, confused, me within the tiny body of the butterfly. I did not dream that I was a butterfly (which would have been perfectly natural after so many months trying to trap one); it was not like that parable where a man dreams he is a butterfly and wakes up not sure whether he is a man who was dreaming he was a butterfly or a butterfly now dreaming it is a man. Another case of bilocation or disintegration, only between man and insect. Like Franz Kafka (in Prague, a city I have visited, as I mentioned earlier), who also dreamt he was an insect. But let me repeat, that was not what I dreamt. I dreamed that this tiny ethereal copy of me entered my body while I was lying on the floor—like in a Disney cartoon—and I got up, went to the table, and sat down to write a long letter, *calamo curente,* my pen flying all night long, page after page falling from the table. I felt like the happiest man in the world: at last I had found the key. I dreamed I was writing the perfect letter, overflowing with ideas. I saw this so clearly in my dream. And I was writing, I want you to know, not with a ballpoint pen, but with a marvelous gold-tipped fountain pen, beautiful strokes following in its wake, full orations, the pen sliding forward with a lovely low sigh.

When I woke up I could not remember a single word of that letter, but I felt perfectly happy, still on the ground, sure that through vigilance I could regain that hypnotic state, that the quest was over . . .

7

LIVADIA

The quest over—as well as all the possible variants, the digressions, the false starts as I picked my way along, which was my method in writing this manuscript, the only possible one: repeating myself, getting at the same idea from a thousand angles, circling around it, creating a pattern like a delicate construction of reeds, through which the story behind is revealed. A sort of monocle, or imagined opera glasses, which sometimes took the shape of V. or of a *Lepidoptera fenestra* (that is, with wings the same size and shape, only higher or lower) and which projects into space like a brand. A red-hot iron blazing through the circumlocutions in all letters, inescapably, like a tiger leaping through a hoop in the circus ring (a perfect example, picture this: before the tiger takes his fateful jump, the flaming hoop is held high by the trainer, and through it a terrible scene is visible, not the smiling public safe in the stands but a masked villain sneaking up on a sleeping girl, a treacherous crime) and landing on its soft paws, without singeing its striped fur (though we were not afraid of that), demonstrating the courage or else the sorrow of a trained tiger. I don't know. The redundancy guaranteed the univocality of the message.

I finally found a letter—almost by chance, in the last shipment from Vladimir Vladimirovich, which I riffled through hurriedly since there was nothing from Mme. Blavatsky—a letter that I copied whole, eventually learning it by heart and reciting it out loud like a poem. This letter was the final proof that women write the most brilliant letters. It wasn't as long as V.'s letters, but was more like them than anything else I'd read, and I immediately took it as a model, an inspiration, showing me what to do to correct this draft, stripping away all the convolutions and immaterial details, cutting to the quick, the innermost grain.

It would be quite enough to copy the letter here, but I will describe the circumstances in which it was written, which will add significance in the eyes of the reader and contribute to a richer understanding.

The story and the letter go back to 1811 (not my oldest source, far from it). In November 1811 Heinrich von Kleist, "the famous poet," sent a letter to his fiancée and cousin Maria von Kleist, to whom he confessed: "I abandoned you for another woman while I was in Berlin, but if it is any consolation, I will tell you that this new friend does not desire to live, but to die with me." Nothing too remarkable about this news except the last few words.

Henriette, his lover, also left a letter, to her husband (she was married, magnifying the tragedy), in which she asked that the bodies, hers and von Kleist's, not be separated in death (just like Heloise and Abelard, it suddenly occurred to me). Kleist, her partner for life, was to be entrusted with her death, killing her and then himself. *In crescendo*.

They prepared to carry out this plan while staying at an inn halfway between Berlin and Potsdam: Henriette wrote a friend saying he would find ten silver talers in her leather case, asking him to use it for a porcelain cup with her name inscribed on it, to be sent to her husband after her death. Kleist wrote to the same friend (a man named Peguilhem), saying that he had forgotten to pay his barber, asking him to use some of the money to settle the debt. The innkeeper stated that the pair did not sleep that night, that they asked for a supply of candles, by which light, it appears, they sat down on the last night of their lives and wrote letters.

The innkeeper's wife stated that the couple went on an excursion to a nearby lake, "and they seemed really happy, calling each other 'my sweet boy,' 'my little girl,' 'my dear thing' the whole time." Until Kleist shot Henriette in the heart, reloaded the pistol, and blew his brains out.

A regrettable incident, certainly, a double suicide. But Henriette's letter is by far the most sensitive and intelligent, the most perfect of all the letters that I read in Livadia. I will use hers to write mine (not that mine will be a suicide note, a farewell letter, heaven help me!; just for the tone, the intensity, the outpouring of emotion). I'll copy out the whole thing:

Letter from Henriette Vogel to Heinrich von Kleist.

Berlin, November 1811

My Heinrich, my sweet music, my bed of hyacinths, my
dawn and my nightfall, my ocean of delights, my aeolian harp,
my morning dew, my rainbow, my dear babe in arms, my
much-loved heart, my joy and my sorrow, my revival, my
freedom, my slavery, my coven of witches, my holy grail, the
air that I breathe, my warmth, my thoughts, my nearest and
farthest desires, my adored sinner, solace of my eyes, my
sweetest worry, my loveliest virtue, my pride, my protector,
my conscience, my bosque, my brilliance, my sword and my
helmet, my generosity, my right hand, my celestial ladder, my
St. John, my knight, my sweet page, my pure poet, my glass,
my fountain of life, my weeping willow, my lord and master,
my hope and my firm purpose, my dear constellation, my
delicate caress, my stronghold, my fortune, my death, my will-

o'-the-wisp, my solitude, my splendid ship, my valley, my
recompense, my Werther, my Lethe, my cradle, my frankin-
cense and myrrh, my voice, my judge, my sweet dreamer, my
longing, my soul, my mirror of gold, my ruby, my Pan pipe,
my crown of thorns, my thousand marvels, my teacher and
my pupil, I love you above all thought. My soul is yours.

Henriette

P.S. My shadow at midday, my spring in the desert, my dear
mother, my religion, the music inside me, my poor sick
Heinrich, my meek and white Paschal Lamb, my door to
heaven.

V. would never come.

I went out into the cold dawn. I walked to the farthest end of the
garden, picking up dried branches and dead leaves as I moved through
the shadows between the double line of beech trees. A box of matches
bulged in the back pocket of my pants. I fished it out and leaned forward, striking one with my index finger. Squatting down, I cupped my
hands around the flame, and set the tiny pile of twigs, leaves, and old
newspapers afire. I had brought my draft with me and also V.'s letters. I read one after another in the firelight. The first letter, which I
received two weeks after I got to Livadia, so beautiful; the second,
which I finished reading in the little restaurant with the bay window,
and in which she told me the story of the long trip from her hometown in Siberia to Jerson and on to Istanbul; the third, an exhaustive
account of our walk and visit to Hagia Sophia, which I received from
Alfiá's hands while on another walk; the fourth, which Petrovich stole
and I recovered; the fifth, false and pathetic ("a confused woman,"
"I've made a mistake"), which the letter carrier brought up to my room
so that she could ask for foreign stamps for her nine-year-old son, who

collected them; the sixth, which surprised me (I figured there would
be five), and which started me writing on odd sheets of paper, whatever came to hand, about my decision to rescue her and the details of
that rescue; and the seventh, in which she went on and on about the
young Artyom, a prisoner, and how good he was and how vile and
calculating I had been—an accusation that infuriated me enough to
put a few accusations of my own in this draft, about her thanklessness
and her treachery, her perfect perfidy—and also offered her explanation for our miraculous salvation, revealing herself splendidly prone
to mystical experience, the mysticism I had taken aim at with science,
until a few hours ago when I was witness to a supernatural event. I
felt my face go red, not from the warmth of the fire but from shame
for having wanted to write "the truth about Mme. Blavatsky." How
could I admit it: right here in Livadia, so far from Tibet, I had under-
gone an experience I could not explain scientifically, no matter how
hard I tried. And after reading her letters, I threw them all into the fire.
I read this draft too, from beginning to end, and all my notes, the quotes
from other people's letters—and then threw them all into the fire. Some
of them rose up, borne along on the hot air, flames licking their edges,
red as butterflies. Yes, butterflies—why not? They ascended quite high
before falling, and then were gone in a second, consumed in the fire.
Finally, I thought about Alfiá, who would cry when she found my
scrawl (just "a few lines," a quick note). I left the suitcase full of V.'s
clothing on the table in my room with a note to Kuzmovna saying it
was for Alfiá (they felt the same size, V. and Alfiá, in the dark). I went
out to the road, empty at this hour, and walked toward Yalta, following the trembling trolley line.

   With the shadowy trees for company, I recited the first words of
that amazing letter: "my sweet music, my bed of hyacinths, my dawn
and my nightfall, my ocean of delights, my aeolian harp, my morning

dew, my rainbow, my dear babe in arms, my much-loved heart, my joy and my sorrow, my revival, my freedom, my slavery, my coven of witches, my holy grail, the air that I breathe . . ."

That is how I would begin my letter to V., free and full of feeling, and without a shadow of a doubt: My dearest Varia: